# Nebula
# Awards 33

# Nebula Awards 33

*The year's best
SF and fantasy
chosen by the
Science-fiction and
Fantasy Writers
of America*

EDITED BY

## Connie Willis

A Harvest Original
Harcourt Brace & Company
*San Diego    New York    London*

Requests for permission to make copies of any part of the work should be mailed to:
Permissions Department, Harcourt Brace & Company, 6277 Sea Harbor Drive,
Orlando, Florida 32887-6777.

The SFWA Nebula Awards is a trademark of the Science-fiction and Fantasy Writers of
America, Inc.

The Library of Congress has cataloged this serial as follows:
The Nebula awards. — No. 18 — New York [N.Y.]: Arbor House, c1983–v.; 22cm.
Annual.
Published: San Diego, Calif.: Harcourt Brace & Company, 1984–
Published for: Science-fiction and Fantasy Writers of America, 1983–
Continues: Nebula award stories (New York, N.Y.: 1982)
ISSN 0741-5567 = The Nebula awards
1. Science fiction. American — Periodicals.
1. Science-fiction and Fantasy Writers of America.
PS648.S3N38    83-647399
813'.0876'08–dc19
AACR 2 MARC-S
Library of Congress [8709r84]rev

ISBN 0-15-100372-6
ISBN 0-15-600601-4 (pbk.)

Text set in Electra
Designed by Kaelin Chappell

Printed in the United States of America
First edition
E D C B A

Permissions acknowledgments appear on pages 271–72, which constitute a continuation of
the copyright page.

IN MEMORIAM

Jerome Bixby

Robert Hoskins

Carl Jacobi

Judith Merril

Samuel A. Peeples

William Rotsler

G. Harry Stine (Lee Correy)

George Turner

# Contents

# Introduction

CONNIE WILLIS

I read my first *Nebula Awards* collection (and *the* first) when I was in college. I had been reading the year's best collections, edited by Anthony Boucher and Judith Merril and Robert P. Mills, since I was thirteen, and I loved them. I even kept a list of my favorite stories from each one: Daniel Keyes's "Flowers for Algernon" and Kit Reed's "The Wait" and Jerome Bixby's "It's a Good Life."

But *Nebula Award Stories 1965* was different. It wasn't just the stories an editor thought were the best—these were the stories the science fiction writers themselves had decided were the best of the year. The best of the best.

And what stories! The very first story in the volume was Roger Zelazny's "The Doors of His Face, the Lamps of His Mouth," a stunning story of a man facing Leviathan. It was followed by Harlan Ellison's pyrotechnic " 'Repent, Harlequin!' Said the Ticktockman," Zelazny's "He Who Shapes," and Brian Aldiss's "The Saliva Tree."

All in one book! And that wasn't all. *Nebula Awards Stories 1965* also included some of the finalists, among them Gordon R. Dickson's chillingly delicious (and completely plausible) "Computers Don't Argue," Larry Niven's "Becalmed in Hell," and J. G. Ballard's haunting "The Drowned Giant." Wow!

I immediately added my favorite stories in the book to my list. And that's how I knew for sure this collection was different. Because every single story in it ended up on my list.

At the time, I knew nothing at all about the science fiction field or SFWA, which gave the awards, or about the authors. I had no idea Brian Aldiss was British or that Roger Zelazny had only been writing professionally for three years or that Harlan Ellison was...Harlan Ellison.

I didn't know anything about the SFWA banquet at which the awards were given, or what the award looked like, or what a witty, intelligent, insane bunch of people science fiction writers were. All I knew was that these stories really were the best of the best. And that I wanted more than anything to have a story in one of those Nebula collections someday.

Now, thirty-three years later, I've been in six Nebula collections and am the editor of this year's volume. Who says dreams don't come true?

I've traveled in Spain with Brian Aldiss, worked with the late Roger Zelazny on an anthology, and sung show tunes with Harlan Ellison. I have met Frank Herbert and Poul Anderson and know all those authors who once were only names to me. I have worked with and been friends with and know great stories about all of them. (Unfortunately, I'm not allowed to tell most of those stories because they also know stories about me.)

Since that first Nebula banquet I attended in New York City—a word of advice to aspiring young writers: Do *not* wear a dress with a Peter Pan collar to your first Nebula banquet. You will *never* live it down.—I've been to countless (and sometimes endless) Nebula banquets in New Orleans and San Francisco, in Kansas City and Santa Fe, and on the *Queen Mary*, where there was a leak in the ceiling from—no, I'm not allowed to tell that story.

I've attended SFWA business meetings, been toastmaster, participated in dinner discussions of everything from artificial intelligence to the religious symbolism in *The Poseidon Adventure*, and even had adventures, like the time Bruce Sterling and I ended up in the hotel kitchen during the banquet, standing in formal dress at the sink and washing off—no, I'm not allowed to tell that story either.

I've listened to keynote speakers (I'm *really* not allowed to tell that story), presented awards, looked admiringly at other people's Nebulas, and told them to hand-carry the award on the plane going home. This is one of the few stories I *can* tell, since it's part of Nebula mythology. Every winner of a Nebula is immediately told by at least nineteen people not to put it in his suitcase because Robert Silverberg—or Theodore Sturgeon or Kate Wilhelm (the story varies from year to year and person to person)—did, and pressure changes in the baggage compartment made the award explode.

I was told this story the first time I won (and every time thereafter—most recently it was Barry Longyear's Nebula) and have told it myself to new winners. I have no idea if it's true. I have not, however, been willing to try it to see whether it is, and neither, I would imagine, has anybody else.

In those thirty-three eventful years, I've won Nebula Awards and lost them (or, as this year's toastmaster, Michael Cassutt, put it, I've been "differently victorious"). And I've read another thirty-one *Nebula Awards* collections and all the stories in them, from Michael Moorcock's "Behold the Man" to Terry Bisson's "Bears Discover Fire" and Mike Resnick's "Seven Views of Olduvai Gorge."

And you know what? I'm just as dazzled, just as awed and impressed by the Nebula Award stories as I was that first time.

That includes this year's Nebula-nominated and -winning stories, which are an amazing mix of fantasy and science fiction, technology and myth, shoes and ships and sealing wax—though the ships are sometimes sailing the methane winds of Jupiter, and the shoes are patent leather and worn by a five-year-old robot.

There are liquid fish and biological copyrights in these stories, Shakespeare and suffragettes and snakes. Merlin's here, and Aristophanes, the *Hindenburg* and Hollywood directors, convicts and dancers and zombies and Greek gods.

The past seems to be on everybody's mind. Is that because, with the millennium rapidly approaching, we're all feeling nostalgic, or is it that everyone's beginning to realize how complex the intertwinings of past and future are, and how much even the teensiest action affects both? Whatever, the past (or pasts) is here in full cry, from Anne Boleyn's murder to JFK's, from Darwin to Davy Crockett to the Cherokees, in such terrific stories as Allen Steele's "...Where Angels Fear to Tread," John Kessel's "The Miracle of Ivar Avenue," and Paul Levinson's "Loose Ends."

This is not to say that there aren't any robots, or space ships, or aliens. They're all here, especially the latter, in fascinating new forms, from Bill Johnson's Traders ("We Will Drink a Fish Together...") to K. D. Wentworth's kreel ("Burning Bright") and Adam-Troy Castro's enigmatic Vlhani ("The Funeral March of the Marionettes"). So is the first contact story, in William Sanders's delightful "The Undiscovered," though in a guise you'd never expect.

I wish I could have included every single story that was on the ballot. I couldn't. I had to accept the fact that the book had a limited amount of space, even though it killed me to leave out wonderful stories such as Eleanor Arnason's enchanting (and enchanted) "The Dog's Story," and Paul Levinson's "The Copyright Notice Case," about a forensic scientist examining a murder involving DNA in a whole new role. I hope after you read this collection, you'll seek out Robert Reed's tale of space exploration and discovery, "Chrysalis." And Allen Steele's "...Where Angels Fear to Tread."

I hope you'll seek them *all* out. This year's Nebula Award–nominated stories were every bit as new, varied, and exciting as 1965's. Damon Knight, in his introduction to *Nebula Award Stories 1965*, said that the stories in the book showed "the quality of modern science fiction, its range, and, I think, its growing depth and maturity."

The exact same thing, I think, can be said of this year's Nebula stories. How do I know? Because every single story made it onto my Favorite Stories List. I hope they make it onto yours, too.

## The 1997 Nebula Awards Final Ballot

### FOR NOVEL

*The Moon and the Sun*, Vonda N. McIntyre (Pocket Books)
*Memory*, Lois McMaster Bujold (Baen Books)
*King's Dragon*, Kate Elliott (DAW Books)
*A Game of Thrones*, George R. R. Martin (Bantam Spectra)
*Ancient Shores*, Jack McDevitt (HarperPrism)
*City on Fire*, Walter Jon Williams (HarperPrism)
*Bellwether*, Connie Willis (Bantam Spectra)

*Indicates winner.

## FOR NOVELLA

*"Abandon in Place," Jerry Oltion (*The Magazine of Fantasy & Science Fiction*)

"The Funeral March of the Marionettes," Adam-Troy Castro (*The Magazine of Fantasy & Science Fiction*)

"Loose Ends," Paul Levinson (*Analog Science Fiction and Fact*)

"Chrysalis," Robert Reed (*Asimov's Science Fiction*)

"Primrose and Thorn," Bud Sparhawk (*Analog Science Fiction and Fact*)

"…Where Angels Fear to Tread," Allen Steele (*Asimov's Science Fiction*)

## FOR NOVELETTE

*"The Flowers of Aulit Prison," Nancy Kress (*Asimov's Science Fiction*)

"The Dog's Story," Eleanor Arnason (*Asimov's Science Fiction*)

"Three Hearings on the Existence of Snakes in the Human Bloodstream," James Alan Gardner (*Asimov's Science Fiction*)

"We Will Drink a Fish Together . . . ," Bill Johnson (*Asimov's Science Fiction*)

"The Miracle of Ivar Avenue," John Kessel (*Intersections*, Tor Books; *Asimov's Science Fiction*)

"The Copyright Notice Case," Paul Levinson (*Analog Science Fiction and Fact*)

"The Undiscovered," William Sanders (*Asimov's Science Fiction*)

## FOR SHORT STORY

*"Sister Emily's Lightship," Jane Yolen (*Starlight 1*, Tor Books)

"The Crab Lice," Gregory Feeley (*Alternate Tyrants*, Tor Books)

"The Elizabeth Complex," Karen Joy Fowler (*Crank!*)

"Itsy Bitsy Spider," James Patrick Kelly (*Asimov's Science Fiction*)

"The Dead," Michael Swanwick (*Starlight 1*, Tor Books)

"Burning Bright," K. D. Wentworth (*Aboriginal SF*)

# Nebula Awards 33

# Sister Emily's Lightship

JANE YOLEN

Jane Yolen is the kind of person I wish I could be. Not only does she accomplish about fifty times as much as the average person— she's written and edited over two hundred books (including my favorites, *Sister Light, Sister Dark* and her terrifying *The Devil's Arithmetic*); been a college teacher, a storyteller, and a critic; had her own imprint at Harcourt Brace; and raised three children, all without turning a hair—but she also accomplishes the impossible. Like getting along with the crochety, eccentric, opinionated, and downright obsessive group known as the Science-fiction and Fantasy Writers of America. She not only was a great SFWA president but is still its best-loved one.

In her spare time, she's won dozens of awards, including the World Fantasy Award, the Regina Medal (for "continued distinguished contributions to children's literature"), the Christopher Award, the Golden Kite Award, and the title "America's Hans Christian Andersen."

About the only award she hadn't won was the Nebula Award, and now she's won that, for this lyrical, lovely tale about one of my favorite writers *by* one of my favorite writers, the winner of this year's Nebula for Best Short Story: "Sister Emily's Lightship."

*I dwell in Possibility.* The pen scratched over the page, making graceful ellipses. She liked the look of the black on white as much as the words themselves. The words sang in her head far sweeter than they sang on the page. Once down, captured like a bird in a cage, the tunes seemed pedestrian, mere common rote. Still, it was as close as she would come to that Eternity, that Paradise that her mind and heart promised. *I dwell in Possibility.*

She stood and stretched, then touched her temples where the poem still throbbed. She could feel it sitting there, beating its wings against her head like that captive bird. Oh, to let the bird out to sing for a moment in the room before she caged it again in the black bars of the page.

Smoothing down the skirt of her white dress, she sat at the writing table once more, took up the pen, dipped it into the ink jar, and added a second line. A *fairer House than…* than what? Had she lost the word between standing and sitting? Words were not birds after all, but slippery as fish.

Then, suddenly, she felt it beating in her head. *Prose! A fairer House than Prose—* She let the black ink stretch across the page with the long dash that lent the last word that wonderful fall of tone. She preferred punctuating with the dash to the hard point, as brutal as a bullet. *I dwell in Possibility.*

She blotted the lines carefully before reading them aloud, her mouth forming each syllable perfectly as she had been taught so many years before at Miss Lyons's Mount Holyoke Female Seminary.

Cocking her head to one side, she considered the lines. *They will do,* she thought, as much praise as she ever allowed her own work, though she was generous to others. Then, straightening the paper and cleaning the nib of her pen, she tore up the false starts and deposited them in the basket.

She could, of course, write any time during the day if the lines came to mind. There was little enough that she had to do in the house. But she preferred night for her truest composition and perhaps that was why she was struggling so. *Then those homey tasks will take me on,* she told herself: supervising the gardening, baking Father's daily bread. Her poetry must never be put in the same category.

Standing, she smoothed down the white skirt again and tidied her hair—"like a chestnut bur," she'd once written imprudently to a friend. It was ever so much more faded now.

But pushing that thought aside, Emily went quickly out of the room as if leaving considerations of vanity behind. Besides the hothouse flowers, besides the bread, there was a cake to be made for tea. After Professor Seelye's lecture there would be guests and her tea cakes were expected.

The tea had been orderly, the cake a success, but Emily headed back upstairs soon after, for her eyes—always sensitive to the light—had begun to tear up. She felt a sick headache starting. Rather than impose her ailments on her guests, she slipped away. They would understand.

Carlo padded up the stairs behind her, so quiet for such a large dog. But how slow he had become these last months. Emily knew that Death would stop for him soon enough. Newfoundlands were not a long-lived breed usually, and he had been her own shaggy ally for the past fifteen years.

Slowing her pace, despite the stabbing behind her eyes, Emily let the old dog catch up. He shoved his rough head under her hand and the touch salved them both.

He curled beside her bed and slept, as she did, in an afternoon made night and close by the window blinds.

It was night in truth when Emily awoke, her head now wonderfully clear. Even the dreadful sleet in her eyes was gone.

She rose and threw on a dressing gown. She owed Loo a letter, and Samuel and Mary Bowles. But still the night called to her. Others might hate the night, hate the cold of November, huddling around their stoves in overheated houses. But November seemed to her the very Norway of the year.

She threw open first the curtains, then the blinds, almost certain of a sight of actual fjords. But though the Gibraltar lights made the village look almost foreign, it was not—she decided—foreign enough.

"That I had the strength for travel," she said aloud. Carlo answered her with a quick drum roll of tail.

Taking that as the length of his sympathy, she nodded at him, lit the already ensconced candle, and sat once again at the writing table. She read over the morning's lines:

*I dwell in Possibility—*
*A fairer House than Prose—*

It no longer had the freshness she remembered, and she sighed.

At the sound, Carlo came over to her and laid his rough head in her lap, as if trying to lend comfort.

"No comfort to be had, old man," she said to him. "I can no longer tell if the trouble is my wretched eyes, sometimes easy and sometimes sad. Or the dis-order of my mind. Or the slant of light on the page. Or the words themselves. Or something else altogether. Oh, my dear dog…" She leaned over and buried her face in his fur but did not weep for she despised private grief that could not be turned into a poem. Still, the touch had a certain efficaciousness, and she stood and walked over to the window.

The Amherst night seemed to tremble in on itself. The street issued a false invitation, the maples standing sentinel between the house and the promise of road.

"Keeping me in?" she asked the dog, "or others out?" It was only her wretched eyes that forced her to stay at home so much and abed. Only her eyes, she was convinced. In fact she planned a trip into town at noon next when the very day would be laconic; if she could get some sleep and if the November light proved not too harsh.

She sat down again at the writing table and made a neat pile of the poems she was working on, then set them aside. Instead she would write a letter. To…to Elizabeth. "Dear Sister," she would start as always, even though their relationship was of the heart, not the blood. "I will tell her about the November light," she said to Carlo. "Though it is much the same in Springfield as here, I trust she will find my observations entertaining."

The pen scratched quickly across the page. *So much quicker,* she thought, *than when I am composing a poem.*

She was deep into the fourth paragraph, dashing "November always seemed to me the Norway…" when a sharp knock on the wall shattered her peace, and a strange insistent whine seemed to fill the room.

And the light. *Oh—the light!* Brighter even than day.

"Carlo!" She called the dog to her, and he came, crawling, trembling. So large a dog and such a larger fright. She fell on him as a drowning person falls on a life preserver. The light made her eyes weep pitchers. Her head began to ache. The house rocked.

And then—as quickly as it had come—it was gone: noise, light, all, all gone.

Carlo shook her off as easily as bath water, and she collapsed to the floor, unable to rise.

Lavinia found her there on the floor in the morning, her dressing gown disordered and her hands over her eyes.

"Emily, my dear, my dear..." Lavinia cried, lifting her sister entirely by herself back onto the bed. "Is it the terror again?"

It was much worse than the night terrors, those unrational fears which had afflicted her for years. But Emily had not the strength to contradict. She lay on the bed hardly moving the entire day while Mother bathed her face and hands with aromatic spirits and Vinnie read to her. But she could not concentrate on what Vinnie read; neither the poetry of Mrs. Browning nor the prose of George Eliot soothed her. She whimpered and trembled, recalling vividly the fierceness of that midnight light. She feared she was, at last, going mad.

"Do not leave, do not leave," she begged first Vinnie, then Mother, then Austin, who had been called to the house in the early hours. Father alone had been left to his sleep. But they did go, to whisper together in the hall. She could not hear what they said but she could guess that they were discussing places to send her away. For a rest. For a cure. For—Ever—

She slept, waked, slept again. Once she asked for her writing tablet, but all she managed to write on it was the word *light* ten times in a column like some mad ledger. They took the tablet from her and refused to give it back.

The doctor came at nine, tall and saturnine, a new man from

Northampton. Vinnie said later he looked more like an undertaker than a physician. He scolded Emily for rising at midnight and she was too exhausted to tell him that for her it was usual. Mother and Vinnie and Austin did not tell him for they did not know. No one knew that midnight was her favorite time of the clock. That often she walked in the garden at midnight and could distinguish, just by the smell, which flowers bloomed and bloomed well. That often she sat in the garden seat and gazed up at the great eight-sided cupola Father had built onto the house. His one moment of monumental playfulness. Or she sat at the solitary hour inside the cupola contemplating night through each of the windows in turn, gazing round at all the world that was hers.

"Stay in bed, Miss Dickinson," warned the doctor, his chapped hands delicately on hers. "Till we have you quite well again. Finish the tonic I am leaving with your mother for you. And then you must eschew the night and its vapors."

Vinnie imitated him quite cruelly after he left. "Oh, the vay-pures, the vay-pures!" she cried, hand to her forehead. Unaccountably, Carlo howled along with her recitation.

Mother was—as usual—silently shocked at Vinnie's mimicry but made no remonstrances.

"He looks—and sounds—quite medieval," Austin commented laconically.

At that Emily began to laugh, a robust hilarity that brought tears to her poor eyes. Austin joined with her, a big stirring hurrah of a laugh.

"Oh, dear Emily," Vinnie cried. "Laugh on! It is what is best for you."

*Best for what?* Emily asked herself, but did not dare say it aloud. But she vowed she would never let the doctor touch her again.

Having slept all day meant that she was awake at midnight; still she did not venture out of the bed. She lay awake fearing to hear once more the horrid knock and feel the house shake and see the piercing white light. A line of poetry ran through her mind: *Me—come! My dazzled face.* But her mind was so befogged that she could not recall if it were her own line or if she had read it somewhere.

At last nothing more happened and she must have fallen back to sleep some time after two. When she woke it was mid-morning and there was a tray by her bed with tea and toast and some of her own strawberry preserves.

She knew she was well again when she realized Carlo was not in the room. He would never have left her side otherwise.

Getting out of the bed was simple. Standing without swaying was not. But she gathered up her dressing gown, made a swift toilette, then went downstairs carrying the tray. Some illnesses she knew, from her months with the eye doctors in Cambridgeport, are best treated like a bad boy at school. Quickly beaten, quicker trained.

If the family was surprised to see her, they knew better than to show it.

"Shall we have Susie and little Ned for tea?" she asked by way of greeting.

Sue came over promptly at four, as much to check up on Emily's progress as to have tea. Austin must have insisted. Heavily pregnant, she walked slowly while Ned, a rambunctious four-year-old, capered ahead.

"Dear critic," Emily said, answering the door herself. She kissed Sue on both cheeks and led her through into the hall. "And who is slower today, you with your royal front or me with my rambling mind."

"Nonsense!" Sue said. "You are indulging yourself in fancies. Neddie, stop jumping about. Your Aunt Emily is just out of a sickbed."

The boy stopped for a moment and then flung himself into Emily's skirts, crying, "Are you hurt? Where does it hurt? Shall I kiss it?"

Emily bent down and said, "Your *Uncle* Emily shall kiss you instead, for I am not hurt at all. We boys never cry at hurts." She kissed the top of his fair head, which sent him into paroxysms of laughter.

Sue made a *tch* sound with her tongue. "And once you said to me that if you saw a bullet hit a bird and he told you he wasn't shot, you might weep at his courtesy, but you would certainly doubt his word."

"Unfair! Unfair to quote me back at me!" Emily said, taking Sue's hands. "Am I not this moment the very pink of health?"

"That is not what Austin said, who saw you earlier today. And there is a white spot between your eyes as if you have lain with a pinched expression all night."

"And all morning, too. Come in here, Sue," Vinnie called from the sitting room. "And do not chastise her any more than I have already. It does no good, you know."

They drank their tea and ate the crumbles of the cake from the day before, though it mortified Emily that they had to do so. But she had had no time to prepare more for their small feast. Neddie had three pieces anyway, two of his own and one Emily gave him from her own plate because suddenly the cake was too sweet, the light too bright, the talk too brittle, and Emily tired past bearing it all.

She rose abruptly. Smiling, she said, "I am going back to bed."

"We have overworn you," Sue said quickly.

"And I you," Emily answered.

"I am not tired, Auntie," Ned said.

"You never are," Vinnie said fondly.

"I am in the evening," Ned conceded. "And sometimes in…"

But Emily heard no more. The stairs effectively muffled the rest of the conversation as she sought the sanctuary of her room.

*I dwell in Possibility—*

She sat at the desk and read the wavering line again. But what possibilities did she, indeed, dwell in? This house, this room, the garden, the lawn between her house and Austin's stately "Evergreens." They were all the possibilities she had. Even the trips to Cambridge-port for eye treatments had held no great promise. All her traveling— and what small journeys they had proved—lay in the past. She was stuck, like a cork in an old bottle without promise of wine. Stuck here in the little town where she had been born.

She went over to the bed and flung herself down on her stomach and wept quietly into the pillow until the early November dark gathered around her.

It was an uncharacteristic and melodramatic scene, and when she sat up at last, her cheeks reddened and quite swollen, she forgave herself only a little.

"Possibly the doctor's tonic has a bite at the bottom," she whispered to Carlo, who looked up at her with such a long face that she had to laugh, her cheeks tight with the salty tears. "Yes, you are right. I have the vay-pures." She stood and, without lighting a lamp, found the wash basin and bathed her face.

She was not hungry, either for food or company, and so she sat in the gathering gloom thinking about her life. Despite her outburst, she quite liked the tidiness of her cocoon. She doubted she had the capacity for wings or the ability for flight.

When it was totally dark, she went back to her bed and lay down, not to sleep but to wait till the rest of the household slept.

The grandfather clock on the landing struck eleven. She waited another fifteen minutes before rising. Grabbing a woolen shawl from the foot of the bed, she rose ghostlike and slipped from the room.

The house breathed silent sleep around her. Mother, Father, Vinnie, Cook had all gone down the corridors of rest, leaving not a pebble behind for her to follow.

She climbed the stairs up to the cupola for she had not the will nor might to brave November's garden. Still, she had to get away from the close surround of family and the cupola was as far as she could go.

She knew which risers creaked alarmingly and, without thinking, avoided them. But behind her Carlo trod on every one. The passage was not loud enough to waken the sleepers who had heard it all before without stirring, yet Emily still held her breath till they reached the top unremarked.

Putting her hand on the dog's head for a moment, to steady them both, she climbed up into the dome of the house. In the summer there was always a fly or two buzzing about the windows and she quite liked them, her "speck pianos." But in November the house was barren of flies. She would have to make all the buzz herself.

Sitting on the bench, she stared out of the windows at the glittering stars beyond the familiar elms. How could she have abjured this peace for possibilities unknown?

"Oh, Carlo," she whispered to the dog, "we must be careful what we say. No bird resumes its egg."

He grunted a response and settled down at her feet for the long watch.

"Like an old suitor," she said, looking down fondly at him. "We are, you know, too long engaged, too short wed. Or some such." She laughed. "I think the prognosis is that my madness is quite advanced."

When she looked up again, there was a flash of light in the far-off sky, a star falling to earth.

"Make a wish, Carlo," she said gaily. "I know I shall."

And then the top of the cupola burst open, a great gush of sound enveloped them, and she was pulled up into the light.

*Am I dead?* she thought at first. Then, *Am I rising to Heaven?* Then, *Shall I have to answer to God?* That would be the prime embarrassment, for she had always held out against the blandishments of her redeemed family, saying that she was religious without that great Eclipse, God. She always told them that life was itself mystery and consecration enough. *Oh, do not let it be a jealous God,* she thought. *I would have too much to explain away.*

Peculiarly this light did not hurt her eyes, which only served to convince her that she was indeed dead. And then she wondered if there would be actual angels as well, further insult to her heresy. *Perhaps they will have butterfly wings,* she thought. *I would like that.* She was amused, briefly, in her dying by these wild fancies.

And then she was no longer going upward, and there was once more a steady ground beneath her feet where Carlo growled but did not otherwise move. Walls, smooth and anonymous, curved away from her like the walls of a cave. *A hallway,* she thought, *but one without signature.*

A figure came toward her, but if *that* were an angel, all of Amherst's Congregational Church would come over faint! It wore no gown of alabaster satin, had no feathery wings. Rather it was a long, sleek, gray man with enormous adamantine eyes and a bulbed head rather like a leek's.

*A leek—I am surely mad!* she thought. All poetry fled her mind.

Carlo was now whining and trembling beyond measure. She bent to comfort him; that he should share her madness was past understanding.

"Do not be afraid," the gray man said. *No—the bulbed thing—* for she now saw it was not a man at all, though like a man it had arms and legs and a head. But the limbs were too long, the body too thin, the head too round, the eyes too large. And though it wore no discernible clothing, it did not seem naked.

"Do not be afraid," it repeated, its English curiously accented. It came down rather heavily on the word *be* for no reason that Emily could tell. Such accentuation did not change the message.

*If not an angel, a demon—* But this her unchurched mind credited even less.

She mustered her strength; she could when courage was called for. "Who—or what—are you?"

The bulb creature smiled. This did not improve its looks. "I am a traveler," it said.

"And where do you travel?" That she was frightened did not give her leave to forget all manners. And besides, curiosity had now succeeded fear.

"From a far..." The creature hesitated. She leaned into its answer. "From a far star."

There was a sudden rip in the fabric of her world.

"Can you show me?" It was not that she did not believe the stranger, but that she did. It was the very possibility that she had, all unknowing, hoped for, wept for.

"Show you?"

"The star."

"No."

The rip was repaired with clumsy hands. She would always see the darn.

"It is too far for sight."

"Oh."

"But I can show you your own star."

"And what do you want from me in exchange?" She knew enough of the world to know this.

For a moment the creature was silent. She feared she had embarrassed it. Or angered it. Then it gave again the grimace that was its smile. "Tell me what it is you do in this place."

She knew this was not an idle question. She chose her answer with care. "I tell the truth," she said. "But I tell it slant."

"Ah..." There was an odd light in the gray creature's eyes. "A poet."

She nodded. "I have some small talent."

"I, myself, make…poems. You will not have heard of me, but my name is…" And here it spoke a series of short, sharp syllables that to her ear were totally unrepeatable.

"Miss Emily Dickinson," she replied, holding out her hand.

The bulb creature took her hand in its and she did not flinch though its hand was far cooler than she expected. Not like something dead but rather like the back of a snake. There were but three long fingers on the hand.

The creature dropped her hand and gave a small bow, bending at its waist. "Tell me, Miss Emily Dickinson, one of your poems."

She folded her hands together and thought for a minute of the dozens of poems shoved into the drawer of her writing table, of the tens more in her bureau drawer. Which one should she recite—for she remembered them all? Which one would be appropriate payment for this gray starfarer?

And then she had it. Her voice—ever light—took on color as she said the poem:

> Some things that fly there be—
> Birds—Hours—the Bumblebee—
> Of these no Elegy.
>
> Some things that stay there be—
> Grief—Hills—Eternity—
> Nor this behooveth me.
>
> There are that resting, rise.
> Can I expound the skies?
> How still the Riddle lies!

When she was done, she did not drop her head modestly as Miss Lyons had taught, but rather stared straight into the starfarer's jeweled eyes.

It did not smile this time and she was glad of that. But it took forever to respond. Then at last it sighed. "I have no poem its equal. But, Miss Emily Dickinson, I can expound the skies."

She did not know exactly what the creature meant.

"Give me your hand again."

And then she knew. "But I cannot leave my dog."

"I cannot vouchsafe the animal."

She misunderstood. "I can. He will not harm you."

"No. I mean more correctly, I do not know what such a trip will do to him."

"I cannot leave him behind."

The gray creature nodded its bulb head, and she unhesitatingly put her hand in its, following down the anonymous corridor and into an inner chamber that was something like a laboratory.

"Sit here," the starfarer said, and when she sat in the chair a webbing grew up out of the arms and bound her with filaments of surprising strength.

"Am I a prisoner?" She was not frightened, just curious.

"The lightship goes many miles quickly. The web is to keep you safe."

She thought how a horse starting too quickly to pull a carriage often knocks its passenger back against the seat, and understood. "And my dog?"

"Ah—now you see the problem."

"Can he sit here in the chair beside me?"

"The chair is not built for so much weight."

"Then he may be badly hurt. I cannot go."

The creature raised one of its long fingers. "I will put your dog in my sleeping chamber for as long as we travel." It took Carlo by the collar and led the unprotesting dog off to a side wall, which opened with the touch of a button, letting down a short bed that was tidily made. "Here," the creature commanded the dog and surprisingly Carlo—who ordinarily obeyed no one but Emily—leaped onto the bed. The starfarer pushed another button and the bed slid back into the wall, imprisoning the now-howling Carlo inside.

"I apologize for my shaggy ally," Emily said.

"There is no need." The gray creature bent over a panel of flashing lights, its six fingers flying between them. When it had finished, it leaned back into its own chair and the webbing held it fast.

"Now I will show you what your own planet looks like from the vantage of space. Do not be afraid, Miss Emily Dickinson."

She smiled. "I am not afraid."

"I did not think *so*," the starfarer said in its peculiar English.

And then, with a great shaking, the lightship rose above Amherst, above Massachusetts, above the great masses of land and water and clouds and air and into the stars.

She lay on her bed remembering. Carlo, still moaning, had not seemed to recover quickly from the trip. But she had. All she could think about was the light, the dark, the stars. And the great green-blue globe—like one of Ned's marbles—that was her home.

What could she tell her family? That she had flown high above them all and seen how small they were within the universe? They would say she had had a dream. *If only I could have returned like Mother from her ramblings, a burdock on her shawl to show where she had been,* she thought.

And then she laughed at herself. Her poems would be her burdocks, clinging stubbornly to the minds of her readers. She sat up in the dark.

*The light. The marble of earth.* She would never be able to capture it whole. Only in pieces. But it was always best to make a start of it. *Begin,* as Cook often said, *as you mean to go on.*

She lit a small candle which was but a memento of that other light. And then she went over to the writing table. Her mind was a jumble of words, images.

*I do not need to travel further than across this room ever again,* she thought. *Or further than the confines of my house.* She had already dwelt in that greatest of possibilities for an hour in a ship made of light. The universe was hers, no matter that she lived only in one tiny world. She would write letters to that world in the form of her poems, even if the world did not fully understand or ever write back. Dipping the pen into the ink jar, she began the first lines of a lifetime of poems:

> *I lost a World—the other day.*
> *Has Anybody found?*
> *You'll know it by the Row of Stars*
> *Around its forehead bound.*

*Of her story, Jane Yolen writes: One cannot live in my part of the Connecticut Valley, twenty minutes from Amherst, and be unaware of Emily Dickinson. Her presence and her poetry are everywhere. The very robins sing her name. ("The Robin's my criterion for tune," she wrote.)*

*Years ago I was reading some of her poetry which was set in a gorgeous book about her life with paintings by the lovingly precise and particularizing Nancy Ekholm Burkert. It was at that moment that I got the idea for Emily and the meeting with the alien. (I always called the story idea "Emily Meets the Martians," but the Red Planet sort of went by the wayside. Literally, as you shall see.)*

*The idea sat around, about one and a half pages worth of typescript, for nearly ten years. I knew it was a good idea, but I never quite got around to it, though I used a lot of Emily's poetry in other ways—in speeches, in articles, and some fiction as well.*

*And then we bought a house in Scotland. Named Wayside.*

*Nice segue!*

*In Scotland I found I was writing a lot about America. And Americans. About alienation, if not aliens. Suddenly I began working on the story of Emily D and her Martian/alien visitor for real.*

*This sudden immersion in the story was complicated by the fact that the holdings at St. Andrews University did not include a whole lot of Emily D scholarship. In fact, the latest critical biography they had was twenty years old! I had to have my own books shipped over to me. (The most expensive way to do research!) I was especially interested in the feminist critics as well as the new research about Emily's long battle with eye problems. I was tickled to discover that she called herself "Uncle Emily" to her nephew Ned. Polly Longsworth, an old friend of mine and a Dickinson biographer of note, had been the first to discover Emily's complicity in her brother Austin's long affair with neighbor Mabel Loomis Todd, but more work had been done since Polly's groundbreaking book and I wanted to read it all! So I read—and wrote—and read some more.*

*And then Patrick and Teresa Nielsen Hayden came for a visit, on their way to the Glasgow WorldCon.*

*I thrust the draft of the story at Patrick. For two days he said not a word. It was agonizing. I do not normally force my attentions on un-*

*willing men editors. At last it was close to the end of their visit and Patrick had just come down the stairs into the living room. I squeaked, "What do you think of my story, Patrick?" He gave me a stricken look and raced back up the stairs.*

*What did that mean? Had I given mortal offense? I had not a clue. But seconds later he raced back down, thrust the manuscript back at me, and said, "I want it. But it needs revision in three places."*

*The three revisions were so slight—a word in one place, a phrase in another, and the deletion of my afterword/historical explanation. I just nodded and gratefully handed over my ten-year-gestated child to its new pa.*

*P.S. Patrick bounced my next story, sent by mail for Starlight 2. Is there a lesson to be learned here?*

# Itsy Bitsy Spider

JAMES PATRICK KELLY

The robot has been a staple of science fiction since *Metropolis* and Karel Capek's *R.U.R.* Exploring this peculiar mix of man and machine (and the uneasy awareness that that's what we are, too) has preoccupied writers from Jack Williamson to Isaac Asimov to Tanith Lee.

Lester del Rey's Helen O'Loy, Gort, Philip K. Dick's rebellious replicants, Ron Goulart's wayward lawagon, the Bicentennial Man, and the intrepid duo of C-3PO and R2-D2 are only a few of the unique and memorable robots science fiction has created. And continues to create, as witness this stunning story by James Patrick Kelly about a little girl named Jen.

"Itsy Bitsy Spider" is Kelly's sixth Nebula-finalist story. He is also the author of *Wildlife,* the Nebula-finalist novella "Mr. Boy," a number of plays, and the Hugo Award–winning novelette "Think Like a Dinosaur."

When I found out that my father was still alive after all these years and living at Strawberry Fields, I thought he'd gotten just what he deserved. Retroburbs are where the old, scared people go to hide. I'd always pictured the people in them as deranged losers. Visiting some fantasy world like the disneys or Carlucci's Carthage is one thing, moving to one is another. Sure, 2038 is messy, but it's a hell of a lot better than nineteen-sixty-whatever.

Now that I'd arrived at 144 Bluejay Way, I realized the place was worse than I had imagined. Strawberry Fields was pretending to be some long, lost suburb of the late twentieth century, except that it had the sterile monotony of cheap VR. It was clean, all right, and neat, but it was everywhere the same. And the scale was wrong. The lots were squeezed together and all the houses had shrunk—like the dreams of their owners. They were about the size of a one-car garage, modular units tarted up at the factory to look like ranches, with old double-hung storm windows and hardened siding of harvest gold, barn red, forest green. Of course, there were no real garages; faux Mustangs and VW buses cruised the quiet streets. Their carbrains were listening for a summons from Barbara Chesley next door at 142, or the Goltzes across the street, who might be headed to Penny Lanes to bowl a few frames, or the hospital to die.

There was a beach chair with blue nylon webbing on the front stoop of 144 Bluejay Way. A brick walk led to it, dividing two patches of carpet moss, green as a dream. There were names and addresses printed in huge lightstick letters on all the doors in the neighborhood; no doubt many Strawberry Fielders were easily confused. The owner of this one was Peter Fancy. He had been born Peter Fanelli, but had legally taken his stage name not long after his first success as Prince Hal in *Henry IV, Part I*. I was a Fancy too; the name was one of the few things of my father's I had kept.

I stopped at the door and let it look me over. "You're Jen," it said.

"Yes." I waited in vain for it to open or to say something else. "I'd like to see Mr. Fancy, please." The old man's house had worse manners than he did. "He knows I'm coming," I said. "I sent him several messages." Which he had never answered, but I didn't mention that.

"Just a minute," said the door. "She'll be right with you."

She? The idea that he might be with another woman now hadn't occurred to me. I'd lost track of my father a long time ago—on purpose. The last time we'd actually visited overnight was when I was twenty. Mom gave me a ticket to Port Gemini, where he was doing the Shakespeare in Space program. The orbital was great, but staying with him was like being underwater. I think I must have held my breath for the entire week. After that there were a few sporadic calls, a couple of awkward dinners—all at his instigation. Then twenty-three years of nothing.

I never hated him, exactly. When he left, I just decided to show solidarity with Mom and be done with him. If acting was more important than his family, then to hell with Peter Fancy. Mom was horrified when I told her how I felt. She cried and claimed the divorce was as much her fault as his. It was too much for me to handle; I was only eleven years old when they separated. I needed to be on *someone's* side, and so I had chosen her. She never did stop trying to talk me into finding him again, even though after a while it only made me mad at her. For the past few years, she'd been warning me that I'd developed a warped view of men.

But she was a smart woman, my mom—a winner. Sure, she'd had troubles, but she'd founded three companies, was a millionaire by twenty-five. I missed her.

A lock clicked and the door opened. Standing in the dim interior was a little girl in a gold-and-white checked dress. Her dark curly hair was tied in a ribbon. She was wearing white ankle socks and black Mary Jane shoes that were so shiny they had to be plastic. There was a Band-Aid on her left knee.

"Hello, Jen. I was hoping you'd really come." Her voice surprised me. It was resonant, impossibly mature. At first glance I'd guessed she was three, maybe four; I'm not much good at guessing kids' ages. Now I realized that this must be a bot—a made person.

"You look just like I thought you would." She smiled, stood on tiptoe, and raised a delicate little hand over her head. I had to bend to shake it. The hand was warm, slightly moist, and very realistic. She had to belong to Strawberry Fields; there was no way my father could afford a bot with skin this real.

"Please come in." She waved on the lights. "We're so happy you're here." The door closed behind me.

The playroom took up almost half of the little house. Against one wall was a miniature kitchen. Toy dishes were drying in a rack next to the sink; the pink refrigerator barely came up to my waist. The table was full-sized; it had two normal chairs and a booster chair. Opposite this was a bed with a ruffled Pumpkin Patty bedspread. About a dozen dolls and stuffed animals were arranged along the far edge of the mattress. I recognized most of them: Pooh, Mr. Moon, Baby Rollypolly, the Sleepums, Big Bird. And the wallpaper was familiar too: Oz figures like Toto and the Wizard and the Cowardly Lion on a field of Munchkin blue.

"We had to make a few changes," said the bot. "Do you like it?"

The room seemed to tilt then. I took a small unsteady step, and everything righted itself. My dolls, my wallpaper, the chest of drawers from Grandma Fanelli's cottage in Hyannis. I stared at the bot and recognized her for the first time.

She was me.

"What is this," I said, "some kind of sick joke?" I felt like I'd just been slapped in the face.

"Is something wrong?" the bot said. "Tell me. Maybe we can fix it."

I swiped at her and she danced out of reach. I don't know what I would have done if I had caught her. Maybe smashed her through the picture window onto the patch of front lawn or shaken her until pieces started falling off. But the bot wasn't responsible, my father was. Mom would never have defended him if she'd known about *this*. The old bastard. I couldn't believe it. Here I was, shuddering with anger, after years of feeling nothing for him.

There was an interior door just beyond some shelves filled with old-fashioned paper books. I didn't take time to look as I went past, but I knew that Dr. Seuss and A. A. Milne and L. Frank Baum would be on those shelves. The door had no knob.

"Open up," I shouted. It ignored me, so I kicked it. "Hey!"

"Jennifer." The bot tugged at the back of my jacket. "I must ask you..."

"You can't have me!" I pressed my ear to the door. Silence. "I'm not this thing you made." I kicked it again. "You hear?"

Suddenly an announcer was shouting in the next room. "*. . . Into the post to Russell, who kicks it out to Havlicek all alone at the top of the key, he shoots... and Baylor with the strong rebound.*" The asshole was trying to drown me out.

"If you don't come away from that door right now," said the bot, "I'm calling Security."

"What are they going to do?" I said. "I'm the long-lost daughter, here for a visit. And who the hell are you, anyway?"

"I'm bonded to him, Jen. Your father is no longer competent to handle his own affairs. I'm his legal guardian."

"Shit." I kicked the door one last time, but my heart wasn't in it. I shouldn't have been surprised that he had slipped over the edge. He was almost ninety.

"If you want to sit and talk, I'd like that very much." The bot gestured toward a banana-yellow beanbag chair. "Otherwise, I'm going to have to ask you to leave."

It was the shock of seeing the bot, I told myself—I'd reacted like a hurt little girl. But I was a grown woman and it was time to start behaving like one. I wasn't here to let Peter Fancy worm his way back into my feelings. I had come because of Mom.

"Actually," I said, "I'm here on business." I opened my purse. "If you're running his life now, I guess this is for you." I passed her the envelope and settled back, tucking my legs beneath me. There is no way for an adult to sit gracefully in a beanbag chair.

She slipped the check out. "It's from Mother." She paused, then corrected herself. "Her estate." She didn't seem surprised.

"Yes."

"It's too generous."

"That's what I thought."

"She must've taken care of you too?"

"I'm fine." I wasn't about to discuss the terms of Mom's will with my father's toy daughter.

"I would've liked to have known her," said the bot. She slid the check back into the envelope and set it aside. "I've spent a lot of time imagining Mother."

I had to work hard not to snap at her. Sure, this bot had at least a human-equivalent intelligence and would be a free citizen someday, assuming she didn't break down first. But she had a cognizor for a brain and a heart fabricated in a vat. How could she possibly imagine my mom, especially when all she had to go on was whatever lies *he* had told her?

"So how bad is he?"

She gave me a sad smile and shook her head. "Some days are

better than others. He has no clue who President Huong is or about the quake, but he can still recite the dagger scene from *Macbeth*. I haven't told him that Mother died. He'd just forget it ten minutes later."

"Does he know what you are?"

"I am many things, Jen."

"Including me."

"You're a role I'm playing, not who I am." She stood. "Would you like some tea?"

"Okay." I still wanted to know why Mom had left my father $438,000 in her will. If he couldn't tell me, maybe the bot could.

She went to her kitchen, opened a cupboard, and took out a regular-sized cup. It looked like a bucket in her little hand. "I don't suppose you still drink Constant Comment?"

His favorite. I had long since switched to rafallo. "That's fine." I remembered when I was a kid, my father used to brew cups for the two of us from the same bag because Constant Comment was so expensive. "I thought they went out of business long ago."

"I mix my own. I'd be interested to hear how accurate you think the recipe is."

"I suppose you know how I like it?"

She chuckled.

"So does he need the money?"

The microwave dinged. "Very few actors get rich," said the bot. I didn't think there had been microwaves in the sixties, but then strict historical accuracy wasn't really the point of Strawberry Fields. "Especially when they have a weakness for Shakespeare."

"Then how come he lives here and not in some flop? And how did he afford you?"

She pinched sugar between her index finger and thumb, then rubbed them together over the cup. It was something I still did, but only when I was by myself. A nasty habit; Mom used to yell at him for teaching it to me. "I was a gift." She shook a teabag loose from a canister shaped like an acorn and plunged it into the boiling water. "From Mother."

The bot offered the cup to me; I accepted it nervelessly. "That's not true." I could feel the blood draining from my face.

"I can lie if you'd prefer, but I'd rather not." She pulled the booster chair away from the table and turned it to face me. "There are many things about themselves that they never told us, Jen. I've always wondered why that was."

I felt logy and a little stupid, as if I had just woken from a thirty-year nap. "She just gave you to him?"

"And bought him this house, paid all his bills, yes."

"But why?"

"*You* knew her," said the bot. "I was hoping you could tell me."

I couldn't think of what to say or do. Since there was a cup in my hand, I took a sip. For an instant, the scent of tea and dried oranges carried me back to when I was a little girl and I was sitting in Grandma Fanelli's kitchen in a wet bathing suit, drinking Constant Comment that my father had made to keep my teeth from chattering. There were knots like brown eyes in the pine walls, and the green linoleum was slick where I had dripped on it.

"Well?"

"It's good," I said absently and raised the cup to her. "No, really, just like I remember."

She clapped her hands in excitement. "So," said the bot. "What was Mother like?"

It was an impossible question, so I tried to let it bounce off me. But then neither of us said anything; we just stared at each other across a yawning gulf of time and experience. In the silence, the question stuck. Mom had died three months ago, and this was the first time since the funeral that I'd thought of her as she really had been—not the papery ghost in the hospital room. I remembered how, after the divorce, she always took my calls when she was at the office, even if it was late, and how she used to step on imaginary brakes whenever I drove her anywhere and how grateful I was that she didn't cry when I told her that Rob and I were getting divorced. I thought about Easter eggs and raspberry Pop-Tarts and when she sent me to Antibes for a year when I was fourteen and that perfume she wore on my father's opening nights and the way they used to waltz on the patio at the house in Waltham.

"*West is walking the ball up court, setting his offense with fifteen seconds to go on the shot clock, nineteen in the half…*"

The beanbag chair that I was in faced the picture window. Behind me, I could hear the door next to the bookcase open.

*"Jones and Goodrich are in each other's jerseys down low, and now Chamberlain swings over and calls for the ball on the weak side…"*

I twisted around to look over my shoulder. The great Peter Fancy was making his entrance.

Mom once told me that when she met my father, he was typecast playing men that women fall hopelessly in love with. He'd had great successes as Stanley Kowalski in *Streetcar* and Sky Masterson in *Guys and Dolls* and the Vicomte de Valmont in *Les Liaisons Dangereuses*. The years had eroded his good looks but had not obliterated them; from a distance he was still a handsome man. He had a shock of close-cropped white hair. The beautiful cheekbones were still there; the chin was as sharply defined as it had been in his first head shot. His gray eyes were distant and a little dreamy, as if he were preoccupied with the War of the Roses or the problem of evil.

"Jen," he said, "what's going on out here?" He still had the big voice that could reach into the second balcony without a mike. I thought for a moment he was talking to me.

"We have company, Daddy," said the bot, in a four-year-old trill that took me by surprise. "A lady."

"I can see that it's a lady, sweetheart." He took a hand from the pocket of his jeans, stroked the touchpad on his belt, and his exolegs walked him stiffly across the room. "I'm Peter Fancy," he said.

"The lady is from Strawberry Fields." The bot swung around behind my father. She shot me a look that made the terms and conditions of my continued presence clear: if I broke the illusion, I was out. "She came by to see if everything is all right with our house." The bot disturbed me even more, now that she sounded like young Jen Fancy.

As I heaved myself out of the beanbag chair, my father gave me one of those lopsided flirting grins I knew so well. "Does the lady have a name?" He must have shaved just for the company, because now that he had come close I could see that he had a couple of fresh nicks. There was a button-sized patch of gray whiskers by his ear that he had missed altogether.

"Her name is Ms. Johnson," said the bot. It was my ex, Rob's, last name. I had never been Jennifer Johnson.

"Well, Ms. Johnson," he said, hooking thumbs in his pants pockets. "The water in my toilet is brown."

"I'll…um…see that it's taken care of." I was at a loss for what to say next, then inspiration struck. "Actually, I had another reason for coming." I could see the bot stiffen. "I don't know if you've seen *Yesterday*, our little newsletter? Anyway, I was talking to Mrs. Chesley next door and she told me that you were an actor once. I was wondering if I might interview you. Just a few questions, if you have the time. I think your neighbors might…"

"Were?" he said, drawing himself up. "*Once?* Madam, I am now an actor and will always be."

"My daddy's famous," said the bot.

I cringed at that; it was something I used to say. My father squinted at me. "What did you say your name was?"

"Johnson," I said. "Jane Johnson."

"And you're a reporter? You're sure you're not a critic?"

"Positive."

He seemed satisfied. "I'm Peter Fancy." He extended his right hand to shake. The hand was spotted and bony and it trembled like a reflection in a lake. Clearly whatever magic—or surgeon's skill—it was that had preserved my father's face had not extended to his extremities. I was so disturbed by his infirmity that I took his cold hand in mine and pumped it three, four times. It was dry as a page of one of the bot's dead books. When I let go, the hand seemed steadier. He gestured at the beanbag.

"Sit," he said. "Please."

After I had settled in, he tapped the touchpad and stumped over to the picture window. "Barbara Chesley is a broken and bitter old woman," he said, "and I will not have dinner with her under any circumstances, do you understand?" He peered up Bluejay Way and down.

"Yes, Daddy," said the bot.

"I believe she voted for Nixon, so she has no reason to complain now." Apparently satisfied that the neighbor wasn't sneaking up on us, he leaned against the windowsill, facing me. "Mrs. Thompson, I think today may well be a happy one for both of us. I have an announcement." He paused for effect. "I've been thinking of Lear again."

The bot settled onto one of her little chairs. "Oh, Daddy, that's wonderful."

"It's the only one of the big four I haven't done," said my father. "I was set for a production in Stratford, Ontario, back in '99; Polly Matthews was to play Cordelia. Now there was an actor; she could bring tears to a stone. But then my wife Hannah had one of her bad times and I had to withdraw so I could take care of Jen. The two of us stayed down at my mother's cottage on the Cape; I wasted the entire season tending bar. And when Hannah came out of rehab, she decided that she didn't want to be married to an underemployed actor anymore, so things were tight for a while. She had all the money, so I had to scramble—spent almost two years on the road. But I think it might have been for the best. I was only forty-eight. Too old for Hamlet, too young for Lear. My Hamlet was very well received, you know. There were overtures from PBS about a taping, but that was when the BBC decided to do the Shakespeare series with that doctor, what was his name? Jonathan Miller. So instead of Peter Fancy, we had Derek Jacobi, whose brilliant idea it was to roll across the stage, frothing his lines like a rabid raccoon. You'd think he'd seen an alien, not his father's ghost. Well, that was another missed opportunity, except, of course, that I was too young. Ripeness is all, eh? So I still have Lear to do. Unfinished business. My comeback."

He bowed, then pivoted solemnly so that I saw him in profile, framed by the picture window. "Where have I been? Where am I? Fair daylight?" He held up a trembling hand and blinked at it uncomprehendingly. "I know not what to say. I swear these are not my hands."

Suddenly the bot was at his feet. "O look upon me, sir," she said, in her childish voice, "and hold your hand in benediction o'er me."

"Pray, do not mock me." My father gathered himself in the flood of morning light. "I am a very foolish, fond old man, fourscore and upward, not an hour more or less; and to deal plainly, I fear I am not in my perfect mind."

He stole a look in my direction, as if to gauge my reaction to his impromptu performance. A frown might have stopped him, a word would have crushed him. Maybe I should have, but I was afraid he'd start talking about Mom again, telling me things I didn't want to know. So I watched instead, transfixed.

"Methinks I should know you"—he rested his hand briefly on the bot's head—"and know this stranger." He fumbled at the controls, and the exolegs carried him across the room toward me. As he drew nearer, he seemed to sluff off the years. "Yet I am mainly ignorant what place this is; and all the skill I have remembers not these garments, nor I know not where I did lodge last night." It was Peter Fancy who stopped before me; his face a mere kiss away from mine. "Do not laugh at me; for, as I am a man, I think this lady to be my child, Cordelia."

He was staring right at me, into me, knifing through make-believe indifference to the wound I'd nursed all these years, the one that had never healed. He seemed to expect a reply, only I didn't have the line. A tiny, sad squeaky voice within me was whimpering, *You left me and you got exactly what you deserve.* But my throat tightened and choked it off.

The bot cried, "And so I am! I am!"

But she had distracted him. I could see confusion begin to deflate him. "Be your tears wet? Yes, faith. I pray…weep not. If you have poison for me, I will drink it. I know you do not love me…"

He stopped and his brow wrinkled. "It's something about the sisters," he muttered.

"Yes," said the bot, " 'for your sisters have done me wrong…' "

"Don't feed me the fucking lines!" he shouted at her. "I'm Peter Fancy, goddamn it!"

After she calmed him down, we had lunch. She let him make the peanut butter and banana sandwiches while she heated up some Campbell's tomato and rice soup, which she poured from a can made of actual metal. The sandwiches were lumpy because he had hacked the bananas into chunks the size of walnuts. She tried to get him to tell me about the daylilies blooming in the backyard and the old Boston Garden and the time he and Mom had had breakfast with Bobby

Kennedy. She asked whether he wanted TV dinner or potpie for dinner. He refused all her conversational gambits. He only ate half a bowl of soup.

He pushed back from the table and announced that it was her nap time. The bot put up a perfunctory fuss, although it was clear that it was my father who was tired out. However, the act seemed to perk him up. Another role for his résumé: the doting father. "I'll tell you what," he said. "We'll play your game, sweetheart. But just once— otherwise you'll be cranky tonight."

The two of them perched on the edge of the bot's bed next to Big Bird and the Sleepums. My father started to sing, and the bot immediately joined in.

*"The itsy bitsy spider went up the water spout."*

Their gestures were almost mirror images, except that his ruined hands actually looked like spiders as they climbed into the air.

*"Down came the rain, and washed the spider out."*

The bot beamed at him as if he were the only person in the world.

*"Out came the sun, and dried up all the rain.*

*"And the itsy bitsy spider went up the spout again."*

When his arms were once again raised over his head, she giggled and hugged him. He let them fall around her, returning her embrace. "That's a good girl," he said. "That's my Jenny."

The look on his face told me that I had been wrong: this was no act. It was as real to him as it was to me. I had tried hard not to, but I still remembered how the two of us always used to play together, Daddy and Jenny, Jen and Dad.

Waiting for Mommy to come home.

He kissed her and she snuggled under the blankets. I felt my eyes stinging.

"But if you do the play," she said, "when will you be back?"

"What play?"

"That one you were telling me. The king and his daughters."

"There's no such play, Jenny." He sifted her black curls through his hands. "I'll never leave you, don't worry now. Never again." He rose unsteadily and caught himself on the chest of drawers.

"Nighty noodle," said the bot.

"Pleasant dreams, sweetheart," said my father. "I love you."

"I love you too."

I expected him to say something to me, but he didn't even seem to realize that I was still in the room. He shambled across the playroom, opened the door to his bedroom, and went in.

"I'm sorry about that," said the bot, speaking again as an adult.

"Don't be," I said. I coughed—something in my throat. "It was fine. I was very...touched."

"He's usually a lot happier. Sometimes he works in the garden." The bot pulled the blankets aside and swung her legs out of the bed. "He likes to vacuum."

"Yes."

"I take good care of him."

I nodded and reached for my purse. "I can see that." I had to go. "Is it enough?"

She shrugged. "He's my daddy."

"I meant the money. Because if it's not, I'd like to help."

"Thank you. He'd appreciate that."

The front door opened for me, but I paused before stepping out into Strawberry Fields. "What about...after?"

"When he dies? My bond terminates. He said he'd leave the house to me. I know you could contest that, but I'll need to sell in order to pay for my twenty-year maintenance."

"No, no. That's fine. You deserve it."

She came to the door and looked up at me, little Jen Fancy and the woman she would never become.

"You know, it's you he loves," she said. "I'm just a stand-in."

"He loves his little girl," I said. "Doesn't do me any good—I'm forty-seven."

"It could if you let it." She frowned. "I wonder if that's why Mother did all this. So you'd find out."

"Or maybe she was just plain sorry." I shook my head. She was a smart woman, my mom. I would've liked to have known her.

"So, Ms. Fancy, maybe you can visit us again sometime." The bot grinned and shook my hand. "Daddy's usually in a good mood after his nap. He sits out front on his beach chair and waits for the ice cream truck. He always buys us some. Our favorite is Yellow

Submarine. It's vanilla with fat butterscotch swirls, dipped in white chocolate. I know it sounds kind of odd, but it's good."

"Yes," I said absently, thinking about all the things Mom had told me about my father. I was hearing them now for the first time. "That might be nice."

**Of his story, James Patrick Kelly writes:** *For years, "Itsy Bitsy Spider" was nothing but a scrap of an envelope that I kept tucked in my wallet. On it was written the title and this sentence: "Dad keeps little girl robot to replace daughter who never visits." From time to time I would find this cryptic note while fumbling for my library card or driver's license and wonder what it meant. I was sure the plot was all about Dad, which is why I couldn't do anything with it. Then a couple of years ago I started writing plays. Working with theater folk made me want to write about acting. Dad became a washed-up actor, but still the story wasn't ready to come out of the wallet.*

*In 1996 my friend John Kessel and I were invited to team teach the last two weeks of Clarion East at Michigan State University. I proposed to John that, to show solidarity with the students, we each try to crank out a new story in our (imaginary) spare time. Then we could put the stories through the workshop so people could see what a professional's first draft looked like. Of course this was lunacy, but I finally took that scrap out of my wallet. Six days later we both were done—and done in. Maybe it was the friendly competition or the sleep deprivation or the Clarion contact high, but the Glimmer Twins caught fire. John's wonderful story, "Gulliver at Home," first appeared in his Tor collection* The Pure Product *and was just reprinted in* The Year's Best Fantasy and Horror. *I sold "Itsy Bitsy Spider" to Gardner Dozois and Sheila Williams at Asimov's.*

# The Nebula Award for Best Novel

CONNIE WILLIS

The first thing I did after I finished reading *Nebula Award Stories 1965* was to go buy a copy of *Dune*, the winner of the Nebula for best novel.

I did the same thing with this year's winner, Vonda McIntyre's *The Moon and the Sun*. It's romantic, fascinating, and beautifully written, and I wish there'd been space in these pages to reprint the whole novel instead of just a section.

In a *perfect* world, there'd be room for all the Nebula finalist novels, as well. They are all great, from Walter Jon Williams's near-future *City on Fire* to George R. R. Martin's epic fantasy *A Game of Thrones*.

The novel finalists this year include stories about alien artifacts, winged horsemen, the Sioux, winters that last forty years, and hula hoops. They are set in the Court of the Sun King, a world-city, the kingdom of Winterfell, and a North Dakota wheat field, and involve computer viruses, buried treasure, ruins restored to life, dragons, and a flock of sheep.

There is high fantasy (Martin's *A Game of Thrones* and Kate Elliott's *King's Dragon*) and historical fantasy (McIntyre's *The Moon and the Sun*) and science fiction (Jack McDevitt's *Ancient Shores*). There is drama (Williams's *City on Fire*) and space adventure (Lois McMaster Bujold's *Memory*) and even comedy (my own novel *Bellwether*). There are quests and conspiracies, civil wars and mysteries, chaos theory and genetic engineering and magic. And inventive plots, fascinating characters, and great reads.

Maybe someday SFWA will be rich enough to come out with a boxed set of the whole final ballot, novels included. In the meantime, here's the list of this year's novels again, for you to cut out (just kidding!) and take with you to the bookstore:

*The Moon and the Sun,* by Vonda N. McIntyre
*Memory,* by Lois McMaster Bujold
*King's Dragon,* by Kate Elliott
*A Game of Thrones,* by George R. R. Martin
*Ancient Shores,* by Jack McDevitt
*City on Fire,* by Walter Jon Williams
*Bellwether,* by Connie Willis

# An excerpt from
# The Moon and the Sun

VONDA N. McINTYRE

To call Vonda McIntyre multifaceted is putting it mildly. She's written *The Exile Waiting,* the *Starfarers* series, five *Star Trek* novels, and any number of wonderful short stories. (Her novellas "Aztecs" and "Transit" were both Nebula Award finalists.) She also edits; writes screenplays; does needlepoint; holds a black belt in Aikido; and knows all about genetics, *Star Trek,* Seattle, and the *New York Times* best-seller list, on which five of her books have appeared.

She also knows all about awards. In 1978 she won the Nebula for her novel *Dreamsnake* (and a Hugo, making it one of that select group of novels to have won both awards). She had previously won a Nebula in 1973 for her novelette "Of Mist, and Grass, and Sand," one of my favorite science fiction stories ever. My first impression when I read it was that it was unlike any science fiction I had read before—that it combined elements of biology and fantasy and folklore into something utterly original.

That's the impression I get every time I read Vonda's work. *The Moon and the Sun,* this year's winner of the Nebula Award for Best Novel, is no exception. Set in seventeenth-century France at the court of Louis XIV, it's part historical novel, part legend, part romance, part science fiction, and, as usual, all original.

Here's a taste of the 1997 Nebula Award–winning novel: Vonda McIntyre's *The Moon and the Sun.*

$\mathcal{S}$unset spread its light across the park of the chateau of Versailles. The moon, waxing gibbous, approached its zenith. Heading for their stables, the coach horses gained their second wind and plunged through the forest along the hard-packed dirt road.

Marie-Josèphe leaned her head against the side of the coach. She wished she had gone with Madame, in Monsieur's crowded carriage. Madame would have all manner of amusing comments about today's journey. Monsieur and Lorraine would engage in their friendly barbed banter. Chartres might ride beside the carriage and tell Marie-Josèphe about his latest experiment in chemistry, for she was surely the only woman and perhaps the only other person at court who understood what he was talking about. Certainly his wife neither understood nor cared. The duchess de Chartres did exactly as she pleased. It had not pleased her to come from the Palais Royale in Paris to join His Majesty's—her father's—procession.

If Chartres spoke to Marie-Josèphe then the duke du Maine might, too. And then the King's grandson Bourgogne and his little brothers would demand their share of paying attention to Marie-Josèphe.

Maine, like Chartres, was married; Bourgogne was barely a youth, and his brothers were children. Besides, they were all unimaginably above Marie-Josèphe's station. Their attention to her could come to nothing.

Nevertheless, Marie-Josèphe enjoyed it.

Bored and lonely and restless, Marie-Josèphe gazed out into the trees. This far from His Majesty's residence, the woods grew unconfined. Fallen branches thrust up through underbrush. The fragile swords of ferns drooped into the roadway. Sunset streaked the world with dusty red-gold rays. If she were riding alone she could stop and listen to the forest, to the twilight burst of birdsong, to the soft dance of bat wings. Instead, her coach drove into the dusk, its driver and its attendants and even her brother all unaware of the music.

The underbrush disappeared; the trees grew farther apart; no branches littered the ground. Hunters could ride headlong through this tame groomed forest. Marie-Josèphe imagined riding along a brushstroke of trail, following the King in pursuit of a deer.

A scream of rage and challenge filled the twilit forest. Marie-

Josèphe clutched the door and the edge of her seat. The horses shied and snorted and leaped forward. The carriage lurched. The exhausted animals tried to outrun the terrible noise. The driver shouted and dragged his team into his control.

The scream of the tiger in His Majesty's menagerie awoke and aroused all the other exotic animals. The elephant trumpeted. The lion coughed and roared. The aurochs bellowed.

The sea monster sang a challenge.

The wild eerie melody quickened Marie-Josèphe's heart. The shrieking warble was as raw, as erotic, as passionate, as the singing of eagles. The tame forests of Versailles hid the same shadows as the wildest places of Martinique.

The sea monster cried again. The menagerie fell silent. The sea monster's song vanished in a whisper.

The carriage rumbled around the arm of the Grand Canal. The canal shimmered with ghostly fog; wavelets lapped against the sides of His Majesty's fleet of miniature ships. Wheels crunched on the gravel of the Queen's Road; the baggage wagons turned down the Queen's Road toward the Fountain of Apollo. Marie-Josèphe's coach continued toward the chateau of Versailles and its formal gardens.

"Driver!"

"Whoa!"

Marie-Josèphe leaned out the window. The heavy, hot breath of tired horses filled the night. The gardens lay quiet and strange, the fountains still.

"Follow my brother, if you please."

"But, mamselle—"

"And then you are dismissed for the evening."

"Yes, mamselle!" He wheeled the horses around.

Yves hurried from one wagon to the other, trying to direct two groups of workers at once.

"You men—take this basin—it's heavy. Stop—you—don't touch the ice!"

Marie-Josèphe opened the carriage door. By the time the footman had climbed wearily down to help her, she was running toward the baggage wagons.

An enormous tent covered the Fountain of Apollo. Candlelight flickered inside, illuminating the silk walls. The tent glowed, an immense lantern.

Rows of candles softly lit the way up the hill to the chateau, tracing the edges of Le Tapis Vert, the Green Carpet. The expanse of perfect lawn split the gardens from Apollo's Fountain to Latona's, flanked by gravel paths and marble statues of gods and heroes.

Marie-Josèphe held her skirts above the gravel and hurried to the baggage wagons. The sea monster's basin and the shroud in the ice divided Yves' attention.

"Marie-Josèphe, don't let them move the specimen till I get back." Yves tossed his command over his shoulder as if he had never left Martinique to become a Jesuit, as if she were still keeping his house and assisting in his experiments.

Yves hurried to the tent. Embroidered on the silken curtains, the gold sunburst of the King gazed out impassively. Two musketeers drew the curtains aside.

"Move the ice carefully," Marie-Josèphe said to the workers. "Uncover the bundle."

"But the Father said—"

"And now I say."

Still the workers hesitated.

"My brother might forget about this specimen till morning," Marie-Josèphe said. "You might wait for him all night."

In nervous silence they obeyed her, uncovering the shroud with their hands. Shards of chopped ice scattered over the ground. Marie-Josèphe took care that the workers caused no damage. She had helped Yves with his work since she was a little girl and he a boy of twelve, both of them learning Greek and Latin, reading Herodotus—credulous old man!—and Galen, and studying Newton. Yves of course always got first choice of the books, but he never objected when she made off with the Principia, or slept with it beneath her pillow. She grieved for the loss of M. Newton's book, yearned for another copy, and wondered what he had discovered about light, the planets, and gravity during the past five years.

The workmen lifted the shrouded figure. Ice scattered onto the path. Marie-Josèphe followed the workmen into the tent. She was anxious to get a clear view of a sea monster, either one that was living or one that was dead.

The enormous tent covered the Fountain of Apollo and a surrounding circle of dry land. Beneath the tent, an iron cage enclosed the fountain. Inside the new cage, Apollo and his golden chariot and the four horses of the sun rose from the water, bringing dawn, heralded by dolphins, by tritons blowing trumpets.

Marie-Josèphe thought, Apollo is galloping west to east, in opposition to the sun.

Three shallow, wide wooden stairs led from the pool's low stone rim to a wooden platform at water's level. The tent, the cage, and the stairs and platform had been built for Yves' convenience, though they spoiled the view of the Dawn Chariot.

Outside the cage, laboratory equipment stood upon a sturdy floor of polished planks. Two armchairs, several armless chairs, and a row of ottomans faced the laboratory.

"You may put the specimen on the table," Marie-Josèphe said to the workers. They did as she directed, grateful to be free of the burden and its sharp odors.

Tall and spare in his long black cassock, Yves stood in the entrance of the cage. His workers wrestled the basin onto the fountain's rim.

"Don't drop it—lay it down—careful!"

The sea monster cried and struggled. The basin ground against stone. One of the workers swore aloud; another elbowed him soundly and cast a warning glance toward Yves. Marie-Josèphe giggled behind her hand. Yves was the least likely of priests to notice rough language.

"Slide it down the stairs. Let water flow in—"

The basin bumped down the steps and onto the platform. Yves knelt beside it, unwrapping the net that surrounded it. Overcome by her curiosity, Marie-Josèphe hastened to join him. The silk of her underskirt rustled against the polished laboratory floor, with a sound as soft and smooth as if she were crossing the marble of the Hall of Mirrors.

Before she reached the cage, the tent's curtains moved aside again. A worker carried a basket of fresh fish and seaweed to the cage, dropped it, and fled. Other workers hauled in ice and a barrel of sawdust.

Her curiosity thwarted, Marie-Josèphe returned to Yves' specimen. She wanted to open its shroud, but thought better of revealing the creature to the tired, frightened workmen.

"You two, cover the bundle with ice, then cover the ice with sawdust. The rest of you, fetch Father de la Croix's equipment from the wagons."

They obeyed, moving the specimen gingerly, for it reeked of preserving spirits and corruption.

Yves will have to carry out his dissection quickly, Marie-Josèphe said to herself. Or he'll have nothing left to dissect but rotten meat on a skeleton.

Marie-Josèphe had grown used to the smell during years of helping her brother with his explorations and experiments. It bothered her not at all. But the workers breathed in short unhappy gasps, occasionally glancing, frightened, toward Yves and the groaning sea monster.

The workers covered the laboratory table with insulating sawdust.

"Bring more ice every day," Marie-Josèphe said. "You understand—it's very important."

One of the workers bowed. "Yes, mamselle, M. de Chrétien has ordered it."

"You may retire."

They fled the tent, repelled by the dead smell and by the live sea monster's crying. The melancholy song drew Marie-Josèphe closer. Yves' workers tilted the basin off the platform. Water trickled into it.

Marie-Josèphe hurried to the fountain.

"Yves, let me see—"

As Yves loosened the canvas restraints, the grinding and creaking of the water pumps shook the night. The fountain nozzles gurgled, groaned, and gushed water. Apollo's fountain spouted water in the shape of a fleur-de-lys. At its zenith, the central stream splashed the tent peak. Droplets rained down on Apollo's chariot, dimpled the pool's surface, and spattered the sea monster. The creature screamed and thrashed and slapped Yves with its tails. Yves staggered backward.

"Turn off the fountain!" Yves shouted.

Snarling, the creature struggled free of the basin. Yves jumped away, evading the sea monster's teeth and claws and tails. The workers ran to do Yves' bidding.

The creature lurched away and tumbled into the water, escaping into its prison in the Fountain of Apollo.

Marie-Josèphe caught Yves' arm. A ripple broke against his foot and flowed around the soles of his boots, as if he walked on water. Water soaked the hem of his cassock.

My brother walks on water, Marie-Josèphe thought with a smile. He ought to be able to keep his clothing dry!

The fountains spurted high, then gushed half as high, then bubbled in their nozzles. The fleur-de-lys wilted. The creaking of the pumps abruptly ceased. No ripple, not even bubbles, marked the surface of the pool.

Yves wiped his sleeve across his face. Marie-Josèphe, standing two steps above him, almost reached his height. She laid her hand on her brother's shoulder.

"You've succeeded," she said.

"I hope so."

Marie-Josèphe leaned forward and peered into the water. A dark shape lay beneath the surface, obscured by the reflections of candlelight.

"It's alive now," Yves said. "How long it will survive…" His worried voice trailed off.

"It need not live long," Marie-Josèphe said. "I want to see it— Call it to you!"

"It won't come to me. It's a beast, it doesn't understand me."

"My *cat* understands," Marie-Josèphe said. "Didn't you train it, all those weeks at sea?"

"I had no time to train it." Yves scowled. "It wouldn't eat—I had to force-feed it." He folded his arms, glaring at the bright water. The sea monster drifted, silent and still. "But I fulfilled His Majesty's wishes. I've done what no one has done in four hundred years. I've brought a living sea monster to land."

Marie-Josèphe leaned closer to the water, straining to see. The creature was long, and sleek, longer and more slender than the dolphins that cavorted off the beach in Martinique. Its tangled hair swirled around its head.

"Whoever heard of a fish with hair?" she exclaimed.

"It's no fish," Yves said. "It breathes air. If it doesn't breathe soon—"

He crossed the rim of the fountain and stepped to the ground. Marie-Josèphe stayed where she was, gazing at the monster.

It gazed back at her, its eyes eerily reflecting the light. It extended its arms, its webbed hands.

Yves' shadow fell across the sea monster. The creature retreated, closing its golden eyes. Yves clenched his fingers around a goad.

"I won't let it drown."

He poked the goad at the sea monster, trying to chivvy the creature into motion.

"Swim, damn you! Surface!"

Its hair drifted about its face. Its tail flukes quivered. The creature trembled.

"Stop, you're scaring it, you'll hurt it!" Marie-Josèphe knelt on the platform and plunged her hands into the water. "Come to me, you're safe here."

The creature's webbed fingers clutched her wrists and pressed heat against her skin. The sea monster's claws touched her like the tips of knives, but never cut.

The sea monster dragged her into the pool.

Yves shouted and jabbed with the goad. The monster floated, just out of reach. Marie-Josèphe struggled to her feet, coughing, soaked. The cold water lifted her full petticoats like the petals of a water lily. She pushed them down. Her underskirt collapsed against her legs, scratchy and ungainly.

"Hurry, take my hand—"

"No, wait," she said. The creature slipped past her, fleeing, then turning back, its voice touching her through the water. "Don't frighten it again." She stretched one hand toward the sea monster. "Come here, come here...."

"Be careful. It's strong, it's cruel—"

"It's terrified!"

The creature's voice brushed against her fingertips. Its song spun from the surface like mist. Barely moving, creeping, floating, the sea monster neared Marie-Josèphe.

"Good sea monster. Fine sea monster."

"His Majesty approaches," Count Lucien said.

Startled, Marie-Josèphe glanced over her shoulder. Count Lucien stood on the fountain's rim. He had come into the tent, crossed the laboratory floor, and entered the sea monster's cage without her noticing him. Yves remained down on the platform at water level, and Count Lucien up on the fountain's rim; the two men stood face to face.

On the other side of the tent, the musketeers held the tent curtains aside. A procession of torches marched along the Green Carpet toward Apollo.

"I'm not ready," Yves said.

Marie-Josèphe returned her attention to the sea monster. It hesitated, just out of her reach. If she snatched at it, it would leap away like a green colt.

"If the King is ready," Count Lucien said, "*you* are ready."

"Yes," Yves said. "Of course."

The sea monster stretched its arms forward. Its claws brushed Marie-Josèphe's fingertips.

"Mlle de la Croix," Count Lucien said, "His Majesty must not see you in this state of disarray."

Marie-Josèphe caught her breath, frightened to realize she might insult His Majesty. She waded toward the platform, clumsy in her soaked skirts, unsteady in her heeled shoes on the uneven bottom of the pond.

The sea monster swam around her, cut her off, and lunged upward before her. It gasped a great gulp of air. Marie-Josèphe stared at it, horrified and fascinated. It splashed down and lay still, gazing at her.

Though its arms and hands mimicked a human's, it was more grotesque than any monkey. Its two tails writhed and kicked. Webs connected its long fingers, which bore heavy, sharp claws. Its long lank hair tangled around its head and over its shoulders and across its chest—its breasts, for it did have flat, wide breasts and small dark nipples. Water beaded on its mahogany skin, gleaming in candlelight.

The monster gazed at Marie-Josèphe with intense gold eyes, the only thing of beauty about it. Grotesque and magnificent, like a gargoyle on a medieval church, its face bore ridged swirls on forehead and cheeks. Its nose was flat and low, its nostrils narrow. The creature's canine teeth projected over its lower lip.

"Splendid." His Majesty spoke, his voice powerful and beautiful. "Splendid and horrible."

*Of her novel, Vonda McIntyre writes: In 1993, when the extraordinary SF writer and fantasist Avram Davidson died, Potlatch (a small, book-oriented West Coast SF convention) hosted his memorial service. His friends remembered him and spoke of him; his biographer, SF writer Eileen Gunn, read some of his letters; via tape recording, Avram lectured us about his researching on mythological sea creatures.*

*Avram was a brilliant (and underappreciated) writer, but he was not an exciting speaker. As the tape unreeled, my mind wandered. I thought, The sailors who reported sea monsters and mermaids were uneducated, and they were superstitious, but they were experienced and they weren't stupid. So what was it that they saw and reported?*

*I dug out a scrap of paper and wrote, "Why do we, today, think that sea monsters never existed, when they obviously did and maybe still do?"*

*That scrap of paper was the basis for* The Moon and the Sun. *It's a novel about sea monsters . . . and what it means to be human.*

The Moon and the Sun *is unusual (for me) in that it exists in two different, more or less simultaneous, forms: novel and screenplay. Recently I was a fellow in the Writers Film Project, a screenwriting workshop for prose writers and playwrights, supported by Amblin Entertainment and Universal Studios, and administered by the Chesterfield Film Company. Early on, Amblin hosted a reception for the workshop. Steven Spielberg, whose support made WFP possible, welcomed us and said something that I think should be repeated to every student of every writing workshop, no matter what the genre. I have certainly quoted him at every workshop time I've taught since my year in Los Angeles.*

*He said: "If you choose to stay in the movie business, right now may be the only time in your career when you can write whatever you want without worrying about whether it's commercial or not. And that's what you should do."*

We had two schools of thought in the workshop about this advice: "He's right," and "He's Steven Spielberg; he has $600 million. He can afford to say that."

I thought he was right. It wasn't my place to decide if The Moon and the Sun *would be too expensive, or too difficult to film, or too uncommercial because it stars a woman and a sea monster, and a male lead rather different from the usual tall and hunky hero.*

I wrote the screenplay version without thinking about bankable stars, special effects, or the cost of filming at a national monument among thousands of visitors.

But a screenplay is closer to a short story than to a novel; in order to keep the script under the dreaded 120-page mark, I had to leave out material I couldn't bear to lose. So I wrote the novel, too. And though a screenplay is shorter than a novel, it takes longer for a screenplay to become a movie than it does for a novel to see print.

The novel is published. The paperback is published. As for the screenplay, taking into account the occasional Hollywood "No" (hysterical enthusiasm followed by endless silence) and the eighty-eleven meetings I've been to about it—including the one that ended, "We'll be in touch with your agent about a deal...."—one of the most important lessons I learned in Hollywood was, "Never hold your breath."

# The Flowers of Aulit Prison

NANCY KRESS

It isn't fair. Not only is Nancy Kress a brilliant writer but she's also gorgeous. And she's so nice you can't even hate her. *And* she not only knows how to write but how to write about how to write. Her "Fiction" columns for *Writer's Digest* and her book on writing, *Beginnings, Middles, and Ends,* are the best essays on writing I've ever read.

But of course it's her own writing that's the best of all. Her novels—*An Alien Light, Brain Rose,* the *Beggars* trilogy, and *Maximum Light*—are wonderful. So are her short stories—subtle, complex, thoughtful, and at the same time wildly readable, qualities that have made her a multiple award winner.

"The Flowers of Aulit Prison" is Kress's third Nebula Award–winning story ("Out of All Them Bright Stars" and her novella "Beggars in Spain" were the first two). With its themes of memory and guilt and wrenched loyalties, its interplay of reality and illusion, "The Flowers of Aulit Prison" reminded me of Philip K. Dick's work, the highest praise that I can give a story. But it is also uniquely and unforgettably a Nancy Kress story. Here is the multilayered and marvelous winner of the 1997 Nebula Award for Best Novelette: Nancy Kress's "The Flowers of Aulit Prison."

My sister lies sweetly on the bed across the room from mine. She lies on her back, fingers lightly curled, her legs stretched straight as elindel trees. Her pert little nose, much prettier than my own, pokes delicately into the air. Her skin glows like a fresh flower. But not with health. She is, of course, dead.

I slip out of my bed and stand swaying a moment, with morning dizziness. A Terran healer once told me my blood pressure was too low, which is the sort of nonsensical thing Terrans will sometimes say—like announcing the air is too moist. The air is what it is, and so am I.

What I am is a murderer.

I kneel in front of my sister's glass coffin. My mouth has that awful morning taste, even though last night I drank nothing stronger than water. Almost I yawn, but at the last moment I turn it into a narrow-lipped ringing in my ears that somehow leaves my mouth tasting worse than ever. But at least I haven't disrespected Ano. She was my only sibling and closest friend, until I replaced her with illusion.

"Two more years, Ano," I say, "less forty-two days. Then you will be free. And so will I."

Ano, of course, says nothing. There is no need. She knows as well as I the time until her burial, when she can be released from the chemicals and glass that bind her dead body and can rejoin our ancestors. Others I have known whose relatives were under atonement bondage said the bodies complained and recriminated, especially in dreams, making the house a misery. Ano is more considerate. Her corpse never troubles me at all. I do that to myself.

I finish the morning prayers, leap up, and stagger dizzily to the piss closet. I may not have drunk pel last night, but my bladder is nonetheless bursting.

At noon a messenger rides into my yard on a Terran bicycle. The bicycle is an attractive design, sloping, with interesting curves. Adapted for our market, undoubtedly. The messenger is less attractive, a surly boy probably in his first year of government service. When I smile at him, he looks away. He would rather be someplace else. Well, if he doesn't perform his messenger duties with more courteous cheer, he will be.

"Letter for Uli Pek Bengarin."

"I am Uli Pek Bengarin."

Scowling, he hands me the letter and pedals away. I don't take the scowl personally. The boy does not, of course, know what I am, any more than my neighbors do. That would defeat the whole point. I am supposed to pass as fully real, until I can earn the right to resume being so.

The letter is shaped into a utilitarian circle, very business-like, with a generic government seal. It could have come from the Tax Section, or Community Relief, or Processions and Rituals. But of course it hasn't; none of those sections would write to me until I am real again. The sealed letter is from Reality and Atonement. It's a summons; they have a job for me.

And about time. I have been home nearly six weeks since the last job, shaping my flowerbeds and polishing dishes and trying to paint a skyscape of last month's synchrony, when all six moons were visible at once. I paint badly. It is time for another job.

I pack my shoulder sack, kiss the glass of my sister's coffin, and lock the house. Then I wheel my bicycle—not, alas, as interestingly curved as the messenger's—out of its shed and pedal down the dusty road toward the city.

Frablit Pek Brimmidin is nervous. This interests me; Pek Brimmidin is usually a calm, controlled man, the sort who never replaces reality with illusion. He's given me my previous jobs with no fuss. But now he actually can't sit still; he fidgets back and forth across his small office, which is cluttered with papers, stone sculptures in an exaggerated style I don't like at all, and plates of half-eaten food. I don't comment on either the food or the pacing. I am fond of Pek Brimmidin, quite apart from my gratitude to him, which is profound. He was the official in R&A who voted to give me a chance to become real again. The other two judges voted for perpetual death, no chance of atonement. I'm not supposed to know this much detail about my own case, but I do. Pek Brimmidin is middle-aged, a stocky man whose neck fur has just begun to yellow. His eyes are gray, and kind.

"Pek Bengarin," he says, finally, and then stops.

"I stand ready to serve," I say softly, so as not to make him even more nervous. But something is growing heavy in my stomach. This does not look good.

"Pek Bengarin." Another pause. "You are an informer."

"I stand ready to serve our shared reality," I repeat, despite my astonishment. Of course I'm an informer. I've been an informer for two years and eighty-two days. I killed my sister, and I will be an informer until my atonement is over, I can be fully real again, and Ano can be released from death to join our ancestors. Pek Brimmidin knows this. He's assigned me every one of my previous informing jobs, from the first easy one in currency counterfeiting right through the last one, in baby stealing. I'm a very good informer, as Pek Brimmidin also knows. What's wrong with the man?

Suddenly Pek Brimmidin straightens. But he doesn't look me in the eye. "You are an informer, and the Section for Reality and Atonement has an informing job for you. In Aulit Prison."

So that's it. I go still. Aulit Prison holds criminals. Not just those who have tried to get away with stealing or cheating or childsnatching, which are, after all, normal. Aulit Prison holds those who are unreal, who have succumbed to the illusion that they are not part of shared common reality and so may do violence to the most concrete reality of others: their physical bodies. Maimers. Rapists. Murderers.

Like me.

I feel my left hand tremble, and I strive to control it and to not show how hurt I am. I thought Pek Brimmidin thought better of me. There is of course no such thing as partial atonement—one is either real or one is not—but a part of my mind nonetheless thought that Pek Brimmidin had recognized two years and eighty-two days of effort in regaining my reality. I have worked so hard.

He must see some of this on my face because he says quickly, "I am sorry to assign this job to you, Pek. I wish I had a better one. But you've been requested specifically by Rafkit Sarloe." Requested by the capital; my spirits lift slightly. "They've added a note to the request. I am authorized to tell you the informant job carries additional compensation. If you succeed, your debt will be considered immediately paid, and you can be restored at once to reality."

Restored at once to reality. I would again be a full member of

World, without shame. Entitled to live in the real world of shared humanity, and to hold my head up with pride. And Ano could be buried, the artificial chemicals washed from her body, so that it could return to World and her sweet spirit could join our ancestors. Ano, too, would be restored to reality.

"I'll do it," I tell Pek Brimmidin. And then, formally, "I stand ready to serve our shared reality."

"One more thing, before you agree, Pek Bengarin." Pek Brimmidin is fidgeting again. "The suspect is a Terran."

I have never before informed on a Terran. Aulit Prison, of course, holds those aliens who have been judged unreal: Terrans, Fallers, the weird little Huhuhubs. The problem is that even after thirty years of ships coming to World, there is still considerable debate about whether *any* aliens are real at all. Clearly their bodies exist; after all, here they are. But their thinking is so disordered they might almost qualify as all being unable to recognize shared social reality, and so just as unreal as those poor empty children who never attain reason and must be destroyed.

Usually we on World just leave the aliens alone, except of course for trading with them. The Terrans in particular offer interesting objects, such as bicycles, and ask in return worthless items, mostly perfectly obvious information. But do any of the aliens have souls, capable of recognizing and honoring a shared reality with the souls of others? At the universities, the argument goes on. Also in market squares and pel shops, which is where I hear it. Personally, I think aliens may well be real. I try not to be a bigot.

I say to Pek Brimmidin, "I am willing to inform on a Terran."

He wiggles his hand in pleasure. "Good, good. You will enter Aulit Prison a Capmonth before the suspect is brought there. You will use your primary cover, please."

I nod, although Pek Brimmidin knows this is not easy for me. My primary cover is the truth: I killed my sister Ano Pek Bengarin two years and eighty-two days ago and was judged unreal enough for perpetual death, never able to join my ancestors. The only untrue part of the cover is that I escaped and have been hiding from the Section police ever since.

"You have just been captured," Pek Brimmidin continues, "and assigned to the first part of your death in Aulit. The Section records will show this."

Again I nod, not looking at him. The first part of my death in Aulit, the second, when the time came, in the kind of chemical bondage that holds Ano. And never ever to be freed—*ever*. What if it were true? I should go mad. Many do.

"The suspect is named 'Carryl Walters.' He is a Terran healer. He murdered a World child, in an experiment to discover how real people's brains function. His sentence is perpetual death. But the Section believes that Carryl Walters was working with a group of World people in these experiments. That somewhere on World there is a group that's so lost its hold on reality that it would murder children to investigate science."

For a moment the room wavers, including the exaggerated swooping curves of Pek Brimmidin's ugly sculptures. But then I get hold of myself. I am an informer, and a good one. I can do this. I am redeeming myself, and releasing Ano. I am an informer.

"I'll find out who this group is," I say. "And what they're doing, and where they are."

Pek Brimmidin smiles at me. "Good." His trust is a dose of shared reality: two people acknowledging their common perceptions together, without lies or violence. I need this dose. It is probably the last one I will have for a long time.

How do people manage in perpetual death, fed on only solitary illusion?

Aulit Prison must be full of the mad.

Traveling to Aulit takes two days of hard riding. Somewhere my bicycle loses a bolt and I wheel it to the next village. The woman who runs the bicycle shop is competent but mean, the sort who gazes at shared reality mostly to pick out the ugly parts.

"At least it's not a *Terran* bicycle."

"At least," I say, but she is incapable of recognizing sarcasm.

"Sneaky soulless criminals, taking us over bit by bit. We should never have allowed them in. And the government is supposed to protect us from unreal slime, ha, what a joke. Your bolt is a nonstandard size."

"Is it?" I say.

"Yes. Costs you extra."

I nod. Behind the open rear door of the shop, two little girls play in a thick stand of moonweed.

"We should kill all the aliens," the repairer says. "No shame in destroying them before they corrupt us."

"Eurummmn," I say. Informers are not supposed to make themselves conspicuous with political debate. Above the two children's heads, the moonweed bends gracefully in the wind. One of the little girls has long brown neck fur, very pretty. The other does not.

"There, that bolt will hold fine. Where you from?"

"Rafkit Sarloe." Informers never name their villages.

She gives an exaggerated shudder. "I would never visit the capital. Too many aliens. They destroy *our* participation in shared reality without a moment's thought! Three and eight, please."

I want to say *No one but you can destroy your own participation in shared reality*, but I don't. Silently I pay her the money.

She glares at me, at the world. "You don't believe me about the Terrans. But I know what I know!"

I ride away, through the flowered countryside. In the sky, only Cap is visible, rising on the horizon opposite the sun. Cap glows with a clear white smoothness, like Ano's skin.

The Terrans, I am told, have only one moon. Shared reality on their world is, perhaps, skimpier than ours: less curved, less rich, less warm.

Are they ever jealous?

Aulit Prison sits on a flat plain inland from the South Coast. I know that other islands on World have their own prisons, just as they have their own governments, but only Aulit is used for the alien unreal, as well as our own. A special agreement among the governments of World makes this possible. The alien governments protest, but of course it does them no good. The unreal is the unreal, and far too painful and dangerous to have running around loose. Besides, the alien governments are far away on other stars.

Aulit is huge and ugly, a straight-lined monolith of dull red stone, with no curves anywhere. An official from R&A meets me and turns me over to two prison guards. We enter through a barred gate, my bicycle chained to the guards', and I to my bicycle. I am led across a wide dusty yard toward a stone wall. The guards of course don't speak to me; I am unreal.

My cell is square, twice my length on a side. There is a bed, a piss pot, a table, and a single chair. The door is without a window, and all the other doors in the row of cells are closed.

"When will the prisoners be allowed to be all together?" I ask, but of course the guard doesn't answer me. I am not real.

I sit in my chair and wait. Without a clock, it's difficult to judge time, but I think a few hours pass totally without event. Then a gong sounds and my door slides up into the ceiling. Ropes and pulleys, controlled from above, inaccessible from inside the cell.

The corridor fills with illusionary people. Men and women, some with yellowed neck fur and sunken eyes, walking with the shuffle of old age. Some young, striding along with that dangerous mixture of anger and desperation. And the aliens.

I have seen aliens before, but not so many together. Fallers, about our size but very dark, as if burned crisp by their distant star. They wear their neck fur very long and dye it strange bright colors, although not in prison. Terrans, who don't even have neck fur but instead fur on their heads, which they sometimes cut into fanciful curves—rather pretty. Terrans are a little intimidating because of their size. They move slowly. Ano, who had one year at the university before I killed her, once told me that the Terrans' world makes them feel lighter than ours does. I don't understand this, but Ano was very intelligent and so it's probably true. She also explained that Fallers, Terrans, and World people are somehow related far back in time, but this is harder to believe. Perhaps Ano was mistaken.

Nobody ever thinks Huhuhubs could be related to us. Tiny, scuttling, ugly, dangerous, they walk on all fours. They're covered with warts. They smell bad. I was glad to see only a few of them, sticking close together, in the corridor at Aulit.

We all move toward a large room filled with rough tables and chairs and, in the corner, a trough for the Huhuhubs. The food is already on the tables. Cereal, flatbread, elindel fruit—very basic, but nutritious. What surprises me most is the total absence of guards.

Apparently prisoners are allowed to do whatever they wish to the food, the room, or each other, without interference. Well, why not? We aren't real.

I need protection, quickly.

I choose a group of two women and three men. They sit at a table with their backs to the wall, and others have left a respectful distance around them. From the way they group themselves, the oldest woman is the leader. I plant myself in front of her and look directly into her face. A long scar ridges her left cheek to disappear into grizzled neck fur.

"I am Uli Pek Bengarin," I say, my voice even but too low to be heard beyond this group. "In Aulit for the murder of my sister. I can be useful to you."

She doesn't speak, and her flat dark eyes don't waver, but I have her attention. Other prisoners watch furtively.

"I know an informer among the guards. He knows I know. He brings things into Aulit for me, in return for not sharing his name."

Still her eyes don't waver. But I see she believes me; the sheer outrage of my statement has convinced her. A guard who had already forfeited reality by informing—by violating shared reality—might easily turn it to less pernicious material advantage. Once reality is torn, the rents grow. For the same reason, she easily believes that I might violate my supposed agreement with the guard.

"What sort of things?" she says, carelessly. Her voice is raspy and thick, like some hairy root.

"Letters. Candy. Pel." Intoxicants are forbidden in prison; they promote shared conviviality, to which the unreal have no right.

"Weapons?"

"Perhaps," I say.

"And why shouldn't I beat this guard's name out of you and set up my own arrangement with him?"

"He will not. He is my cousin." This is the trickiest part of the cover provided to me by R&A Section; it requires that my would-be protector believe in a person who has kept enough sense of reality to honor family ties but will nonetheless violate a larger shared reality. I told Pek Brimmidin that I doubted that such a twisted state of mind would be very stable, and so a seasoned prisoner would not believe in it. But Pek Brimmidin was right and I was wrong. The woman nods. "All right. Sit down."

She does not ask what I wish in return for the favors of my supposed cousin. She knows. I sit beside her, and from now on I am physically safe in Aulit Prison from all but her.

Next, I must somehow befriend a Terran.

This proves harder than I expect. The Terrans keep to themselves, and so do we. They are just as violent toward their own as all the mad doomed souls in Aulit; the place is every horror whispered by children trying to shock each other. Within a tenday, I see two World men hold down and rape a woman. No one interferes. I see a Terran gang beat a Faller. I see a World woman knife another woman, who bleeds to death on the stone floor. This is the only time guards appear, heavily armored. A priest is with them. He wheels in a coffin of chemicals and immediately immerses the body so that it cannot decay to release the prisoner from her sentence of perpetual death.

At night, isolated in my cell, I dream that Frablit Pek Brimmidin appears and rescinds my provisional reality. The knifed, doomed corpse becomes Ano; her attacker becomes me. I wake from the dream moaning and weeping. The tears are not grief but terror. My life, and Ano's, hang from the splintery branch of a criminal alien I have not yet even met.

I know who he is, though. I skulk as close as I dare to the Terran groups, listening. I don't speak their language, of course, but Pek Brimmidin taught me to recognize the cadences of "Carryl Walters" in several of their dialects. Carryl Walters is an old Terran, with gray head fur cut in boring straight lines, wrinkled brownish skin, and sunken eyes. But his ten fingers—how do they keep the extra ones from tangling them up?—are long and quick.

It takes me only a day to realize that Carryl Walters's own people leave him alone, surrounding him with the same nonviolent respect that my protector gets. It takes me much longer to figure out why. Carryl Walters is not dangerous, neither a protector nor a punisher. I don't think he has any private shared realities with the guards. I don't understand until the World woman is knifed.

It happens in the courtyard, on a cool day in which I am gazing hungrily at the one patch of bright sky overhead. The knifed woman screams. The murderer pulls the knife from her belly and blood shoots out. In seconds the ground is drenched. The woman doubles over. Everyone looks the other way except me. And Carryl Walters runs over with his old-man stagger and kneels over the body, trying uselessly to save the life of a woman already dead anyway.

Of course. He is a healer. The Terrans don't bother him because they know that, next time, it might be they who have need of him.

I feel stupid for not realizing this right away. I am supposed to be *good* at informing. Now I'll have to make it up by immediate action. The problem, of course, is that no one will attack me while I'm under Afa Pek Fakar's protection, and provoking Pek Fakar herself is far too dangerous.

I can see only one way to do this.

I wait a few days. Outside in the courtyard, I sit quietly against the prison wall and breathe shallowly. After a few minutes I leap up. The dizziness takes me; I worsen it by holding my breath. Then I ram as hard as I can into the rough stone wall and slide down it. Pain tears through my arm and forehead. One of Pek Fakar's men shouts something.

Pek Fakar is there in a minute. I hear her—hear all of them—through a curtain of dizziness and pain.

"—just *ran* into the wall, I saw it—"

"—told me she gets these dizzy attacks—"

"—head broken in—"

I gasp, through sudden real nausea, "The healer. The Terran—"

"The Terran?" Pek Fakar's voice, hard with sudden suspicion. But I gasp out more words, "… disease … a Terran told me … since childhood…without help I…" My vomit, unplanned but useful, spews over her boots.

"Get the Terran," Pek Fakar rasps to somebody. "And a towel!"

Then Carryl Walters bends over me. I clutch his arm, try to smile, and pass out.

When I come to, I am lying inside, on the floor of the eating hall, the Terran cross-legged beside me. A few World people hover near the far wall, scowling. Carryl Walters says, "How many fingers you see?"

"Four. Aren't you supposed to have five?"

He unbends the fifth from behind his palm and says, "You fine."

"No, I'm not," I say. He speaks childishly, and with an odd accent, but he's understandable. "I have a disease. Another Terran healer told me so."

"Who?"

"Her name was Anna Pek Rakov."

"What disease?"

"I don't remember. Something in the head. I get spells."

"What spells? You fall, flop on floor?"

"No. Yes. Sometimes. Sometimes it takes me differently." I look directly into his eyes. Strange eyes, smaller than mine, and that improbable blue. "Pek Rakov told me I could die during a spell, without help."

He does not react to the lie. Or maybe he does, and I don't know how to read it. I have never informed on a Terran before. Instead he says something grossly obscene, even for Aulit Prison: "Why you unreal? What you do?"

I move my gaze from his. "I murdered my sister." If he asks for details, I will cry. My head aches too hard.

He says, "I sorry."

Is he sorry that he asked, or that I killed Ano? Pek Rakov was not like this; she had some manners. I say, "The other Terran healer said I should be watched carefully by someone who knows what to do if I get a spell. Do you know what to do, Pek Walters?"

"Yes."

"Will you watch me?"

"Yes." He is, in fact, watching me closely now. I touch my head; there is a cloth tied around it where I bashed myself. The headache is worse. My hand comes away sticky with blood.

I say, "In return for what?"

"What you give Pek Fakar for protection?"

He is smarter than I thought. "Nothing I can also share with you." She would punish me hard.

"Then I watch you, you give me information about World."

I nod; this is what Terrans usually request. And where information is given, it can also be extracted. "I will explain your presence to

Pek Fakar," I say, before the pain in my head swamps me without warning, and everything in the dining hall blurs and sears together.

Pek Fakar doesn't like it. But I have just given her a gun, smuggled in by my "cousin." I leave notes for the prison administration in my cell, under my bed. While the prisoners are in the courtyard—which we are every day, no matter what the weather—the notes are replaced by whatever I ask for. Pek Fakar had demanded a "weapon"; neither of us expected a Terran gun. She is the only person in the prison to have such a thing. It is to me a stark reminder that no one would care if all we unreal killed each other off completely. There is no one else to shoot; we never see anyone not already in perpetual death.

"Without Pek Walters, I might have another spell and die," I say to the scowling Pek Fakar. "He knows a special Terran method of flexing the brain to bring me out of a spell."

"He can teach this special method to me."

"So far, no World person has been able to learn it. Their brains are different from ours."

She glares at me. But no one, even those lost to reality, can deny that alien brains are weird. And my injuries are certainly real: bloody head cloth, left eye closed from swelling, skin scraped raw the length of my left cheek, bruised arm. She strokes the Terran gun, a boringly straight-lined cylinder of dull metal. "All right. You may keep the Terran near you—if he agrees. Why should he?"

I smile at her slowly. Pek Fakar never shows a response to flattery; to do so would be to show weakness. But she understands. Or thinks she does. I have threatened the Terran with her power, and the whole prison now knows that her power extends among the aliens as well as her own people. She goes on glaring, but she is not displeased. In her hand, the gun gleams.

And so begin my conversations with a Terran.

Talking with Carryl Pek Walters is embarrassing and frustrating. He sits beside me in the eating hall or the courtyard and publicly scratches his head. When he is cheerful, he makes shrill horrible whistling noises between his teeth. He mentions topics that belong only among kin: the state of his skin (which has odd brown lumps on it) and his lungs (clogged with fluid, apparently). He does not know enough to begin conversations with ritual comments on flowers. It is like talking to a child, but a child who suddenly begins discussing bicycle engineering or university law.

"You think individual means very little, group means everything," he says.

We are sitting in the courtyard, against a stone wall, a little apart from the other prisoners. Some watch us furtively, some openly. I am angry. I am often angry with Pek Walters. This is not going as I'd planned.

"How can you say that? The individual is very important on World! We care for each other so that no individual is left out of our common reality, except by his own acts!"

"Exactly," Pek Walters says. He has just learned this word from me. "You care for others so no one left alone. Alone is bad. Act alone is bad. Only together is real."

"Of course," I say. Could he be stupid after all? "Reality is always shared. Is a star really there if only one eye can perceive its light?"

He smiles and says something in his own language, which makes no sense to me. He repeats it in real words. "When tree falls in forest, is sound if no person hears?"

"But—do you mean to say that on your star, people believe they…" What? I can't find the words.

He says, "People believe they always real, alone or together. Real even when other people say they dead. Real even when they do something very bad. Even when they murder."

"But they're not real! How could they be? They've violated shared reality! If I don't acknowledge you, the reality of your soul, if I send you to your ancestors without your consent, that is proof that I don't understand reality and so am not seeing it! Only the unreal could do that!"

"Baby not see shared reality. Is baby unreal?"

"Of course. Until the age when children attain reason, they are unreal."

"Then when I kill baby, is all right, because I not kill real person?"

"Of course it's not all right! When one kills a baby, one kills its chance to become real, before it could even join its ancestors! And also all the chances of the babies to which it might become ancestor. No one would kill a baby on World, not even these dead souls in Aulit! Are you saying that on Terra people would kill babies?"

He looks at something I cannot see. "Yes."

My chance has arrived, although not in a form I relish. Still, I have a job to do. I say, "I have heard that Terrans will kill people for science. Even babies. To find out the kinds of things that Anna Pek Rakov knew about my brain. Is that true?"

"Yes and no."

"How can it be yes *and* no? Are children ever used for science experiments?"

"Yes."

"What kinds of experiments?"

"You should ask, what kind children? Dying children. Children not born yet. Children born...wrong. With no brain, or broken brain."

I struggle with all this. Dying children...he must mean not children who are really dead, but those in the transition to join their ancestors. Well, that would not be so bad, provided the bodies were then allowed to decay properly and release the souls. Children without brains or with broken brains...not bad, either. Such poor unreal things would be destroyed anyway. But children not born yet...in or out of the mother's womb? I push this away, to discuss another time. I am on a different path.

"And you never use living, real children for science?"

He gives me a look I cannot read. So much of Terran expression is still strange. "Yes. We use. In some experiments. Experiments who not hurt children."

"Like what?" I say. We are staring directly at each other now. Suddenly I wonder if this old Terran suspects that I am an informer seeking information, and that is why he accepted my skimpy story about having spells. That would not necessarily be bad. There are ways to bargain with the unreal once everyone admits that bargaining is what is taking place. But I'm not sure whether Pek Walters knows that.

He says, "Experiments who study how brain work. Such as, how memory work. Including shared memory."

"Memory? Memory doesn't 'work.' It just is."

"No. Memory work. By memory-building pro-teenz." He uses a Terran word, then adds, "Tiny little pieces of food," which makes no sense. What does food have to do with memory? You don't eat memories, or obtain them from food. But I am further down the path, and I use his words to go further still.

"Does memory in World people work with the same...'pro-teenz' as Terran memory?"

"Yes and no. Some same or almost same. Some different." He is watching me very closely.

"How do you know that memory works the same or different in World people? Have Terrans done brain experiments on World?"

"Yes."

"With World children?"

"Yes."

I watch a group of Huhuhubs across the courtyard. The smelly little aliens are clustered together in some kind of ritual or game. "And have you, personally, participated in these science experiments on children, Pek Walters?"

He doesn't answer me. Instead he smiles, and if I didn't know better, I'd swear the smile was sad. He says, "Pek Bengarin, why you kill your sister?"

The unexpectedness of it—now, so close to almost learning something useful—outrages me. Not even Pek Fakar had asked me that. I stare at him angrily. He says, "I know, I not should ask. Wrong for ask. But I tell you much, and answer is important—"

"But the question is obscene. You should not ask. World people are not so cruel to each other."

"Even people damned in Aulit Prison?" he says, and even though I don't know one of the words he uses, I see that yes, he recognizes that I am an informer. And that I have been seeking information. All right, so much the better. But I need time to set my questions on a different path.

To gain time, I repeat my previous point. "World people are not so cruel."

"Then you—"

The air suddenly sizzles, smelling of burning. People shout. I look up. Afa Pek Fakar stands in the middle of the courtyard with the

Terran gun, firing it at the Huhuhubs. One by one they drop as the beam of light hits them and makes a sizzling hole. The aliens pass into the second stage of their perpetual death.

I stand and tug on Pek Walters's arm. "Come on. We must clear the area immediately or the guards will release poison gas."

"Why?"

"So they can get the bodies into bondage chemicals, of course!" Does this alien think the prison officials would let the unreal get even a little bit decayed? I thought that after our several conversations, Pek Walters understood more than that.

He rises slowly, haltingly, to his feet. Pek Fakar, laughing, strolls toward the door, the gun still in her hand.

Pek Walters says, "World people not cruel?"

Behind us, the bodies of the Huhuhubs lie sprawled across each other, smoking.

The next time we are herded from our cells into the dining hall and then the courtyard, the Huhuhub corpses are of course gone. Pek Walters has developed a cough. He walks more slowly, and once, on the way to our usual spot against the far wall, he puts a hand on my arm to steady himself.

"Are you sick, Pek?"

"Exactly," he says.

"But you are a healer. Make the cough disappear."

He smiles, and sinks gratefully against the wall. " 'Healer, heal own self.' "

"What?"

"Nothing. So you are informer, Pek Bengarin, and you hope I tell you something about science experiments on children on World."

I take a deep breath. Pek Fakar passes us, carrying her gun. Two of her own people now stay close beside her at all times, in case another prisoner tries to take the gun away from her. I cannot believe anyone would try, but maybe I'm wrong. There's no telling what the unreal will do. Pek Walters watches her pass, and his smile is gone. Yesterday Pek Fakar shot another person, this time not even an alien. There is a note under my bed requesting more guns.

I say, "*You* say I am an informer. I do not say it."

"Exactly," Pek Walters says. He has another coughing spell, then closes his eyes wearily. "I have not an-tee-by-otics."

Another Terran word. Carefully I repeat it. " 'An-tee-by-otics'?"

"Pro-teenz for heal."

Again that word for very small bits of food. I make use of it. "Tell me about the pro-teenz in the science experiments."

"I tell you everything about experiments. But only if you answer questions first."

He will ask about my sister. For no reason other than rudeness and cruelty. I feel my face turn to stone.

He says, "Tell me why steal baby not so bad for make person un-real always."

I blink. Isn't this obvious? "To steal a baby doesn't damage the baby's reality. It just grows up somewhere else, with some other people. But all real people of World share the same reality, and any-way after the transition, the child will rejoin its blood ancestors. Baby stealing is wrong, of course, but it isn't a really serious crime."

"And make false coins?"

"The same. False, true—coins are still shared."

He coughs again, this time much harder. I wait. Finally he says, "So when I steal your bicycle, I not violate shared reality too much, be-cause bicycle still somewhere with people of World."

"Of course."

"But when I steal bicycle, I violate shared reality a little?"

"Yes." After a minute I add, "Because the bicycle is, after all, *mine*. You…made my reality shift a little without sharing the decision with me." I peer at him; how can all this not be obvious to such an in-telligent man?

He says, "You are too trusting for be informer, Pek Bengarin."

I feel my throat swell with indignation. I am a *very good* in-former. Haven't I just bound this Terran to me with a private shared reality in order to create an exchange of information? I am about to de-mand his share of the bargain when he says abruptly, "So why you kill your sister?"

Two of Pek Fakar's people swagger past. They carry the new guns. Across the courtyard a Faller turns slowly to look at them, and even I can read fear on that alien face.

I say, as evenly as I can manage, "I fell prey to an illusion. I thought that Ano was copulating with my lover. She was younger, more intelligent, prettier. I am not very pretty, as you can see. I didn't share the reality with her, or him, and my illusion grew. Finally it exploded in my head, and I ... did it." I am breathing hard, and Pek Fakar's people look blurry.

"You remember clear Ano's murder?"

I turn to him in astonishment. "How could I forget it?"

"You cannot. You cannot because of memory-building pro-teenz. Memory is strong in your brain. Memory-building pro-teenz are strong in your brain. Scientific research on World children for discover what is structure of pro-teenz, where is pro-teenz, how pro-teenz work. But we discover different thing instead."

"What different thing?" I say, but Pek Walters only shakes his head and begins coughing again. I wonder if the coughing spell is an excuse to violate our bargain. He is, after all, unreal.

Pek Fakar's people have gone inside the prison. The Faller slumps against the far wall. They have not shot him. For this moment, at least, he is not entering the second stage of his perpetual death.

But beside me, Pek Walters coughs blood.

He is dying. I am sure of it, although of course no World healer comes to him. He is dead anyway. Also, his fellow Terrans keep away, looking fearful, which makes me wonder if his disease is catching. This leaves only me. I walk him to his cell, and then wonder why I can't just stay when the door closes. No one will check. Or, if they do, will care. And this may be my last chance to gain the needed information, before either Pek Walters is coffined or Pek Fakar orders me away from him because he is too weak to watch over my supposed blood sickness.

His body has become very hot. During the long night he tosses on his bunk, muttering in his own language, and sometimes those strange alien eyes roll in their sockets. But other times he is clearer, and he looks at me as if he recognizes who I am. Those times, I question him. But the lucid times and unlucid ones blur together. His mind is no longer his own.

"Pek Walters. Where are the memory experiments being conducted? In what place?"

"Memory...memories..." More in his own language. It has the cadences of poetry.

"Pek Walters. In what place are the memory experiments being done?"

"At Rafkit Sarloe," he says, which makes no sense. Rafkit Sarloe is the government center, where no one lives. It is not large. People flow in every day, running the Sections, and out to their villages again at night. There is no square measure of Rafkit Sarloe that is not constantly shared physical reality.

He coughs, more bloody spume, and his eyes roll in his head. I make him sip some water. "Pek Walters. In what place are the memory experiments being done?"

"At Rafkit Sarloe. In the Cloud. At Aulit Prison."

It goes on and on like that. And in the early morning, Pek Walters dies.

There is one moment of greater clarity, somewhere near the end. He looks at me, out of his old, ravaged face gone gaunt with his transition. The disturbing look is back in his eyes, sad and kind, not a look for the unreal to wear. It is too much sharing. He says, so low I must bend over him to hear, "Sick brain talks to itself. You not kill your sister."

"Hush, don't try to talk..."

"Find...Brifjis. Maldon Pek Brifjis, in Rafkit Haddon. Find..." He relapses again into fever.

A few moments after he dies, the armored guards enter the cell, wheeling the coffin full of bondage chemicals. With them is the priest. I want to say, *Wait, he is a good man, he doesn't deserve perpetual death*—but of course I do not. I am astonished at myself for even thinking it. A guard edges me into the corridor and the door closes.

That same day, I am sent away from Aulit Prison.

"Tell me again. Everything," Pek Brimmidin says.

Pek Brimmidin is just the same: stocky, yellowing, slightly stooped. His cluttered office is just the same. Food dishes, papers, overelaborated sculptures. I stare hungrily at the ugly things. I hadn't realized how much I'd longed, in prison, for the natural sight of curves. I keep my eyes on the sculptures, partly to hold back my question until the proper time to ask it.

"Pek Walters said he would tell me everything about the experiments that are, yes, going on with World children. In the name of science. But all he had time to tell me was that the experiments involve 'memory-building pro-teenz,' which are tiny pieces of food from which the brain constructs memory. He also said the experiments were going on in Rafkit Sarloe and Aulit Prison."

"And that is all, Pek Bengarin?"

"That is all."

Pek Brimmidin nods curtly. He is trying to appear dangerous, to scare out of me any piece of information I might have forgotten. But Frablit Pek Brimmidin can't appear dangerous to me. I have seen the real thing.

Pek Brimmidin has not changed. But I have.

I ask my question. "I have brought to you all the information I could obtain before the Terran died. Is it sufficient to release me and Ano?"

He runs a hand through his neck fur. "I'm sorry I can't answer that, Pek. I will need to consult my superiors. But I promise to send you word as soon as I can."

"Thank you," I say, and lower my eyes. *You are too trusting for be informer, Pek Bengarin.*

Why didn't I tell Frablit Pek Brimmidin the rest of it, about "Maldon Pek Brifjis" and "Rafkit Haddon" and not really killing my sister? Because it is most likely nonsense, the ravings of a fevered brain. Because this "Maldon Pek Brifjis" might be an innocent World man, who does not deserve trouble brought to him by an unreal alien. Because Pek Walters's words were personal, addressed to me alone, on his deathbed. Because I do not want to discuss Ano with Pek Brimmidin's superiors one more useless painful time.

Because, despite myself, I trust Carryl Pek Walters.

"You may go," Pek Brimmidin says, and I ride my bicycle along the dusty road home.

I make a bargain with Ano's corpse, still lying in curled-finger grace on the bed across from mine. Her beautiful brown hair floats in the chemicals of the coffin. I used to covet that hair desperately, when we were very young. Once I even cut it all off while she slept. But other times I would weave it for her, or braid it with flowers. She was so pretty. At one point, when she was still a child, she wore eight bid rings, one on each finger. Two of the bids were in negotiation between the boys' fathers and ours. Although older, I have never had a single bid.

Did I murder her?

My bargain with her corpse is this: If the Reality & Atonement Section releases me and Ano because of my work in Aulit Prison, I will seek no further. Ano will be free to join our ancestors; I will be fully real. It will no longer matter whether or not I killed my sister, because both of us will again be sharing in the same reality as if I had not. But if Reality & Atonement holds me unreal still longer, after all I have given them, I will try to find this "Maldon Pek Brifjis."

I say none of this aloud. The guards at Aulit Prison knew immediately when Pek Walters died, inside a closed and windowless room. They could be watching me here, now. World has no devices to do this, but how did Pek Walters know so much about a World man working with a Terran science experiment? Somewhere there are World people and Terrans in partnership. Terrans, as everyone knows, have all sorts of listening devices we do not.

I kiss Ano's coffin. I don't say it aloud, but I hope desperately that Reality & Atonement releases us. I want to return to shared reality, to the daily warmth and sweetness of belonging, now and forever, to the living and dead of World. I do not want to be an informer anymore.

Not for anyone, even myself.

The message comes three days later. The afternoon is warm and I sit outside on my stone bench, watching my neighbor's milkbeasts eye her sturdily fenced flowerbeds. She has new flowers that I don't recognize, with blooms that are entrancing but somehow foreign—could they be Terran? It doesn't seem likely. During my time in Aulit Prison, more people seem to have made up their minds that the Terrans are unreal. I have heard more mutterings, more anger against those who buy from alien traders.

Frablit Pek Brimmidin himself brings the letter from Reality & Atonement, laboring up the road on his ancient bicycle. He has removed his uniform, so as not to embarrass me in front of my neighbors. I watch him ride up, his neck fur damp with unaccustomed exertion, his gray eyes abashed, and I know already what the sealed message must say. Pek Brimmidin is too kind for his job. That is why he is only a low-level messenger boy all the time, not just today.

These are things I never saw before.

*You are too trusting for be informer, Pek Bengarin.*

"Thank you, Pek Brimmidin," I say. "Would you like a glass of water? Or pel?"

"No, thank you, Pek," he says. He does not meet my eyes. He waves to my other neighbor, fetching water from the village well, and fumbles meaninglessly with the handle of his bicycle. "I can't stay."

"Then ride safely," I say, and go back in my house. I stand beside Ano and break the seal on the government letter. After I read it, I gaze at her a long time. So beautiful, so sweet-natured. So loved.

Then I start to clean. I scrub every inch of my house, for hours and hours, climbing on a ladder to wash the ceiling, sloshing thick soapsuds in the cracks, scrubbing every surface of every object and carrying the more intricately shaped outside into the sun to dry. Despite my most intense scrutiny, I find nothing that I can imagine being a listening device. Nothing that looks alien, nothing unreal.

But I no longer know what is real.

Only Bata is up; the other moons have not risen. The sky is clear and starry, the air cool. I wheel my bicycle inside and try to remember everything I need.

Whatever kind of glass Ano's coffin is made of, it is very tough. I have to swing my garden shovel three times, each time with all my strength, before I can break it. On the third blow the glass cracks, then falls leisurely apart into large pieces that bounce slightly when they hit the floor. Chemicals cascade off the bed, a waterfall of clear liquid that smells only slightly acrid.

In my high boots I wade close to the bed and throw containers of water over Ano to wash off chemical residue. The containers are waiting in a neat row by the wall, everything from my largest wash basin to the kitchen bowls. Ano smiles sweetly.

I reach onto the soggy bed and lift her clear.

In the kitchen, I lay her body—limp, soft-limbed—on the floor and strip off her chemical-soaked clothing. I dry her, move her to the waiting blanket, take a last look, and wrap her tightly. The bundle of her and the shovel balances across the handles of my bicycle. I pull off my boots and open the door.

The night smells of my neighbor's foreign flowers. Ano seems weightless. I feel as if I can ride for hours. And I do.

I bury her, weighted with stones, in marshy ground well off a deserted road. The wet dirt will speed the decay, and it is easy to cover the grave with reeds and toglif branches. When I've finished, I bury my clothes and dress in clean ones in my pack. Another few hours of riding and I can find an inn to sleep in. Or a field, if need be.

The morning dawns pearly, with three moons in the sky. Everywhere I ride are flowers, first wild and then cultivated. Although exhausted, I sing softly to the curving blooms, to the sky, to the pale moonlit road. Ano is real, and free.

Go sweetly, sweet sister, to our waiting ancestors.

Two days later I reach Rafkit Haddon.

It is an old city, sloping down the side of a mountain to the sea. The homes of the rich either stand on the shore or perch on the mountain, looking in both cases like rounded great white birds. In between lie a jumble of houses, market squares, government buildings, inns, pel shops, slums, and parks, the latter with magnificent old trees and shabby old shrines. The manufacturing shops and warehouses lie to the north, with the docks.

I have experience in finding people. I start with Rituals & Processions. The clerk behind the counter, a pre-initiate of the priesthood, is young and eager to help. "Yes?"

"I am Ajma Pek Goranalit, attached to the household of Menanlin. I have been sent to inquire about the ritual activity of a citizen, Maldon Pek Brifjis. Can you help me?"

"Of course." She beams. An inquiry about ritual activity is never written; discretion is necessary when a great house is considering honoring a citizen by allowing him to honor their ancestors. A person so chosen gains great prestige—and considerable material wealth. I picked the name "Menanlin" after an hour's judicious listening in a crowded pel shop. The family is old, numerous, and discreet.

"Let me see," she says, browsing among her public records. "Brifjis ... Brifjis ... it's a common name, of course ... which citizen, Pek?"

"Maldon."

"Oh, yes...here. He paid for two musical tributes to his ancestors last year, made a donation to the Rafkit Haddon Priest House...Oh! And he was chosen to honor the ancestors of the house of Choulalait!"

She sounds awe-struck. I nod. "We know about that, of course. But is there anything else?"

"No, I don't think so...wait. He paid for a charity tribute for the ancestors of his clu merchant, Lam Pek Flanoe, a poor man. Quite a lavish tribute, too. Music, and three priests."

"Kind," I said.

"Very! Three priests!" Her young eyes shine. "Isn't it wonderful how many truly kind people share reality?"

"Yes," I say. "It is."

I find the clu merchant by the simple method of asking for him in several market squares. Sales of all fuels are of course slow in the summer; the young relatives left in charge of the clu stalls are happy to chat with strangers. Lam Pek Flanoe lives in a run-down neighborhood just behind the great houses by the sea. The neighborhood is home to servants and merchants who provide for the rich. Four more glasses of pel in three more pel shops, and I know that Maldon Pek Brifjis is currently a guest in the home of a rich widow. I know the widow's address. I know that Pek Brifjis is a healer.

A healer.

*Sick brain talks to itself. You not kill your sister.*

I am dizzy from four glasses of pel. Enough. I find an inn, the kind where no one asks questions, and sleep without the shared reality of dreams.

It takes me a day, disguised as a street cleaner, to decide which of the men coming and going from the rich widow's house is Pek Brifjis. Then I spend three days following him, in various guises. He goes a lot of places and talks to a lot of people, but none of them seem unusual for a rich healer with a personal pleasure in collecting antique water carafes. On the fourth day I look for a good opportunity to approach him, but this turns out to be unnecessary.

"Pek," a man says to me as I loiter, dressed as a vendor of sweet flatbreads, outside the baths on Elindel Street. I have stolen the sweets before dawn from the open kitchen of a bake shop. I know at once that the man approaching me is a bodyguard, and that he is very good. It's in the way he walks, looks at me, places his hand on my arm. He is also very handsome, but that thought barely registers. Handsome men are never for such as me. They are for Ano.

Were for Ano.

"Come with me, please," the bodyguard says, and I don't argue. He leads me to the back of the baths, through a private entrance, to a small room apparently used for private grooming of some sort. The only furniture is two small stone tables. He checks me, expertly but gently, for weapons, looking even in my mouth. Satisfied, he indicates where I am to stand, and opens a second door.

Maldon Pek Brifjis enters, wrapped in a bathing robe of rich imported cloth. He is younger than Carryl Walters, a vigorous man in a vigorous prime. His eyes are striking, a deep purple with long gold lines radiating from their centers. He says immediately, "Why have you been following me for three days?"

"Someone told me to," I say. I have nothing to lose by an honest shared reality, although I still don't fully believe I have anything to gain.

"Who? You may say anything in front of my guard."

"Carryl Pek Walters."

The purple eyes deepen even more. "Pek Walters is dead."

"Yes," I say. "Perpetually. I was with him when he entered the second stage of death."

"And where was that?" He is testing me.

"In Aulit Prison. His last words instructed me to find you. To…ask you something."

"What do you wish to ask me?"

"Not what I thought I would ask," I say, and realize that I have made the decision to tell him everything. Until I saw him up close, I wasn't completely sure what I would do. I can no longer share reality with World, not even if I went to Frablit Pek Brimmidin with exactly the knowledge he wants about the scientific experiments on children. That would not atone for releasing Ano before the Section agreed. And Pek Brimmidin is only a messenger, anyway. No, less than a messenger: a tool, like a garden shovel, or a bicycle. He does not share the reality of his users. He only thinks he does.

As I had thought I did.

I say, "I want to know if I killed my sister. Pek Walters said I did not. He said 'sick brain talks to itself,' and that I had not killed Ano. And to ask *you*. Did I kill my sister?"

Pek Brifjis sits down on one of the stone tables. "I don't know," he says, and I see his neck fur quiver. "Perhaps you did. Perhaps you did not."

"How can I discover which?"

"You cannot."

"Ever?"

"Ever." And then, "I am sorry."

Dizziness takes me. The "low blood pressure." The next thing I know, I lie on the floor of the small room, with Pek Brifjis's fingers on my elbow pulse. I struggle to sit up.

"No, wait," he says. "Wait a moment. Have you eaten today?"

"Yes."

"Well, wait a moment anyway. I need to think."

He does, the purple eyes turning inward, his fingers absently pressing the inside of my elbow. Finally he says, "You are an informer. That's why you were released from Aulit Prison after Pek Walters died. You inform for the government."

I don't answer. It no longer matters.

"But you have left informing. Because of what Pek Walters told you. Because he told you that the skits-oh-free-nia experiments might have…no. It can't be."

He too has used a word I don't know. It sounds Terran. Again I struggle to sit up, to leave. There is no hope for me here. This healer can tell me nothing.

He pushes me back down on the floor and says swiftly, "When did your sister die?" His eyes have changed once again; the long golden flecks are brighter, radiating from the center like glowing spokes. "Please, Pek, this is immensely important. To both of us."

"Two years ago, and 152 days."

"Where? In what city?"

"Village. Our village. Gofkit Ilo."

"Yes," he says. "*Yes*. Tell me everything you remember of her death. Everything."

This time I push him aside and sit up. Blood rushes from my head, but anger overcomes the dizziness. "I will tell you nothing. Who do you people think you are, ancestors? To tell me I killed Ano, then tell me I didn't, then say you don't know—to destroy the hope of atonement I had as an informer, then to tell me there is no other hope—no, there might be hope—no, there's *not*—how can you live with yourself? How can you twist people's brains away from shared reality and offer *nothing to replace it!*" I am screaming. The bodyguard glances at the door. I don't care; I go on screaming.

"You are doing experiments on children, wrecking their reality as you have wrecked mine! You are a murderer—" But I don't get to scream all that. Maybe I don't get to scream any of it. For a needle slides into my elbow, at the inner pulse where Maldon Pek Brifjis has been holding it, and the room slides away as easily as Ano into her grave.

A bed, soft and silky, beneath me. Rich wall hangings. The room is very warm. A scented breeze whispers across my bare stomach. Bare? I sit up and discover I am dressed in the gauzy skirt, skimpy bandeau, and flirting veil of a prostitute.

At my first movement, Pek Brifjis crosses from the fireplace to my bed. "Pek. This room does not allow sound to escape. Do not resume screaming. Do you understand?"

I nod. His bodyguard stands across the room. I pull the flirting veil from my face.

"I am sorry about that," Pek Brifjis says. "It was necessary to dress you in a way that accounts for a bodyguard carrying a drugged woman into a private home without raising questions."

A private home. I guess that this is the rich widow's house by the sea. A room that does not allow sound to escape. A needle unlike ours: sharp and sure. Brain experiments. "Skits-oh-free-nia."

I say, "You work with the Terrans."

"No," he says. "I do not."

"But Pek Walters..." It doesn't matter. "What are you going to do with me?"

He says, "I am going to offer you a trade."

"What sort of trade?"

"Information in return for your freedom."

And he says he does not work with Terrans. I say, "What use is freedom to me?" although of course I don't expect him to understand that. I can never be free.

"Not that kind of freedom," he says. "I won't just let you go from this room. I will let you rejoin your ancestors, and Ano."

I gape at him.

"Yes, Pek. I will kill you and bury you myself, where your body can decay."

"You would violate shared reality like that? For *me?*"

His purple eyes deepen again. For a moment, something in those eyes looks almost like Pek Walters's blue ones. "Please understand. I think there is a strong chance you did not kill Ano. Your village was one where...subjects were used for experimentation. I think that is the true shared reality here."

I say nothing. A little of his assurance disappears. "Or so I believe. Will you agree to the trade?"

"Perhaps," I say. Will he actually do what he promises? I can't be sure. But there is no other way for me. I cannot hide from the government all the years until I die. I am too young. And when they find me, they will send me back to Aulit, and when I die there they will put me in a coffin of preservative chemicals...

I would never see Ano again.

The healer watches me closely. Again I see the Pek Walters look in his eyes: sadness and pity.

"Perhaps I will agree to the trade," I say, and wait for him to speak again about the night Ano died. But instead he says, "I want to show you something."

He nods at the bodyguard, who leaves the room, returning a few moments later. By the hand he leads a child, a little girl, clean and well-dressed. One look makes my neck fur bristle. The girl's eyes are flat and unseeing. She mutters to herself. I offer a quick appeal for protection to my ancestors. The girl is unreal, without the capacity to perceive shared reality, even though she is well over the age of reason. She is not human. She should have been destroyed.

"This is Ori," Pek Brifjis says. The girl suddenly laughs, a wild demented laugh, and peers at something only she can see.

"Why is it here?" I listen to the harshness in my own voice.

"Ori was born real. She was made this way by the scientific brain experiments of the government."

"Of the government! That is a lie!"

"Is it? Do you still, Pek, have such trust in your government?"

"No, but..." To make me continue to earn Ano's freedom, even after I had met their terms...to lie to Pek Brimmidin...those offenses against shared reality are one thing. The destruction of a real person's physical body, as I had done with Ano's (had I?) is another, far far worse. To destroy a *mind*, the instrument of perceiving shared reality...Pek Brifjis lies.

He says, "Pek, tell me about the night Ano died."

"Tell me about this...thing!"

"All right." He sits down in a chair beside my luxurious bed. The thing wanders around the room, muttering. It seems unable to stay still.

"She was born Ori Malfisit, in a small village in the far north—"

"What village?" I need desperately to see if he falters on details.

He does not. "Gofkit Ramloe. Of real parents, simple people, an old and established family. At six years old, Ori was playing in the forest with some other children when she disappeared. The other children said they heard something thrashing toward the marshes. The family decided she had been carried off by a wild kilfreit—there are still some left, you know, that far north—and held a procession in honor of Ori's joining their ancestors.

"But that's not what happened to Ori. She was stolen by two men, unreal prisoners promised atonement and restoration to full reality, just as you were. Ori was carried off to Rafkit Sarloe, with eight other children from all over World. There they were given to the

Terrans, who were told that they were orphans who could be used for experiments. The experiments were ones that would not hurt or damage the children in any way."

I look at Ori, now tearing a table scarf into shreds and muttering. Her empty eyes turn to mine, and I have to look away.

"This part is difficult," Pek Brifjis says. "Listen hard, Pek. The Terrans truly did not hurt the children. They put ee-lek-trodes on their heads ... you don't know what that means. They found ways to see which parts of their brains worked the same as Terran brains and which did not. They used a number of tests and machines and drugs. None of it hurt the children, who lived at the Terran scientific compound and were cared for by World childwatchers. At first the children missed their parents, but they were young, and after a while they were happy."

I glance again at Ori. The unreal, not sharing in common reality, are isolated and therefore dangerous. A person with no world in common with others will violate those others as easily as cutting flowers. Under such conditions, pleasure is possible, but not happiness.

Pek Brifjis runs his hand through his neck fur. "The Terrans worked with World healers, of course, teaching them. It was the usual trade, only this time we received the information and they the physical reality: children and watchers. There was no other way World could permit Terrans to handle our children. Our healers were there every moment."

He looks at me. I say, "Yes," just because something must be said.

"Do you know, Pek, what it is like to realize you have lived your whole life according to beliefs that are not true?"

"No!" I say, so loudly that Ori looks up with her mad, unreal gaze. She smiles. I don't know why I spoke so loud. What Pek Brifjis said has nothing to do with me. Nothing at all.

"Well, Pek Walters knew. He realized that the experiments he participated in, harmless to the subjects and in aid of biological understanding of species differences, were being used for something else. The roots of skits-oh-free-nia, misfiring brain sir-kits—" He is off on a long explanation that means nothing to me. Too many Terran words, too much strangeness. Pek Brifjis is no longer talking to me. He is talking to himself, in some sort of pain I don't understand.

Suddenly the purple eyes snap back to mine. "What all that means, Pek, is that a few of the healers—our own healers, from World—found out how to manipulate the Terran science. They took it and used it to put into minds memories that did not happen."

"Not possible!"

"It is possible. The brain is made very excited, with Terran devices, while the false memory is recited over and over. Then different parts of the brain are made to...to recirculate memories and emotions over and over. Like water recirculated through mill races. The water gets all scrambled together.... No. Think of it this way: different parts of the brain send signals to each other. The signals are forced to loop together, and every loop makes the unreal memories stronger. It is apparently in common use on Terra, although tightly controlled."

*Sick brain talks to itself.*

"But—"

"There are no objections possible, Pek. It is real. It happened. It happened to Ori. The World scientists made her brain remember things that had not happened. Small things, at first. That worked. When they tried larger memories, something went wrong. It left her like this. They were still learning; that was five years ago. They got better, much better. Good enough to experiment on adult subjects who could then be returned to shared reality."

"One can't plant memories like flowers, or uproot them like weeds!"

"These people could. And did."

"But—*why?*"

"Because the World healers who did this—and they were only a few—saw a different reality."

"I don't—"

"They saw the Terrans able to do everything. Make better machines than we can, from windmills to bicycles. Fly to the stars. Cure disease. Control nature. Many World people are afraid of Terrans Pek. And of Fallers and Huhuhubs. Because their reality is superior to ours."

"There is only one common reality," I say. "The Terrans just know more about it than we do!"

"Perhaps. But Terran knowledge makes people uneasy. And afraid. And jealous."

*Jealous. Ano saying to me in the kitchen, with Bata and Cap bright at the window, "I will too go out tonight to see him! You can't stop me! You're just jealous, a jealous ugly shriveled thing that not even your lover wants, so you don't wish me to have any—" And the red flood swamping my brain, the kitchen knife, the blood—*

"Pek?" the healer says. "Pek?"

"I'm...all right. The jealous healers, they hurt their own people, World people, for revenge on the Terrans—that makes no sense!"

"The healers acted with great sorrow. They knew what they were doing to people. But they needed to perfect the technique of inducing controlled skits-oh-free-nia...they *needed* to do it. To make people angry at Terrans. Angry enough to forget the attractive trade goods and rise up against the aliens. To cause war. The healers are mistaken, Pek. We have not had a war on World in a thousand years; our people cannot understand how hard the Terrans would strike back. But you must understand: the outlaw scientists thought they were doing the right thing. They thought they were creating anger in order to save World.

"And another thing—with the help of the government, they were careful not to make any World man or woman permanently unreal. The adults manipulated into murder were all offered atonement as informers. The children are all cared for. The mistakes, like Ori, will be allowed to decay someday, to return to their ancestors. I will see to that myself."

Ori tears the last of the scarf into pieces, smiling horribly, her flat eyes empty. What unreal memories fill her head?

I say bitterly, "Doing the right thing...letting me believe I killed my sister!"

"When you rejoin your ancestors, you will find it isn't so. And the means of rejoining them was made available to you: the completion of your informing atonement."

But now that atonement never will be completed. I stole Ano and buried her without Section consent. Maldon Pek Brifjis, of course, does not know this.

Through my pain and anger I blurt, "And what of *you*, Pek Brifjis? You work with these criminal healers, aiding them in emptying children like Ori of reality—"

"I don't work with them. I thought you were smarter, Pek. I work against them. And so did Carryl Walters, which is why he died in Aulit Prison."

"Against them?"

"Many of us do. Carryl Walters among them. He was an informer. And my friend."

Neither of us says anything. Pek Brifjis stares into the fire. I stare at Ori, who has begun to grimace horribly. She squats on an intricately woven curved rug that looks very old. A reek suddenly fills the room. Ori does not share with the rest of us the reality of piss closets. She throws back her head and laughs, a horrible sound like splintering metal.

"Take her away," Pek Brifjis says wearily to the guard, who looks unhappy. "I'll clean up here." To me he adds, "We can't allow any servants in here with you."

The guard leads away the grimacing child. Pek Brifjis kneels and scrubs at the rug with chimney rags dipped in water from my carafe. I remember that he collects antique water carafes. What a long way that must seem from scrubbing shit, from Ori, from Carryl Walters coughing out his lungs in Aulit Prison, among aliens.

"Pek Brifjis—did I kill my sister?"

He looks up. There is shit on his hands. "There is no way to be absolutely sure. It is possible you were one of the experiment subjects from your village. You would have been drugged in your house, to awake with your sister murdered and your mind altered."

I say, more quietly than I have said anything else in this room, "You will really kill me, let me decay, and enable me to rejoin my ancestors?"

Pek Brifjis stands and wipes the shit from his hands. "I will."

"But what will you do if I refuse? If instead I ask to return home?"

"If you do that, the government will arrest you and once more promise you atonement—if you inform on those of us working to oppose them."

"Not if I go first to whatever part of the government is truly working to end the experiments. Surely you aren't saying the *entire* government is doing this…thing."

"Of course not. But do you know for certain which Sections, and which officials in those Sections, wish for war with the Terrans, and which do not? *We* can't be sure. How can you?"

Frablit Pek Brimmidin is innocent, I think. But the thought is useless. Pek Brimmidin is innocent, but powerless.

It tears my soul to think that the two might be the same thing.

Pek Brifjis rubs at the damp carpet with the toe of his boot. He puts the rags in a lidded jar and washes his hands at the washstand. A faint stench still hangs in the air. He comes to stand beside my bed.

"Is that what you want, Uli Pek Bengarin? That I let you leave this house, not knowing what you will do, whom you will inform on? That I endanger everything we have done in order to convince you of its truth?"

"Or you can kill me and let me rejoin my ancestors. Which is what you think I will choose, isn't it? That choice would let you keep faith with the reality you have decided is true, and still keep yourself secret from the criminals. Killing me would be easiest for you. But only if I consent to my murder. Otherwise, you will violate even the reality you have decided to perceive."

He stares down at me, a muscular man with beautiful purple eyes. A healer who would kill. A patriot defying his government to prevent a violent war. A sinner who does all he can to minimize his sin and keep it from denying him the chance to rejoin his own ancestors. A believer in shared reality who is trying to bend the reality without breaking the belief.

I keep quiet. The silence stretches on. Finally it is Pek Brifjis that breaks it. "I wish Carryl Walters had never sent you to me."

"But he did. And I choose to return to my village. Will you let me go, or keep me prisoner here, or murder me without my consent?"

"Damn you," he says, and I recognize the word as one Carryl Walters used, about the unreal souls in Aulit Prison.

"Exactly," I say. "What will you do, Pek? Which of your supposed multiple realities will you choose now?"

It is a hot night, and I cannot sleep.

I lie in my tent on the wide empty plain and listen to the night noises. Rude laughter from the pel tent, where a group of miners drinks far too late at night for men who must bore into hard rock at dawn. Snoring from the tent to my right. Muffled lovemaking from a tent farther down the row, I'm not sure whose. The woman giggles, high and sweet.

I have been a miner for half a year now. After I left the northern village of Gofkit Ramloe, Ori's village, I just kept heading north. Here on the equator, where World harvests its tin and diamonds and pel berries and salt, life is both simpler and less organized. Papers are not necessary. Many of the miners are young, evading their government service for one reason or another. Reasons that must seem valid to them. Here government sections rule weakly, compared to the rule of the mining and farming companies. There are no messengers on Terran bicycles. There is no Terran science. There are no Terrans.

There are shrines, of course, and rituals and processions, and tributes to one's ancestors. But these things actually receive less attention than in the cities, because they are more taken for granted. Do you pay attention to air?

The woman giggles again, and this time I recognize the sound. Awi Pek Crafmal, the young runaway from another island. She is a pretty thing, and a hard worker. Sometimes she reminds me of Ano.

I asked a great many questions in Gofkit Ramloe. *Ori Malfisit*, Pek Brifjis said her name was. *An old and established family.* But I asked and asked, and no such family had ever lived in Gofkit Ramloe. Wherever Ori came from, and however she had been made into that unreal and empty vessel shitting on a rich carpet, she had not started her poor little life in Gofkit Ramloe.

Did Maldon Pek Brifjis know I would discover that, when he released me from the rich widow's house overlooking the sea? He must have. Or maybe, despite knowing I was an informer, he didn't understand that I would actually go to Gofkit Ramloe and check. You can't understand everything.

Sometimes, in the darkest part of the night, I wish I had taken Pek Brifjis's offer to return me to my ancestors.

I work on the rock piles of the mine during the day, among miners who lift sledges and shatter solid stone. They talk, and curse, and revile the Terrans, although few miners have as much as seen one. After work the miners sit in camp and drink pel, lifting huge mugs with dirty hands, and laugh at obscene jokes. They all share the same reality, and it binds them together, in simple and happy strength.

I have strength, too. I have the strength to swing my sledge with the other women, many of whom have the same rough plain looks as

I, and who are happy to accept me as one of them. I had the strength to shatter Ano's coffin, and to bury her even when I thought the price to me was perpetual death. I had the strength to follow Carryl Walters's words about the brain experiments and seek Maldon Pek Brifjis. I had the strength to twist Pek Brifjis's divided mind to make him let me go.

But do I have the strength to go where all of that leads me? Do I have the strength to look at Frablit Pek Brimmidin's reality, and Carryl Walters's reality, and Ano's, and Maldon Pek Brifjis's, and Ori's—and try to find the places that match and the places that don't? Do I have the strength to live on, never knowing if I killed my sister, or if I did not? Do I have the strength to doubt everything, and live with doubt, and sort through the millions of separate realities on World, searching for the true pieces of each—assuming that I can even recognize them?

Should anyone have to live like that? In uncertainty, in doubt, in loneliness. Alone in one's mind, in an isolated and unshared reality.

I would like to return to the days when Ano was alive. Or even to the days when I was an informer. To the days when I shared in World's reality, and knew it to be solid beneath me, like the ground itself. To the days when I knew what to think, and so did not have to.

To the days before I became—unwillingly—as terrifyingly real as I am now.

*Of her novelette, Nancy Kress writes: I don't know how or why this story came to be written; sometimes it happens that way. I do remember writing the first paragraph whole, as it came to me, all at once. Then I looked at it and said, "Her sister's dead? How did that happen?" In the course of finding out how that happened, I also found out that World has a far different belief system than do the Terrans who explore it.*

*That's one version, anyway. Another, just as valid, might be that belief systems fascinate me, so I'm more or less constantly mulling them over. Mine, his, hers, my dentist's. When I write, the mulling becomes a story, because the preliminary groundwork has already been done.*

*Also, I have a younger sister with long brown hair. You use what's available.*

# The Crab Lice

GREGORY FEELEY

Science fiction has always been almost as interested in the past as it is in the future, writing not only time-travel-to-the-past stories, but also "what if" alternate history stories in which the South wins the Civil War, Castro plays major-league baseball, and Hitler invades Britain.

All of these stories turn on events—battles, errors, and coincidences—and on externals. No one, to my knowledge, has ever written an alternate history based on how internal changes like thought might affect the course of history. Until now.

Gregory Feeley—a well-known critic and essayist for the *Washington Post,* the *New York Times,* and the *Atlantic*—is the author of "The Weighing of Ayre," the Philip K. Dick finalist novel *The Oxygen Barons,* and numerous short stories, all of which reflect his well-read, analytical, and original mind.

Especially this Nebula-finalist story, "The Crab Lice," an extraordinary tale about a journey into both the past and the future and about the over- (and under-) estimated effect of literature.

Transfixed (respectively) with rage and triumph, the tyrant and his tormentor ride home to their beds where, tossing in uneasy sleep, they experience the same dream, although it comes in different guises. For what is to Aristophanes a mere *enupnion,* a phantasm compounded of wish-fulfillment and anxiety (for who would wish finally to displace his enemy, assuming a position so lately proven vulnerable?), is for Cleon a very *oneiros*, a sent vision (prophecy, or mere warning?) of his deepest dreads. Let a snake kill an eagle as in Homer, foretelling the leader's destruction at the hands of his enemies (or worse, his own people), but for the horsefly to emerge from beneath the saddle where it has so long stung to sit upon it—O monstrous!—like a warrior: this is an abomination.

Let the wheel of fortune that bore me up now cast me down and crush me, thinks Cleon (standing apart from the dream's action even as he experiences it), but do not let me be undone by an outrage of nature. Let *ate* and *hubris* consume me: let my *hamartia* crush me utterly; but do not let Aristophanes of Pandionis be the agent of my overthrow. My citizens can fall upon me; I can bear exile and even death; but if the profaner of the City Dionysia usurps me I shall be *anathema*: worse, I shall be ridiculous.

Aristophanes, ears yet ringing with the laughter that greeted his *Phtheires*, regards his unlikely elevation with a more complex disquiet. He has been charged with winning peace for Athens (the particulars of Cleon's downfall are not given, as the dream has begun in medias res), and the *Ekklesia*—whose front benches are, in the odd logic of dreams, here filled with the cast of his play—is looking to him for results. "You don't have to wear masks in the *Ekklesia*," he thinks to himself, but feels unaccountably embarrassed to say so. He is engaged in an explanation of how to bring the Spartans to the peace table—it involves inviting them to the Great Dionysian Festival, where the merits of peace will be presented dramatically—but the members of his chorus are, bewilderingly, raising successive objections, which Aristophanes must rebut in the manner of Socrates, drawing out each questioner (who are, he realizes with mild alarm, no brighter than any actor) so that he comes to an appreciation of his error. Aristophanes is growing entangled in the coils of his argument, and the scene steadily congeals into clammy dream-anxiety; shouldn't the chorus be speaking *his* words?

Dionysos, god of vegetative rites and hence of comedy, sees his disparate champions thrashing in epiphenomenal torment and is amused. Evading the Heraclitian flux of the material universe, he slips through interstices in tenspace and links the dreamers' psyches through a wormhole thinner than an atomic nucleus. Mediating between the standing wave fronts (which else would collapse into each other like air bubbles), Dionysos appears, vivider than real: a Theophany.

The Pnyx vanishes and before them stands the god, slight of frame yet perfectly formed, his brow garlanded with berries and an ivy wand held in one hand. Cleon imagines for a confused instant that his dream has taken a fortuitous turn: Dionysos breaking in to restore him to his proper eminence; but Aristophanes—the scent of sandalwood and incense in his nostrils, and the drape of the god's short cape visible in extraordinary detail—knows this to be no dream. He has imagined since childhood how he would comport himself upon encountering a god, but now finds himself tongue-tied.

"Author of others' words," declaims Dionysos in a clear, lovely voice; "and actions," with a nod toward Cleon, whom Aristophanes can see only from the corner of his eye. "Do you mortals so covet each other's stations? Misery is drawn swiftly in the wake of granted wishes."

While Aristophanes pauses to frame a reply, Cleon—who has little experience discoursing with gods but knows the wisdom of establishing alliances with the powerful—speaks up. "O great Dionysos, witness the injustice done to me! This scribbler maligns his city's leaders in time of war—and at your festival! He likens Athens' generals to vermin before visiting delegations and sows dissent when we must unite against our enemies!"

The god favors him with an easy smile. "All this is true, General," he says. "And had you added that he moreover bores his audience, I should look upon him with displeasure. But I am the god of fertility, not war, and Aristophanes has made my revelers laugh. You should feel honored to have been the occasion of such mirth."

"It may not be your province to worry about the affairs of state, great Dionysos, but it is mine," the demagogue declares. "Why are not the *Spartan* generals costumed as body lice? Why can our citizens not laugh at our foes, who do not permit plays at all? This cub Aristophanes mocks those who protect him, and lends comfort to comedy's real enemy!"

"Your general is skilled in debate," says the god mildly, turning to Aristophanes as if for comment.

"Skilled in stealing the rhetorical power of his betters," Aristophanes replies in his ringing actor's voice. "Cleon and his cohorts attacked Pericles to the end of his life—dogs pulling down a stag—and now he struts before the *Ekklesia* seeking to sway his audience with the great man's music. Yet it is but a *leather skin* that Cleon pounds, producing not melody but noise."

"There!" cries Cleon, goaded at last. "He mocks me for my merchant origins, as though the wisdom of policy were dependent on family fortunes. Like Pericles, he would keep Athens' affairs in the hands of its soft-handed aristocracy."

"But I myself am of noble birth," observes the god, "so must look upon Aristophanes' viewpoint with sympathy."

At this Cleon scowls, to Aristophanes' inexpressible delight, and makes to speak. Let him upbraid the god, Aristophanes prays, and be transformed into a frog.

"Men are not gods," Cleon growls, checking his anger. "Our ways are not yours, as the interaction between gods and mortals has long shown."

This is better said than the playwright would have wished, though still lame. For a second he had feared that Cleon would remind Dionysos that he was also born of the simple nymph Semele, who was cruelly tricked unto death by Hera for having been seduced by Zeus. But the demagogue's ill-schooling undoes him, and any sympathy the god may have for poor mortals goes unstirred.

"Indeed men are not gods," says Aristophanes boldly, "for no god may challenge Zeus, while any Athenian might question the wisdom of his leaders, who govern only at popular sufferance." Cleon scowls at this, but dares not interrupt while Dionysos is listening politely. Heartened, Aristophanes presses further. "Perhaps someday a playwright will topple the tyrant he satirizes. Is that not so, O Dionysos?"

"Never!" cries Cleon, fists doubled. "The gods would not permit it."

"Don't be too sure what we'd do," advises Dionysos. "Apollo oversaw your city's law-making, but he didn't lift a finger when Aristophanes mocked you last spring with his *Cavaliers*. Though my rather priggish half-brother loves order, he would likelier avenge its overthrow than prevent it, and then only if it seemed a personal affront."

"But it could happen, great one?" Aristophanes persists.

"You mean in the future?" The young god seems faintly bemused. "I suppose. Couldn't you ask an oracle?"

"What could an oracle see that the son of Zeus cannot?" It sounds flattering even to Aristophanes' ears, although he meant it seriously.

"I suppose I could look," says Dionysos with a slight frown. With a horrible thrill, Aristophanes realizes that the god is not terribly bright.

"This is nonsense," Cleon bellows. "The future is not laid out like the past."

"Why, of course it is," says Dionysos. He turns as if to point, then realizes that the direction is not one the mortals can see.

"Were men's fates not somewhere written," says Aristophanes smugly, "how could mad Cassandra see them, or the sibyls foretell their outlines?" He is not sure that he believes this himself, but is not about to relinquish the advantage.

"Defeatist cynicism!" cries Cleon. "Strong men are the authors of their—"

"Oh, hush." Dionysos gestures with his wand and Cleon vanishes with a pop, to be replaced by a large mottled frog. "*Brekekekek,*" croaks the tyrant, eyes bulging.

"You're right, of course," the god continues, producing a wineskin from somewhere. He plants his feet apart, leans backward, and squirts a crimson jet into his open mouth. "Once you have entered into the world of time and space, you can move freely along any axis. We can, that is." He wipes his mouth with the back of his wrist, then hands the skin to Aristophanes. "So you want to know your future, whether one of your plays will someday overthrow the state? I can look and tell you that."

"I was wondering rather whether any play would," says Aristophanes nervously. He isn't sure that he wants his own future read, or even to hear that it is readable. He hefts the wineskin, which is so wondrously supple that it sloshes in his hand like a jellyfish, and inexpertly squeezes a spurt over his mouth and chin.

"That's harder," says the god meditatively. "It means sorting all the...well, you don't really have a word for it. It won't take any longer, of course." And he laughs carelessly, an ingenuous youth.

Aristophanes scarcely hears him; the freshet of wine is shockingly good. He lowers the skin, his senses tingling, and sees Dionysos wave a hand in farewell. The god flickers, as a figure seen by firelight will when an ember bursts, and suddenly is standing in a slightly different position.

"You're back already?" Aristophanes asks.

"Returned to the moment whence I left," the god explains. His expression is also different. "What was your question again? Oh, yes," he says, reaching for the skin, "playwrights toppling tyrants." There was no mistaking the weariness with which he lifts it.

"I take it you traveled beyond next year," Aristophanes ventures, finding the phrase charming.

Dionysos drinks long. "Oh, yes," he says, pausing at last, "aeons beyond: farther into the future than Homer lies in the past." The god is speaking an archaic dialect, Greek as Homer may have spoken it. "And every intervening year was sampled, as a ship sailing to Nubia crosses every wave. You, Aristophanes, shall never drive generals into exile, although your *Pæderastoi* will cause a scandal such as *Phtheires* and even *Eirene*—which you prudently produce only after Cleon's death—never approach."

"I will write a play called *The Buttfuckers?*"

"Not about Cleon's regime," Dionysos says absently, his accent fading. "The golden boy, the one of your own class—Alcibiades."

"Alcibiades shall be tyrant?" Nothing Aristophanes has heard astonished him more than this.

"Stop trying to deflect me," the god says pettishly. "You asked about playwrights overthrowing their targets, did you not?"

"I beg your pardon, O Dionysos," says Aristophanes at once, as abjectly as he can manage. Sweet Zeus, he thinks, my mouth is going to get me killed.

"That's better." The god's good humor is promptly restored. "Let me explain this while I still can hold it in my head." He reaches for the skin, then thinks better of it. "The lore is all there, but it's hard to keep straight: I can sail up the river of time, but the fishing line of memory wants to stretch only downstream." He catches Aristophanes' bewildered expression and shrugs. "Outside time and space, such matters are much simpler."

"How far upriver lies the age in which a playwright overthrows his persecutors?" Aristophanes suggests.

Dionysos shudders like a wet dog, a ripple from shoulder to hips. "Farther than I hope again to see," he says, raising the skin and drinking. "An Age of Man past heroes, where cacophony and noise shout down the arts. Do you want to hear their panegyric to spring?" Without waiting for an answer, Dionysos strikes a pose and declaims:

> Syeringae-sprouting Thargelion,
> Root-wetting, compounding eros with mnemosyne,
> is the cruelest month.
> I sing of the shadowed dust beneath the rock,
> Crueler still, which you should fear,
> But fear you also water:
> It certainly killed that Phoenician.

"That's a panegyric?" asks Aristophanes.

"It gains something in translation," says the god sourly.

Aristophanes isn't really interested in posterity's lyrical shortcomings. "Are there any *plays* that celebrate spring's awakening?" he asks, thinking to return to his theme by degrees.

"Celebrate?" The god's expression is quite horrible. "Spring seems to fall upon them as a calamity. Only one was a comedy: something called *Pollen Allergies.* I couldn't understand it. No plays about the gods: the tragedies are all about *mortals. Common* mortals." Dionysos is as bewildered as he is indignant.

Aristophanes is realizing that what he really wants to know is whether his own plays would still be performed. There doesn't seem any way to ask this question, and he knows that the god will not volunteer the answer.

"Do the actors dance well?" he asks diplomatically. (Dionysos loves dancing, and Aristophanes likes to think that his own chorus gave the god pleasure.)

"The actors don't dance, the dancers don't act." Dionysos is speaking rapidly now, his face flushed. "Few poems are sung, and most music has no words." He drinks again from the skin, which shows no sign of emptying.

"How can music have no—"

The god gestures, and Aristophanes is plunged into darkness. Discordant shrieks, like a lyre being pulled apart, rise to a crescendo from a pit before him. On a raised stage lit by unflickering torches, naked dancers disport themselves with jointless abandon. Aristophanes stares at their painted bodies and features. Although no *phallopharoi*, the dancers—several of them, he realizes with a further shock, women—manage in their sinuous twinings to create the semblance of inhuman energy, like saplings straining to rut. The effect is plainly felt on the audience members around him, who leap to their feet and begin shouting incomprehensibly at the stage.

An instant later the theater (an indoor theater, thinks Aristophanes in wonder: like a temple) vanishes, and Aristophanes finds himself in a nondescript place, not dark, but without visible features.

"Those weren't mortals," he ventures after a moment, their startling leaps still vivid before him. "They must have been sylphs."

"They were human," Dionysos says from somewhere. "Celebrating spring. They are enacting a rite, one they don't believe in."

Aristophanes is untroubled by the notion of performers lacking piety for their work, but can see how the god might feel differently. "Was that dance strophe to the play proper?" he inquires.

"No play, just dance. The arts are torn asunder, and their unhealed wounds dry them up." Dionysos may sense Aristophanes' indifference, for his next words hold a hint of malice. "Would you like to see what has become of the art of drama in this distant tomorrow?"

"Well," says Aristophanes, but he is again hurled into a darkened chamber. Before him a large window looks onto a country scene, from which all color has been leached. Two barbarians are speaking; Aristophanes is startled less that their language is incomprehensible than by how loud it is. At once the scene changes: disoriented, Aristophanes finds himself looking upon a different vantage, as though the window has changed place with another. An instant later it happens again.

Head reeling, Aristophanes puts out his hand, which grazes the shoulder of Dionysos. "Consider it a frieze that moves," the god whipers.

At this Aristophanes understands: the rectangle is not a window, but a panel upon the wall; its tableau moves as in life. Every few seconds the vantage shifts. He feels like a playgoer sitting in the center of the stage, whose gaze is directed violently from one angle to another by a strong man grasping his head.

Much of the story is incomprehensible, but it involves a young maiden who is raped and killed by men who then take refuge in her father's house. Aristophanes has never heard of the story, and the pain shown in the actors' maskless faces—the worried mother learns of her child's death when the killer tries to sell her the maiden's stolen peplos—is almost unbearable. Could Sophocles have torn a greater rent in the human heart?

The story is not ended when the theater again disappears, and Aristophanes finds himself alone with Dionysos, like a child yanked from play. "A pretty comedy, eh?" he demands.

Aristophanes would have liked to see the tale through to its exodos, but a god's impatience cannot be denied. "Surely that was a tragedy, great Dionysos?" he suggests. "The hypothesis—"

"The tale is called *Virgin Spring*," the god says implacably. "Did you notice that it wasn't even in verse? Like listening to two alewives argue outside a door."

"It is plainly a barbarian's art, so—"

"That drama," Dionysos says precisely, "is by the greatest master ever to ply that medium. It is, moreover, the art that displaces yours: for the moving frieze will drive real drama into obscurity."

Aristophanes gapes at him. "What, that? How—"

The god smiles grimly. "Like a fresco, the moving frieze can be enjoyed at any time, whether it is a festival day or not. And it requires no rehearsals, nor archon to fund the chorus: the tale can be opened as readily as a scroll, and you don't even have to know how to read. High drama for slaves and barbarians alike!"

Aristophanes feels his head reeling. "But you said this was the era when a playwright finally—"

"Yes, but what of it? I scan through history to find you a playwright-insurgent and look up to find myself in a godless, shattered desert at the far end of time!" Drunk (there is now no doubt about it), Dionysos regards his celebrant with truculent injury.

"Do they even read plays?" asks Aristophanes, a bit desperately.

"Do they read *yours*, you mean." Dionysos suddenly grins. "Of all the plays you have written, only *Cavaliers* shall survive unto posterity. Your *Party Animals* will be known in name only, while *The Crab Lice* shall be utterly lost, its very existence forgotten. For all the labors you have made, you will be known best for a play that angered Cleon."

Aristophanes draws himself up, although it requires an effort. "Perhaps such a civilization is not worthy of my work," he says with dignity.

Gods don't stand upon dignity. "You love the applause and prizes," Dionysos says, pointing a perfect finger. "You want your name to outlive you, like Homer's."

"Perhaps." Aristophanes' sorrow, thickening around him like a cloud, will allow no darts to reach him. "We share that desire, don't we? You called the future godless, and you're right. They have forgotten you, and pray to other gods. Woe that you looked so far as to see that."

Dionysos stiffens at this, but Aristophanes cannot be concerned by the prospect of becoming a frog: he is preoccupied by the coils of his own anagnorisis. Fittingly, it comes in the guise of comedy: there is nothing more comic than the man made miserable by getting to see what he wanted.

The god takes a last drink and tosses aside the wineskin, which disappears without a sound. "Spacetime scums the palate, like curds," he mutters. "Too soon the need to rinse."

Aristophanes turns his head, the thread of his attention snagged. "Rinse?" he asks.

"When we return to Olympos, all we have learned here falls away, like mud from a soiled garment." Dionysos moves as though to take a step, then hesitates. "Eventually, after the feasts and tumbles, the accumulation of contingency becomes oppressive. With departure, the slate is wiped clean."

Aristophanes can hardly believe this. "You abandon all your recollections, like bad debts? Great Zeus," he mutters to himself, "no wonder the gods never seem to learn."

The patron of comedy casts Aristophanes a reproachful look. "You shouldn't talk, scornful one. When this dream is ended you shall let drop your unhappy knowledge, just as Cleon shall forget the ordeal of being a frog. I leave behind this time no quickened nymph, no punished mortals. Who, earwig, are *you* to rebuke me?"

The world around them begins to break up, and Aristophanes feels a vertiginous swoop as the ground beneath him heaves. *Earwig?* he thinks as he scrambles for footing, then understands. The louse at least sucks blood to live; the earwig bites merely from spite.

Dionysos is holding himself with exaggerated care as the firmament dissolves, like a drunkard steeling himself to step into a busy street. "Aeons pass," he says, "and the shards of divinity that once were Zeus alone and now are scattered across dozens shall again be drawn into a solitary Godhead. Shall I experience this as oblivion? Rebirth?"

The god's voice is taking on a peculiar quality, as though reaching Aristophanes across a long distance. The playwright cups his hands and shouts. "But what will happen to us?"

Dionysos seems mildly surprised at the question. "Like a fly springing from an entangling web, I send ripples throughout the plenum in departing. Perhaps the shades of unborn maybes will feel a shiver at my passing, but only for an instant."

"No," Aristophanes screams as the god's figure begins to swell but grows thinner, like watered wine. "What will happen to *me?*"

If Great Dionysos hears his celebrant, he does not deign to answer. Shall I die? thinks Aristophanes as the wave fronts collapse and the shock wave blows him away. Perhaps his spirit, like a turtle wandered into a dead end, is simply being lifted and set a few feet back, to find a different path.

But *No*, he thinks in a rage. If this last hour is taken from him, Aristophanes as he knows himself must surely perish, and a truncated self will awaken ignorant of his murder. A leaf in a gale, he spins away and is lost.

A wet leaf molders and dissolves, its nutrients spread through the soil and are infused by questing roots, their atomies organized anew. Aristophanes of Pandionis, untroubled by anxieties of posterity, is asleep in his bed, breath redolent of wine, with an erection. Beneath his blanket a bedbug bites, and his sleeping hand moves to scratch it.

The four-dimensional ganglion of Dionysos' search path quivers at his departure from tenspace, a strummed chord that vibrates too faintly for all but its principals to sense.

Gnaeus Naevius, riding into the exile his last attack on Roman nobility provoked, feels the brief gaze of otherworldly attention light upon him, as though he had attracted a zephyr's fleeting curiosity. Gerhard Bloch, who mounted a burlesque to incite journeymen to rise against the town council of Muhlhausen, experiences a moment of supernal regret, illuminating the lineaments of his failure like a searchlight from heaven, as he is driven by soldiers' pikes to a terrible death. Bertolt Brecht, putting the finishing touches on a poem (which he has no intention of publishing) that comments ironically on the success of his adopted country in crushing a workers' rebellion, feels a spasm of inexplicable loss, an unalterable conviction that he has taken his life down a wrong turning from which he will never find his way back.

And in Hermanice Prison, political prisoner Václav Havel suddenly looks up from his bunk as something flits through his mind. A letter from his brother Ivan reports that Samuel Beckett has written a play in his honor, and the convicted subverter of the republic muses on the enigmatic account of the play's minimal action that Ivan has recounted. Rubbing his chafed fingertips against the paper (he spends his days running a sanding machine, presumably that he might ponder how steadily repeated abrasion will wear away even hardwood), Havel was reflecting on the platonic essence of drama when the fancy flashes and vanishes, the stream bottom turned cloudy with the flick of a fin. What—it's gone already—was that?

Folding away the letter and picking up his pen (a cheap ballpoint, but not easily replaced), he wonders: Would I rather defeat the regime with my plays or by my example? Posed thus, it is an easy question: he remembers being taught about the novels by Dickens and Zola that provoked social reforms, and which proved poorer works than novels his teachers never mentioned. Great literature exerts only indirect influence; downpours may buffet the landscape, but shifts in the water table transform it.

The choice, moreover, has already been made for him: His works—future as well as past—must await the government's downfall before being produced, so can play no role in that unlikely event. In any case, he has not written a play in years.

Still, it's a tempting fantasy: Rouse the people with your dramatic genius, storm the Winter Palace! It certainly beats rotting in prison, a single stone sunk to encourage a future breakwater.

"It is a stupid conceit," he says aloud. All the same, he scribbles something on the wall beside his bunk, then blinks at it, startled:

Cleon — in Greek letters — is a louse!

*Of his story, Gregory Feeley writes: "The Crab Lice" was written as a commission for an anthology about "alternate tyrants." The assignment was a troubling one; as alternate history has grown over the past twenty years from one of the genre's exotic variants to a major category (as ubiquitous in science fiction as cats are in fantasy), its morally objectionable nature has become unmistakable. The favorite subgenre of armchair Civil War strategists and guys who relish stories of the Nazis winning World War II, alternate history takes the history of violent conflict — that inexpungible mural of human misery — and plays games with it.*

*It's hardly accidental that "alternate history" is concerned almost exclusively with replaying the outcomes of wars, usually the coffee-table book favorites. Devotees claim they are engaging in "thought experiments," but really, alternate history novels about the victory of the Third Reich are no more serious — and no less offensive in their appeal — than thrillers about secret plans for the Fourth Reich.*

*I dithered for some weeks about producing an alternate history story that overcame these objections (and began pondering one about Rosa Luxemburg's unhappy last days as a minister of the German Soviet Republic in 1921) but finally decided that I didn't want to play by the enemy's rules. "The Crab Lice" is a meditation, I guess, on the question Aristophanes asks: Will an artist ever bring down a bad regime by the force of his art?*

*The answer I put in Václav Havel's mouth — "It's a stupid conceit" — is, at the very least, a reasonable one. But of course it's what we wish for nonetheless.*

*I owe thanks to Mike Resnick for publishing a story that must seem a rebuke to his entire series of alternate history anthologies. It's good to see editors break rules.*

# The 1997 Author Emeritus: Nelson Bond

## CONNIE WILLIS

Science fiction has a short but glorious past, and we are intensely proud of the writers who invented the paradigms of the field and defined its parameters. There is no better proof of this than SFWA's many programs to honor the pioneers and early settlers of the field. Witness SFWA's Grand Master Awards, its *Science Fiction Hall of Fame* anthologies, and its *Best of the Nebulas* collection.

In 1994, in one of the best ideas it had ever had, SFWA decided to honor veteran writers who were no longer writing and publishing and who were important to science fiction's past, by choosing an Author Emeritus each year. This Author Emeritus is invited to attend the SFWA Nebula Awards Weekend, is honored at the banquet, and is given a special award. The Author Emeritus program has previously honored Emil Petaja, Wilson Tucker, and Judith Merril.

This year's Author Emeritus is Nelson Bond, the author of *Mr. Mergenthwirker's Lobblies and Other Fantastic Tales*, *The Thirty-first of February*, *No Time Like the Future*, *Nightmares and Daydreams*, and *Exiles of Time*. From the thirties through the fifties, he wrote hundreds of inventive and delightful stories, among them his Lancelot Biggs and Pat Pending series, and his groundbreaking Meg the Priestess stories, including "Pilgrimage" and "Magic City."

Not only was Meg a strong, smart protagonist in a time when women in science fiction were nearly always alien bait and/or scientists' daughters, but the world she inhabited, with its wrecked cities, insular tribes, lost technologies, and degraded language, was the forerunner of such post-apocalyptic worlds as Leigh Brackett's *The Long Tomorrow* and John Wyndham's *Re-birth*.

Bond also wrote for *Scribner's, Esquire, Blue Book*, and other literary magazines; aired numerous radio plays (including two series); and adapted his *Mr. Mergenthwirker's Lobblies* into the first-ever network-broadcast teleplay. His plays include a stage version of Orwell's *Animal Farm*, still internationally active. He collected books, too, and gave writing advice to a very young Isaac Asimov and published a bibliography of James Branch Cabell's work.

And, in between, he wrote dozens and dozens of stories—about Horsesense Hank and Squaredeal Sam McGhee, about stairways that ascend to other dimensions and little green men that nobody else can see, about baseballs hit so hard they come down two weeks in the future and invisible beasts and clocks that run backward—all composed in a clever and breezy style that tells us he was having as much fun as the reader.

And still is. Easily the most animated and articulate writer at the 1997 Nebula Awards Weekend in Santa Fe, Bond signed books, chatted with everyone, and was the evening's most inspirational speaker. "I think one day we will go to Venus, we will go to Mars, we will go to the moons of Jupiter," he said in his acceptance speech, "and when we do, you will have sent them there."

And you helped us get to where we are today, Nelson Bond, and reminded us not only of a past to be proud of but a future to look forward to.

# The Bookshop

NELSON BOND

One of my favorite kinds of SF stories has always been the "mysterious little shop" story. Strange things happen when you stumble into this unassuming little shop, and you can find almost anything there: love potions, a willing buyer for your soul, sometimes even a gateway to another galaxy.

Dozens of science fiction authors have led us into these shops, including Avram Davidson, Mildred Clingerman, and Howard Fast, but none has taken us to any place odder and more wonderful than Nelson Bond does in this story, first published in 1940: "The Bookshop."

In the dead sultriness of Manhattan midsummer there was no incentive to write. Marston's apartment was like the inside of a kiln. Two hours ago he had stripped off his damp shirt and sat down before his typewriter. Now, for all his labors, he had nothing to show but a dozen crumpled balls of bond paper flung haphazardly in and at the wastepaper basket.

"Damn novels!" muttered Marston. "And damn editors with deadlines. And *damn* this heat!"

He swept a handful of white and yellow sheets from the tray before him, leafed through them bitterly. It was a good idea, his plot for this novel. He read again the three chapters he had completed. It was good work; some of the best he had ever done; smoothly written. *The*

*Underlings.* A psychological story of defeat, and of ones who let them-selves be defeated. *"The fault, dear Brutus, is not with our stars—"*

A good theme. And so far, a good job. But—

This heat! This overwhelming, enervating heat. He was, Marston realized with a sudden petulant anger, ill. Actually and physically ill. He gave up. With a final despairing glance at the white sheet shining in the platen roll, he rose. He was shocked to find his exhaustion so deep that as he stood up there danced before his eyes a black vertigo, brief but frightening.

There could be only suffocation and discomfort so long as he re-mained here. Out of doors it would be hot, too, but there might be a ghost of a breeze stirring in the shaded streets down by the river.

Marston put on shirt and coat, and went out.

He had not remembered the bookshop was along this way—had, in-deed, quite forgotten the little shop until suddenly there it was, just a few paces before him. Then he recalled the several occasions on which, before, he had seen it and planned to drop in for a browse. Each time, circumstances had prevented his doing so.

The bookshop was far from prepossessing in appearance. It was ancient and musty, and its only lure was the faint aura of mystery ever attendant to dark neglected places. How long it had been a fixture in this neighborhood, Marston had no way of knowing. It did, apparently, but a slight business, for of the scores who passed it by, none save him-self so much as turned a head to peer into its dusty window.

He had seen it first a year ago or so—that afternoon when, with poor Thatcher, he had been riding by here on a bus. Thatcher was a minor poet; not a very good one, but an ardent one. He had been re-galing Marston with an enthusiastic preview of his latest masterpiece, soon to be released.

"Very soon, Marston. Just a few more stanzas and it goes to the publisher. It…it's a good work, Marston. Oh, I know that sounds brag-gart, coming from me. But a writer can tell when his work is good or bad. This isn't like anything I've done before. It's poetry this time. *Real poetry—"*

His tone was pathetically eager. Marston murmured, "I'm sure it is, Thatcher."

"I *know* it is. I'm calling it *Songs of a New Century*. It will make me, Marston. Up to now, I've just been a versifier. This book will give me a reputation. See if I'm not right...Oh, I say!"

He stopped suddenly. Marston, glancing up swiftly, remembered that Thatcher's health was reportedly on the thin edge. The man didn't look at all well. His cheeks were too pale, his eyes too dark and sunken. "What is it, old man? You all right?"

"What?" Thatcher recovered his poise, ventured the slimmest excuse for a smile. "Oh...oh, yes, quite!" But he pressed the buzzer that drew the bus to the curb and rose, Marston thought, a little abruptly. "I'm fine, thanks. But I just remembered a little errand. Chap I have to see. In there."

And he pointed to the shop before which Marston now stood.

Marston insisted, "You're sure you feel well? Perhaps I should come along—?"

"Now, don't you worry about me. I'll be all right. Chap's an old friend of mine." Thatcher climbed down from the bus. He called back over his shoulder, "See you later, Marston. Watch for the *Songs*—"

But he had, thought Marston regretfully, been mistaken. On both counts. They never met again. Nor did the new book ever appear. Poor Thatcher was not so well as he had hopefully claimed. It was his heart. The next day Marston read his name in the obituary column.

All of a year ago, that had been. Since then, Marston had thought often of the little bookshop. It held a sort of macabre fascination for him; an association of ideas Marston could not explain even to himself. Into that little shop Thatcher had disappeared. Marston had never seen him again. It made the bookshop a—a sort of symbol.

Silly, of course. But last winter when Marston lay ill of the flu and tossed for restless hours in delirium, it had become almost an obsession with him. A compulsion clung to him; he experienced an insensate desire to climb from his sickbed and visit it. A curious urge, but one so powerful that when finally he recovered, he *did* make a special trip to the little shop.

But he had chosen a poor time. It was closed. The door was latched and bolted, and the shades drawn tight.

Now, however, it was not closed. The shade was up, the door an inch or so invitingly ajar. And though the shop was small, there would be coolness in its musty depths. The sun poured down on Marston's head and pressed on his shoulders with a ponderable strength. His head ached, and a dull nausea was upon him.

He opened the door and went in.

The transition from glaring sunlight to shaded dark was abrupt; at first he could see nothing. Somewhere in the back of the shop a bell jangled softly; ancient silences seemed to well in upon the cheerful, tinny sound, engulfing, stilling it.

Marston, stumbling forward, bumped against a table. Surprise brought a small "Oh!" to his lips, and he clung to the table, waiting for his moment of blindness to pass. Out of the shadows before him came a quiet, sympathetic voice.

"Did you hurt yourself, my friend?"

Marston complained, "It's dark in here."

"Dark?" A moment's silence. Then, "Dark, yes. It is, I suppose. But peaceful."

Marston could see more plainly now. He stood in the center of a small, low-ceilinged room walled on either side with shelves of books. The table before him also was piled high with bound volumes. Some were old and faded; others, he was surprised to notice, were brightly new.

Beyond the table was a tiny desk, and at the desk a quiet figure sat, imperturbably scratching with an old goose-quill in a ledger open before him. In the ill light Marston could not clearly see the proprietor's face, but he saw bent shoulders, and white hair shining like a halo in the gloom. There was, he felt, something vaguely familiar about the old man's features—something tantalizingly near the fringes of his memory....

It slipped away even as he tried to grasp it. And the proprietor looked up.

"Is there anything in particular, my friend?"

"Just looking," said Marston. Like all book-lovers, he loathed efficiency in the management of a bookstore. He preferred seeking, in his own good time and at his own whim, whatever of literary interest the shop might hold for him.

The old man nodded.

"There is no need for haste," he said, and returned to his interminable scribbling. The goose-quill pen scraped dryly but not unpleasantly. Marston turned to the shelves.

It did not occur to him at once that there was anything unusual about the books on which he looked. That realization came upon him gradually; hence it came as a slow, growing wonder and not with any deep, sharp sense of shock. There are so many books, so many authors. Their names are legion; easily forgotten. Marston's eyes had traveled over perhaps a full row before there awakened in his mind the awareness that he had viewed something strange and puzzling, something that did not ring quite true.

He glanced back along the row. The proprietor apparently had made no effort to separate his stock according to subject matter. Poetry, plays and novels, essays and texts stood side by side in scrambled heterogeneity. Titles heretofore unknown by Marston. New names and old...old thoughts and new.

Then he saw a thin volume, brown with age. The title, *Agamemnon*. And the author...William Shakespeare!

*Agamemnon*...by Shakespeare? Marston knew of no such title. The hot spark ever latent in the heart of the book-worshiper leaped suddenly into blaze. One of two things: he had stumbled across either the most amazing discovery of the century or the greatest hoax ever perpetrated in the name of art. His pulse quickening with excitement, Marston reached for the volume.

Then his hand, in reaching, stayed. For now he saw, senses sharpened by his discovery, still other titles; books equally unknown and equally amazing. *Cap'n Catfish*, by Mark Twain. *The Leprechaun*, by Donn Byrne. John Galsworthy's *Feet of Clay*, and *Darkling Moors*, by Charlotte Brontë.

Swiftly his gaze dropped to another shelf. He saw with a vast, incredulous incomprehension *Christopher Crump*, by Charles Dickens, *The Gargoyle's Eye*, by Edgar Allan Poe, Thackeray's *Colonel Cowperthwaite*, and *The Private Casebook of Sherlock Holmes*, by Sir Arthur Conan Doyle.

He had heard no footsteps, but now he was aware that at his side stood the proprietor of the little shop. There was quiet pleasure in the old man's voice.

"You admire my books, young friend?"

Marston could only wave a hand at the shelves. His speech was stammering, confused.

"But...these! I don't understand!"

"You are Robert Marston, aren't you? Fantasy is your field. You should appreciate these others."

Marston's gaze helplessly followed the proprietor's gesture. He looked upon names well known to him as his own, but at titles never before dreamed of. *The Troglodytes*, by Jules Verne, Charles Fort's *What Unseen Presence?*, *Hanuman, the First God*, by Ignatius Donnelly, Weinbaum's *Conquest of Space*, and Lovecraft's bulky *Complete History of Demonology*.

And under these a smaller volume; a thin, bright volume with untarnished book jacket. Its title... *Songs of a New Century*. Its author...David Thatcher.

It was then, suddenly, that Marston understood. A great dull prescience filled him, and to his host he said in a voice that was strangely tired, "I suppose, then *it—it*, too, is here?"

And the old man nodded gravely.

"*The Underlings?* Yes, my son; it, too, is here."

There was but one copy, fresh and shining new as if it had at this very moment come from the publisher's office. The dust jacket was brave and fair. Even in this shaken hour, Marston's heart knew a swift, high lift of pride in this, his book.

He reached for it—then hesitated. And of his aged host he asked, "May I?"

"It is your book," said the old man.

And Marston took it down....

Oh, some changes had been made, he found, in the opening chapters. But they were minor editings. In the main, those scenes were as he had written them. With shaking hands he turned the clean white pages. His eyes sought avidly words that heretofore had never known the permanence of print, read thoughts that up till now had existed only in his mind.

And swiftly though he read, he knew with a fierce, bright joy that he had not erred in claiming this his finest work.

There was no mediocrity in this book; no faltering, no stumbling confusion of ideas. Each sentence was perfect; no word or thought or phrase but shone with lustrous purity. This was the book Marston had always meant to write; it was the book he had always known lay somewhere deep within him. Here was the triumphant accomplishment of his writing powers. And Marston, who knew books, knew that this book was great, and that in it, at the end, his skill had attained its full fruition....

*At the end!*

He closed the book, and its closing was a small and startling sound in the fusty silence. He stared at his host, knowing now wherein that face and form had been familiar. A coldness was upon him, and a sudden fear, and he said loudly, "But no! Not now, old man! Not before it is finished—"

The old man said quietly, "Surely you see it cannot be finished over *there*, Marston? Nothing is ever perfect on that side. Only in this bookshop are stories and songs high and sweet and true as their authors dreamed them.

"There *The Underlings* would be but another book—a clothbound, crippled symbol of a dream that died aborning. Thoughts as lofty as the stars faltering on words too weak to bear them. Tales finished over there are never truly great. Always they lack the wings on which their authors envisioned them.

"Only in the library of the left-undone may a story reach the heights intended by its creator. Here—beside an epic Homer ever meant to write, a play that Marlowe planned but did not put into words, Galsworthy's last and greatest romance, ten thousand tales unwritten by a thousand dreamers—here *The Underlings* can take its rightful place in the imperishable library of might-have-been.

"It is the final price for perfection. And a small one."

His voice soughed into silence like the last faint whisper of the moondrawn tide. And it seemed to Marston that a new sound reached his ears; it was as though voices spoke to him from some not distant place, voices greeting him in good fellowship, bidding him come and join their camaraderie. He heard—or thought he did—the laughing voice of Thatcher.

*"What's all the fuss, old boy? My soul, but you're making an issue of a simple matter—"*

Now the old man held out his hand to Marston.

"Are you ready, my friend?" he asked.

But—there was the book in his hand. And suddenly there swept into Marston's brain a thought so daring that an ague seized his limbs.

It was not yet too late! Nor would it be until that ancient hand met his. Could he but reach the street outside—and with this book— *The Underlings* might yet be given to the world in all its dreamed perfection!

A swift decision stirred him. With a sudden cry he stepped back from the ancient's proffered clasp, whirled, and stumbled toward the doorway. The worn knob slipped beneath his palm; the door held, and in panic desperation he tugged, panting, at the barrier. Behind him the soft voices rose in a wailing crescendo of dismay. A sigh whispered in his ear, "There's no escape, my son. You but delay—"

Then the door was open; and the sunlight, raw, hot, and heavy as the crush of a monstrous fist, was blinding-gold in his eyes. With the precious volume clenched in his hands, he cried aloud his triumph, staggered into the street wildly, heedlessly.

He did not hear the voices raised in swift warning, nor the startled rasp of the Klaxon, nor the screaming grind of futile brakes. He heard only the deafening tumult of a world flaming into oblivion ... then the soft peace once more, and the chiding voice of the ancient one. "You but delay, my son. Are you ready, now?"

And a cool hand meeting his own...

"Couldn't *help* hittin' him!" said the truckman. "I swear to God I couldn't help it! This guy seen it—he'll tell you. He come bustin' right out in front o' me, shoutin' like he was crazy or somethin'. I tried to stop, but—"

"OK," said the big man in blue. "OK. It wasn't your fault. Anybody else see it happen? Where'd he come from, anyhow?"

A witness, white of lip, lifted horror-fascinated eyes from the figure on the asphalt. He pointed a shaking finger.

"Over there, Officer. That vacant lot across the street. I saw him wandering around in there, mumbling to himself. I think he must have had a sunstroke the way he acted. That property has been vacant for years. Why he'd want to go in there—"

"I'll take your name," said the policeman. "Anybody recognize him? Let's see that book he was carrying. Maybe it's got his name in it."

Someone handed the book to him.

He leafed through the volume briefly, tilted back his cap, and scratched his forehead.

"Hey, now! This is the queerest looking damn book I ever saw! Look! Only the first three chapters printed...and the rest of it nothing but blank pages!"

# Three Hearings on the Existence of Snakes in the Human Bloodstream

JAMES ALAN GARDNER

Science fiction loves to divide itself into subgenres—Golden Age, New Wave, cyberpunk, post-cyberpunk, alternate history, space opera, high fantasy, urban fantasy, hard SF, soft SF, downright mushy SF—defining and dividing its stories into neat categories.

But there are also authors who refuse to be defined, stories that defy description. R. A. Lafferty springs to mind, and Howard Waldrop, and Carol Emshwiller. "The Lottery," and "The Drowned Giant," and Walter M. Miller's classic, *A Canticle for Leibowitz*.

And James Alan Gardner's Nebula-finalist story, "Three Hearings on the Existence of Snakes in the Human Bloodstream." It's an alternate history...no, it's a parody of...it's hard science, but not exactly...it's about biology, politics, religion...no, it's actually... well, uncategorizable. And great.

"Three Hearings..." is Gardner's first story to appear on the Nebula Awards final ballot. He is the author of *Expendable* and *Commitment Hour*.

*1. Concerning an Arrangement of Lenses, So Fashioned as to Magnify the View of Divers Animalcules, Too Tiny to Be Seen with the Unaided Eye:*

His Holiness, Supreme Patriarch Septus XXIV, was an expert on chains.

By holy law, chains were required on every defendant brought to the Court Immaculate. However, my Lord the Jailer could exercise great latitude in choosing which chains went on which prisoners. A man possessed of a healthy fortune might buy his way into nothing more than a gold link necklace looped loosely around his throat; a beautiful woman might visit the Jailer privately in his chambers and emerge with thin and glittering silver bracelets—chains, yes, but as delicate as thread. If, on the other hand, the accused could offer neither riches nor position nor generous physical charms…well then, the prison had an ample supply of leg-irons, manacles, and other such fetters, designed to show these vermin the grim weight of God's justice.

The man currently standing before Patriarch Septus occupied a seldom-seen middle ground in the quantity of restraints: two solid handcuffs joined by an iron chain of business-like gauge, strong enough that the prisoner had no chance of breaking free, but not so heavy as to strain the man's shoulders to the point of pain. Clearly, my Lord the Jailer had decided on a cautious approach to this particular case; and Septus wondered what that meant. Perhaps the accused was nobody himself but had sufficient connections to rule out unwarranted indignities…a sculptor or musician, for example, who had won favor with a few great households in the city. The man certainly had an artistic look—fierce eyes in an impractical face, the sort of high-strung temperament who could express passion but not use it.

"Be it known to the court," cried the First Attendant, "here stands one Anton Leeuwenhoek, a natural philosopher who is accused of heresy against God and Our Lady, the Unbetombed Virgin. Kneel, Supplicant, and pray with His Holiness, that this day shall see justice."

Septus waited to see what Leeuwenhoek would do. When thieves and murderers came before the court, they dropped to their knees immediately, making gaudy show of begging God to prove their innocence. A heretic, however, might spit defiance or hurl curses at the Patriarchal throne—not a good way to win mercy, but then, many heretics came to this chamber intent on their own martyrdom. Leeuwenhoek had the eyes of such a fanatic, but apparently not the convictions; without so much as a grimace, he got to his knees and bowed his head. The Patriarch quickly closed his own eyes and intoned the words he had recited five times previously this morning:

"God grant me the wisdom to perceive the truth. Blessed Virgin, grant me the judgment to serve out meet justice. Let us all act this day to the greater glory of Thy Divine Union. Amen."

Amens sounded around the chamber: attendants and advocates following the form. Septus glanced sideways toward Satan's Watchboy, an ominous title for a cheerfully freckle-faced youth, the one person here excused from closing his eyes during the prayer. The Watchboy nodded twice, indicating that Leeuwenhoek had maintained a proper attitude of prayer and said Amen with everyone else. Good—this had just become a valid trial, and anything that happened from this point on had the strength of heavenly authority.

"My Lord Prosecutor," Septus said, "state the charges."

The prosecutor bowed as deeply as his well-rounded girth allowed, perspiration already beading on his powdered forehead. It was not a hot day, early spring, nothing more...but Prosecutor ben Jacob was a man famous for the quantity of his sweat, a trait that usually bothered his legal adversaries more than himself. Many an opposing counsel had been distracted by the copious flow streaming down ben Jacob's face, thereby overlooking flaws in the prosecutor's arguments. One could always find flaws in ben Jacob's arguments, Septus knew— dear old Abraham was not overly clever. He was, however, honest, and could not conceive of winning personal advancement at the expense of those he prosecuted; therefore, the Patriarch had never dismissed the man from his position.

"Your Holiness," ben Jacob said, "this case concerns claims against the Doctrine of the, uhh...Sleeping Snake."

"Ah." Septus glanced over at Leeuwenhoek. "My son, do you truly deny God's doctrine?"

The man shrugged. "I have disproved the doctrine. Therefore, it can hardly be God's."

Several attendants gasped loudly. They perceived it as part of their job to show horror at every sacrilege. The same attendants tended to whisper and make jokes during the descriptions of true horrors: murders, rapes, maimings. "The spectators will remain silent," Septus said wearily. He had recited those words five times this morning too. "My Lord Prosecutor, will you please read the text?"

"Ummm...the text, yes, the text."

Septus maintained his composure while ben Jacob shuffled through papers and parchments looking for what he needed. It was, of course, standard procedure to read any passages of scripture that a heretic denied, just to make sure there was no misunderstanding. It was also standard procedure for ben Jacob to misplace his copy of the relevant text in a pile of other documents. With any other prosecutor, this might be some kind of strategy; with ben Jacob, it was simply disorganization.

"Here we are, yes, here we are," he said at last, producing a dog-eared page with a smear of grease clearly visible along one edge. "Gospel of Susannah, chapter twenty-three, first verse." Ben Jacob paused while the two Verification Attendants found the passage in their own scripture books. They would follow silently as he read the text aloud, ready to catch any slips of the tongue that deviated from the holy word. When the attendants were ready, ben Jacob cleared his throat and read:

*"After the procession ended, they withdrew to a garden outside the walls of Jerusalem. And in the evening, it happened that Matthias beheld a serpent there, hidden by weeds. He therefore took up a stone that he might crush the beast; but Mary stayed his hand, saying, 'There is no danger, for look, the beast sleeps.'*

*'Teacher,' Matthias answered, 'it will not sleep forever.'*

*'Verily,' said Mary, 'I promise it will sleep till dawn; and when the dawn comes, we will leave this place and all the serpents that it holds.'*

*Yet still, Matthias kept hold of the stone and gazed upon the serpent with fear.*

*'O ye of little faith,' said Mary to Matthias, 'why do you concern yourself with the sleeping creature before you, when you are blind to the serpents in your own heart? For I tell you, each drop of your blood courses with a legion of serpents, and so it is for every Child of Dust. You are all poisoned with black venoms, poisoned unto death. But if you believe in me, I will sing those serpents to sleep; then will they slumber in peace until you leave this flesh behind, entering into the dawn of God's new day.'"*

Ben Jacob lowered his page and looked to the Verifiers for their confirmation. The Patriarch turned in their direction too, but he didn't need their nods to tell him the scripture had been read correctly. Septus knew the passage by heart; it was one of the fundamental texts of Mother Church, the Virgin's promise of salvation. It was also one of the most popular texts for heretics to challenge. The presumption of original sin, of damnation being inherent in human flesh...that was anathema to many a fiery young soul. *What kind of God,* they asked, *would damn an infant to hell merely for being born?* It was a good question, its answer still the subject of much subtle debate; but the Virgin's words were unequivocal, whether or not theologians had reasoned out all the implications.

"Anton Leeuwenhoek," Septus said, "you have heard the verified word of scripture. Do you deny its truth?"

Leeuwenhoek stared directly back. "I must," he answered. "I have examined human blood in meticulous detail. It contains no serpents."

The toadies in the courtroom had their mouths open, ready to gasp again at sacrilege; but even they could hear the man was not speaking in deliberate blasphemy. He seemed to be stating...a fact.

How odd.

Septus straightened slightly in the Patriarchal throne. This had the prospect of more interest than the usual heresy trial. "You understand," he said to Leeuwenhoek, "this passage is about original sin. The Blessed Virgin states that all human beings are poisoned with sin and can only be redeemed through her."

"On the contrary, Your Holiness." Leeuwenhoek's voice was sharp. "The passage states there are snakes in human blood. I know there are not."

"The snakes are merely..." Septus stopped himself in time. He had been on the verge of saying the snakes were merely a metaphor; but this was a public trial, and any pronouncements he made would have the force of law. To declare that any part of scripture was not the literal truth...no Patriarch had ever done so in open forum, and Septus did not intend to be the first.

"Let us be clear on this point," Septus said to Leeuwenhoek. "Do you deny the Doctrine of Original Sin?"

"No—I could never make heads or tails of theology. What I understand is blood; and there are no snakes in it."

One of the toadies ventured a small gasp of horror, but even a deaf man could have told the sound was forced.

Prosecutor ben Jacob, trying to be helpful, said, "You must appreciate that the snakes would be very, very small."

"That's just it," Leeuwenhoek answered with sudden enthusiasm. "I have created a device that makes it possible to view tiny things as if they were much larger." He turned quickly toward Septus. "Your Holiness is familiar with the telescope? The device for viewing objects at long distances?"

The Patriarch nodded in spite of himself.

"My device," Leeuwenhoek said, "functions on a similar principle—an arrangement of lenses that amplify one's vision to reveal things too small to see with the naked eye. I have examined blood in every particular; and while it contains numerous minute animalcules I cannot identify, I swear to the court there are no snakes. Sleeping or otherwise."

"Mm." Septus took a moment to fold his hands on the bench in front of him. When he spoke, he did not meet the prisoner's eyes. "It is well-known that snakes are adept at hiding, are they not? Surely it is possible that a snake could be concealed behind...behind these other minute animalcules you mention."

"A legion of serpents," Leeuwenhoek said stubbornly. "That's what the text said. A legion of serpents in every drop of blood. Surely they couldn't *all* find a place to hide; and I have spent hundreds of hours searching, Your Holiness. Days and weeks and months."

"Mm."

Troublesome to admit, Septus didn't doubt the man. The Patriarch had scanned the skies with an excellent telescope, and had seen a universe of unexpected wonders—mountains on the moon, hair on the sun, rings around the planet Cronus. He could well believe Leeuwenhoek's magnifier would reveal similar surprises...even if it didn't show serpents in the bloodstream. The serpents were merely a parable anyway; who could doubt it? Blessed Mary often spoke in poetic language that every educated person recognized as symbolic rather than factual.

Unfortunately, the church was not composed of educated persons. No matter how sophisticated the clergy might be, parishioners came from humbler stock. Snakes in the blood? If that's what Mary said, it must be true; and heaven help a Patriarch who took a less dogmatic stance. The bedrock of the church was Authority: ecclesiastic authority, scriptural authority. If Septus publicly allowed that some doctrines could be interpreted as mere symbolism—that a fundamental teaching was metaphor, not literal fact—well, all it took was a single hole in a wineskin for everything to leak out.

On the other hand, truth was truth. If there were no snakes, there were no snakes. God made the world and all the people in it; if the Creator chose to fashion human lifeblood a certain way, it was the duty of Mother Church to accept and praise Him for it. Clinging to a lie in order to preserve one's authority was worse than mere cowardice; it was the most damning blasphemy.

Septus looked at Leeuwenhoek, standing handcuffed in the dock. A living man with a living soul; and with one word, Septus could have him executed as a purveyor of falsehood.

But where did the falsehood truly lie?

"This case cannot be decided today," Septus announced. "Mother Church will investigate the claims of the accused to the fullest extent of her strength. We will build magnifier devices of our own, properly blessed to protect against Satan's interference." Septus fought back a smile at that; there were still some stuffy inquisitors who believed the devil distorted what one saw through any lens. "We shall see what is there and what is not."

Attendants nodded in agreement around the courtroom, just as they would nod if the sentence had been immediate acquittal or death. But ben Jacob said, "Your Holiness—perhaps it would be best if the court were to...to issue instructions that no other person build a magnification device until the church has ruled in this matter."

"On the contrary," Septus replied. "I think the church should make magnifiers available to all persons who ask. Let them see for themselves."

The Patriarch smiled, wondering if ben Jacob understood. A decree suppressing magnifiers would simply encourage dissidents to build them in secret; on the other hand, providing free access to such devices would bring the curious *into* the church, not drive them away. Anyway, the question would only interest the leisured class, those with time and energy to wonder about esoteric issues. The great bulk of the laity, farmers and miners and ostlers, would never hear of the offer. Even if they did, they would hardly care. Minute animalcules might be amusing curiosities, but they had nothing to do with a peasant's life.

Another pause for prayer and then Leeuwenhoek was escorted away to instruct church scholars in how to build his magnification device. The man seemed happy with the outcome—more than escaping a death sentence, he would now have the chance to show others what he'd seen. Septus had met many men like that: grown-up children, looking for colorful shells on the beach and touchingly grateful when someone else took an interest in their sandy little collections.

As for Leeuwenhoek's original magnifier—Septus had the device brought to his chambers when the court recessed at noon. Blood was easy to come by: one sharp jab from a pin and the Patriarch had his sample to examine. Eagerly he peered through the viewing lens, adjusting the focus in the same way as a telescope.

Animalcules. How remarkable.

Tiny, tiny animalcules…countless schools of them, swimming in his own blood. What wonders God had made! Creatures of different shapes and sizes, perhaps predators and prey, like the fishes that swam in the ocean.

And were there snakes? The question was almost irrelevant. And yet…very faintly, so close to invisible that it might be a trick of the eye, something as thin as a hair seemed to flit momentarily across the view.

Then it was gone.


*2. The Origin of Serpentine Analogues in the Blood of Papist Peoples:*


Her Britannic Majesty, Anne VI, rather liked the Star Chamber. True, its power had been monstrously abused at times in the past five centuries—secret trials leading to secret executions of people who were probably more innocent than the monarchs sitting on the judgment seat—but even in the glorious Empire, there was a place for this kind of hearing. The queen on this side of the table, one of her subjects on the other…it had the air of a private chat between friends: a time when difficulties could get sorted out, one way or another.

"Well, Mr. Darwin," she said after the tea had been poured, "it seems you've stirred up quite a hornet's nest. Have you not?"

The fiercely bearded man across the table did not answer immediately. He laid a finger on the handle of his cup as if to drink or not to drink was some momentous decision; then he said, "I have simply spoken the truth, ma'am…as I see it."

"Yes; but different people see different truths, don't they? And a great many are upset by the things you say are true. You are aware there has been…unpleasantness?"

"I know about the riots, ma'am. Several times they have come uncomfortably close to me. And of course, there have been threats on my life."

"Indeed." Anne lifted a tiny slice of buttered bread and took what she hoped would seem a thoughtful nibble. For some reason, she always enjoyed eating in front of the accused here in the Star Chamber; they themselves never had any appetite at all. "The threats are one reason We invited you here today. Scotland Yard is growing rather weary of protecting you; and Sir Oswald has long pondered whether your life is worth it."

That got the expected reaction—Darwin's finger froze on the cup handle, the color draining away from his face. "I had not realized … " His eyes narrowed. "I perceive, ma'am, that someone will soon make a decision on this issue."

"Exactly," the queen said. "Sir Oswald has turned to the crown for guidance, and now We turn to you." She took another tiny bite of the bread. "It would be good of you to explain your theories—to lay out the train of reasoning that led to your … unsettling public statements."

"It's all laid out in my book, ma'am."

"But your book is for scientists, not queens." Anne set down the bread and allowed herself a small sip of tea. She took her time doing so, but Darwin remained silent. "Please," she said at last. "We wish to make an informed decision."

Darwin grunted ... or perhaps it was a hollow chuckle of cynicism. An ill-bred sound in either case. "Very well, Your Majesty." He nodded. "It is simply a matter of history."

"History is seldom simple, Mr. Darwin; but proceed."

"In ... 1430-something, I forget the exact year, Anton Leeuwenhoek appeared before Supreme Patriarch Septus to discuss the absence of snakes in the bloodstream. You are familiar with that, ma'am?"

"Certainly. It was the pivotal event in the Schism between Our church and the Papists."

"Just so."

Anne could see Darwin itching to leap off his chair and begin prowling about the room, like a professor lecturing to a class of dull-lidded schoolboys. His strained impetuosity amused her; but she hoped he would keep his impulses in check. "Pray continue, Mr. Darwin."

"It is common knowledge that the Patriarch's decision led to a ... a deluge, shall we say, of people peering at their own blood through a microscope. Only the upper classes at first, but soon enough it spread to the lower levels of society too. Since the church allowed anyone to look into a microscope without cost, I suppose it was a free source of amusement for the peasantry."

"An opiate for the masses," Anne offered. She rather liked the phrase—Mr. Marx had used it when *he* had his little visit to the Star Chamber.

"I suppose that must be it," Darwin agreed. "At any rate, the phenomenon far outstripped anything Septus could have foreseen; and even worse for the Patriarchy, it soon divided the church into two camps—those who claimed to see snakes in their blood and those who did not."

"Mr. Darwin, We are well aware of the fundamental difference between Papists and the Redeemed."

"Begging your pardon, ma'am, but I believe the usual historical interpretation is...flawed. It confuses cause and effect."

"How can there be confusion?" Anne asked. "Papists have serpents in their blood; that is apparent to any child looking into a microscope. We Redeemed have no such contaminants; again, that is simple observational fact. The obvious conclusion, Mr. Darwin, is that Christ

Herself marked the Papists with Her curse, to show one and all the error of their ways."

"According to the Papists," Darwin reminded her, "the snakes are a sign of God's blessing: a sleeping snake means sin laid to rest."

"Is that what you think, Mr. Darwin?"

"I think it more practical to examine the facts before making any judgment."

"That is why we are here today," Anne said with a pointed glance. "Facts...and judgment. If you could direct yourself to the heart of the matter, Mr. Darwin?"

"The heart of the matter," he repeated. "Of course. I agree that *today* any microscope will show that Papists have snakes in their bloodstream ... or as scientists prefer to call them, serpentine analogues, since it is highly unlikely the observed phenomena are actual reptiles—"

"Let us not bandy nomenclature," Anne interrupted. "We accept that the entities in Papist blood are unrelated to cobras and puff adders; but they have been called snakes for centuries, and the name is adequate. Proceed to your point, Mr. Darwin."

"You have just made my point for me, ma'am. Five centuries have passed since the original controversy arose. What we see *now* may not be what people saw *then*." He took a deep breath. "If you read the literature of that long-ago time, you find there was great doubt about the snakes, even among the Papists. Serpentine analogues were extremely rare and difficult to discern...unlike the very obvious entities seen today."

"Surely that can be blamed on the equipment," Anne said. "Microscopes of that day were crude contrivances compared to our fine modern instruments."

"That is the usual argument." Darwin nodded. "But I believe there is a different explanation."

"Yes?"

"My argument, ma'am, is based on my observations of pigeons."

Anne blinked. "Pigeons, Mr. Darwin?" She blinked again. "The birds?" She bit her lip. "The filthy things that perch on statues?"

"Not wild pigeons, Your Majesty, domestic ones. Bred for show.

For example, some centuries ago, a squire in Sussex took it into his head to breed a black pigeon from his stock of gray ones."

"Why ever would he want a black pigeon?"

"That remains a mystery to me too, ma'am; but the historical records are clear. He set about the task by selecting pigeons of the darkest gray he could find, and breeding them together. Over many generations, their color grew darker and darker until today, the squire's descendants boast of pigeons as black as coal."

"They boast of that?"

"Incessantly."

Darwin seized up a piece of bread and virtually stuffed it into his mouth. The man had apparently become so engrossed in talking, he had forgotten who sat across the table. *Good*, Anne thought; he would be less guarded.

"We understand the principles of animal husbandry," Anne said. "We do not, however, see how this pertains to the Papists."

"For the past five centuries, Your Majesty, the Papists have been going through exactly the same process...as have the Redeemed, for that matter. Think, ma'am. In any population, there are numerous chance differences between individuals; the squire's pigeons, for example, had varying shades of gray. If some process of selection chooses to emphasize a particular trait as desirable, excluding other traits as undesirable—if you restrict darker birds to breeding with one another and prevent lighter ones from contributing to the bloodline—the selected characteristic will tend to become more pronounced with each generation."

"You are still talking about pigeons, Mr. Darwin."

"No, ma'am," he said triumphantly, "I am talking about Papists and the Redeemed. Let us suppose that in the times of Patriarch Septus, some people had almost imperceptible serpentine analogues in their bloodstream—a chance occurrence, just as some people may have curls in their hair while others do not."

Anne opened her mouth to say that curls were frequently not a chance occurrence at all; but she decided to remain silent.

"Now," Darwin continued, "what happened among the people of that day? Some saw those tiny, almost invisible snakes; others did not. Those who saw them proclaimed, *This proves the unshakable word of*

*Mother Church.* Those who saw nothing said, *The scriptures cannot be taken literally—believers must find the truth in their own hearts.* And so the Schism split the world, pitting one camp against another."

"Yes, Mr. Darwin, We know all that."

"So, ma'am, you must also know what happened in subsequent generations. The rift in belief created a similar rift in the population. Papists only married Papists. The Redeemed only married the Redeemed."

"Of course."

"Consequently," Darwin stressed the word, "those who could see so-called snakes in their blood only married those of similar condition. Those who saw nothing married others who saw nothing. Is it any wonder that, generation by generation, snakes became more and more visible in Papist blood? And less and less likely to be seen in the Redeemed? It is simply a matter of selective breeding, ma'am. The Papists are not different from us because the Virgin put her mark on them; they are different because they selected to *make* themselves different. To *emphasize* the difference. And the Redeemed have no snakes in their blood for the same reason—simply a side effect of our ancestors' marital prejudice."

"Mr. Darwin!" Anne said, aghast. "Such claims! No wonder you have angered the Papists as much as your own countrymen. To suggest that God's sacred sign is a mere barnyard accident..." The Queen caught her breath. "Sir, where is your decency?"

"I have something better than decency," he answered in a calm voice. "I have proof."

"Proof? How could you prove such a thing?"

"Some years ago, ma'am," he said, "I took passage on a ship sailing the South Seas; and during that voyage, I saw things that completely opened my eyes."

"More pigeons, Mr. Darwin?"

He waved his hand dismissively. "The birds of the Pacific Islands are hardly fit study for a scientist. What I observed were the efforts of missionaries, ma'am; both Papists and the Redeemed, preaching to the natives who lived in those isles. Have you heard of such missions?"

"We sponsor several of those missions personally, Mr. Darwin."

"And the results, ma'am?"

"Mixed," Anne confessed. "Some tribes are open to Redemption, while others..." She shrugged. "The Papists do no better."

"Just so, Your Majesty. As an example, I visited one island where the Papists had been established for thirty years, yet the local priest claimed to have made no *true* converts. Mark that word, *true*. Many of the natives espoused Papist beliefs, took part in Papist worship, and so on...but the priest could find no snakes in their blood, so he told himself they had not truly embraced Mother Church."

"You would argue with the priest's conclusion?"

"Certainly," Darwin replied. "In my eyes, the island tribe was simply a closed population that for reasons of chance never developed serpentine analogues in their blood. If you interbreed only white pigeons, you will never develop a black."

Anne said, "But—" then stopped stone-still, as the words of a recent mission report rose in her mind. *We are continually frustrated in our work on this island; although the people bow before God's altar, their blood continues to show the serpent-stain of the Unclean....*

"Mr. Darwin," Anne murmured, "could there possibly be islands where all the people had snakes in their blood, regardless of their beliefs?"

"There are indeed, ma'am." Darwin nodded. "Almost all the island populations are isolated and homogeneous. I found some tribes with snakes, some without—no matter which missionaries ministered there. When the Papists land among a people who already have analogues in their bloodstream, they soon declare that they have converted the tribe and hold great celebrations. However, when they land among a people whose blood is clear...well, they can preach all they want, but they won't change the effects of generations of breeding. Usually, they just give up and move on to another island where the people are more receptive...which is to say, where they have the right blood to begin with."

"Ah."

Anne lowered her eyes. Darwin had been speaking about the Papists, but she knew the same was true of Redeemed missionaries. They tended to stay a year in one place, do a few blood tests, then move on if they could not show results—because results were exclusively measured in blood rather than what the people professed. If missionaries, her own missionaries, had been abandoning sincere believers because they didn't believe the conversions were "true" ... what would God think of that?

But Darwin hadn't stopped talking. "Our voyage visited many islands, Your Majesty, a few of which had never received missionaries of any kind. Some of those tribes had serpentine analogues in their blood, while some did not...and each island was homogeneous. I hypothesize that the potential for analogues might have been distributed evenly through humankind millennia ago; but as populations grew isolated, geographically or socially—"

"Yes, Mr. Darwin, We see your point." Anne found she was tapping her finger on the edge of the table. She stopped herself and stood up. "This matter deserves further study. We shall instruct the police to find a place where you can continue your work without disturbance from outside sources."

Darwin's face fell. "Would that be a jail, ma'am?"

"A comfortable place of sanctuary," she replied. "You will be supplied with anything you need—books, paper, all of that."

"Will I be able to publish?" he asked.

"You will have at least one avid reader for whatever you write." She favored him with the slightest bow of her head. "You have given Us much to think about."

"Then let me give you one more thought, Your Majesty." He took a deep breath, as if he was trying to decide if his next words would be offensive beyond the pale. Then, Anne supposed, he decided he had nothing to lose. "Papists and the Redeemed have been selectively breeding within their own populations for five hundred years. There may come a time when they are too far removed from each other to be...cross-fertile. Already there are rumors of an unusually high mortality rate for children with one Papist parent and one Redeemed. In time—millennia perhaps, but in time—I believe the two populations may split into separate species."

"Separate species? Of humans?"

"It may happen, Your Majesty. At this very moment, we may be witnessing the origin of two new species."

Queen Anne pursed her lips in distaste. "The origin of species, Mr. Darwin? If that is a joke, We are not amused."

*3. The Efficacy of Trisulphozymase for Preventing SA Incompatibility Reactions in Births of Mixed-Blood Parentage:*

The hearing was held behind closed doors—a bad sign. Julia Grant had asked some of her colleagues what to expect and they all said, *Show trial, Show trial.* Senator McCarthy loved to get his name in the papers. And yet the reporters were locked out today; just Julia and the Committee.

A very bad sign.

"Good afternoon, Dr. Grant," McCarthy said after she had sworn to tell the truth, the whole truth, and nothing but the truth. His voice had a smarmy quality to it; an unpleasant man's attempt at charm. "I suppose you know why you're here?"

"No, senator."

"Come now, doctor," he chided, as if speaking to a five-year-old. "Surely you must know the purpose of this Committee? And it therefore follows that we would take great interest in your work."

"My work is medical research," she replied tightly. "I have no political interests at all." She forced herself to stare McCarthy in the eye. "I heal the sick."

"There's sickness and there's sickness." The senator shrugged. "We can all understand doctors who deal with sniffles and sneezes and heart attacks…but that's not your field, is it?"

"No," she answered. "I'm a hematologist, specializing in SA compatibility problems."

"Could you explain that for the Committee?"

The doctor suspected that every man on the Committee—and they were all men—had already been briefed on her research. If nothing else, they read the newspapers. Still, why not humor them?

"All human blood," she began, "is either SA-positive or SA-negative—"

"SA stands for Serpentine Analogue?" McCarthy interrupted.

"Yes. The name comes from the outdated belief—"

"—That some people have snakes in their bloodstream," McCarthy interrupted again.

"That's correct."

"*Do* some people have snakes in their bloodstream?" McCarthy asked.

"Snake-like entities," another senator corrected ... probably a Democrat.

"Serpentine analogues are not present in anyone's bloodstream," Julia said. "They don't appear until blood is exposed to air. It's a specialized clotting mechanism, triggered by an enzyme that encourages microscopic threads to form at the site of an injury—"

"In other words," McCarthy said, "SA-positive blood works differently from SA-negative. Correct?"

"In this one regard, yes." Julia nodded.

"Do you think SA-positive blood is *better* than SA-negative?"

"It provides slightly more effective clotting at wounds—"

"Do you *admire* SA-positive blood, doctor?"

Julia stared at him. Mentally, she counted to ten. "I am fascinated by all types of blood," she answered at last. "SA-positive clots faster...which is useful to stop bleeding but gives a slightly greater risk of stroke. Overall, I'd say the good points and the bad even out. If they didn't, evolution would soon skew the population strongly one way or the other."

McCarthy folded his hands on the table in front of him. "So you believe in evolution, Dr. Grant?"

"I'm a scientist. I also believe in gravity, thermodynamics, and the universal gas equation."

Not a man on the Committee so much as smiled.

"Doctor," McCarthy said quietly, "what blood type are you?"

She gritted her teeth. "The Supreme Court ruled that no one has to answer that question."

In sudden fury, McCarthy slammed his fist onto the table. "Do you see the Supreme Court in here with us? Do you? Because if you do, show me those black-robed faggots and I'll boot their pope-loving asses straight out the window." He settled back in his chair. "I don't think you appreciate the seriousness of your situation, Dr. Grant."

"What situation?" she demanded. "I am a medical researcher—"

"And you've developed a new drug, haven't you?" McCarthy snapped. "A new *drug*. That you want to loose on the public. I wonder if the person who invented heroin called herself a medical researcher too?"

"Mr. McCarthy, trisulphozymase is not a narcotic. It is a carefully developed pharmaceutical—"

"Which encourages miscegenation between Papists and the Redeemed," McCarthy finished. "That's what it does, doesn't it, doctor?"

"No!" She took a deep breath. "Trisulphozymase combats certain medical problems that occur when an SA-positive father and an SA-negative mother—"

"When a Papist man sires his filthy whelp on a Redeemed woman," McCarthy interrupted. "When a Papist *fucks* one of the Saved! *That's* what you want to encourage, doctor? That's how you'll make the world a better place?"

Julia said nothing. She felt her cheeks burn like a child caught in some forbidden act; and she was infuriated that her reaction was guilt rather than outrage at what McCarthy was saying.

*Yes*, she wanted to say, *it* will *make the world a better place to stop separating humanity into hostile camps.* Most people on the planet had no comprehension of either Papist or Redeemed theology; but somehow, the poisonous idea of blood discrimination had spread to every country of the globe, regardless of religious faith. Insanity! And millions recognized it to be so. Yet the McCarthys of the world found it a convenient ladder on which they could climb to power, and who was stopping them? Look at Germany. Look at Ireland. Look at India and Pakistan.

Ridiculous…and deadly, time and again throughout history. Perhaps she should set aside SA compatibility and work on a cure for the drive to demonize those who were different.

"A doctor deals with lives, not lifestyles," she said stiffly. "If I were confronted with a patient whose heart had stopped beating, I would attempt to start it again, whether the victim were an innocent child, a convicted murderer, or even a senator." She leaned forward. "Has anyone here ever seen an SA incompatibility reaction? How a newborn infant dies? How the mother goes into spasm and usually dies too? Real people, gentlemen; real screams of pain! Only a monster could witness such things and still rant about ideology."

A few Committee members had the grace to look uncomfortable, turning away from her gaze; but McCarthy was not one of them. "You think this is all just ideology, doctor? A lofty discussion of philosophical doctrine?" He shook his head in unconvincing sorrow. "I wish it were...I truly wish it were. I wish the Papists weren't trying to rip down everything this country stands for, obeying the orders of their foreign masters to corrupt the spirit of liberty itself. Why should I care about a screaming woman, when she's whored herself to the likes of them? *She* made her decision; now she has to face the consequences. No one in this room invented SA incompatibility, doctor. *God* did...and I think we should take the hint, don't you?"

The sharp catch of bile rose in Julia's throat. For a moment, she couldn't find the strength to fight it; but she couldn't be sick, not in front of these men. Swallowing hard, she forced herself to breathe evenly until the moment passed. "Senators," she said at last, "do you actually intend to suppress trisulphozymase? To withhold life-saving treatment from those who need it?"

"Some might say it's a sign," McCarthy answered, "that a Redeemed man can father a child on a Papist without complications, but it doesn't work the other way around. Doesn't that sound like a sign to you?"

"Senators," she said, ignoring McCarthy, "does this Committee intend to suppress trisulphozymase?"

Silence. Then McCarthy gave a little smile. "How does trisulphozymase work, doctor?"

Julia stared at him, wondering where this new question was going. Warily, she replied, "The drug dismantles the SA factor enzyme into basic amino acids. This prevents a more dangerous response from the mother's immune system, which might otherwise produce antibodies to the enzyme. The antibodies are the real problem, because they may attack the baby's—"

"So what you're saying," McCarthy interrupted, "is that this drug can destroy the snakes in a Papist's bloodstream?"

"I told you, there *are* no snakes! Trisulphozymase temporarily eliminates the extra clotting enzyme that comes from SA-positive blood."

"It's only temporary?"

"That's all that's needed. One injection shortly before the moment of birth—"

"But what about repeated doses?" McCarthy interrupted. "Or a massive dose? Could you *permanently* wipe out the SA factor in a person's blood?"

"You don't administer trisulphozymase to an SA-positive person," Julia said. "It's given to an SA-negative mother to prevent—"

"But suppose you *did* give it to a Papist. A *big* dose. *Lots* of doses. Could it destroy the SA factor forever?" He leaned forward eagerly. "Could it make them like us?"

And now Julia saw it: what this hearing was all about. Because the Committee couldn't really suppress the treatment, could they? Her results were known in the research community. Even if the drug were banned here, other countries would use it; and there would eventually be enough public pressure to force re-evaluation. This wasn't about the lives of babies and mothers; this was about clipping the devil's horns.

Keeping her voice steady, she said, "It would be unconscionable to administer this drug or any other to a person whose health did not require it. Large doses or long-term use of trisulphozymase would have side effects I could not venture to guess." The faces in front of her showed no expression. "Gentlemen," she tried again, "in an SA-positive person, the enzyme is *natural*. A natural component of blood. To interfere with a body's natural functioning when there is no medical justification..." She threw up her hands. "Do no harm, gentlemen. The heart of the Hippocratic Oath. At the very least, doctors must do no harm."

"Does that mean," McCarthy asked, "that you would refuse to head a research project into this matter?"

"Me?"

"You're the top expert in your field." McCarthy shrugged. "If anybody can get rid of the snakes once and for all, it's you."

"Senator," Julia said, "have you no shame? Have you no shame at all? You want to endanger lives over this...triviality? A meaningless difference you can only detect with a microscope—"

"Which means they can walk among us, doctor! Papists can walk *among* us. Them with their special blood, their snakes, their damned inbreeding—they're the ones who care about what you call a triviality! They're the ones who flaunt it in our faces. They say they're God's Chosen. With God's Mark of Blessing. Well, I intend to *erase* that mark, with or without your help."

"Without," Julia told him. "Definitely without."

McCarthy's gaze was on her. He did not look like a man who had just received an absolute no. With an expression far too smug, he said, "Let me tell you a secret, doctor. From our agents in the enemy camp. Even as we speak, the Papists are planning to contaminate our water supply with their damned SA enzyme. Poison us or make us like *them*...one way or the other. We *need* your drug to fight that pollution; to remove the enzyme from our blood before it can destroy us! What about *that*, Dr. Grant? Will your precious medical ethics let you work on a treatment to keep us safe from their damned Papist toxins?"

Julia grimaced. "You know nothing about the human metabolism. People couldn't 'catch' the SA factor from drinking water; the enzyme would just break down in your stomach acid. I suppose it might be possible to produce a methylated version that would eventually work its way into the bloodstream...." She stopped herself. "Anyway, I can't believe the Papists would be so insane as to—"

"Right now," McCarthy interrupted, "sitting in a committee room of some Papist hideaway, there are a group of men who are just as crazy as we are. Believe that, doctor. Whatever *we* are willing to do to them, they are willing to do to *us*; the only question is, who'll do it *first*." McCarthy settled back and cradled his hands on his stomach. "Snakes all 'round, Dr. Grant. You can make a difference in who gets bitten."

It was, perhaps, the only true thing McCarthy had said since the hearing had begun. Julia tried to doubt it, but couldn't. SA-positive or -negative, you could still be a ruthless bastard.

She said nothing.

McCarthy stared at her a few moments more, then glanced at the men on both sides of him. "Let's consider this hearing adjourned, all right? Give Dr. Grant a little time to think this over." He turned to look straight at her. "A *little* time. We'll contact you in a few days...find out who scares you more, us or them."

He had the nerve to wink before he turned away.

The other senators filed from the room, almost bumping into each other in the hurry to leave. Complicitous men...weak men, for all their power. Julia remained in the uncomfortable "Witness Chair," giving them ample time to scurry away; she didn't want to lay eyes on them again when she finally went out into the corridor.

Using trisulphozymase on an SA-positive person...what would be the effect? Predictions were almost worthless in biochemistry—medical science was a vast ocean of ignorance dotted with researchers trying to stay afloat in makeshift canoes. The only prediction you could safely make was that a large enough dose of *any* drug would kill the patient.

On the other hand, better to inject trisulphozymase into SA-positive people than SA-negative. The chemical reactions that broke down the SA enzyme also broke down the trisulphozymase—mutual assured destruction. If you didn't have the SA enzyme in your blood, the trisulphozymase would build up to lethal levels much faster, simply because there was nothing to stop it. SA-positive people could certainly tolerate dosages that would kill a...

Julia felt a chill wash through her. She had created a drug that would poison SA-negatives but not SA-positives...that could selectively massacre the Redeemed while leaving the Papists standing. And her research was a matter of public record. How long would it take before someone on the Papist side made the connection? One of those men McCarthy had talked about, just as ruthless and crazy as the senator himself.

How long would it take before they used her drug to slaughter half the world?

There was only one way out: put all the snakes to sleep. If Julia could somehow wave her hands and make every SA-positive person SA-negative, then the playing field would be level again. No, not the playing field—the killing field.

Insanity ... but what choice did she have? Sign up with McCarthy; get rid of the snakes before they began to bite; pray the side effects could be treated. Perhaps, if saner minds prevailed, the process would never be deployed. Perhaps the threat would be enough to force some kind of bilateral enzyme disarmament.

Feeling twenty years older, Dr. Julia Grant left the hearing room.

The corridor was empty; through the great glass entryway at the front of the building, she could see late afternoon sunlight slanting across the marble steps. A single protester stood on the sidewalk, mutely holding a sign aloft—no doubt what McCarthy would call a Papist sympathizer, traitorously opposing a duly appointed congressional committee.

The protester's sign read, *"Why do you concern yourself with the sleeping creature before you, when you are blind to the serpents in your own heart?"*

Julia turned away, hoping the building had a back door.

*Of his story, James Alan Gardner writes: It's seldom that I can actually trace the genesis of a story, but "Three Hearings ..." is an exception. The night of January 1, 1996, I couldn't sleep; and when I got out of bed to find something to do with myself, I happened to pick up a how-to-write-poetry book that I'd been meaning to read. (There's this nagging voice in the back of my head that keeps saying, "Jeez, I really should know something about poetry. And microbiology. And Chinese folklore." That voice is why I keep writing science fiction instead of something respectable, like murder mysteries.)*

*Anyway, I opened the poetry book at random and found a short poem called "The Oxen" by Thomas Hardy, of all people. The poem is based on a folk tradition that oxen supposedly kneel on Christmas Eve, just as they knelt before the baby Jesus on the first Christmas. Hardy wistfully thinks about the legend and says that he would like someone to come to him and say, "Let's go out into the fields to see the oxen kneeling"... and he would like to go there and see that they are kneeling. To me, the poem was about becoming tired of modern sophistication: nostalgically wishing for simple faith and simple proofs of faith.*

*This led me to think of a point in history where a simple article of faith was suddenly exposed as a lie. My notes say, "Someone has invented a telescope or a microscope which shows the belief is not true, and that person is pulled in front of the High Priest to judge his heresy. The High Priest is a sophisticated man and feels that the symbolic truth is more important than the literal; but he knows that for some people, this tiny thing will undermine their faith."*

*That's a pretty stock situation in science fiction: the moment when* science confronts religion. But then I decided things would be more interesting if, for some people, the microscope/telescope did confirm their simple faith. Some metaphoric claim of something in a person's blood...and with the poor quality of early microscopes, some people saw what their religion claimed would be there. Over the generations, those who saw something would associate with each other, tending to reinforce the trait within that population....

A pattern immediately presented itself: first Leeuwenhoek with the microscope; then Darwin explaining how a selection process had emphasized the trait; and finally, a modern scientist who could lay the whole situation out with real chemistry. The parallels with RH+ and RH– blood were just begging to be exploited...and the story pretty well wrote itself from there. Thanks to everyone at Asimov's, thanks to the readers, and thanks to SFWA. I like the story myself and am very happy it's been so well received.

# The Dead

MICHAEL SWANWICK

The dystopia is probably science fiction's strongest suit. The endless possibilities for disaster in the very near future have led to some of science fiction's finest work. Authors from George Orwell to William Gibson, from Harry Harrison to Pat Cadigan, have envisioned frightening futures for us to live in.

So has Michael Swanwick, who has imagined the dark side of the future in such works as *Griffin's Egg, Jack Faust,* and *Vacuum Flowers*. His gritty techno-future visions have won him the Theodore Sturgeon Memorial Award, the World Fantasy Award, and the Nebula Award for his novel *Stations of the Tide*.

But none of his many fascinating futures is more frightening than the one he imagines in this year's Nebula-finalist short story "The Dead." Or more thought provoking. Or more possible.

Three boy zombies in matching red jackets bussed our table, bringing water, lighting candles, brushing away the crumbs between courses. Their eyes were dark, attentive, lifeless; their hands and faces so white as to be faintly luminous in the hushed light. I thought it in bad taste, but "This is Manhattan," Courtney said. "A certain studied offensiveness is fashionable here."

The blond brought menus and waited for our order.

We both ordered pheasant. "An excellent choice," the boy said in a clear, emotionless voice. He went away and came back a minute later with the freshly strangled birds, holding them up for our approval. He couldn't have been more than eleven when he died and his skin was of that sort connoisseurs call "milk-glass," smooth, without blemish, and all but translucent. He must have cost a fortune.

As the boy was turning away, I impulsively touched his shoulder. He turned back. "What's your name, son?" I asked.

"Timothy." He might have been telling me the *specialité de maison*. The boy waited a breath to see if more was expected of him, then left.

Courtney gazed after him. "How lovely he would look," she murmured, "nude. Standing in the moonlight by a cliff. Definitely a cliff. Perhaps the very one where he met his death."

"He wouldn't look very lovely if he'd fallen off a cliff."

"Oh, don't be unpleasant."

The wine steward brought our bottle. "Château Latour '17." I raised an eyebrow. The steward had the sort of old and complex face that Rembrandt would have enjoyed painting. He poured with pulse-less ease and then dissolved into the gloom. "Good lord, Courtney, you *seduced* me on cheaper."

She flushed, not happily. Courtney had a better career going than I. She outpowered me. We both knew who was smarter, better connected, more likely to end up in a corner office with the historically significant antique desk. The only edge I had was that I was a male in a seller's market. It was enough.

"This is a business dinner, Donald," she said, "nothing more."

I favored her with an expression of polite disbelief I knew from experience she'd find infuriating. And, digging into my pheasant, murmured, "Of course." We didn't say much of consequence until dessert, when I finally asked, "So what's Loeb-Soffner up to these days?"

"Structuring a corporate expansion. Jim's putting together the financial side of the package, and I'm doing personnel. You're being headhunted, Donald." She favored me with that feral little flash of teeth she made when she saw something she wanted. Courtney wasn't a beautiful woman, far from it. But there was that fierceness to her, that sense of something primal being held under tight and precarious control that made her hot as hot to me. "You're talented, you're thuggish, and you're not too tightly nailed to your present position. Those are all qualities we're looking for."

She dumped her purse on the table, took out a single-folded sheet of paper. "These are the terms I'm offering." She placed it by my plate, attacked her torte with gusto.

I unfolded the paper. "This is a lateral transfer."

"Unlimited opportunity for advancement," she said with her mouth full, "if you've got the stuff."

"Mmm." I did a line-by-line of the benefits, all comparable to what I was getting now. My current salary to the dollar—Ms. Soffner was showing off. And the stock options. "This can't be right. Not for a lateral."

There was that grin again, like a glimpse of shark in murky waters. "I knew you'd like it. We're going over the top with the options because we need your answer right away—tonight preferably. Tomorrow at the latest. No negotiations. We have to put the package together fast. There's going to be a shitstorm of publicity when this comes out. We want to have everything nailed down, present the fundies and bleeding hearts with a *fait accompli*."

"My God, Courtney, what kind of monster do you have hold of now?"

"The biggest one in the world. Bigger than Apple. Bigger than Home Virtual. Bigger than HIVac-IV," she said with relish. "Have you ever heard of Koestler Biological?"

I put my fork down.

"Koestler? You're peddling corpses now?"

"Please. Postanthropic biological resources." She said it lightly, with just the right touch of irony. Still, I thought I detected a certain discomfort with the nature of her client's product.

"There's no money in it." I waved a hand toward our attentive waitstaff. "These guys must be—what?—maybe two percent of the annual turnover? Zombies are luxury goods: servants, reactor cleanups, Hollywood stunt deaths, exotic services"—we both knew what I meant—"a few hundred a year, maybe, tops. There's not the demand. The revulsion factor is too great."

"There's been a technological breakthrough." Courtney leaned forward. "They can install the infrasystem and controllers and offer the product for the factory-floor cost of a new subcompact. That's way below the economic threshold for blue-collar labor.

"Look at it from the viewpoint of a typical factory owner. He's already downsized to the bone and labor costs are bleeding him dry. How can he compete in a dwindling consumer market? Now let's imagine he buys into the program." She took out her Mont Blanc and began scribbling figures on the tablecloth. "No benefits. No liability suits. No sick pay. No pilferage. We're talking about cutting labor costs by at least two thirds. Minimum! That's irresistible, I don't care how big your revulsion factor is. We project we can move five hundred thousand units in the first year."

"Five hundred thousand," I said. "That's crazy. Where the hell are you going to get the raw material for—?"

"Africa."

"Oh, God, Courtney." I was struck wordless by the cynicism it took to even consider turning the sub-Saharan tragedy to a profit, by the sheer, raw evil of channeling hard currency to the pocket Hitlers who ran the camps. Courtney only smiled and gave that quick little flip of her head that meant she was accessing the time on an optic chip.

"I think you're ready," she said, "to talk with Koestler."

At her gesture, the zombie boys erected projector lamps about us, fussed with the settings, turned them on. Interference patterns moiréd, clashed, meshed. Walls of darkness erected themselves about us. Courtney took out her flat and set it up on the table. Three taps of her nailed fingers and the round and hairless face of Marvin Koestler appeared on the screen. "Ah, Courtney!" he said in a pleased voice. "You're in—New York, yes? The San Moritz. With Donald." The slightest pause with each accessed bit of information. "Did you have the antelope medallions?" When we shook our heads, he kissed his fingertips. "Magnificent! They're ever so lightly braised and then smothered in buffalo mozzarella. Nobody makes them better. I had the same dish in Florence the other day, and there was simply no comparison."

I cleared my throat. "Is that where you are? Italy?"

"Let's leave out where I am." He made a dismissive gesture, as if it were a trifle. But Courtney's face darkened. Corporate kidnapping being the growth industry it is, I'd gaffed badly. "The question is— what do you think of my offer?"

"It's…interesting. For a lateral."

"It's the start-up costs. We're leveraged up to our asses as it is. You'll make out better this way in the long run." He favored me with a sudden grin that went mean around the edges. Very much the financial buccaneer. Then he leaned forward, lowered his voice, maintained firm eye-contact. Classic people-handling techniques. "You're not sold. You know you can trust Courtney to have checked out the finances. Still, you think: It won't work. To work the product has to be irresistible, and it's not. It can't be."

"Yes, sir," I said. "Succinctly put."

He nodded to Courtney. "Let's sell this young man." And to me, "My stretch is downstairs."

He winked out.

Koestler was waiting for us in the limo, a ghostly pink presence. His holo, rather, a genial if somewhat coarse-grained ghost afloat in golden light. He waved an expansive and insubstantial arm to take in the interior of the car and said, "Make yourselves at home."

The chauffeur wore combat-grade photomultipliers. They gave him a buggish, inhuman look. I wasn't sure if he was dead or not. "Take us to Heaven," Koestler said.

The doorman stepped out into the street, looked both ways, nodded to the chauffeur. Robot guns tracked our progress down the block.

"Courtney tells me you're getting the raw materials from Africa."

"Distasteful, but necessary. To begin with. We have to sell the idea first—no reason to make things rough on ourselves. Down the line, though, I don't see why we can't go domestic. Something along the lines of a reverse mortgage, perhaps, life insurance that pays off while you're still alive. It'd be a step toward getting the poor off our backs at last. Fuck 'em. They've been getting a goddamn free ride for too long; the least they can do is to die and provide us with servants."

I was pretty sure Koestler was joking. But I smiled and ducked my head, so I'd be covered in either case. "What's Heaven?" I asked, to move the conversation onto safer territory.

"A proving ground," Koestler said with great satisfaction, "for the future. Have you ever witnessed bare-knuckles fisticuffs?"

"No."

"Ah, now there's a sport for gentlemen! The sweet science at its sweetest. No rounds, no rules, no holds barred. It gives you the real measure of a man—not just of his strength but his character. How he handles himself, whether he keeps cool under pressure—how he stands up to pain. Security won't let me go to the clubs in person, but I've made arrangements."

Heaven was a converted movie theater in a rundown neighborhood in Queens. The chauffeur got out, disappeared briefly around the back, and returned with two zombie bodyguards. It was like a conjurer's trick. "You had these guys stashed in the *trunk?*" I asked as he opened the door for us.

"It's a new world," Courtney said. "Get used to it."

The place was mobbed. Two, maybe three hundred seats, standing room only. A mixed crowd, blacks and Irish and Koreans mostly, but with a smattering of uptown customers as well. You didn't have to be poor to need the occasional taste of vicarious potency. Nobody paid us any particular notice. We'd come in just as the fighters were being presented.

"Weighing two-five-oh, in black trunks with a red stripe," the ref was bawling, "tha gang-bang *gangs*ta, the bare-knuckle *brawla*, the man with tha—"

Courtney and I went up a scummy set of back stairs. Bodyguard–us–bodyguard, as if we were a combat patrol out of some twentieth–century jungle war. A scrawny, potbellied old geezer with a damp cigar in his mouth unlocked the door to our box. Sticky floor, bad seats, a good view down on the ring. Gray plastic matting, billowing smoke.

Koestler was there, in a shiny new hologram shell. It reminded me of those plaster Madonnas in painted bathtubs that Catholics set out in their yards. "Your permanent box?" I asked.

"All of this is for your sake, Donald—you and a few others. We're pitting our product one-on-one against some of the local talent. By arrangement with the management. What you're going to see will settle your doubts once and for all."

"You'll like this," Courtney said. "I've been here five nights straight. Counting tonight." The bell rang, starting the fight. She leaned forward avidly, hooking her elbows on the railing.

The zombie was gray-skinned and modestly muscled, for a fighter. But it held up its hands alertly, was light on its feet, and had strangely calm and knowing eyes.

Its opponent was a real bruiser, a big black guy with classic African features twisted slightly out of true so that his mouth curled up in a kind of sneer on one side. He had gang scars on his chest and even uglier marks on his back that didn't look deliberate but like something he'd earned on the streets. His eyes burned with an intensity just this side of madness.

He came forward cautiously but not fearfully, and made a couple of quick jabs to get the measure of his opponent. They were blocked and countered.

They circled each other, looking for an opening.

For a minute or so, nothing much happened. Then the gangster feinted at the zombie's head, drawing up its guard. He drove through that opening with a slam to the zombie's nuts that made me wince.

No reaction.

The dead fighter responded with a flurry of punches, and got in a glancing blow to its opponent's cheek. They separated, engaged, circled around.

Then the big guy exploded in a combination of killer blows, connecting so solidly it seemed they would splinter every rib in the dead fighter's body. It brought the crowd to their feet, roaring their approval.

The zombie didn't even stagger.

A strange look came into the gangster's eyes then, as the zombie counterattacked, driving him back into the ropes. I could only imagine what it must be like for a man who had always lived by his strength and his ability to absorb punishment to realize that he was facing an opponent to whom pain meant nothing. Fights were lost and won by flinches and hesitations. You won by keeping your head. You lost by getting rattled.

Despite his best blows, the zombie stayed methodical, serene, calm, relentless. That was its nature.

It must have been devastating.

The fight went on and on. It was a strange and alienating experience for me. After a while I couldn't stay focused on it. My thoughts kept slipping into a zone where I found myself studying the line of Courtney's jaw, thinking about later tonight. She liked her sex just a little bit sick. There was always a feeling, fucking her, that there was something truly repulsive that she *really* wanted to do but lacked the courage to bring up on her own.

So there was always this urge to get her to do something she didn't like. She was resistant; I never dared try more than one new thing per date. But I could always talk her into that one thing. Because when she was aroused, she got pliant. She could be talked into anything. She could be made to beg for it.

Courtney would've been amazed to learn that I was not proud of what I did with her—quite the opposite, in fact. But I was as obsessed with her as she was with whatever it was that obsessed her.

Suddenly Courtney was on her feet, yelling. The hologram showed Koestler on his feet as well. The big guy was on the ropes, being pummeled. Blood and spittle flew from his face with each blow. Then he was down; he'd never even had a chance. He must've known early on that it was hopeless, that he wasn't going to win, but he'd refused to take a fall. He had to be pounded into the ground. He went down raging, proud and uncomplaining. I had to admire that.

But he lost anyway.

That, I realized, was the message I was meant to take away from this. Not just that the product was robust. But that only those who backed it were going to win. I could see, even if the audience couldn't, that it was the end of an era. A man's body wasn't worth a damn anymore. There wasn't anything it could do that technology couldn't handle better. The number of losers in the world had just doubled, tripled, reached maximum. What the fools below were cheering for was the death of their futures.

I got up and cheered too.

In the stretch afterward, Koestler said, "You've seen the light. You're a believer now."

"I haven't necessarily decided yet."

"Don't bullshit me," Koestler said. "I've done my homework, Mr. Nichols. Your current position is not exactly secure. Morton-Western is going down the tubes. The entire service sector is going down the tubes. Face it, the old economic order is as good as fucking gone. Of course you're going to take my offer. You don't have any other choice."

The fax outed sets of contracts. "A Certain Product," it said here and there. Corpses were never mentioned.

But when I opened my jacket to get a pen Koestler said, "Wait. I've got a factory. Three thousand positions under me. I've got a motivated workforce. They'd walk through fire to keep their jobs. Pilferage is at zero. Sick time practically the same. Give me one advantage your product has over my current workforce. Sell me on it. I'll give you thirty seconds."

I wasn't in sales and the job had been explicitly promised me already. But by reaching for the pen, I had admitted I wanted the position. And we all knew whose hand carried the whip.

"They can be catheterized," I said — "no toilet breaks."

For a long instant Koestler just stared at me blankly. Then he exploded with laughter. "By God, that's a new one! You have a great future ahead of you, Donald. Welcome aboard."

He winked out.

We drove on in silence for a while, aimless, directionless. At last Courtney leaned forward and touched the chauffeur's shoulder.

"Take me home," she said.

Riding through Manhattan I suffered from a waking hallucination that we were driving through a city of corpses. Gray faces, listless motions. Everyone looked dead in the headlights and sodium vapor streetlamps. Passing by the Children's Museum I saw a mother with a stroller through the glass doors. Two small children by her side. They all three stood motionless, gazing forward at nothing. We passed by a stop-and-go where zombies stood out on the sidewalk drinking forties in paper bags. Through upper-story windows I could see the sad rainbow trace of virtuals playing to empty eyes. There were zombies in the park, zombies smoking blunts, zombies driving taxies, zombies sitting on stoops and hanging out on street corners, all of them waiting for the years to pass and the flesh to fall from their bones.

I felt like the last man alive.

Courtney was still wired and sweaty from the fight. The pheromones came off her in great waves as I followed her down the hall to her apartment. She stank of lust. I found myself thinking of how she got just before orgasm, so desperate, so desirable. It was different after she came, she would fall into a state of calm assurance; the same sort of calm assurance she showed in her business life, the aplomb she sought so wildly during the act itself.

And when that desperation left her, so would I. Because even I could recognize that it was her desperation that drew me to her, that made me do the things she needed me to do. In all the years I'd known her, we'd never once had breakfast together.

I wished there was some way I could deal her out of the equation. I wished that her desperation were a liquid that I could drink down to the dregs. I wished I could drop her in a wine press and squeeze her dry.

At her apartment, Courtney unlocked her door and in one complicated movement twisted through and stood facing me from the inside. "Well," she said. "All in all, a productive evening. Good night, Donald."

"Good night? Aren't you going to invite me inside?"

"No."

"What do you mean, no?" She was beginning to piss me off. A blind man could've told she was in heat from across the street. A chimpanzee could've talked his way into her pants. "What kind of idiot game are you playing now?"

"You know what no means, Donald. You're not stupid."

"No I'm not, and neither are you. We both know the score. Now let me in, goddamnit."

"Enjoy your present," she said, and closed the door.

I found Courtney's present back in my suite. I was still seething from her treatment of me and stalked into the room, letting the door slam behind me so that I was standing in near-total darkness. The only light was what little seeped through the draped windows at the far end of the room. I was just reaching for the light switch when there was a motion in the darkness.

*'Jackers!* I thought, and all in a panic lurched for the light switch, hoping to achieve I don't know what. Credit-jackers always work in trios, one to torture the security codes out of you, one to phone the numbers out of your accounts and into a fiscal trapdoor, a third to stand guard. Was turning the lights on supposed to make them scurry for darkness, like roaches? Nevertheless, I almost tripped over my own feet in my haste to reach the switch. But of course it was nothing like what I'd feared.

It was a woman.

She stood by the window in a white silk dress that could neither compete with nor distract from her ethereal beauty, her porcelain skin. When the lights came on, she turned toward me, eyes widening, lips parting slightly. Her breasts swayed ever so slightly as she gracefully raised a bare arm to offer me a lily. "Hello, Donald," she said huskily. "I'm yours for the night." She was absolutely beautiful.

And dead, of course.

Not twenty minutes later I was hammering on Courtney's door. She came to the door in a Pierre Cardin dressing gown and from the way she was still cinching the sash and the disarray of her hair I gathered she hadn't been expecting me.

"I'm not alone," she said.

"I didn't come here for the dubious pleasures of your fair white body." I pushed my way into the room. (But couldn't help remembering that beautiful body of hers, not so exquisite as the dead whore's, and now the thoughts were inextricably mingled in my head: death and Courtney, sex and corpses, a Gordian knot I might never be able to untangle.)

"You didn't like my surprise?" She was smiling openly now, amused.

"No, I fucking did not!"

I took a step toward her. I was shaking. I couldn't stop fisting and unfisting my hands.

She fell back a step. But that confident, oddly expectant look didn't leave her face. "Bruno," she said lightly. "Would you come in here?"

A motion at the periphery of vision. Bruno stepped out of the shadows of her bedroom. He was a muscular brute, pumped, ripped, and as black as the fighter I'd seen go down earlier that night. He stood behind Courtney, totally naked, with slim hips and wide shoulders and the finest skin I'd ever seen.

And dead.

I saw it all in a flash.

"Oh, for God's sake, Courtney!" I said, disgusted. "I can't believe you. That you'd actually...That thing's just an obedient body. There's nothing there—no passion, no connection, just...physical presence."

Courtney made a kind of chewing motion through her smile, weighing the implications of what she was about to say. Nastiness won.

"We have equity now," she said.

I lost it then. I stepped forward, raising a hand, and I swear to God I intended to bounce the bitch's head off the back wall. But she didn't flinch—she didn't even look afraid. She merely moved aside, saying, "In the body, Bruno. He has to look good in a business suit."

A dead fist smashed into my ribs so hard I thought for an instant my heart had stopped. Then Bruno punched me in my stomach. I doubled over, gasping. Two, three, four more blows. I was on the ground now, rolling over, helpless and weeping with rage.

"That's enough, baby. Now put out the trash."

Bruno dumped me in the hallway.

I glared up at Courtney through my tears. She was not at all beautiful now. Not in the least. You're getting older, I wanted to tell her. But instead I heard my voice, angry and astonished, saying, "You...you goddamn, fucking necrophile!"

"Cultivate a taste for it," Courtney said. Oh, she was purring! I doubted she'd ever find life quite this good again. "Half a million Brunos are about to come on the market. You're going to find it a lot more difficult to pick up *living* women in not so very long."

I sent away the dead whore. Then I took a long shower that didn't really make me feel any better. Naked, I walked into my unlit suite and opened the curtains. For a long time I stared out over the glory and darkness that was Manhattan.

I was afraid, more afraid than I'd ever been in my life.

The slums below me stretched to infinity. They were a vast necropolis, a neverending city of the dead. I thought of the millions out there who were never going to hold down a job again. I thought of how they must hate me—me and my kind—and how helpless they were before us. And yet. There were so many of them and so few of us. If they were to all rise up at once, they'd be like a tsunami, irresistible. And if there was so much as a spark of life left in them, then that was exactly what they would do.

That was one possibility. There was one other, and that was that nothing would happen. Nothing at all.

God help me, but I didn't know which one scared me more.

*Of his story, Michael Swanwick writes: There's really very little I can say about this story. I wrote it at a time when corporations were responding to record profits by firing thousands of their employees, and I wrote it in anger. I was so pleased with the result that I gave it the best name I could imagine for a zombie story—that of James Joyce's single finest short work ever. And I'm extremely happy it made the ballot.*

*That's it, though. I don't think I've ever written a story that speaks as clearly for itself as this one. Anything I might say about it is already contained within the text, written down in black and white.*

*A word, however, about its venue. The original anthology holds a place of honor in our field as the incubator of much of our finest work. (On a personal level, my first published story, "The Feast of Saint Janis," appeared in Robert Silverberg's* New Dimensions *series.) These things have, they tell me, never made a lot of money. So, in today's market particularly, publishing such a series is a work of love and courage.* Starlight *deserves your support. I urge you to give it. Any literary era gets the original anthology series it deserves. To judge by the first volume of this one, we're not doing too badly at all.*

# Rhysling Award Winners

W. GREGORY STEWART
TERRY A. GAREY

The Rhysling Awards are given by the Science Fiction Poetry Association for "excellence in speculative, science-oriented, SF, fantasy, horror, and related poetry published during the preceding year." Awards are given in two categories: best short poem (under fifty lines) and best long poem (over fifty lines).

The Rhysling Award is named after the wandering Blind Singer of the Spaceways who was created by Robert A. Heinlein. Rhysling, who appears in his short story "The Green Hills of Earth," was brilliant, bawdy, brave, and as poverty-stricken as most of today's poets.

Previous Rhysling Award winners have included Joe Haldeman, Susan Palwick, and Robert Frazier. This year's winners are W. Gregory Stewart and Terry A. Garey.

W. Gregory Stewart, the author of the Rhysling Award for Best Short Poem, is a four-time Rhysling Award winner whose poetry has appeared in *Asimov's Science Fiction*, *Amazing Stories*, *Thin Ice*, and in various e-zines online. In "Day Omega," he explores a much older world than the one we inhabit.

This year's winner of the Rhysling Award for Best Long Poem is Terry A. Garey's "Spotting UFOs While Canning Tomatoes." Garey is the author of numerous poems, the editor of *Time Frames* and *Time Gum*, with Eleanor Arnason, and the author of *The Joy of Home Winemaking*.

In "Spotting UFOs While Canning Tomatoes," Garey gives instructions for something far more important than canned tomatoes.

## Day Omega
*for Frederik Pohl*
W. GREGORY STEWART

maybe your mitochondria
will be left them on that day
(but even this day these
are not yours, really,
hitching their ride from
past to future with now
just another onramp on the way, and you
just another stranger
who stopped to pick them up,
as far as you're going,
if that'll help),

but they will not think of you
as ancestor, any more
than you think of some barely formed
bit of organic twitch as ancestor,
or some tree-thing as ancestor,
eye-wide in the dark,
not like you think
of Grampy Joe, who still
has an appendix, or had one, anyway,
and five fingers and five toes,
each hand or foot,
they will not, could not
think of you that way,
even charitably.

oh, they are beyond day million, they
are so far past that, past human
and day billion and beyond,
you would not know them
for the fruit of the fruit
in their myriad forms
on worlds that do not even exist
in your time.

maybe your mitochondria,
that you'd picked up at evolution's yard sale
and handed on—that essence
of ape and earlier that's been in the family
for years (and now the great-grandchildren
don't know what to do with it),
maybe that strange life will still be there
on day Omega, hiding inside
and thinking the tiniest thoughts,
and smug, as the stars go out—

which is only as far as you were going, anyway.

*Of his poem,* **W. Gregory Stewart** *writes: I've always admired Frederik Pohl—wait. I have vastly enjoyed Frederik Pohl's writing over the years. That's better—admiration takes some knowledge of the* man, *and I only know his pages. Oh. Yeah. So, then. I have* always *admired Frederik Pohl....*

*So I suppose there must have been something happening back among the nether neurons when the title "Day Omega" came to me. (That came first, by the way.) Consciously, I wasn't thinking about "Day Million," but—well, given the end results, I suppose I must have been, subwise. When I finally realized it, I put in the "day million" bit, for proper acknowledgment—and homage. And completed the title. So. I suppose I had to have seen something there, some fodder for the poetic process.*

*And if I have seen fodder, it is because I was looking over the shoulder of giants....*

## Spotting UFOs While Canning Tomatoes
*For Karen Schaffer, Laurie Winter, and Eleanor Arnason*
TERRY A. GAREY

First, get your tomatoes
this is not always as easy as it seems
if you are going to go to all that trouble
they might as well be good ones:
    red, full of flavor, perfectly ripe
    not a lot of bruises
grow them yourself
or get them from a farmers' market:
    Big Boy, Big Girl, Roma, Royal Chico
    Super Beefsteak, Early Pick, Lady Luck, Rutgers,
I've canned them all
just be sure they're good

pick a cool evening to do this if you can
unfortunately
cool evenings and tomatoes rarely go together
think of your pioneer grandmothers
indian grandmothers
slave grandmothers
immigrant grandmothers,
putting up whole gardens for families of ten
and the hired hands

think of winter and canned tomatoes from the store
    tasting of tin
purse your lips in disgust
roll up your sleeves
and get to work
(a friend taught me to do this
long ago
when I was young and poor but had plenty of tomatoes
she put my tomato destiny in my own hands
as well as my peach, pear, applesauce and jelly destiny)

make sure you have enough jars, lids, rings and time
read through the instructions
(you know what your memory is like)
then fire up the canner and go for it

it's still the same hot water bath
taking too much room on the stove
a battered saucepan for scalding lids
bigger saucepan for scalding tomatoes
to make them easier to peel

then it's peel and core, my girl, peel and core
chop those tomatoes down
slip off the skins, keep the water hot

paring knife nicks, seeds spurt out
acids sting my skin
adds to the general redness

mere mortals should clear the kitchen
order out pizza—if they want to eat
it's like a marathon:
          sweat, determination, endurance
          going for the long distance—
          you have to remember to drink water
          so you don't dehydrate

as I go along, lift hot jars, dump water
push in the tomatoes, wipe the rims
leave a space for expansion
try to guess how much is enough
when I tighten down the lids
as I go along
          I philosophize
on the meaning of life
meditate on the smile of my grandmother
female bonding
female machisma
think about the farm women doing four times as much as this

every day all summer
and gasp, shake my head
I'll never understand how they did it

while the first batch boils I get ready for the next
try to stockpile against time and weariness
shift from one sore foot to another
wad up the newspapers, wipe up flooding juice
save skins for the compost

I glance out the kitchen window and spot moving lights in the sky
an airplane, I think,
then as the steam rises around my head I realize
there are no flight patterns out my kitchen window
my hands clench, I think: UFOs, Flying Saucers,
aliens, green monsters
tentacled sentient creatures who need women to:
        can tomatoes?
The heck with them. Let them can their own tomatoes.

the kitchen's a mess
I've burned myself twice
used a Band-Aid
        scalded the inside of my arm with steam
but there are the first seven jars
and one by one
        ping!
        goes the beat of my heart as they seal down

take that, alien invaders

I work on into the night—not talking much—
hit a plateau
where it seems I'll never see the last bushel done
but finally
it's over
last jar is sealed
I dump the five gallons of hot water down the drain
so the canner won't rust

wipe down the counters
clean off the stove top
    touch once more all the women
everywhere, even outerspace aliens,
who put something aside for winter

*Of her poem, Terry A. Garey writes:* "Spotting UFOs While Canning Tomatoes" *was first published in* Serve It Forth: Cooking with Anne McCaffrey, *in 1996. It was the only poem in the cookbook. I still can't believe they took it. This year I am growing Big Boy, Mom's Royal Chico, and Brandywine tomatoes, while watching the skies.*

# The Elizabeth Complex

KAREN JOY FOWLER

You very rarely see articles on "The Rules of Science Fiction." This is because science fiction constantly reinvents itself—breaking the old rules, making new ones, then promptly breaking those—and has been doing so since the field began. From C. L. Moore and Henry Kuttner to Samuel R. Delany to Kurt Vonnegut Jr., the field has been blessed with innovators and rule smashers.

I'd say Karen Joy Fowler follows in that tradition, except that I'm not sure shattering tradition can *be* a tradition. Every story she writes is absolutely original, from her short story collection, *Artificial Things,* to her critically acclaimed novels *Sarah Canary* and *The Sweetheart Season,* to "Lieserl" and "The Faithful Companion at Forty," both nominated for the Nebula Award.

And this story, "The Elizabeth Complex," is like no other you've ever read.

*"Love is particularly difficult to study clinically."*
*—Nancy J. Chodorow*

*"Fathers love as well.—Mine did, I know,—*
*but still with heavier brains."* *—Elizabeth Barrett Browning*

There is no evidence that Elizabeth ever blamed her father for killing her mother. Of course, she would hardly have remembered her mother. At three months, Elizabeth had been moved into her own household with her own servants; her parents became visitors rather than caretakers. At three years, the whole affair was history—her mother's head on Tower Green, her father's re-marriage eleven days later. Because the charge was adultery and, in one case, incest, her own parentage might easily have come into question. But there has never been any doubt as to who her father was. "The lion's cub," she called herself, her father's daughter, and from him she got her red hair, her white skin, her dancing, her gaiety, her predilection for having relatives beheaded, and her sex.

Her sex was the problem, of course. Her mother's luck at cards had been bad all summer. But the stars were good, the child rode low in the belly, and the pope, they had agreed, was powerless. They were expecting a boy.

After the birth, the jousts and tournaments had to be cancelled. The musicians were sent away, except for single pipe, frolicsome, but thin. Her mother, spent and sick from childbirth, felt the cold breath of disaster on her neck.

Her father put the best face on it. Wasn't she healthy? Full weight and lusty? A prince would surely follow. A poor woman gave the princess a rosemary bush hung all with gold spangles. "Isn't that nice?" her mother's ladies said brightly, as if it weren't just a scented branch with glitter.

Elizabeth had always loved her father. She watched sometimes when he held court. She saw the deference he commanded. She saw how careful he was. He could not allow himself to be undone with passion or with pity. The law was the law, he told the women who came before him. A woman's wages belonged to her husband. He could mortgage her property if he liked, forfeit it to creditors. That his children were hungry made no difference. The law acknowledged the defect of her sex. Her father could not do less.

He would show the women these laws in his books. He would show Elizabeth. She would make a little mark with her fingernail in the margin beside them. Some night when he was asleep, some night when she had more courage than she had ever had before, she would slip into the library and cut the laws she had marked out of the books. Then the women would stop weeping and her father would be able to do as he liked.

Her father read to her *The Taming of the Shrew*. He never

seemed to see that she hated Petruchio with a passion a grown woman might have reserved for an actual man. "You should have been a boy," he told her, when she brought home the prize in Greek, ahead of all the boys in her class.

Her older brother died when she was a small girl. Never again was she able to bear the sound of a tolling bell. She went with her father to the graveyard, day after day. He threw himself on the grave, arms outstretched. At home, he held her in his arms and wept onto her sleeve, into her soft brown hair. "My daughter," he said. His arms tightened. "If only you had been a boy."

She tried to become a boy. She rode horseback, learned Latin. She remained a girl. She sewed. She led the Presbyterian Girls' Club. The club baked and stitched to earn the money to put a deserving young man through seminary. When he graduated, they went as a group to see him preach his first sermon. They sat in the front. He stood up in the clothes they had made for him. "I have chosen my text for today," he said from the pulpit. "1 Tim 2:12. 'I suffer not a woman to teach, nor to usurp authority over the man, but be in silence.'"

Elizabeth rose. She walked down the long aisle of the church and out into the street. The sun was so fiery it blinded her for a moment. She stood at the top of the steps, waiting until she could see them. The door behind her opened. It opened again and again. The Presbyterian Girls' Club had all come with her.

She rode horseback, learned Latin and also Greek, which her father had never studied. She had, they said, a pride like summer. One winter day she sat with all her ladies in the park, under an oak, under a canopy, stitching, with her long, beautiful, white fingers. If the other ladies were cold, if they wished to be inside, they didn't say so. They sat and sewed together and one of them sang aloud and the snowflakes flew about the tent like moths. Perhaps Elizabeth was herself cold and wouldn't admit it, or perhaps, even thin as she was, she was not cold and this would be an even greater feat. There was no way to know which was true.

Perhaps Elizabeth was merely teasing. Her fingers rose and dipped quickly over the cloth. From time to time, she joined her merry voice to the singer's. She had a strong, animal aura, a force. Her spirits were always lively. John Knox denounced her in church for her fiddling and flinging. She and her sister both, he said, were incurably addicted to joyosity.

Her half-brother had never been lusty. When he died, some years after her father, long after his own mother, hail the color of fire fell in the city, thunder rolled low and continuous through the air. This was a terrible time. It was her time.

Her father opposed her marriage. It was not marriage itself, he opposed; no, he had hoped for that. It was the man. A dangerous radical. An abolitionist. A man who would never earn money. A man who could then take her money.

Hadn't she sat in his court and seen this often enough with her very own eyes?

For a while she was persuaded. When she was strong enough, she rebelled. She insisted that the word *obey* be stricken from the ceremony. Nor would she change her name. "There is a great deal in a name," she wrote her girlfriend. "It often signifies much and may involve a great principle. This custom is founded on the principle that white men are lords of all. I cannot acknowledge this principle as just; therefore I cannot bear the name of another." She meant her first name by this. She meant Elizabeth.

Her family's power and position went back to the days when Charles I sat on the English throne. Her father was astonishingly wealthy, spectacularly thrifty. He wasted no money on electricity, bathrooms, or telephones. He made small, short-lived exceptions for his youngest daughter. She bought a dress; she took a trip abroad. She was dreadfully spoiled, they said later. But spinsters are generally thought to be entitled to compensatory trips abroad and she had reached the age where marriage was unlikely. Once men had come to court her in the cramped parlor. They faltered under the grim gaze of her father. There is no clear evidence that she ever blamed him for this, although there is, of course, the unclear evidence.

She did not get on with her step-mother. "I do not call her mother," she said. She, herself, was exactly the kind of woman her father esteemed—quiet, reserved, respectful. Lustless and listless. She got from him her wide beautiful eyes, her sky-colored eyes, her chestnut hair.

When Elizabeth was one year old, her father displayed her, quite naked, to the French ambassadors. They liked what they saw. Negotiations began to betroth her to the Duke of Angouleme, negotiations that foundered later for financial reasons.

She was planning to address the legislature. Her father read it in the paper. He called her into the library and sat with her before the fire. The blue and orange flames wrapped around the logs, whispering into smoke. "I beg you not to do this," he said. "I beg you not to disgrace me in my old age. I'll give you the house in Seneca Falls."

She had been asking for the house for years. "No," Elizabeth said.

"Then I'll disinherit you entirely."

"If you must."

"Let me hear this speech."

As he listened his eyes filled with tears. "Surely, you have had a comfortable and happy life," he cried out. "Everything you could have wanted has been supplied. How can someone so tenderly brought up feel such things? Where did you learn such bitterness?"

"I learnt it here," she told him. "Here, when I was a child, listening to the women who brought you their injustices." Her own eyes, fixed on his unhappy face, spilled over. "Myself, I am happy," she told him. "I have everything. You've always loved me. I know this."

He waited a long time in silence. "You've made your points clear," he said finally. "But I think I can find you even more cruel laws than those you've quoted."

Together they reworked the speech. On towards morning, they kissed each other and retired to their bedrooms. She delivered her words to the legislature. "You are your father's daughter," the senators told her afterwards, gracious if unconvinced. "Today, your father would be proud."

"Your work is a continual humiliation to me," he said. "To me, who's had the respect of my colleagues and my country all my life. You have seven children. Take care of them." The next time she spoke publicly he made good on his threats and removed her from his will.

"Thank god for a girl," her mother said when Elizabeth was born. She fell into an exhausted sleep. When she awoke she looked more closely. The baby's arms and shoulders were thinly dusted with dark hair. She held her eyes tightly shut, and when her mother forced them open, she could find no irises. The doctor was not alarmed. The hair was hypertrichosis, he said. It would disappear. Her eyes were fine. Her father said that she was beautiful.

It took Elizabeth ten days to open her eyes on her own. At the moment she did, it was her mother who was gazing straight into them. They were already violet.

When she was three years old they attended the silver jubilee for George V. She wore a Parisian dress of organdie. Her father tried to point out the royal ladies. "Look at the King's horse!" Elizabeth said instead. The first movie she was ever taken to see was *The Little Princess* with Shirley Temple.

Her father had carried her in his arms. He dressed all in joyous yellow. He held her up for the courtiers to see. When he finally had a son, he rather lost interest. He wrote his will to clarify the order of succession. At this point, he felt no need to legitimize his daughters, although he did recognize their place in line for the throne. He left Elizabeth an annual income of three thousand pounds. And if she ever married without sanction, the will stated, she was to be removed from the line of succession, "as though the said Lady Elizabeth were then dead."

She never married. Like Penelope, she maintained power by promising to marry first this and then that man; she turned her miserable sex to her advantage. She made an infamous number of these promises. No other woman in history has begun so many engagements and died a maid. "The Queen did fish for men's souls and had so sweet a bait that no-one could escape from her network," they said at court. She had a strong animal aura.

A muskiness. When she got married for the first time her father gave her away. She was only seventeen years old, and famously beautiful, the last brunette in a world of blondes. Her father was a guest at her third wedding. "This time I hope her dreams come true," he told the reporters. "I wish her the happiness she so deserves." He was a guest at her fifth wedding, as well.

Her parents had separated briefly when she was fourteen years old. Her mother, to whom she had always been closer, had an affair with someone on the set; her father took her brother and went home to his parents. Elizabeth may have said that his moving out was no special loss. She has been quoted as having said this.

She never married. She married seven different men. She married once and had seven children. She never married. The rack was in constant use during the latter half of her reign. Unexplained illnesses plagued her. It was the hottest day of the year, a dizzying heat. She went into the barn for Swansea pears. Inexplicably the loft was cooler than the house. She said she stayed there half an hour in the slatted light, the half coolness. Her father napped inside the house. "I perceive you think of our father's death with a calm mind," her half-brother, the new king, noted.

"It was a pleasant family to be in?" the Irish maid was asked. Her name was Bridget but she was called Maggie by the girls, because they had once had another Irish maid they were fond of and she'd had that name.

"I don't know how the family was. I got along all right."

"You never saw anything out of the way?"

"No, sir."

"You never saw any conflict in the family?"

"No, sir."

"Never saw the least—any quarreling or anything of that kind?"

"No, sir."

The half hour between her father settling down for his nap and the discovery of murder may well be the most closely examined half hour in criminal history.

The record is quite specific as to the hours when Bridget left the house, she looked at the clock. As she ran, she heard the city hall bell toll. Only eight minutes are unaccounted for.

After the acquittal she changed her name to Lizbeth. "There is one thing that hurts me very much," she told the papers. "They say I don't show any grief. They say I don't cry. They should see me when I am alone."

Her father died a brutal, furious, famous death. Her father died quietly of a stroke before her sixth wedding. After her father died, she discovered he had reinserted her into his will. She had never doubted that he loved her. She inherited his great fortune, along with her sister. She found a sort of gaiety she'd never had before.

She became a devotee of the stage, often inviting whole casts home for parties, food, and dancing. Her sister was horrified; despite the acquittal they had become a local grotesquerie. The only seemly response was silence, her sister told Lizbeth, who responded to this damp admonition with another party.

The sound of a pipe and tabor floated through the palace. Lord Semphill went looking for the source of the music. He found the queen dancing with Lady Warwick. When she had become queen, she had taken a motto. Semper Eadem, it was. Always the Same. This motto had first belonged to her mother.

She noticed Lord Semphill watching her through the drapes. "Your father loved to dance," he said awkwardly, for he had always been told this. He was embarrassed to be caught spying on her.

"Won't you come and dance with us?" she asked. She was laughing at him. Why not laugh? She had survived everything and everyone. She held out her arms. Lord Semphill was suddenly, deeply moved to see the queen, at her age, bending and leaping into the air like the flame on a candle, twirling this way and then that, like the tongue in a lively bell.

*Of her story, Karen Joy Fowler writes: Francis Galton, a biologist, founder of eugenics, and cousin of Charles Darwin, probably made the first composite photographs in 1877. He believed he was studying the physical impact of race and character. In one such work, Galton combined eight different faces. Eighty seconds was the required exposure time, so each face was exposed for ten seconds. Only those characteristics common to all eight received the amount of time required.*

*Galton found the composite more beautiful than any of the individuals and noted that "the points of similarity far outweigh the points of dissimilarity."*

*A year or so ago, my daughter Shannon told me about the work of Nancy Burson, a conceptual artist who uses computer programs and digital imaging techniques to create photographs of people who don't exist. Much of Burson's early work also involved composite portraits. In one composite, she combined the faces of John Wilkes Booth, Lee Harvey Oswald, and Sirhan Sirhan. "I expected a portrait of evil," she said about the piece, "and ended up with the boy next door."*

*"The Elizabeth Complex" is my own attempt to create a composite character. The Elizabeth in the story is composed of pieces of Elizabeth I, Elizabeth Cady Stanton, Lizzie Borden, and Elizabeth Taylor. The title is intended to extend the story farther back in time, by alluding to Electra, an early ancestress of my character.*

*It was Jung who first used the term Electra complex; in doing so, he was creating his own sort of composite. In both the complex and in my story, the point of exposure is the relationship between father and daughter. When I worked on the story, I thought, like Galton and Jung, that the similarities were in the foreground. When I finished, it seemed to me that the points of dissimilarity ultimately dominate.*

*The final version is intended to trace the decreasing power of fathers as measured in units of famous Elizabeths.*

# Abandon in Place

JERRY OLTION

Over the years, there have been lots of stories about space travel in science fiction, and stories about strange supernatural happenings, and stories with a "gee whiz!" sense of wonder, and hard-science "no nonsense" stories about NASA's space program, and "soft-science" stories about memory and regret and longing. There have been plots involving trips to the Moon and plots involving ghosts and plots involving NASA.

But I think this is the first time they've all been in the same story. And only a writer like Jerry Oltion could pull it off. The author of nine novels, including *Frame of Reference* and two in the *Isaac Asimov's Robot City: Robots and Aliens* series, and over seventy short stories, Oltion is a regular contributor to *Analog,* and obviously an expert on the space program.

"Abandon in Place," the winner of this year's Nebula Award for Best Novella, is Oltion's first Nebula, and his second nomination. In his acceptance speech, he said that he had told his editor the story was "a wish-fulfillment story. And now, because of this," he said, holding up his glittering Nebula, "it really is."

It certainly is. For everyone who reads it.

Six hours after Deke Slayton, the astronaut, died of cancer, his racing airplane took off from a California airport and never came down. The pilot didn't respond to the control tower, and the plane vanished from radar shortly after takeoff, but witnesses clearly identified it as Slayton's. Which was impossible, because that same airplane was in a museum in Nevada at the time.

The story made the rounds at the Cape. Engineers and administrators and astronauts all passed it along like scouts telling ghost stories around a campfire, but nobody took it seriously. It was too easy to mistake one plane for another, and everyone knew how fast rumors could get started. They had heard plenty of them over the years, from the guy who'd claimed to be run off the road by Grissom's Corvette after the *Apollo* 1 fire to the Australian who'd supposedly found a piece of Yuri Gagarin's spacesuit in the debris that rained over the outback when *Skylab* came down. This was just one more strange bit of folklore tacked onto the Apollo era, which was itself fast fading into legend.

Then Neil Armstrong died, and a Saturn V launched itself from pad 34.

Rick Spencer was there the morning it went up. He had flown his T-38 down from Arlington right after the funeral, grabbed a few hours of sleep right there at the Cape, then driven over to the shuttle complex before dawn to watch the ground crew load a communications satellite into the *Atlantis*. The ungainly marriage of airplane and rocket on pad 39A would be his ticket to orbit in another week if they ever got the damned thing off the ground, but one of the technicians forgot to mark a step off his checklist and the whole procedure shut down while the foreman tried to decide whether to back up and verify the job or take the tech at his word when he said he'd done it. Rick was getting tired of waiting for somebody to make a decision, so he went outside the sealed payload mating bay for a breath of fresh air.

The sun had just peeked over the horizon. The wire catwalk beneath his feet and the network of steel girders all around him glowed reddish gold in the dawn light. The hammerhead crane overhead seemed like a dragon's long, slender neck and head leaning out to sniff curiously at the enormous winged orbiter that stood there sweating with dew beneath its gaze. The ground, nearly two hundred feet below, was still inky black. Sunlight hadn't reached it yet, wouldn't for a few more minutes. The ocean was dark, too, except near the horizon where the brilliant crescent of sun reflected off the water.

From his high catwalk Rick looked down the long line of launch pads to the south, the tops of their gantries projecting up into the light as well. Except for pads 34 and 37. Those two had been decommissioned after the Apollo program, and now all that remained were the concrete bunkers and blast deflectors that couldn't be removed, low gray shapes still languishing in the shadow of early dawn. Just like the whole damned space program, Rick thought. Neil had been given a hero's burial, and the President's speech had been full of promise for renewed support of manned exploration in space, but it was all a lot of hot air and everyone knew it. The aging shuttle fleet was all America had, and all it was likely to get for the foreseeable future. Even if NASA could shake off the bureaucratic stupor it had fallen into and propose a new program, Congress would never pass an appropriations bill for the hardware.

Rick looked away, but a flicker of motion drew his attention back to pad 34, where brilliant floodlights now lit a gleaming white rocket and its orange support tower. Rick blinked, but it didn't go away. He stepped closer to the railing and squinted. Where had *that* come from? Over half of it rose above the dawn line; Rick looked over the edge of the *Atlantis*'s gantry and made a quick guess based on his own height. That rocket had to be over three hundred feet tall.

Three hundred and sixty-three, to be exact. Rick couldn't measure it that closely, but he didn't need to. He recognized the black-striped Saturn V instantly, and he knew its stats by heart. He had memorized them when he was a kid, sitting in front of his parents' black-and-white TV set while he waited for the liftoffs. Three hundred sixty-three feet high, weighing over three thousand tons when fueled, the five F-1 engines in its first stage producing seven and a half *million* pounds of thrust—it was the biggest rocket ever built.

And it had also been over thirty years since the last of them flew. Rick closed his eyes and rubbed them with his left hand. Evidently Neil's death had affected him more than he thought. But when he looked to the south again, he still saw the brilliant white spike standing there in its spotlight glare, mist swirling down its side as the liquid oxygen in its tanks chilled the air around the massive rocket.

Rick was alone on the gantry. Everyone else was inside, arguing about the payload insertion procedure. He considered going in and asking someone to come out and tell him if he was crazy or not, but he abandoned that thought immediately. One week before his first flight, he wasn't about to confess to hallucinations.

It sure looked real. Rick watched the dawn line creep down the Saturn's flank, sliding over the ever-widening stages until it reached the long cylinder of the main body. The spectacle was absolutely silent. The only sound came from closer by: the squeak and groan of the shuttle gantry expanding as it began to warm under the light.

Then, without warning, a billowing cloud of reddish white smoke erupted from the base of the rocket. The eye-searing brightness of RP-1 and oxygen flame lit up the cloud from within, and more exhaust blasted sideways out of the flame deflectors.

Rick felt the gantry vibrate beneath him, but there was still no sound. The exhaust plume rose nearly as high as the nose cone, roiling like a mushroom cloud over an atomic blast, then slowly the rocket began to lift. Bright white flame sprayed the entire launch pad as the thundering booster, gulping thousands of gallons of fuel per second, rose into the sky. Only when the five bell-shaped nozzles cleared the gantry—nearly ten seconds after liftoff—did the solid beam of flame grow ragged at the edges. A few final tongues of it licked the ground, then the rocket lifted completely into the air.

The shuttle gantry beneath Rick's feet shook harder. He grabbed for support just as the sound reached him: a thunderous, crackling assault that sent him staggering back against the catwalk's inner railing, his hands over his ears. The gantry shook like a skyscraper in an earthquake, knocking him to his knees on the non-skid grating. He didn't try to rise again, just stared upward in awe as the Saturn V dwindled rapidly now and the roar of its engines tapered off with distance.

The glare left afterimages when he blinked. He didn't care. He watched the rocket arc over and begin its long downrange run, picking up orbital velocity now that it had cleared the thickest part of the atmosphere.

The door behind him burst open and a flood of white-jacketed technicians scrambled out. The first few stopped when they saw the enormous plume of exhaust rising into the sky, and the ones behind them piled into their backs, forcing them forward until everyone was packed near the railing. Molly, the payload foreman, gave Rick a hand up, and bent close to his ear to shout over the roar of the rocket and the babble of voices, "What the hell was that?"

Rick shook his head. "Damned if I know."

"There wasn't supposed to be a launch today," she said.

Rick looked up at the dwindling rocket, now just a bright spark aiming for the sun, and said, "Something tells me Control was just as surprised as we were." He pointed toward the base of the exhaust plume, where the cloud had spread out enough to reveal the gantry again.

"What?" Molly asked, squinting to see through the billowing steam. Then she realized what he was pointing at. "Isn't that pad thirty-four?"

Molly and her payload crew reluctantly trooped back into the mating bay to see if the shaking had damaged their satellite, but since Rick was on his own time he rode the cage elevator down to the ground, climbed into his pickup, and joined the line of cars streaming toward the launch site.

The scrub oak and palmetto that lined the service road prevented anyone from seeing the pad until they had nearly reached it. Rick thought he should have been able to see the 400-foot gantry, at least, but when he arrived at the pad he realized why he hadn't. It had vanished just as mysteriously as it had arrived, leaving not a trace.

Rick drove across the vast concrete apron to the base of the old launch pedestal. It looked like an enormous concrete footstool: four squat legs holding a ten-foot-thick platform forty feet in the air, with a thirty-foot-wide hole in the platform for the rocket exhaust to pour through. Off to the side stood the foundation and the thick blast protection wall of the building that had once housed propellant pumps and service equipment. Now both structures looked old and weathered. Rust streaks ran down their gray sides, and stenciled on the pitted concrete, the paint itself fading now, were the words "ABANDON IN PLACE."

Weeds grew out of cracks in the apron, still green and vigorous even right up next to the pedestal. Rick was beginning to doubt what he'd seen, because obviously nothing had launched from this pad for at least a decade.

But the contrail still arched overhead, high-altitude winds snaking it left and right, and when Rick opened the door and stepped out of his pickup he smelled the unmistakable mixture of RP-1 smoke and steam and scorched cement that came with a launch.

Doors slammed as more people got out of their cars. Dozens of them were there already, and more arrived every minute, but what should have been an unruly mob was strangely quiet. Nobody wanted to admit what they'd seen, especially in the face of so much conflicting evidence.

Rick recognized Tessa McClain, an experienced astronaut whom he'd dated a few times in the last couple of months, climbing out of the back of a white van along with half a dozen other people from the vehicle assembly building. When she saw him she jogged across the concrete to his side and said, "Did you see it?" Her face glowed with excitement.

"Yeah," Rick said. "I was up on the gantry at thirty-nine."

She looked up at the contrail overhead, her straight blond hair falling back over her shoulders. "Wow. That must have been a hell of a sight. I felt it shake the ground, but I didn't get outside until it was already quite a ways up." She looked back down at him. "It was a Saturn Five, wasn't it?"

"That's what it looked like," he admitted.

"God, this is incredible." She turned once around, taking in the entire launch pad. "A Moon rocket! I never expected to see anything like it ever again."

"Me either," Rick said. He struggled to find the words to express what he was thinking. "But how could we possibly have seen anything? There's no tower here, no fuel tanks, nothing. And the launch pedestal is too small for a fully fueled Saturn Five. This complex was for the S-One B's."

She grinned like a child at Christmas. "I'm sure whoever—or whatever—staged this little demonstration was able to make all the support hardware they needed. And take it away again when they were done with it."

Rick shook his head. "But that's impossible."

Tessa laughed. "We all saw it." She pointed upward. "And the contrail's still there." Suddenly her eyes grew even wider.

"What?" Rick asked.

She looked across the rolling hummocks of palmetto toward the fifty-story-high vehicle assembly building—and the launch control center at its base. "I wonder if it's sending back telemetry?"

I t took a while to find out. Nobody remembered what frequencies the Apollo spacecraft broadcast on or what protocols the data streams used, and the ground controllers had to dig through archived manuals to find out. It took still more time to set up the receivers to accept the signals, but when the technicians eventually tuned into the right frequencies they found a steady information flow. They couldn't decode most of it, since the software to do that had been written for the old RCA computer system, but they did at least establish that the rocket had not vanished along with its ground support structures.

Rick and Tessa were in the launch control center now, watching the overhead monitors while programmers in the central instrumentation building frantically attempted to adapt the old programs to the new machines. What they saw was mostly a lot of numbers, but every few minutes one of the programmers would patch in another section of translated code and another display would wink into place on the screen. They had already figured out cabin temperature and pressure, fuel level in the upper stage tanks, and a few of the other simple systems.

By this point in a normal flight the whole project would rightfully belong to Mission Control in Houston, but there was nothing normal about this launch. When the Houston flight director heard what the Kennedy team was doing, he wanted nothing to do with it anyway. He intended to keep his own neck well out of the way when heads started rolling after this crazy debacle was over.

But the spacecraft stubbornly refused to disappear. Radar tracked it through one complete orbit and part of another, when its altitude and velocity began to rise. At the same time, the fuel levels in the third stage tanks began to drop. That could mean only one thing: The booster was firing again.

"Translunar injection," Tessa whispered. "They're going for the Moon."

"Who's 'they'?" Rick asked. So far none of the telemetry indicated a live—or even a ghostly—passenger in the command module.

"It's got to be Neil," Tessa said. "And who knows who else is going with him."

"Neil is in a box in Arlington cemetery," Rick said. "I saw them put him there."

"And you saw the launch this morning," Tessa reminded him. "Neil being on board it is no more impossible than the rocket itself."

"Good point." Rick shrugged. Every dead astronaut from Gagarin on could be in the mystery Apollo capsule for all he knew. This bizarre manifestation was completely new territory; nobody knew the rules yet.

Enough people claimed to, of course. Psychics seemed to crawl out of the woodwork over the next few days, each with their own interpretation of the event. NASA had to close the gates and post guards around the perimeter of the space center to keep it from being overrun by curious mystics, but that merely fueled speculation that they were developing a new super-secret space vehicle at the taxpayers' expense.

The administration tried the silent approach at first, but when that charge was leveled they reluctantly admitted that for once the fruitcakes were closer to the truth than the whistleblowers. In a carefully worded press release, NASA's public relations spokesman said, "What appeared to be a Saturn Five Moon rocket seemed to launch from the deserted complex thirty-four. This alleged launch was not authorized by NASA, nor was it part of any program of which NASA is aware. A complete investigation of the incident is being made, and our findings will be made public as soon as we learn what actually occurred."

That was Bureauspeak for, "We don't have a clue either." Rick spent days with the investigation team, going over his story again and again—careful to say "appeared to" and "looked like" at all the appropriate spots—until he could recite it in his sleep, but no one was the wiser afterward. They examined the launch pad, which revealed no sign of a liftoff. All they could do was listen to the telemetry coming from the spacecraft and speculate.

Three days after its launch, the ghost Apollo entered lunar orbit.

A few hours after that, the lunar module separated from the command module and made a powered descent toward the surface. It wasn't headed for the Sea of Tranquility. It appeared to be landing at Copernicus, one of the sites proposed for further Apollo missions before the last three had been cancelled. But when it reached 500 feet, the telemetry suddenly stopped.

"What the hell happened?" demanded Dale Jackson, the impromptu flight director for the mission. He stood beside one of the consoles on the lowest of the terraced rows, looking around at the dozens of technicians who were scrambling to reacquire the signal.

Tessa and Rick were watching from farther up, sitting side by side at unused consoles and holding hands like teenagers on a date at the best movie of all time. When the telemetry stopped, Tessa flinched as if a monster had just jumped out of a closet.

"What happened?" Rick asked. "Did it blow up?"

Tessa shook her head. "Everything stopped," she said. "The command module too, and it was still in orbit."

"Five hundred feet," Rick said. Something about that figure nagged at him. What happened at five hundred feet in a normal lunar descent? "Got it!" he said, loudly enough that everyone in the room looked back up at the screens. When they saw no data there, they turned to him.

"Five hundred feet was 'low gate,' when the pilot was supposed to take over from the descent computer and actually land the LEM," he told them. "The computer couldn't take it all the way to the surface. It wasn't sophisticated enough to choose a landing site."

Jackson asked, "So, what, you think it crashed? It was still five hundred feet up."

Rick hesitated. He'd been biting his tongue for days now, afraid of knocking himself off the *Atlantis* mission with a poorly chosen phrase, but he had grown tired of being timid. He cleared his throat and said, "I think when the time came for a human to take over, it went back to wherever it came from."

"Sure it did." Jackson turned to the technicians. "Get me that signal."

They tried, but it quickly became apparent that there simply wasn't a signal any longer. Not even radar could find any sign of the spacecraft. The mysterious Apollo had vanished without a trace.

NASA held back Rick's *Atlantis* mission an extra week while the ground crew checked the ship for damage from the shaking it had received, but at last they pronounced it ready to fly. On the morning of the launch, Rick and four other astronauts rode the elevator up the gantry, climbed in through the hatch in the side of the orbiter, and strapped themselves into their acceleration chairs. After a countdown that was only interrupted twice due to a defective pressure sensor in a fuel line, they finally lit the three main engines and the two solid rocket boosters and rode America's space truck into orbit.

It was Rick's first time in space. He had expected to be excited, and he was, but somehow not so excited as he had imagined. Instead of watching the Earth slide past beneath him, he spent most of his free time watching the Moon, now just past full. It had been lunar dawn at the landing site when the Apollo had lifted off, just the way it had been for the real flights over a quarter of a century earlier. That was to give the crew the best lighting angle for landing, and to make sure they had plenty of daylight to explore in. And to make emergency repairs if anything went wrong.

What a wild time that must have been, he thought as he floated between the pilot's and copilot's chairs and looked out the forward windows at the white disk a quarter million miles away. Flying by the seat of your pants, your life right at your fingertips and the entire world watching over your shoulder to see if you had the wits to keep yourself alive. Aldrin had accidentally snapped off the pin of the ascent engine arming switch with his backpack, and he'd had to poke a felt pen into the hole to arm the engines before he and Armstrong could leave the Moon. A felt pen! If something like that happened on the shuttle, ground control would probably order the crew to conserve power and wait for a rescue—except they still couldn't launch a second shuttle within a month of the first one. Maybe they could get the Russians to come up and push the button for them with one of *their* felt pens.

He was being unfair. The Hubble telescope repair had taken some real ingenuity, and the Spacelab scientists were always fixing broken equipment. But none of that had the same dazzle as flying to the Moon. Nowadays the shuttle astronauts seemed more like appliance repairmen than intrepid explorers. Rick had convinced himself that the shuttle was doing some valuable science, but now, after seeing a Saturn V launch only two weeks earlier, he realized that science wasn't what had thrilled him when he'd watched them as a kid, and it wasn't why he was here now. He was in space because he wanted to explore it, and this—barely two hundred miles off the ground—was the farthest into it he could get.

He wished Tessa were on his flight. She would know what he was feeling. On their dates, they had talked a lot about their reasons for becoming astronauts, and she had admitted to the same motives as he. But she had been scheduled for *Discovery*'s next launch in a month and a half.

He heard a shout from the mid-deck. "Merde!" A moment later, Pierre Renaud, the Canadian payload specialist whose company had paid for his ticket, floated through the hatchway onto the flight deck.

"What's the matter?" Rick asked when he saw the look of dismay on Pierre's face.

"The toilet has broken," Pierre said.

Rick was on post-flight vacation in Key West when the next one went up. The phone woke him from a sound sleep just after dawn, and when he fumbled the receiver to his ear and answered it, Dale Jackson's gravelly voice said, "There's been another Saturn launch. Get your ass up here so we can compare notes with the last time."

Rick came instantly awake. Less than an hour later he was in the air headed north. By the time he crossed Lake Okeechobee he could see the ragged remains of the contrail, and when he arrived at the Cape the place looked like an anthill that had just been kicked. Cars zoomed up and down the service roads, and the public highways outside the gates were packed in all directions.

Two wide-eyed Air Force cadets escorted him from the airport to a meeting room in the headquarters building, where NASA's administrator, flight director, range safety officer, and at least a dozen other high-ranking officials were already deep in discussion over the incident. Rick noted with amusement that the flight surgeon was also present, and presumably taking notes. Jackson, the flight director, was talking about the difficulty of decommissioning a fully fueled Saturn V on the pad, should another one appear.

"We don't even have facilities there to store the fuel anymore, much less pump it," he was saying. "Especially not in the fifteen minutes or so that these things stick around. That's barely time enough to hook up the couplings."

Tessa was there as well, and she smiled wide and waved when she saw Rick. He edged around the conference table and pulled up a chair beside her. "What are you doing here?" he whispered.

"Getting the third degree," Tessa answered. "I was at the pad when this one lifted off."

"Which pad?"

"Thirty-four."

"You're kidding. You'd be toast if you were that close to the launch."

"I was in the blockhouse."

Rick supposed that would offer some protection. And besides, even that might not be necessary. The weeds hadn't been charred or blown away in the first launch. "Why were you there?" he asked. "How did you know it would happen again?"

She grinned, obviously proud of herself. "Because ghosts usually repeat themselves until they get whatever they came for, and today was the next launch window."

At the head of the table, Jackson was still talking. "...Nor do we have crawler capability to remove the rocket even if we *could* pump it dry. We'd have to completely rebuild the access road, and in the meantime we'd be left with a thirty-six-story embarrassment."

Rick sized up the meeting in an instant. NASA saw these ghost rockets as a threat, and wanted them stopped.

"Why don't we just put astronauts in them instead?" he asked. "There's time enough to ride up the gantry and climb inside before launch."

Jackson squinted down the table at him. "In a completely unknown and untested vehicle? No way."

"It's not unknown or untested," said Tessa. "It's a Saturn Five."

"It's a goddamned mystery," Jackson said, "and there's no valid reason to risk anyone's life on one, either on the ground or in space."

"What do you propose to do, then?" the range safety officer asked. "Shoot them down?"

Nervous laughter broke out around the table but quickly died out. Jackson shook his head. "I propose we let them go. Assuming there are any more. They aren't harming anything except our image."

Warren Altman, latest in a string of five new administrators in the last two years, said, "Yes, precisely. Our image. We're in enough trouble as it is without Congress thinking things are out of control down here." He paused to take off his glasses, and used one of the earpieces for a pointer as he continued, "No, Dale, we can't afford to do nothing. No matter how bizarre this situation is, we've got to take control of it, show Congress that we're handling it, or we'll lose even more credibility than we already have. That means decommissioning the damned things, and if we can't do it on the ground then we'll just have to do it in orbit."

"How?" asked Jackson.

"Just as Rick suggested. Put an astronaut in one, and let him interrupt the mission once it reaches Earth orbit. We'll already have a shuttle up there next month; it can rendezvous with the Apollo and our astronaut can return on the shuttle."

"Leaving the third stage and the rest of the spacecraft in orbit," Jackson pointed out.

"Better there than on the pad," Altman replied. "Besides, maybe we can figure out a use for it. *Skylab* was just an empty Saturn third stage." He laughed. "Hell, if this continues for a few months, we could have all the habitat modules we need to build a real space station."

"And what if they disappear on us just like the last one?"

Altman's eyes narrowed. He hadn't thought of that. But he just shrugged and said, "We'll worry about that later. Chances are the damned things will fade out as soon as we interfere anyway. That's what usually happens with ghosts." He pointed his glasses at Rick. "It's your idea; do you want to volunteer?"

"Of course I do!" Rick said.

"You lucky bastard," Tessa whispered.

He thought so, too, until the training started. For the next month, Jackson kept him on sixteen-hour days in the simulators, training for a mission that hadn't even been considered in over two decades. He learned every switch and dial in the Apollo command module until he could operate the ship with his eyes closed, and he practiced every contingency that the flight engineers could come up with, including a lunar flyby and slingshot back to Earth in case the rocket wouldn't let him shut it down before translunar injection. They had plenty of data already for that kind of abort: Apollo 13 had done a slingshot return when an oxygen tank had blown on the way to the Moon.

Rick even argued them into letting him train in a mockup lunar module, reasoning that he might be able to use it as a lifeboat in case of a similar emergency. They also let him practice using the descent and ascent engines for emergency thrust, and after he wheedled with them for a few days they even let him practice landing.

"Only because it'll help you get a feel for the controls," Jackson told him. "You couldn't actually land even if you wanted to, because if you separate the lunar module from the command module, you're dead. Rendezvous and docking is done from the command module, and you won't have a pilot."

Rick wondered about that. They didn't know who or what might inhabit the capsule atop the enormous rocket. It might be anything from Armstrong's preserved corpse to the Ghost of Christmas Future. The only thing NASA knew for sure was that they weren't going to risk more than one person on this flight.

So Rick found himself standing alone at the base of the concrete pedestal during the hour before dawn on the morning of the next launch window. He wore a shuttle spacesuit modified to allow him to lie in an Apollo couch—the best they could come up with in only a month, since the few remaining Apollo suits in the Smithsonian and other museums were over thirty years old and wouldn't hold air without major refurbishing. He also wore a parachute strapped to his back. The parachute was Jackson's idea, in case the whole Saturn V, gantry and all, faded away when Rick tried to enter the capsule 350 feet off the ground.

Pad 34 was spooky in the pre-dawn twilight. Little gusts of wind rattled the bushes that grew out of the cracks in the concrete, and Rick felt eyes watching him. Most of those belonged to the NASA personnel who waited in the blockhouse nearly a thousand feet away, but the tingling at the back of his neck made Rick wonder if other eyes were watching him as well, and maybe judging him. What would they make of him? He'd been barely ten years old when the *Eagle* landed, was never a military pilot like the first astronauts, never even a soldier. Just a kid who'd always dreamed of becoming an astronaut. And now here he stood with his spacesuit on, holding his suitcase-sized portable ventilator like a banker with his briefcase waiting at a subway stop, while the empty launch pad mocked his every breath.

Even the pads to the north were empty. *Discovery* had already lifted off three days ago, taking Tessa and five others into orbit with the Spacelab, where they were to study the effects of free fall on fruit fly mating habits—and also to await Rick's arrival. They had put themselves in the most likely orbit for the Apollo to take, but it was still a gamble and everyone knew it. If they had guessed wrong, Rick would have to go to plan B: re-entry using the Apollo capsule.

There would be no rescue if that didn't work. None of the other shuttles were even close to being ready for launch; *Atlantis* was still at Edwards, waiting for a ride home that might never come because the 747 carrier plane had developed cracks in the wing struts, and *Columbia* and *Endeavor* were both in the vehicle assembly building with their supposedly reusable engines scattered across acres of service bay while the technicians tried to match enough parts to get one complete set to work.

At least Rick was there. His heart was pounding, but he was there and ready to fly. He squared his shoulders and checked his watch. Any time now.

Suddenly, silently, the rocket appeared. Spotlight glare blinded Rick until he lowered his sun visor, then he turned once around to orient himself. The gantry was right where he'd expected it to be, and the Saturn V...Rick tilted his head back and felt his heart skip a beat. It was colossal. From right there at the base of it, the thing looked like it already reached to the Moon.

He didn't have time to gawk. He ran awkwardly for the gantry, his boots slapping the concrete, then climbed inside the elevator cage and rode it all the way to the top, nervously watching the ground drop far-ther and farther away. Two-thirds of the way up, he crossed into sun-light.

The metal structure squeaked and groaned around him, just like the shuttle gantry did. The grating underfoot scuffed against his boots as he crossed over on the swing arm bridge to the white room and the capsule. The hatch was open, as if waiting for him. Normally a crew of technicians would be there to help him into his seat, but he was com-pletely alone. Nobody waited inside the capsule, either. Quickly, lest the rocket launch with him on the gantry, he climbed in, unplugged his ventilator and tossed it back out the hatch, and plugged one of the ship's three umbilicals into his suit. He jounced up and down on the seat a time or two. Banged on the hatch frame with his gloved hand. Solid. Satisfied, he tossed the parachute out after the ventilator, pulled the hatch closed, sealed it, and sank back into the center couch.

The instrument panel was a forest of switches and knobs before him, uncomfortably close to his face. He scanned the readouts, look-ing for anomalies, while he took a deep breath and smelled the cool, metallic scent of pressurized air. His suit umbilical was working, then. He should have a radio link now, too. He spoke into his suit's micro-phone. "Control, this is Apollo, do you read?"

"Loud and clear," Jackson's voice said.

"Ready for liftoff," Rick told him.

"Good. Estimated time to launch…uh, call it two minutes."

"Roger." Rick's pulse rate was sky high. He tried to calm himself down, but the lack of a real countdown somehow underscored how crazy this whole thing was. He was sitting on top of a ghost!

He forced himself to concentrate on the instruments in front of him. Main power bus, green. Cabin temperature, nominal. Fuel pres-sure—

Amber lights blinked on, and a low rumble vibrated the walls.

"Ignition sequence starting," Jackson said.

"Roger. I feel it."

"All engines running."

Through the hatch window Rick saw the swing arm glide away, and the cabin seemed to sway slightly to the right.

"Liftoff. We have liftoff."

The rumble grew louder, and now Rick felt the acceleration begin to build. The launch tower slid downward out of sight, and then all he could see was blue morning sky. He had expected the gees to slam him back into the seat, but they built gently as the booster burned its fuel and the rocket grew lighter. When the second stage ignited there was a lurch and the gees grew stronger, but they were still bearable.

This time Houston had gotten in the act. Mission Control took over the flight now, and Laura Turner, the capsule communicator, said, "You're looking good, Apollo. Escape tower jettison in twenty seconds."

Rick felt the thump right on schedule, and now that the tower and its boost protection cover were gone he could see out the side windows as well. Florida was a long ways down already, and receding fast.

The third stage ignited a few minutes later, propelling the spaceship on into orbit. "Right on target," Laura said. "We track you one hundred miles uprange of *Discovery* and closing."

"Roger."

And now it was time for Rick to earn his ride. He didn't have to do much; NASA wouldn't let him fly the Apollo toward the shuttle. It was his job to disarm the engines and let Tessa bring the shuttle to him. Holding his breath, he reached out to the too-close instrument panel with his gloved index finger. Would the ship let him take over now, or would it hold him prisoner all the way to the Moon? Or would it vanish in a puff of smoke the moment he touched the controls?

Only one way to tell. The switches clicked home with a satisfying thunk, and the indicator lights showed those circuits dead. The rest of the instruments, and the capsule itself, remained undisturbed. Rick took a breath, then reported, "Engines disarmed. Apollo is now safe for rendezvous."

"Roger, Apollo. Sit back and enjoy the ride, Rick."

He unstrapped himself and drifted free of the acceleration couch. The Apollo capsule might be cramped compared to the shuttle, but with only one person in it he had enough room to float from window to window and look at the blue and white Earth below.

And at the Moon, once again in its crescent phase. It beckoned to him stronger now than ever, for here he sat in a spaceship that could take him there. Take him there and land, if only he had two more astronauts to fly with him.

The shuttle was a bright speck against the solid black of space, drawing steadily closer. Rick watched until it resolved into the familiar stubby-winged orbiter.

"Apollo, this is *Discovery*," Tessa said over the radio. "Do you read?" Her voice sounded excited, as well it might. Not every day did she get the chance to rendezvous with a ghost.

Rick smiled at the sound of her voice. He had always wanted to fly a mission with her. He had always assumed when it happened he would be the low man on the duty roster, cleaning rat droppings out of cages on a Spacelab flight or something, but here he was, commander of his own ship, making space history.

He said, "*Discovery*, this is Apollo. I read you loud and clear. Good to see you, Tessa."

"Are you ready for EVA?"

EVA. Extra-vehicular activity. They couldn't actually dock the Apollo and the shuttle; Rick would have to transfer across on his own, leaving the Apollo to coast onward alone, its engines silenced, its mission—whatever that might be—unfulfilled.

But if NASA really turned it into another *Skylab*, that might mollify whoever or whatever was behind these launches. Then maybe it wouldn't go to waste.

Rick shook his head. Who was he kidding? NASA would never use this ship for anything. He'd known it ever since he saw the look on Altman's face when Jackson asked what they would do if it faded away. Altman just wanted to show Congress—and the power behind the new Apollo—that NASA was still in control. He expected this to be the last of the mystery ships, now that Rick had deactivated it.

"Apollo, do you copy?" Tessa asked.

Rick swallowed. If he screwed with the flight plan, it would be the last time he ever flew. Worse, the spaceship could turn into gossamer and cobwebs at any moment, stranding him in cislunar space with nothing but a pressure suit, slowly suffocating as his air supply ran out. Or it could wait until he reached the Moon before fading out, just as the last two had done, the first over Copernicus and the second over the Aristarchus plateau. But if he didn't at least try it, could he live with himself for the rest of his life, knowing that he'd once had the opportunity to go to the Moon but had turned it down?

He had always wanted to explore the unknown; well, this was certainly his opportunity for it. He had no idea whose ghost this was or what its purpose might be, but it was his ship now, by right of conquest if nothing else. So what was he going to do with it?

Tessa called again. "Hello, Apollo, are you ready for EVA?"

He took a deep breath. "Negative," he said. "Negative. In fact, I think I'm going to need a little help over here."

"What sort of help, Apollo?"

Looking out at the brilliant white crescent, he said, "I need someone to ride with me to the Moon. Preferably two someones. You know anybody who wants to go?"

Tessa's shriek was inarticulate, a primal whoop of surprise or relief or laughter, but before Rick could ask her which it was, Laura, in Houston, said, "Don't even *think* it, Rick. You do not have authorization for an extended mission. Is that clear?"

Rick sighed. But he could already hear the roar of bridges burning. "Clear as space itself, Laura, but I'm going. And if I can take a full crew with me, then I'm going to land when I get there. There's nothing you can do to stop me."

"Negative, Rick. You need ground control. Now that you've disarmed the engines, you have no assurance that any aspect of the mission will proceed normally. You'll have to re-arm and fire the engines yourself, but without us you won't know when to do that. Even after you're on your way, you'll need our radar for tracking, and you'll need our computers to calculate course corrections, and—"

"I get the point, capcom." By the quickness of her response, Laura had obviously considered all this beforehand, but it didn't matter. "You're bluffing," Rick told her. "You wouldn't let us die out here if you could prevent it."

She didn't answer. Rick took that as answer enough. Tessa evidently did too; she said, "We're coming over."

A new voice, Dale Jackson's, said, "You're staying right there.

Rick, Tessa, we will not provide tracking for a lunar flight. I don't care if you drift straight out of the solar system, we will not jeopardize the entire space program just to satisfy your curiosity."

"What space program?" Tessa asked. "We're breeding fruit flies over here." That wasn't exactly fair; one of the payload specialists was an astronomer who was running a free-flying instrument platform— but she was from Japan.

"I'm not going to argue with you. Tessa, if you leave *Discovery*, you will be charged with dereliction of duty and reckless endangerment of the rest of the crew. And I'm not bluffing; if you attempt to leave Earth orbit in that Apollo, you'll be on your own."

Rick looked at the empty seats on either side of him. In a cramped alcove behind them was the navigation equipment—a telescope and sextant and a primitive guidance computer—that could theoretically provide him with enough measurements and computing ability to stay on course. But he hadn't trained to use them, and he bet neither Tessa nor whoever was coming with her knew how to calculate their trajectory with them, either.

"What do you think, Tessa?" he asked. "Can we do it without ground control?"

"I don't—"

"That will not be necessary," a new voice said, drowning her out. It had a heavy accent, but Rick couldn't place it immediately. Some foreign ham operator broadcasting on the Tracking and Data Relay Satellite frequencies?

"Who's that?" he asked.

"I am Gregor Ivanov, of the Russian Space Agency in Kaliningrad. I have been monitoring your signal, and am prepared to offer assistance."

Houston was evidently receiving his signal, too. "You can't do that!" Jackson yelled.

The Russian laughed. "I certainly can. In fact, I must. International treaties legally require that Russia offer help to any craft that has been disabled or abandoned either at sea or in space."

"You stay out of this!" Jackson yelled again. "That craft is neither disabled nor abandoned."

"Oh? Perhaps I mis-heard you. Do you plan to offer ground radar support for the lunar landing mission?" Gregor laughed again, clearly enjoying his position.

Jackson wasn't amused. "Get off this frequency, Russkie," he growled. "You're creating an international incident."

"I certainly hope so," Gregor replied. "Apollo, I repeat my offer. Kaliningrad control will provide your ground support for a lunar landing and sample return mission. Do you wish our assistance?"

Rick felt a laugh bubbling up from his own throat. Could he trust the Russians to guide an Apollo to the Moon? Would they actually help an American crew reenact the mission that had embarrassed their country over thirty years ago? Probably. The cold war was dead and buried, with the Berlin Wall for a tombstone. Whether or not they could actually perform was the big question. Their computer equipment was nearly as antiquated as the 36K of wire-wrapped core memory under the navigation console.

But Rick really didn't have much choice. Houston would fight him every step of the way. And besides, an international mission sounded kind of nice about now. Rick would need someone on his side when he returned. If he returned. Shaking his head, he said, "Any port in a storm, Kaliningrad. I accept your offer."

"This is treason!" Jackson shouted, but Rick ignored him.

Tessa said, "We're coming across, Apollo."

"You're already suited up?" It took two hours of pre-breathing pure oxygen to purge the nitrogen from a shuttle astronaut's bloodstream before they could exit the ship; Tessa and whoever else was coming with her must have started before Rick had even launched.

"Contingency planning," Tessa replied, amusement in her voice. "You might have needed rescue, you know."

"Ah, of course," Rick said.

Jackson tried again. "Tessa, think about this. You're throwing away your whole career for nothing."

"I wouldn't call a lunar landing 'nothing.' "

"It's a goddamned ghost! It's worse than nothing. You could be killed!"

"Yes, I could, couldn't I?" Tessa said. "We could all be killed. Or worse yet, we could all give up the dream and keep flying shuttles into low orbit until they all wear out and Congress decides that manned space flight is a waste of time. I don't want to die in a geriatric ward, wishing I'd taken my one big chance at a real space mission."

She grunted with effort, and Rick saw the shuttle's airlock door swing open. A white spacesuited figure slowly emerged, then another. Rick wondered who the second person was. Another of the shuttle's regular crewmembers? Unlikely. They needed someone to fly the thing back home. That left the Spacelab scientists. Rick ran down the list in his mind and came up with the obvious choice: Yoshiko Sugano, the Japanese astronomer. Her instrument pallet was designed to fly free of the shuttle's annoying vibration and surface glow, and she had been trained to guide it by remote control. She understood docking maneuvers better than most of the regular astronauts; she would make a perfect command module pilot. Besides which, she would make the mission a truly international effort, a point that Tessa had no doubt considered long before Kaliningrad got into the act.

Sure enough, when the two spacesuited figures bumped up against the Apollo and crawled around to the open hatch, Rick saw Tessa's grinning face through her bubble helmet, and behind her, swimming a bit in the one-size-fits-most shuttle suit, was Yoshiko. She didn't look nearly as pleased with herself as Tessa, but she had come along.

"Request permission to come aboard," she said somewhat breathlessly.

"Yes, yes, of course!" Rick said, helping her and Tessa through the narrow rectangle. It was a tight fit; his modified suit had made it okay, but regular shuttle suits had never been designed to fit through an Apollo hatch. Rick felt a moment's panic run through him as he suddenly wondered if they would fit through the *lander's* hatch. They could make it all the way to the Moon only to get stuck in the doorway.

It was too late to worry about that. Like Aldrin and Armstrong and the engine arming switch, they would just have to figure out something on the scene.

As they struggled to fit themselves into the three seats, Jackson tried one last grandstand act, threatening to charge them and the entire Russian Federation with piracy, but Rick said, "NASA doesn't own this ship. Nobody does. Or maybe everyone does. Either way, if you're not going to help us then get off this frequency, because we need it to communicate with ground control."

"*We're* ground control, damn it!" Jackson shouted, "and I'm telling you to return to the mission profile."

"Sorry," Rick said. "Kaliningrad is now in control of this flight. Please get off the air."

Jackson said something else, but Gregor Ivanov also spoke at the same time, and neither transmission was intelligible.

"Say again, Kaliningrad, say again," Rick said, and this time Jackson stayed quiet.

Gregor said, "You still have a chance to make your original launch window if you can prepare for boost within the next fifty minutes. Do you think that is possible?"

Rick looked at Tessa, who nodded and gave the thumbs up. Yoshiko, her eyes wide, only shrugged. This was her first space flight, and it was obviously not turning out the way she'd expected.

"We'll have to get out of these damned suits," Tessa said. "Ours aren't modified for these chairs, and the TLI boost would probably break our necks if we tried it suited up."

"Remove your suits, then," Gregor said, "and prepare for acceleration in fifty-three minutes."

"Roger." Rick made sure the hatch was sealed, then repressurized the cabin. When the gauge neared five pounds, he twisted his helmet until the latches clicked free and pulled it off. Tessa and Yoshiko did the same.

Their three helmets alone nearly filled the space between their heads and the control panels. Removing their suits became a comedy in a closet as they elbowed each other and bumped heads and shoulders in their struggle. The control switches all had guards surrounding them, round loops of metal like old-style flip tops from pop cans sticking out on either side of the toggles to keep people from accidentally tripping them, but Rick still winced each time someone brushed a panel with a hand or a foot.

"This is ridiculous," Tessa said, giggling. "Let's unsuit one at a time, and help each other out."

"Right," said Rick. "You first." He and Yoshiko unsealed the waist ring around Tessa's suit and lifted the top half over her head, then Yoshiko held her shoulders while Rick worked the lower half off her legs. That left her in the spandex cooling and ventilation suit; not as comfortable as regular clothing, with its woven-in plastic tubes and air hoses snaking along all four limbs, but better than the spacesuit. She also left her communications carrier "Snoopy hat" on so she could still hear the radio signals from the ground. Rick stuffed the suit in the equipment bay behind the seats, then he and Tessa helped Yoshiko out of hers, and finally the two women helped him unsuit as well. It was still clumsy business, and at one point Rick found his face pressed against Yoshiko's right breast, but when he said, "Oops, sorry!" and pulled away, he bonked his head on the control panel.

Yoshiko laughed and said, "Don't worry about it. I think we will all become very familiar with one another before this is finished." Rick glanced at Tessa, with whom he'd already become pretty familiar on the ground, and saw that she was grinning.

"In your dreams, Rick," she said. "There's barely room enough in here to pick your nose."

Yoshiko blushed, and so did Rick. He said, "That's not what I was thinking."

"Sure it wasn't. Watch yourself, Yo. He's insatiable. Fortunately, the checklist will keep him too busy to paw us much."

Yoshiko laughed nervously, and Rick realized he'd been had. Nothing he could say would redeem him.

Luckily, Tessa was right about the checklist. Besides stowing the spacesuits, they had to move the Apollo away from the shuttle—which was already receding on its own as well—then orient the ship correctly for the burn that would send them out of orbit, all while making sure the rest of the electronic and mechanical equipment was functioning.

Just over half an orbit later, their panel green and the moment of truth approaching, they waited nervously for the last few minutes to tick by. The engines were armed, the guidance computer was on line, and Kaliningrad had calculated the proper start time and duration for the burn just in case they had to go to manual control. As Rick, in the left seat, hovered with his finger near the manual fire button, Tessa said, "Hey, we haven't named the ship yet. We can't launch for the Moon without a name."

"No, that would be bad luck," Yoshiko agreed.

They both looked at Rick, who shrugged and said, "I don't know. I hadn't even thought about it. How about 'The Ghost,' or 'The Spook?'"

Tessa shook her head. "No, that sends the wrong message. We need something positive, hopeful. Like 'Second Chance,' or, or—"

"Yes, you said it: 'Hope,'" Yoshiko said. Then, looking at Rick, she said, "or 'The Spirit of Hope' if you want to keep the ghost aspect."

Rick nodded. "Yeah. I like it."

"Me too." Tessa licked her forefinger, tapped the overhead hatch in the docking collar—the farthest forward point she could reach— and said, "I christen thee *The Spirit of Hope.*"

Gregor's voice came over the radio. "Very good, *Spirit of Hope.* Stand by for Trans-Lunar Injection in thirty seconds."

The DSKY, the primitive display/keyboard, flashed, "Go/No-go?" This was their last chance to abort. Rick hardly hesitated at all before he pushed the Proceed button. He had already committed himself.

The three astronauts kept their eyes on the controls, watching for signs of trouble, as Gregor counted down the time. The seconds seemed to stretch out forever, but at last Gregor said, "Now!" and right on cue, the Saturn IV-B third stage engine automatically fired for the last time, pressing them back into their seats with a little over a gee of thrust. Rick let his hand fall away from the manual fire button and tucked it against the armrest.

The cabin rumbled softly, the acceleration much smoother than during the ride up through the atmosphere. Rick glanced out the side window at the Earth, but the gee force blurred his vision until it was just a smear of blue and white.

The burn went on and on, over five minutes of thrust, propelling them from 17,000 miles per hour to 25,000, enough to escape the Earth's pull. Near the end of the burn, Rick forced his hand out to the cutoff button, just in case the computer didn't shut it off at the right moment, but Gregor's "Now!" and the sudden silence came simultaneously. Rick's hand leaped forward with the cessation of thrust and pushed the button anyway, but it wasn't necessary. They were coasting now, headed for the Moon.

A s soon as they unbuckled from their couches, they began taking stock. They had three days of coasting to do before they reached the Moon, plenty of time to explore every nook and cranny in the tiny capsule. Every cubic inch of it seemed filled with something, and the only way to find out what was there was to unpack it, inspect it, and put it back into place. There was no room to leave things out; in fact, there was hardly room enough for them all to explore the ship at once.

Yoshiko had been right: within the first half hour they had ceased to worry about bumping into one another. In fact, attempting to avoid it just made them all the more aware of each other, so they simply ignored the forced intimacy and went on with their work, gently brushing aside the stray elbows and feet and other body parts that got in their way. Their spandex cooling and ventilation suits at least allowed the illusion of modesty, which was really all they could ask for in such a tiny space.

Rick didn't mind brushing against Tessa, nor did she seem to mind it when he did. Both of them were grinning like newlyweds, and the air between them seemed charged with a thousand volts. They kissed once while Yoshiko was busy in the equipment bay, just a quick touch of the lips, but it sent a thrill down Rick's spine nonetheless. This was better than any shuttle flight with her would have been.

In most ways, at least. Rick's conviction wavered a bit when Yoshiko found the food, which came in vacuum-packed plastic bags with little accordion necks to squirt water in through to rehydrate it—and to squirt the gooey result out into the astronaut's mouth. Rick and Tessa laughed at her incredulous expression when she saw how it worked. "Like toothpaste?" she asked, and Rick, who had eaten the commercially available version in his school lunches throughout the fall of '69, laughed and said, "It tastes about like it, too."

"It'll keep us alive," Tessa said. "That's what counts. I doubt I'll taste a thing anyway."

She was fiddling with something she had found in a locker. Suddenly she laughed and said, "Smile!" and when Rick and Yoshiko looked up, they saw that she had a TV camera aimed at them. "Hey, Gregor, are you getting a picture?" she asked, panning from Rick to Yoshiko and back.

"Da, affirmative," Gregor said. "Very clear signal."

"Great!" Tessa panned slowly around the cabin, then went to a window and shot some footage of the Earth, already much smaller behind them.

"Wonderful!" Gregor said. "Perfect. We're getting it all on tape, but if you'll wait a few minutes I think we can broadcast you live on national television."

"You're kidding," Tessa said, turning the camera back inside.

"Nyet. We are working on it right now. It's late night in most of Russia; so what if we interrupt a few old horror movies? This is much more interesting."

"Wow. Hear that, Houston? The Russians are showing us live on TV."

Mission Control had been silent since before the TLI burn, but now Laura Turner, the regular capcom, said, "We read you, ah ... *Hope.* We're receiving your signal, too. Hi, Rick. Hi, Yoshiko."

"Hi." Rick and Yo waved at the camera. They could hear some sort of commotion going on in the background, either in Houston or Kaliningrad, but they couldn't tell which.

Yoshiko said, "I wonder if anyone in Japan is receiving this?"

A few seconds later, a new voice said, "Yes, we are. This is Tomi-ichi Amakawa at Tanegashima Space Center, requesting permission to join communication."

"Granted," Gregor said. "And welcome to the party."

"Thank you. We, too, are arranging to broadcast your signal. And, Yoshiko, I have a message for you from your colleagues at university. They are very angry at you for abandoning their observatory, and they also wish you good luck."

She grinned. "Give them my apologies, and my thanks. And tell them if any of them would have done differently, they have rocks where their hearts should be."

"Hah! They envy you. We all do."

"You should. This is an incredible experience."

Gregor said, "We are ready. Perhaps you should give an introduction, so people will know why we are suddenly getting pictures from space."

"Right," said Tessa. She pointed the camera at Rick. "Go for it, Rick. You know as much about this as any of us."

Rick swallowed, suddenly nervous. All of Russia and Japan were watching. And who knew who else? Anybody with a satellite dish and the right receiver could pick up their signal. He slicked his hair back, licked his lips nervously, and said, "Uh, right. Okay, well, hi, I'm Rick Spencer, an American astronaut, and this is Yoshiko Sugano from Japan, and Tessa McClain behind the camera, also from America." Tessa turned the camera around, let it drift free, and backed up to get into the shot. She waved, tilting slowly sideways until she bumped her head against the back of a couch. All three astronauts laughed, and Rick felt himself relax a bit. When Tessa retrieved the camera and aimed it at him again, he said, "As you've probably heard by now, NASA has been plagued with ghosts for the last three months. Ghost Apollo rockets. Well, we decided to see if somebody could ride one into orbit, and once I got there I picked up Tessa and Yoshiko from the *Discovery*, and here we are." He neglected to mention that they were defying orders; let NASA say so if they wanted to. At this point, they would look like the Grinch if they tried it.

Rick said, "Despite its mysterious origin, it seems to behave like a regular Apollo spacecraft. It's every bit as solid as the original article"—he thumped one of the few bare stretches of wall with his knuckles—"and as you can see, every bit as cramped. But there's an amazing amount of stuff in this little thirteen-foot-wide cone. Let's show you some of it." With that for an introduction, Rick led the camera on a tour through the command module, pointing out all the controls and the few amenities, including the waste collection bags, about which he said, "They're primitive, but guaranteed not to break down at a delicate moment, like the shuttle toilet does half the time." He waved at the control panels again, at the hundreds of switches and knobs and gauges, and said, "That's the whole Apollo concept in a nutshell: nothing fancy, but it got the job done. And God willing—or whoever is responsible for this—it'll get the job done again."

Tessa held the camera on the control panel until Gregor said, "Thank you, Rick. We've been thumbing through the manual down here, and it looks like it's just about time for you to dock with the lunar module. Are you ready for that?"

Rick wondered what manual they were consulting. Probably a copy of Aldrin's *Men from Earth*, or one of the later books published around the twenty-fifth anniversary of the first landing. Or it was conceivable that they had copies of the actual checklists from the original flights. The Soviets had had a good spy network back in the sixties.

It didn't matter. They needed to dock with the LM, that much was obvious. Rick looked to Yoshiko. "How about it?" he asked. "I've trained a little on these thrusters in the simulator, but you're our resident expert in docking maneuvers. You want to have a go at it?"

She gulped, realizing that this was her first big moment to either shine or screw up, but she nodded and said, "Yes, certainly," and she pulled herself down into the pilot's chair.

Rick and Tessa strapped themselves into their own chairs, and with Gregor's coaching they blew the bolts separating the command and service module from the S-IV-B booster, exposing the lunar module that had ridden just beneath them all this way. Yoshiko experimented for a few minutes with the hand controller, getting the feel of the thrusters, while Tessa filmed the whole process, showing the people back home the ungainly, angular LM perched atop the spent third stage booster and Yoshiko peering out the tiny windows as she concentrated on bringing the CSM around until the docking collar at the top of the capsule pointed at the hatch on top of the LM. A gentle push with the forward thrusters brought them toward it at a few feet per second, drifting slightly to the side, but she corrected for that with another attitude jet, and they drove straight in for the last few feet. The docking rings met a few inches off center, but the angled guide bars sticking out from the top of the command module did their job and with a little sideways lurch and a solid clang of metal on metal, the two spaceships met.

"Latches engaged," Rick reported when the indicators lit up. He reached out and squeezed Yoshiko's hand. "That was great," he said. "Kaliningrad, we're in business!"

Yoshiko sighed and closed her eyes for the first time in minutes, and over the radio Gregor said, "Congratulations. And thank you for the live coverage. It might interest you to know that millions of people in Russia and across most of Europe were watching over your shoulders."

"And Japan, too," Tomiichi Amakawa said.

Tessa whistled softly. "Wow. People are watching a space mission? Who'd have thought. Just like old times, eh?"

Yoshiko said, "It has been a long time. A whole new generation has been born who have never seen a lunar flight. People are interested again."

Rick looked out the window at a footpad of the LM angling through his view of the Earth. People were interested again? After years of shuttle flights, the astronauts taping science shows that were only broadcast on the educational channels after they ran out of cooking and painting programs, that was hard to believe. It was evidently true, though. For now, at least, people all over the world were once more looking up into the sky.

The Earth seemed to grow brighter, more distinct, as he gazed at it. Rick blinked his eyes, then flinched when Tessa screamed in his ear.

Rick whipped his head around toward her, and she pointed at the control panel. "It's fading out!" she said.

Sure enough, the entire spaceship had taken on a hazy translucence. Earth could be seen right through the middle of it, without need for windows. It was like looking through heavily tinted glass, but it grew lighter even as they watched.

"Holy shit," Rick whispered. His heart was suddenly pounding. They hadn't lost any air yet, but if the ship kept fading...

"Spacesuits!" Yoshiko yelled, reaching around to pull one from behind the seats.

"*Hope*, what is happening?" Gregor asked, his voice tense.

"We've got—" Rick began before his voice failed. He swallowed and said, "Kaliningrad, we have a problem." He helped Yoshiko with her suit, but he knew that they would be dead anyway if the ship vanished. In just their spacesuits they could survive for seven hours, maximum, before they ran out of air.

"What kind of problem?" Gregor asked.

"The ship is fading out on us," Rick said, holding the lower half of Yoshiko's suit while she stuffed her feet into it.

"Can you see it on the TV transmission?" Tessa asked, aiming the camera at the bright Earth through the spaceship's walls. She was breathing hard, but after that initial scream she had brought herself firmly under control.

"Yes, we can," Gregor answered.

"Damn. It's really happening, then."

Rick was having a lot more trouble than Tessa in keeping his fear from controlling him, but a sudden thought made him forget about his own predicament for a moment. "Cut the transmission," he said to her.

"Why?"

"You want another *Challenger*?"

"Oh." Tessa shut off the camera. She understood him perfectly. The biggest catastrophe with the *Challenger*, in terms of the space program as a whole, was not that it blew up, but that millions of people *watched* it blow up. NASA had never really recovered from that. If the whole world saw the *Spirit of Hope* kill its crew, it could destroy any renewed interest in space they had managed to create as well.

"It's too late," Tessa told him. "They already know what killed us."

But even as she said it, the walls grew distinct again. Yoshiko stopped struggling into her suit, and Rick simply stared at the metal walls that once again enclosed them.

"*Hope*, what is your status?" Gregor asked.

"It's back," Rick said. "The ship is solid again."

"What happened? Do you know what caused it?"

"Negative, negative. It just faded out, then came right back."

"Did you do anything that might have influenced it?"

Rick looked at Tessa, then at Yoshiko. Both women shook their heads. "Hard to tell," Rick said. "We screamed. We scrambled for spacesuits. Tessa shut off the camera."

"We all realized we were going to die," Tessa added, and when Rick frowned at her she said, "Well, we're dealing with a ghost here. Maybe that's important."

"Maybe so," Rick admitted.

Gregor said, "Do you have any abnormal indications now?"

Rick scanned the controls for any other clues, but there were none. No pressure loss, no power drain, nothing. "Negative, Kaliningrad," he said. "According to the dashboard, we've got a green bird up here."

Gregor laughed a strained, harsh laugh. "I begin to regret my hasty decision to oversee this mission. Never fear! I will not desert you. But this is troubling. Should I consult the engineers, or a medium?"

"Why don't you try both?" Rick said.

Gregor paused a moment, then said, "Yes, of course. You are absolutely right. We will get right to work on it."

The astronauts sat still for a moment, letting their breath and heart rates fall back toward normal. Rick looked over at his two companions: Yoshiko half into her spacesuit, Tessa holding the TV camera as if it were a bomb that might explode at any moment. Yoshiko reached out and touched the control panel, reassuring herself that it was solid again, then she turned up the cabin temperature. "I'm cold," she said.

Rick chuckled. "That's not surprising. Ghosts are supposed to make people feel cold."

Tessa narrowed her eyes.

"What?"

"I was just thinking. Ghosts make people feel cold. They repeat themselves. What else do they do? If we can figure out the rules, maybe we can keep this one from disappearing on us again until we get home."

Maybe it was just relief at still being alive after their scare, but the intense look in Tessa's eyes was kind of a turn-on. All the same, Rick tried to pay attention to what she was saying. They did need to understand the rules. "Well," he said, "they sometimes make wailing noises."

Tessa nodded. "And they leave slime all over everything."

Rick wiped at the edge of his couch. Bare metal and rough nylon webbing. No slime. "I don't think we're dealing with that kind of ghost," he said.

Yoshiko asked, "Aren't ghosts supposed to be the result of unfulfilled destiny?"

"Yeah," Rick said. "I think that's pretty clear in this case, anyway."

"You mean Neil Armstrong, right?"

"Who else?"

"I don't know. Armstrong doesn't make sense. He already made it to the Moon. If this was his unfulfilled destiny, I'd think it would be a Mars ship, or a space station or something."

"Good point," Tessa said. "But if it isn't Armstrong's ghost, then whose is it?"

Rick snorted. "Well, NASA thinks it's theirs. Maybe the organization is really dead, and we just don't know it."

"Was there another budget cut in Congress?" Tessa asked facetiously.

Rick laughed, but Yoshiko shook her head vigorously. "No, no, I think you have it!"

"What, it's NASA's ghost?"

"In a sense, yes. What if it's the ghost of your entire space program? When Neil Armstrong died, so did the dreams of space enthusiasts all over your nation. Maybe all over the world. It reminded them that you had once gone to the Moon, but no longer could. Maybe the unfulfilled dreams of all those people created this spaceship."

Rick looked out his tiny triangular window at the Earth again. Could he be riding in some kind of global wish-fulfillment fantasy? "No," he said. "That can't be. Ghosts are individual things. Murder victims. People lost in storms."

"Shipwrecks," Tessa said. "They can be communal."

"Okay," Rick admitted, "but they need some kind of focus. An observer. They don't just pop into being all by themselves."

Tessa's hair drifted out in front of her face; she pushed it back behind her ears and said, "How do you know? If a ghost wails in the forest..."

"Yeah, yeah. But something made it fade out just now and come back again a minute later. That seems like an individual sort of phenomenon to me, not some nebulous gestalt."

Yoshiko was nodding wildly. "What?" Rick asked her.

"I think you're right. And if so, then I know whose ghost this is."

"Whose?"

"It's yours."

Rick, expecting her to name anyone but himself, laughed. "Me?"

"Yes, you. You're the commander; it makes sense that you would control the, um, more spiritual aspects of the mission as well."

Both women looked at him appraisingly. A moment ago Rick had found Tessa's intensity compelling, but now those same eyes seemed almost accusatory. "That's ridiculous," he said. "I don't have any control over this ship. Except for the usual kind," he amended before anyone could argue the point. "Besides, the first two launches didn't have anybody on board. And I wasn't even there for the second one."

Tessa said, "No, but you were there for the first one, the day after Neil's funeral. And you'd just gotten back from your shuttle flight—depressed about all the things that went wrong—when the second one went up. If anybody was convinced the space program was dead, it was you."

Rick steadied himself with the grab handle at the top of the control panel. "What, you think I'm channeling the combined angst of all the Trekkies and fourteen-year-old would-be astronauts in the world?"

"Maybe. What were you thinking just now?"

"When it faded? I was thinking—" Rick wrinkled his forehead, trying to remember. "I was thinking how good it felt to have people interested in space again."

"There, you see?"

"No, I don't see," Rick said, exasperated. "What does that have to do with anything?"

"It's a perfect correlation. When you thought nobody cared, that space exploration was dead, you got your own personal Apollo, but when you thought maybe the rest of the world did want to go into space after all, it went away."

Yoshiko said, "And it came back when you thought our deaths would ruin that renewed interest."

Rick's head felt thick, abuzz with the crazy notion that he might be responsible for all this. The way Tessa and Yoshiko presented it made a certain sort of sense, but he couldn't bring himself to believe it. "Come on," he said. "This is a *spaceship*, not some...some vague shadow in the mist. It's got rivets, and switches, and...and...well, hardware." He gestured at the angular walls enclosing them.

Tessa said, "So? We already know it's a ghost. That's not the question. The question is whether or not you're behind it."

"I'm not," Rick said.

"No? I think you are. And it'd be easy enough to test. Let's experiment and find out."

Rick felt his heart skip a beat. Any emotion he had felt for Tessa a moment ago was drowned out now by unreasoning panic. Ghostly hardware was one thing—he could accept that even if he didn't understand it—but the notion that he might somehow exert some kind of subconscious control over it scared him to death. "Let's not," he said.

Tessa pulled herself closer to him. "You agreed that we should figure out the rules so we can keep it from disappearing on us again. We've got a theory now, so let's experiment and see if we're right."

Rick looked out the window again. Black space all around. No stars. Earth visibly receding. He shivered at the sight. For the first time since the launch, he really understood how far they were from help. Whether or not he was responsible for the ghost, he was now responsible for three lives. And maybe, just maybe, a few dreams back home as well. He turned back inside and said, "We've got plenty to do already without crazy experiments. We've got to get this ship rotating or we'll overheat on the side facing the sun, and we've got to take a navigational fix, and check out the lunar module, and so on. Right, Kaliningrad?"

"Yes," Gregor said. "Portside skin temperature is rising. Also—" Voices just out of microphone range made him pause, then he said, "Our engineers agree with your theory, but suggest that you refrain from testing it at this time."

"Your *engineers* agree?" Tessa asked.

"That is correct."

"You're kidding, right?"

"Nyet. I—" More voices, then Gregor said, "—I cannot tell you anything more yet. But please give us more time to study the problem here before you do anything, ah, unusual."

Rick nodded and pulled himself down into his couch again. Gregor was obviously hiding something, but whether he was hiding information or ignorance, Rick couldn't tell. Either way, he was glad to be let off the hook. He said, "I agree one hundred percent. All right, then, let's get to work. Roll maneuver first, so strap in."

Tessa looked as if she might protest, but after a few seconds she stowed the camera and belted herself into her couch as well. Yoshiko smiled and shook her head. "You beg the question," she said, but she strapped in, too.

Rick knew she was right. As they worked to set the spacecraft spinning, he considered what Yoshiko and Tessa had said. Logically, if any single person were responsible for the Apollo manifestations then he was as good a candidate as anyone, but despite his fear of uninformed experimentation he couldn't make himself believe it. He didn't *feel* responsible for anything; certainly not the fade-out they had just seen. His own life was on the line, after all, and he didn't have a death wish.

He began to wonder about that as they went through their checklist. Would he be here if he didn't? So many things could go wrong, nearly all of them deadly. Even the most routine tasks contained elements of danger. For instance, when they blew the bolts separating the spent S-IV-B third stage from beneath their lunar module, the long tube began to tumble, spinning end over end and spraying unused propellent uncomfortably close to them. They had to use the thrusters twice to push themselves away from it before they finally watched it recede into space. The "barbecue roll" went off without a hitch, and the ship's skin temperature evened out, but when Rick unbuckled and pulled himself over to the navigation instruments in the equipment bay he discovered that all their maneuvering had driven them off course.

"It looks like we're closer to a polar trajectory than an equatorial one," he reported to Kaliningrad after he had sighted on a guide star and a lunar landmark and let the computer calculate their position. A polar course was no good; landing and rendezvous would be much easier if they stayed close to the Moon's equator. That way the command module would pass over the landing site on every orbit, and they would have a launch window every two hours without having to do a fuel-wasting plane change.

Gregor said, "Da, our radar confirms your measurement. Wait a moment, and we will calculate a correction burn for you."

"Roger." Rick strapped back into his couch and they used a short burst from the service propulsion system engine to bring themselves back onto an equatorial course. That, at least, provided some relief from another nagging worry; the SPS engine was the last link in the multi-stage chain that had brought them this far, and if it had failed to ignite they wouldn't be able to brake into lunar orbit, or even make course corrections for a slingshot trajectory back home.

After the burn they had to check out the lunar module. With Yoshiko steadying her feet, Tessa opened the hatch between the two spaceships, then removed the docking probe so they could fit through the tunnel. Rick stowed the probe in the equipment bay and followed the two women into the lander, but it had even less room than the command module so he stayed in the tunnel, feeling a bit disoriented as he looked down from above on the angular instrument panel and flight controls. The ascent engine was a big cylinder between the slots where pilot and copilot stood, sort of like the way the engine in an older van stuck out between the driver and the passenger.

"Is this what you sit on during descent?" Yoshiko asked.

Tessa laughed. "No, you fly it standing up, with bungee cords holding your feet to the deck."

"You're kidding."

"Nope."

Yoshiko looked around at the spartan furnishings. To save weight, everything not absolutely essential had been omitted, including switch covers and wiring conduit. Bundles of wires were tied into place, fuel and air lines ran exposed along the walls, and the few storage areas were covered with nylon nets rather than metal panels. The whole ship looked fragile, and in fact it was. A person could shove a screwdriver through the walls if they wanted to. Yoshiko said, "I think I'm glad you two are flying this one."

They hadn't talked before this about who would stay in the command module while the other two went down to the Moon. Though keeping Yoshiko in the command module where her docking skills would be most useful was the logical choice, Rick said, "Are you sure? I was prepared to draw straws for it if you wanted."

She shook her head. "No. This is adventure enough. And who knows, if we inspire enough people I may have another chance to land later, when my own country sends a mission."

Rick wondered what a Japanese lander would look like. Probably a lot slicker than this, he figured, though to be fair he had to admit that *anybody's* lander would be slicker if it were built with modern materials. Most of the equipment—the engines and the computers and so forth—could be bought straight off the shelf nowadays. It would be so much easier to build a lunar lander now than it had been the first time, if people just wanted to.

Well, maybe they would. Who could say?

"You'll certainly have a better chance than we will," Tessa said. "Rick and I will be lucky to stay out of prison when we get—whoa!"

For a second, the Moon had shone brightly through the flight control panel. It was just a flicker, gone as soon as it had appeared, but the ship had done it again.

"It *is* you," Tessa said, pointing accusingly at Rick. "You were thinking positive again, weren't you?"

His heart had begun to pound, and a cold sweat broke out on his body as he said, "Jail isn't exactly my favorite dream."

"No, but I'll bet money you were thinking good stuff just before that."

"Well, yeah, but—"

"But nothing. Every time you think we're going to jump-start the space program with this little stunt, the ship disappears, and every time you think we're not, it comes back. Admit it."

Rick suddenly felt claustrophobic in the narrow access tunnel. He said, "No way! There are a million other factors that could be operating here. My optimism or pessimism isn't controlling the ship."

"I think it is."

They stared at one another for a few seconds, then Gregor said over the radio, "Tessa's theory may be correct. Our studies indicate that ghosts are often closely tied to emotional states."

"Your studies of *what?*" Rick asked. "You can't put ghosts in a lab."

Gregor laughed. "No, but you can sometimes take the lab to the ghosts. You forget, Russia has been studying paranormal phenomena since the cold war. We may not know everything about them, but we have learned a thing or two."

Rick and Tessa looked at each other, both clearly amazed. The Russians had actually gotten *results*? Impossible. Rick said, "I don't believe you for a second."

The Japanese controller, Tomiichi, had not spoken up for some time, but now he said, "Believe it. The Russians aren't the only ones to investigate these matters."

The Japanese, too? Rick looked at Yoshiko, but she merely shrugged and said, "I am an astronomer, not a parapsychologist."

"True enough," Rick muttered, wondering why she hadn't remembered that before when she and Tessa were brainstorming their crazy explanation for all of this. But evidently someone in Russia — and maybe Japan, too — thought they had a handle on it. "So what if you're right, Kaliningrad?" Rick asked. "What do you suggest we do?"

"Be aware that you could die out there," Gregor said. "And if Tessa is correct, then you should remind yourself occasionally that your death will also kill any chance of a resurgence in popularity for manned space flight."

"I'm the one who made her turn off the camera," Rick reminded him. To Tessa he said, "I know we're in danger out here."

"You've got to *feel* it," Tessa said. "That's what matters to a ghost. You've got to remind yourself all the time that this isn't some kind of picnic."

Rick shuddered at the thought of the ship disappearing again, maybe for good, and the three of them blowing away in opposite directions in the last puff of breathing air. "That won't be hard," he told her.

It turned out to be tougher than he thought. Over the next two days, as they coasted toward the Moon, the ship faded out twice more, once to almost transparency before whatever was responsible brought it back. Maybe it *was* him, Rick thought after the second time. It had happened while he was asleep, and when Yoshiko had shaken him awake he had to admit that he had indeed been dreaming about a colony on the Moon.

Both Yoshiko and Tessa were looking at him like hostages in a bank robbery or something. Those accusing looks, combined with the adrenaline rush from waking to their screams and his own fear of death, suddenly pissed him off. As he rubbed the sleep from his eyes, he said, "All right, damn it, maybe I *am* in control of this thing. And if you're right about that, maybe you're right about experimenting with it, too."

"What do you mean?" Tessa asked nervously.

"I mean if I'm God all of a sudden, then why don't I use it for something? Like make us a bigger ship, or at least a more modern one. Something with a shower, for instance. Or how about the *Millennium Falcon*? Maybe we could go to Alpha Centauri as long as we're out here."

"Nyet!" Gregor said loudly. "Do not experiment! It is more dangerous than you can imagine."

Rick snorted loudly. "Well, comrade, if I'm in the dark, then it's because you guys are holding back on me. If you know what's going on up here, then tell me. Why shouldn't I dream up a nice, big fantasy instead of this cramped little can?"

"E equals MC squared, that's why," Gregor said. "Your ghost cannot violate the known laws of physics. We do not know where the energy comes from to create the...ah, the physical manifestation, but we do know that a clumsy attempt to manipulate it can result in a violent release of that energy."

"You do, eh? And how do you know that?"

Gregor conferred for a moment with someone else in the control room with him, then came back on line. "Let us just say that not all of our underground explosions in the 1970s were nuclear."

Rick looked out the window at black space. "You've made a weapon out of ghosts?" he asked quietly.

Gregor said, "Is an industrial accident a weapon? It is not useful unless you can direct it, and that's what I'm trying to tell you now. You are the focus of this phenomenon, but not its master. If you are careful you can maintain it, but if you attempt to manipulate it, the result will be disastrous."

"So you say."

"So we have come to understand. We do not have all the answers either."

Rick's mad was wearing off, but frustration made him say, "Well, why don't you come up with some? I'm getting tired of being the scapegoat up here."

Gregor laughed softly. "We are doing our best, but you will understand if that is too little and too late. We are having trouble reproducing your situation in our flight simulators."

"Hah. I'll bet you are." Rick took a deep breath and let it out slowly. "All right," he said, "I'll try to be good. But if you learn anything more about how this works, I want to know it instantly. Agreed?"

"Agreed," Gregor said.

Rick rubbed his eyes again and unstrapped from his chair. Looking pointedly at Tessa and Yoshiko, he said, "Okay, then unless anybody has an objection, I think I'll have some breakfast."

"No problem," Tessa said, holding her hands out. Yoshiko nodded. They both turned away, either to give him some privacy or to escape his anger, but whichever it was he really didn't care.

Tessa pulled herself into the equipment bay and began taking a navigational reading while he rehydrated a bag of dried scrambled eggs.

"Hey," she said a few minutes later. "We're on a polar trajectory again." She looked directly at Rick, who was sucking on a packet of orange juice.

"It's not me," he protested. "A polar orbit means we can't land. The command module wouldn't pass over our landing site again for an entire lunar day." That was twenty-eight Earth days, far too long for a crew to wait on the surface. In order to rendezvous with the command module, they would have to make an orbital plane-change in mid-launch, a much more tricky and fuel-costly maneuver. Either that or the command module would have to make a plane change, which was equally difficult.

Yoshiko acquired a rapt expression for a few seconds, then said, "Unless you land at the pole. The command module would pass over both poles on every orbit."

"We can't land at the...can we?"

"Absolutely not," Gregor's voice said. "Even I will not allow that kind of risk. You would have bad lighting, extremes of temperature, no margin for error in landing sites, possibly even fog obscuring your vision on final approach."

"Fog?" asked Tessa.

"It is possible. Current theory predicts water ice in some of the deeper craters near the pole, where sunlight can never reach them."

"Wow," whispered Rick. "Ice on the Moon. That would make supporting a colony a lot easier."

"Rick." Tessa was looking intently at the walls, but they remained solid.

"Look, it's a fact," Rick told her, still put out with the whole situation. "Ice would make it easier to set up a colony. We wouldn't have to fly all our water up from Earth. That doesn't mean I think we're actually going to build one, okay?"

"All right," Tessa said. "I just want you to be careful." She looked out the window at the Earth, now just a tiny blue and white disk in the void. "So, Kaliningrad, what do you suggest?"

Gregor said, "Give us a minute." He took longer than that, but when he came back he said, "We want to check your guidance computer's program. Perhaps we can discover where it intends to take you."

So Rick, who had at least trained with the primitive keyboard and display, pulled himself down into the equipment bay and ran the computer while Kaliningrad talked him through the procedure, and sure enough, the program was indeed for a polar trajectory. And when they checked the computer in the lander, they learned that it was programmed for a descent to the rim of the Aitken Basin, a six-mile-deep crater right on the Moon's south pole.

"That's ridiculous," Rick said when he heard the news. "How could we be expected to land on the south pole? Like Gregor said, the light would be coming in sideways. Shadows would extend for miles, and every little depression would be a black hole."

Tessa, who had been running the computer in the lander, said, "Well, maybe this switch labeled 'Na inject' could provide a clue. If it sprays sodium into the descent engine's exhaust plume, it would probably light up like a candle flame and provide all the light we need."

"You're kidding." Rick pulled his way through the docking collar into the lunar module to look for himself, and sure enough there was the switch, right next to one labeled "Hi-int Floods."

Tessa said, "It looks like landing lights to me. Two separate systems for redundancy."

"Those weren't on the simulator I trained with," Rick said.

"Of course not. NASA would never plan a polar landing. Too dangerous."

They knew that NASA had been listening in on their broadcast all along, and sure enough, now Laura Turner in Houston said, "Well, maybe not, Tessa. We've been digging through the old paperwork here, and in fact one of the mission proposals *was* for a polar landing. You're right, there was a lot of argument against it, but it was considered a possibility for a later mission after we'd gained enough experience with the easy ones. Of course it got axed along with everything else when the budget cuts came down, but if we'd had the support for it, we would eventually have gone."

Rick felt a shiver run up his spine. "The last two ghosts went to Copernicus and Aristarchus. Those were on the list, too, weren't they?"

"That's right."

"So basically we're reenacting what the U.S. should have done all along."

"That's a matter of opinion, but yeah, I guess you could say that."

Gregor asked, "Houston, can those guidance computers be reprogrammed for a less difficult landing site?"

"Negative," Laura said. "The programs are hard-wired in core memory. There's only two kilobytes of erasable memory, and they need that for data storage."

"So it's a polar landing or nothing," Rick said, his breath coming short. He looked at the controls again. They were solid as a rock now.

"Looks that way," Tessa said. She grinned at him. Even with the added danger, it was obvious what she would choose.

Rick gulped. Her wide smile and intense, almost challenging stare were incredibly alluring, but at the same time he couldn't help wondering how deep a hole they could dig themselves into on this flight, anyway. Deeper, apparently, than he had first thought. But they were already in quite a ways; he couldn't back out now. "All right, then," he said. "A polar landing it is. I just hope we find something worth the risk."

Tessa laughed, and leaned forward to kiss him. "Just going is worth the risk," she said. "That's what exploring is all about."

Both Houston and Kaliningrad were unhappy with their choice, but Houston didn't have any say in the matter anymore, and Kaliningrad was caught in a dilemma of its own making, for bailing out now would amount to abandoning an international rescue in the middle of the attempt. So they reluctantly set up their own computers to match the course wired into the onboard ones, and on the eighty-third hour of the flight, Rick, Tessa, and Yoshiko strapped themselves into their couches for the long rocket burn that would slow them into orbit around the Moon. That had to happen after they had rounded the horizon, which meant they would be cut off from Earth for the burn. The computer would count down the time and fire the engine automatically, but just in case it didn't, they all set their watches to keep track as well.

The last few minutes dragged by. The Moon wasn't visible in the windows; they had turned the ship end-for-end so it was behind them now, their course missing the horizon by a mere hundred miles. Rick kept glancing at his watch, then at the computer display, then at the attitude indicators, making sure they were still lined up properly for the burn.

Yoshiko took careful notes. If Rick and Tessa crashed or couldn't return from the surface, she would have to fire the trans-Earth injection burn herself and make the homeward flight alone.

Just before the burn, the computer asked, "Go/No-go?" again, and Rick pushed "Proceed." The three astronauts watched the countdown continue to zero, but Rick didn't feel the engine kick in. He stabbed at the manual fire button hard enough to break his fingernail on it, and then he felt the thrust.

Tessa looked over at him, her mouth open. "The computer didn't fire it on time?"

"I didn't feel it," Rick said. "Not until I—"

"It did," Yoshiko said. "I felt it before you pushed the button. The computer's okay."

"Are you sure?" It had been a split-second impression on Rick's part, and his body was so high on adrenaline that he might not have felt the thrust immediately, but he'd have sworn it hadn't fired until he hit the button.

"I'm sure," Yoshiko said.

Rick looked to Tessa, who shrugged. "Too close to call, for me."

Rick laughed a high-pitched, not-quite-panicky laugh. "What the hell," he said. "We got it lit; that's what counts. Are we still go for landing?"

Tessa nodded. "I am."

"You still comfortable with the idea of staying up here by yourself for a day?" Rick asked Yoshiko.

"Yes," she said.

"All right, then, let's do it."

They didn't mention the possible computer glitch to Gregor when they rounded the back side of the Moon and reacquired his signal. They reported only that they had achieved orbit and were ready to proceed. Gregor had them fire another burn to circularize their orbit, and that one went off automatically, so Rick began to relax about that anyway. He had plenty else to keep him occupied. The flight out had been a picnic compared to the constant checklists they had to follow and the navigational updates they had to key into the computers before they could separate the two ships. They hardly had time to look out at the Moon, its gray cratered surface sliding silently past below. But finally after two more orbits, two hours each in the lighter lunar gravity instead of the hour and a half they were used to in Earth orbit, they were ready.

They had named the lunar module *Faith*, to go along with *Hope* and to signify their trust that it would set them down and bring them back again safely. So when Gregor was satisfied that everything was ready, he radioed to the astronauts, "You are go for separation, *Faith*."

"Roger," said Rick. He and Tessa were both suited up again and standing elbow to elbow in front of the narrow control panel.

In the command module, Yoshiko said, "Going for separation," and she released the latches that held the two ships together. A shudder and a thump echoed in the tiny cabin, and they were free.

*Faith*'s computer rotated them around to the right angle, and when the proper time came, the engine lit for a thirty-second burn that lowered their orbit to within eight miles of the surface. They coasted down the long elliptical track, watching the cratered surface grow closer and closer, until their radar began picking up return signals and Gregor finally said, "You are go for powered descent."

Rick pushed "proceed" on the keyboard, and the computer fired the engine again, slowing them to less than orbital velocity. They were committed now.

Tessa reached out and punched Rick in the shoulder. "Break a leg, buddy," she said. "It's showtime."

It was indeed. Rick gave her a quick hug, clumsy in the suits but nonetheless heartfelt, then gave his attention completely to the controls. Their course was bending rapidly now, curving down toward the surface, which this close to the pole was a stark pattern of white crater rims holding pools of absolute blackness. Rick's gloved finger hovered near the sodium inject switch, but he didn't flip it yet. He didn't know how much he had, and he wanted to save it for the actual landing.

Tessa called out their altitude, dropping rapidly at first, then slower and slower, until at six hundred feet they were only falling at twenty feet per second. Five seconds later she whispered, "Low gate," and Rick rocked the controller in his hand, switching out the computer.

He held his breath. This was when the previous two lunar modules had disappeared, at the point where the pilot had to take over. He waited for that to happen again, but the lander dropped another fifty feet, then seventy-five, and it was still there.

"Whew," he said. "We made it."

"What do you mean?" demanded Tessa. "We're still four hundred feet up!"

"Piece of cake," Rick said, looking out the window at the landscape slowly moving past. It was impossible to tell which little arc of crater rim was their target, and the tiny triangular windows were too small to give them an overview of the larger picture, so Rick just picked one that looked reasonably wide and brought the lander down toward it. It was strewn with boulders, but there were plenty of clear spaces between them, if he could just hit one.

"Quantity light," Tessa called out. He had only a minute of fuel left, less than he was supposed to have at this altitude, but it was still plenty at their rate of fall.

He slowed their descent to ten feet per second and rotated them once around. One big boulder right on the rim had a wide flat spot beside it, so he angled over toward it. Flying the lander felt just like the simulator, save for the shifting of weight, and that actually helped him get a feel for the controls.

"Two hundred feet, eleven down," Tessa said.

Too fast. Rick throttled up the engine a bit.

"One eighty, six down. One seventy, three down. One sixty-five, zero down—we're going back up!"

"Sorry," Rick said, dropping the thrust again. While he was at it, he flipped on the sodium injector, and sure enough, the landscape exploded in bright yellow light. Even the bottoms of the craters were visible now, though they seemed fuzzy, out of focus.

No time to sightsee now, though. Tessa kept reading off the numbers, her voice rising a little in pitch. "Forty-five seconds. One sixty feet, four down. One fifty, five down; one forty, six down...you're picking up too much speed!"

"Got it," Rick said, nudging their thrust up a bit.

"One hundred, five down. Thirty seconds."

Rick did the math in his head. At this rate of descent he had ten seconds of fuel to spare. Far less than regulation, but still enough if he didn't waste any more. "Piece of cake," he said again, holding it steady for the spot he had chosen.

The descent went smoothly through the next fifty feet, but with only fifty feet to go, the ground began to grow indistinct. "What's that, are we kicking up dust?" Rick asked.

"I don't know," Tessa said. "It looks more like fog."

"Fog? Damn, Gregor was right." Rick held the controls steady, but they were descending into a white mist. The big boulder he'd been using for a marker disappeared in the cloud swirling up from the crater floor. Rick couldn't tell if they were still going to miss it or not; they could be drifting right over it for all he could tell.

Tessa's hand hovered near the Abort Stage button. That would fire the ascent stage's engine, smashing the lower half of the lander into the surface as it blasted the top half free and back into orbit.

"We're too low for that," Rick said. "We'd crash with the descent stage if we tried it. Just hang on and call out the numbers."

"Roger. Twenty, five down."

That was pretty fast, but Rick didn't budge the controller. If he shifted them sideways in the process, they could hit the boulder.

"Fifteen...ten...contact light!"

The feelers at the ends of the landing legs had touched the surface. Rick let the engine run for another half second, then shut it down. The lander rocked sideways just a bit, then lurched as they hit the surface hard. "Engine off," Rick said, his eyes glued to the ascent engine fuel level. It held steady. No leaks, then, from the shaking, and no warning lights on any other systems. Looking over at the descent engine's fuel gauge, he saw that they had six seconds left.

Tessa glared at him. "Piece of cake?" she asked. "Piece of *cake?*"

Rick, at a loss for words, could only shrug.

Yoshiko's voice came over the radio. "*Faith*, are you down?"

Tessa laughed. "Yes, we're down. Through fog as thick as soup, with six seconds of fuel left."

Fog. There was water on the Moon. Rick looked out the window, pointed. "Look, it's blowing away."

Without the rocket exhaust and the harsh sodium light to heat the ice in the crater floor, what had already vaporized was rapidly expanding into the vacuum, revealing the rubble-strewn crater rim on which the lander had touched down. Rick looked for his landmark boulder, saw it out of the corner of his window, only a few feet away from the side of the lander. They had barely missed it. In fact two of the legs had straddled it. If one of them had hit it, the lander would have tipped over.

Rick put it out of his mind. They were down, and they had more important things to worry about.

Time seemed to telescope on them as they ran through another checklist to make sure the ascent stage was ready to go in an emergency, then they depressurized the lander and popped open the hatch to go outside. Rick went first, not because it was his Apollo or because he was in any way more deserving, but for the same reason that Neil Armstrong went first on *Apollo 11*: because in their bulky spacesuits it was too difficult for the person on the right to sidle past the person on the left in order to reach the door.

It was a tight squeeze, but he made it through the hatch. The corrugated egress platform and ladder were in shadow, so Rick had to climb down by feel. He pulled the D-ring that lowered the outside camera, and Gregor radioed that they were receiving its signal back on

Earth. Rick figured he was probably just a silhouette against the side-lit background, but he supposed that was about as good as the grainy picture of Neil taking his first step.

He was on the last rung when he realized he hadn't thought up anything historic to say. He paused for a moment, thinking fast, then stepped off onto the landing pad and then from there onto the frozen lunar soil. It crunched beneath his feet; he could feel it, though he couldn't hear it in the vacuum.

Tessa had made it through the hatch, too, and was watching from the platform, obviously waiting for him to speak, so he held his hand up toward her—and symbolically toward Earth, he hoped—and said, "Come on out. The water's fine!"

The water was indeed fine. Fine as powdered sugar, and about the same consistency. Brought to the Moon's surface in thousands of comet strikes over the millennia, it had accumulated molecule by molecule as the vaporized water and methane and other gasses froze out in the shadowed crater bottoms at the poles. It was too cold, and the Moon's gravity was too light, for it to pack down into solid ice, so it remained fluffy, like extremely fine snow. When Rick and Tessa walked out into it they sank clear to their thighs, even though they only weighed about fifty pounds, and they would probably have sunk further if they'd gone on. But they could feel the cold seeping into their legs already, so they had to scoop up what samples they could in special thermos bottles designed for the purpose and turn back. The sample equipment packed in the lander was designed for a polar mission, but their spacesuits were made to keep them warm in vacuum, not against ice that could conduct heat away.

So they walked around the crater rim, bounding along in the peculiar kangaroo-hop gait that worked so well in light gravity, looking for anything else that might prove interesting. That was just about everything, as far as Rick was concerned. He was on the Moon! Every aspect of it, from the rocky, cratered ground underfoot to the sharp, rugged horizon, reminded him that he was walking on another world. He looked out toward the Earth, about two-thirds of it visible above the horizon, about two-thirds of that lit by the sun, and he felt a shiver run down his spine at the sight. He had thought he would never see it like that except in thirty-year-old pictures.

They were making pictures of their own now. Tessa carried the TV camera and gave a running commentary as they explored. Gregor said that everyone in Russia and Europe was watching, and Tomiichi said the same for Japan. And surprisingly, Laura said the same about the United States. "They even preempted *Days of Our Lives* for you," she told them.

"Hah. Maybe there's hope for our country yet," Rick muttered.

"Watch it," Tessa said, but whether for fear of him offending their watchers or for fear of him getting too hopeful, she didn't say.

Rick didn't care. He felt an incredible sense of well-being that had nothing at all to do with whether or not they made it back alive. They were on the Moon, he and Tessa, at the absolute pinnacle of achievement for an astronaut. Higher than anything either of them had ever expected to achieve, at any rate. No matter what they faced on the way home, or after they got there, nothing could alter the fact that they were here now. And Rick couldn't think of anyone he would rather share the experience with. He and Tessa would be spoken of in the same breath forever, and that was fine with him. He watched the way she bounded along in the low gravity, listened to her exclaim with delight with each new wonder she discovered, and he smiled. He wouldn't mind at all sharing a page in the history books with her.

They collected rocks and more ice from all along their path. At one stop Rick packed a handful of snow into a loose ball and flung it at Tessa, who leaped nearly five feet into the air to avoid it. When the snowball hit on the sunlit side of the crater, it burst into a puff of steam.

"Wow," Tessa said as she bounced to a stop, "did you see that? Do it again."

Rick obligingly threw another snowball past her, and she followed it with the camera until it exploded against a rock.

"Did you guys back home see it, too?" she asked. "What makes them blow up like that?"

Gregor said, "Heat, I'd guess. And vacuum. Without an atmosphere to attenuate the sunlight, a rock will heat up just as much there at the pole as it would at the equator, so when the snow touches the hot rock it flashes into steam."

"Hah, I suppose so. Looks pretty wild."

"It might also give us a good idea what gasses are in the snow. Rick, could you set a sample down a bit more gently on a sunlit surface and let us see how it boils off?"

Rick did as he asked, packing a double-handful of snow and setting it on a boulder's slanted face. Steam immediately began to rise from it, then stopped after a few seconds. The snowball shifted slightly and more steam sublimed off, then another few seconds passed before the remaining snow melted into a bubbling puddle.

"Aha!" Gregor said. "Three separate fractions, at least. I would guess methane for the first, then ammonia or carbon dioxide, and finally water. That is wonderful news! All four gasses will be useful to a colony."

"If we ever send one," Rick said, trying to suppress his silly grin so Tessa wouldn't grow afraid of his optimism, but that in itself made him laugh out loud.

"Damn it, Rick, you're scaring me half to death!" she said. They both turned to look at the lander, glittering like a gold and silver sculpture on the concrete gray crater rim, but it remained solid.

"Don't worry," Rick told her. "I may be having fun, but I'm still just as scared as you are."

"Good."

They explored for another hour, but before they had even made it a tenth of the way around the crater they had to turn back. The suits only held another two hours of oxygen, and they would need that time to return to the lander, climb back inside, and pressurize the cabin again. And after that their time on the Moon would be over, because they had to get back to *Hope* as quickly as possible and blast off for Earth again before the plane of their polar orbit shifted too far away from a return path. Their SPS engine had enough fuel for a plane change of a few degrees, but the longer they waited the more it would take.

They had done enough already. They had discovered water on the Moon, and had gone a long way toward proving that it could sustain a colony if humanity wanted to send one. Now all they had to do was get home alive, but that in itself was a big enough job to keep them occupied full-time.

Yet as he waited for Tessa to climb up the ladder and kick the dust from her boots, Rick thought of one more thing he could do. His heart leaped in his throat at the thought, but it would be the perfect cap to a perfect day—provided he really wanted to do it. And provided he'd read Tessa's signals right as well.

He had no time to decide. It was now or never. He gulped, muttered, "He who hesitates is lost," and moved back away from the lander.

"What?" Tessa asked. She had reached the egress platform.

"Don't go inside yet." Rick paced a few yards away, then began scuffing five-foot-high letters into the crunchy soil with his boot. They showed up beautifully in the low-angled light.

"What are you doing?" she asked him.

He didn't answer. It would become obvious in a moment, if he could just remember how to spell. That was no sure bet; his head buzzed like an alarm going off, and his breath came in ragged gasps that had nothing to do with the exertion of drawing in the dirt. This would change his life even more than the trip to the Moon. Maybe.

"Oh, Rick," Tessa said when he completed the first line, but she grew silent when she saw him begin a second. She was still silent when he finished his message:

*Tessa, I love you.*
*Will you marry me?*

He was still standing on the final dot below the question mark. He looked up at her, a dark silhouette against the darker sky, her gold-mirrored faceplate reflecting his own sunlit form and the words he'd written. He couldn't see her expression through it, couldn't tell what she was thinking. He waited for some indication, but after the silence stretched on so long that Gregor asked, "Rick? Tessa? Are you okay?" she began to climb down the ladder again.

"Stand by, Kaliningrad," Rick said.

Tessa stepped back onto the lunar surface, walked slowly and deliberately over to stand beside Rick. Even this close, he couldn't see her face, but he heard her sniff.

"Tess?"

She didn't answer him, at least not over the radio. But she shook her head a little and stepped to the side far enough to scratch a single word in the soil:

*Yes.*

Rick echoed it aloud. "Yes!" All his apprehension died in an instant. He bounded over to her and wrapped her in a bear hug. "Tessa, I love you!"

"Oh, Rick."

"Are you two getting mushy again?" Yoshiko asked.

Rick laughed. "Mushy, hell, we're getting married."

The radio burst into a jumble of voices as everyone spoke at once, then Gregor's voice cut through the rest. "My sincere congratulations," he said, "but your launch window is fast approaching."

"Roger," Rick said. "We're going inside now."

He helped Tessa climb back into the lander, then he climbed up and kicked off as much dust as he could. Before he ducked in through the hatch he looked down at the words they had written on the ground, their declaration clearly written for all to see. Those words could stay there for a billion years or so, the way things weathered on the Moon. Or if people actually came up and mined the crater for ice, they could be obliterated within a decade. That would depend quite a bit on what happened on the trip home.

Rick thought again of all the things that could yet go wrong. Engine failures, docking failures, computer failures—the list seemed endless. Despite his excitement over his and Tessa's future, if their personal welfare over the next few days made any difference then he would have no trouble staying sufficiently pessimistic to keep the ghost from fading away on them.

The number of possible disasters shrank with each stage of the mission: *Faith's* ascent engine carried them into orbit, and Yoshiko docked smoothly with the lander, and the SPS engine fired on time to send them back homeward; but the way Rick figured it, infinity minus a few was still infinity. Plenty of things could still go wrong.

Including, of course, the ghost disappearing. Twice more on the return trip, both times right after Gregor reported that "Moon fever" was once more gripping the world, the spacecraft's walls grew indistinct around them, and both times they came back only after Rick convinced himself that their deaths could still squelch humanity's renewed enthusiasm for space. All the evidence seemed to support Yoshiko and Tessa's theory that he was somehow in control of the apparition, whether or not he was directly responsible for it.

Gregor would say no more about it, save that he should listen to them. Tessa took that as carte blanche to control his every action, including sleep, which she wouldn't let him do. She was afraid he would start dreaming of the bold new age of space exploration and they would all die of explosive decompression before he could wake up. She refused to let Gregor or Tomiichi or Laura tell them anything more about the situation on Earth, and she kept inventing elaborate new scenarios in which humanity would decide not to follow their lead after all. And now that they were engaged, she seemed to think Rick's personal space was hers to invade in whatever imaginative ways she could think of as well. She would tickle him if she thought he was drifting off, or kiss him, or brush against him seductively. Rick found it alternately amusing and annoying, depending on which stage of his sleep deprivation cycle he was in at the time.

To keep himself busy, and to keep his mind on other things, he made her an engagement ring out of one of the switch guards, which were already nearly the right size and shape. He snapped one off from beside a third-stage booster control that didn't connect to anything anymore, and with a little filing on a zipper he buffed the rough edges down enough for her to wear it.

"I'll treasure it forever," she told him when he slid it onto her finger, but Rick was too befuddled from lack of sleep to know if she was fooling or serious.

Finally, less than a day out from Earth, Tessa could no longer stay awake either. As she drifted off to sleep, she admonished Yoshiko to continue the job, but as soon as her breathing slowed, Yoshiko told

Rick, "Go ahead and sleep if you want. I think you'll be more valuable to us tomorrow if you get some rest now."

Rick, groggy with fatigue, tried to focus on her face. "Why?" he asked. "What's tomorrow?"

She grinned diabolically. "Re-entry. Twenty-five thousand miles an hour, *smack* into the atmosphere. Sleep well."

Rick slept, but just as Yoshiko had intended, all his dreams were of burning up in a fireball as the Apollo capsule hit the atmosphere at too steep an angle, or of skipping off into interplanetary space if they hit too shallow. Or of hitting their window square on and still burning up when the ghost ship proved incapable of withstanding the heat. The gunpowdery smell of the lunar dust they had tracked inside on their spacesuits didn't help any, either; it only provided another sensory cue that they were on fire.

When he woke, Earth was only a couple hours away. It still looked much smaller than it had from the shuttle, but it felt so much closer and it looked so inviting after his hours of bad dreams that Rick almost felt as if he was home already.

With that thought, the capsule grew indistinct again. Tessa screamed, "Rick!" and punched him in the chest, and Yoshiko said quickly, "Remember the consequences!"

The ship solidified once more, and Rick rubbed his sore sternum where Tessa's ring had jabbed him. "Jeez, you don't have to kill me," he said. "I get scared just fine on my own when that happens."

Tessa snorted. "Hah. If you were as scared as I am, the ship would never disappear in the first place."

"Well, I'm sorry; I'll try to be more terrified from now on." Rick turned away from her, but there was no place to go to be alone in an Apollo capsule. After a few minutes of silence, he looked back over at her and said, "Okay, I'll try harder to control this. But don't look at me so accusingly when it happens, okay? I'm not trying to make it disappear."

Tessa sighed. "I know you're not. It's just—I don't know. I don't have any control over it, except what little control I have over you. My life is in your hands. Hell, at this point the entire space program is in your hands. And all you have to do to kill it is get cocky."

"No pressure," Rick said sarcastically.

Yoshiko laughed. "Whether you like it or not, you embody the spirit of exploration. When we get back, that spirit will probably pass on to someone else, but right now it resides in you, and you have to bring it safely home."

"With all due respect," Rick said, "that sounds like a bunch of tabloid speculation to me."

She shook her head. "No, this is really no different than any space mission. Every time someone goes into space, their nation's spirit flies with them. When *Apollo 1* killed its crew, your nation faltered for two years before going on, and when the *Challenger* blew up it took three more. When the Soviets' Moon rocket blew up in 1969, they completely scrapped their lunar program and shifted to space stations. It's like that all over the world. Every astronaut who has ever flown has had your ability, and your responsibility; yours is just more obvious than most, made physical by the same power that created this ship."

Rick studied the industrial gray control panel before him while he considered what she'd said. The truth of it seemed undeniable, at least in principle. The details could be argued—retooling after an accident wasn't exactly backing off—but it was true that exploration stopped each time an accident happened, and when it started again it almost always took a new, more conservative direction.

"Well," Rick said at last, "I'll try my best to pass the baton without fumbling. We've only got a couple hours left; after that it's somebody else's problem."

They spent the time before re-entry stowing all the equipment and debris that had accumulated in the cabin throughout their week in space. While they worked, the Earth swelled from a blue and white ball to the flatter, fuzzy-edged landscape they were familiar with from the shuttle flights. At that point they only had a few minutes left before atmospheric contact, just time enough to jettison the cylindrical service module with its spent engine and fuel tanks, then reorient the command module so it would hit the atmosphere blunt end first.

All three of them were breathing hard as the last few seconds ticked away. They weren't wearing their spacesuits; the gee forces would be too severe for that, and besides, if anything happened to the capsule they would burn up instantly anyway, spacesuits or no. Rick reached out and held Tessa's hand, wishing he could reassure her that they would be okay, but he knew that a phrase like "Don't worry" coming from him would only make her worry all the more. So he merely said, "Ready with the marshmallows?"

"Very funny," she replied.

Yoshiko laughed, though, and said, "Never mind marshmallows, I'm getting out my bathing suit. Hawaii, here we come!"

Their splashdown target was about a thousand miles west of there, but that would be their first landfall after the recovery ship picked them up. There were two recovery ships, actually, one Russian and one American, but the Russians had agreed to let the Americans pick up the capsule if they wished. NASA wished very much, so they got the prize, though neither Rick nor Tessa looked forward to the official reception.

The unofficial one, however, would be worth every minute of NASA's wrath. The main reason for the Russian ship's presence was to televise the splashdown for the curious world, which Gregor said was even more excited now that the last, most perilous stage of the mission was about to commence. The love story didn't hurt their ratings, either.

Despite the extra danger from the publicity, Rick was glad for the attention; he was counting on public support to keep him and Tessa out of serious trouble, and maybe even provide them with a source of income from the lecture circuit until the new space program got started. Their careers in the shuttle program were certainly dead now, and only hero status would ever let them fly again.

Contact. The capsule shuddered and the seats pressed up against them. The force eased off for a second, then built again, stronger and stronger, until it was well over a gee. Air heated to incandescence shot past the windows, lighting up the inside of the capsule like a fluorescent tube, and the ship began to rock from side to side. Some of that was no doubt the guidance computer fine-tuning their trajectory with shots from the attitude control jets, but every few seconds the capsule would lurch violently as it hit a pocket of denser air. The deeper they plunged into the atmosphere, the greater their deceleration, until they were pulling nearly seven gees and struggling just to breathe.

Long minutes dragged past as the three astronauts remained

pinned to their couches, barely able to move. Rick kept his hand near the manual controls mounted on the end of his armrest, but even when the buffeting became severe and the automatic system seemed to be overreacting, he didn't take over control. He trusted the ghost more than he trusted his own instincts. It wouldn't let them die now, not this close to the end of the mission.

The cabin walls flickered momentarily at that thought, and Rick cringed as he waited for a blast of flame to engulf him, but the fade-out only lasted for an eyeblink. Tessa and Yoshiko both gasped, but they said nothing. Speech was impossible with the incredible weight pressing them into their couches.

The ionized gas roaring by had cut off communications with the ground. Rick heard only static in his headphones, but the shriek of air around the blunt edge of the heat shield nearly drowned out even that. Up through the window he could see a twisting tail of white-hot flame stretching away for miles into a sky that grew steadily bluer as they fell.

Finally after six minutes the gee force began to ease off, and the flames streaming past the windows faded away. They had slowed to terminal velocity now, still plenty fast but not fast enough to burn away any more of their heat shield.

Rick looked at the altimeter at the top of the control panel. At 25,000 feet, just as the needle passed the black triangle on the gauge, the drogue parachutes opened with a soft jolt. Rick watched them flutter overhead, stabilizing the craft and slowing them just a bit more, then at 10,000 feet the main chutes streamed out and snapped open in three orange and white striped canopies. The capsule lurched as if it had hit solid ground, but then it steadied out and hung there at the bottom of the shroud lines, swaying slightly from side to side as it drifted.

The sun was only a few hours above the horizon, and waves scattered its light like millions of sparkling jewels below them. Rick let out a long sigh. "Home sweet home," he said.

"Don't relax yet," Tessa said, eyeing the altimeter. "We're still a couple miles up."

"Yes, Mom."

A new voice over the radio said, "Apollo, this is the *U.S.S. Nimitz*. We have you in visual."

"Roger, visual contact," Rick said. He loosened his harness and peered out the windows, but he couldn't spot the ship, nor the Russian one. It was a big ocean.

The altimeter dropped steadily, swinging counter-clockwise through five thousand feet, then four, three, two…

"All right," Rick said. "We're going to make it."

"Rick!" Tessa shot him an angry look. "We're still at a thousand feet."

Rick looked out at the ocean, now seeming close enough to touch. "I don't care. I've played doublethink with the supernatural the whole way to the Moon and back; well now I'm done with that. We could survive a fall from here, so unless this thing sinks right on out of sight with us in it, I say superstition be damned: we're home safe and sound." He banged on the hatch for emphasis. It made a solid enough thud when he hit it, but a moment later it began to shimmer like a desert mirage.

"Rick, stop it!" Tessa yelled, and Yoshiko said, "Not yet, damn it, not yet!"

"I take it all back!" Rick shouted, but this time the capsule continued to fade. It supported their weight for another few seconds, but that was all. The control panel grew indistinct, the altimeter going last like the grin of the Cheshire cat, its needle dropping toward the last few tic marks, and then the couches gave way beneath them, pitching all three astronauts out into the air.

Rick flailed his arms wildly to keep from tumbling. His right hand struck one of the spacesuits and it bounced away from him, spinning around with arms and legs extended. The other two spacesuits had remained solid, too, and for a moment Rick wondered why they hadn't faded along with the ship, but then he remembered that he and Tessa and Yoshiko had worn them aboard.

He twisted around, looking frantically for the only other non-ghostly items in the capsule, and he saw them just below, falling like the rocks they were: the samples he and Tessa had collected from the lunar surface.

"No!" he shouted, reaching for them as if he could snatch at least one rock out of the air, but he suddenly got a face full of water and he choked and coughed. The sample containers had been part of the ship, and they had disappeared, too, splashing him with their contents. He smelled ammonia, and something else he couldn't identify before the wind whipped it away.

Everything they had collected, everything they had done, had vanished in one moment of arrogant pride. They were returning to Earth with nothing more than what they had taken with them.

Except the entire world knew they had gone and knew what they'd seen; nothing could take that away.

Tessa was a few feet to the side, but she had spread her arms and legs out to slow her fall. As she swept upward, her hair streaming out behind her, Rick shouted, "Don't hit like that!"

"Of course not," she yelled back at him. "I'll dive at the last minute."

Yoshiko was windmilling her arms to keep from going in headfirst, but she was tumbling too fast. "Cannonball!" Rick yelled at her, but he didn't see if she tucked into the position or not. He barely had time to twist around so his own feet were pointed downward.

The ocean came up at them fast. Rick looked away, and this time he saw the ships, two enormous gray aircraft carriers plowing side by side through the waves toward him, their decks covered with sailors. And reporters. And scientists, and bureaucrats, and who knew what else.

Rick closed his eyes and braced for the impact he knew was coming.

*Of his story, Jerry Oltion writes: Kathy and I were watching a TV documentary on Deke Slayton, and it ended with this hokey bit about a ghostly airplane taking off shortly after he died and disappearing into the clouds. I said, "Yeah, right," in a sarcastic voice, whereupon Kathy asked me, "What would it take to make you believe in ghosts?"*

*"A really big, obvious one," I said. "Like the ghost of a Saturn V launching in front of a crowd and sending back telemetry even after it was out of sight."*

*"That sounds like a story to me," she replied.*

*So I wrote it. It was about seven thousand words long the first time around, because I was done with the idea the moment the characters decided to fly the ghost to the Moon, but when I sent it to Kris Rusch at*

F&SF *she sent it back and told me to finish the story. Twenty-three thousand words later, I got the characters* almost *to a splashdown in the Pacific and figured that was enough. Kris thought so, too, and bought the story. But when it came out in the magazine, readers kept writing and asking "What happens next?" so I'm expanding it some more. As of this writing, Rick and Tessa are being held captive while the bad guys try to force them to make another ghost. I think Rick will probably do that the hard way, but I'm not sure yet. That's what I love about this story: The possibilities are endless! If it ever gets published at novel length, you'll see what I mean.*

# The Grand Master Award: Poul Anderson

CONNIE WILLIS

And, finally, the Grand Master. The SFWA Lifetime Achievement Award. The honor of honors, given only to the giants of the field: Robert A. Heinlein, Arthur C. Clarke, Alfred Bester, Andre Norton, A. E. van Vogt. And now, very fittingly, to Poul Anderson.

Poul Anderson has been called "science fiction's historian, past, present, and alternative," and "the backbone of the field." He is one of our finest and steadiest writers, producing classic after classic over a period of fifty years. James Blish called him "the enduring explosion."

Explode he does, in all directions: science fiction, fantasy, farce, mystery, horror, poetry, parody, politics. He is that rare author who is equally good at history and the future, at solid science and high fantasy, swashbuckling adventure and subtle psychological drama.

He has written about the Dark Ages and the end of the universe, about a vast intergalactic empire and about a world in which Shakespeare's characters are real, where Prospero is at war with Cromwell. He has written about warlocks and physicists and Scandinavian warriors, about Mercury and mermaids and the Franco-Prussian War.

Not only is he expert at many forms of fiction, but he's also adept at all of its techniques. He is famous for his gift of characterization. All of his characters, from the tough old soldier Mackenzie in "No Truce with Kings" to the grieving pilot in "Vulcan's Forge," are fully imagined people, highly individualized, and even quirky, and yet at the same time characters you can identify with, characters whose fates you care about.

Careers have been built around such characters, but characterization is not Anderson's only strength. There is also his prose—elegant and evocative, a style that has prompted people to describe him as "the bard of science fiction." It's impossible to describe. Lines such as the Queen of Air and Darkness's contemptuous dismissal of human life—"prison days, angry nights, works that crumble in the fingers, loves that turn to rot or stone or driftweed"—or the beginning of "Goat Song"—"Three women: one is dead; one is alive; one is both and neither, and will never live and never die, being immortal in SUM"—only hint at it. His inspired use of language is perhaps most evident in his titles, which are, quite simply, the best in the business: *The Stars Are Also Fire, The Corridors of Time, No Truce with Kings, The Winter of the World.*

And then there is his skill in constructing storylines: building parallel plots of practical problems and psychological conflicts, then producing an ending that resolves both, using a scientific situation to illuminate a metaphysical one, interweaving a variety of viewpoints to examine a story from all angles.

In "The Queen of Air and Darkness" (my favorite Poul Anderson story of all time), he not only tricks his characters into believing an illusion and then reveals the sobering reality behind it, he does the same thing to you as you read the story, so that the characters' betrayal and dismay become yours.

In "Kings Who Die," he begins with the simple, matter-of fact line "Luckily, Diaz was looking the other way when the missile exploded" and then leads you into a harsh tale of a war that can't be won and a soldier who is betrayed into betrayal by his own best instincts. By the time that first line is repeated again at the very end of the story, its meaning has been transmuted into something ironic and terrible.

Plot, character, and prose are not, however, his greatest ability, believe it or not. His true grandeur lies in his wonderful ideas. Only Poul Anderson would think of placing Titania and Caliban in the real world, of seeing Jupiter's surface as beautiful, of having a feudal baron hijack a spaceship. Only Anderson would imagine a Time Patrol whose job is to keep the continuum from sliding off-track. Only he would think of having our first contact with the superior race who will threaten our existence take the form of a charming child, asking, "Please, mister, could I have a cracker for my oontatherium?"

Only Anderson would think of making a witch and a warlock stand for logic and order, or of looking at history as a logarithmic curve, or of using a computer to retell the myth of Orpheus. "He thinks clear across the spectrum," Theodore Sturgeon said of him. It's true, and a little frightening. Sometimes, reading an Anderson story, you feel like you're on the spaceship *Leonora Christie* in *Tau Zero*, going faster and faster till you're about to burst through to another universe altogether.

I'm so happy that Poul Anderson was chosen to be Grand Master in the year that I got to edit the *Nebula Awards* collection. He's a wonderful, wonderful writer. If you've never read him, start with the story that follows, and then read "The Queen of Air and Darkness." And *Tau Zero*. And "Kings Who Die." And "Turning Point." And *The Boat of a Million Years*. And everything else, by this treasure of the field, this true Grand Master: Poul Anderson.

# A Tribute to Poul Anderson

JACK WILLIAMSON

It was only fitting that Jack Williamson should be the one to present the Grand Master Award to Poul Anderson at the Nebula Awards
ceremony. The author of such classics as "Nonstop to Mars" and the
Hugo Award–winning *Wonder's Child,* and the inventor of terraform-
ing, androids, and antimatter, Williamson is one of science fiction's
founding fathers.

He is also one of its first Grand Masters, and so it is especially
fitting that he present this tribute to the newest Grand Master, Poul
Anderson.

Poul Anderson's Grand Master Nebula has been amply
earned. In the half century since his first sale ("Tomorrow's
Children" to *Astounding*) in 1947, while he was still an undergraduate,
he has published some fifty books and hundreds of stories. He has won
eight Hugos, three Nebulas, the Gandalf Award, the Tolkien Award for
Lifetime Achievement. He has been president of the Science-fiction
and Fantasy Writers of America.

His wife is Karen. They live in Orinda, east of San Francisco.
Their daughter, Astrid, is married to Greg Bear. Born in Pennsylvania
in 1926, he lived briefly in Denmark and grew up in Minnesota, ab-
sorbing the history and literature of his Scandinavian forebears. He
earned his degree in physics from the University of Minnesota in 1948.

The sagas and the science, I think, have made him what he is, the physicist as epic poet.

Summing him up is a difficult challenge because he has made himself the master of so much that any dominant theme is hard to find. He has written the hardest of hard science fiction. *Tau Zero* is a novel I recall for the sheer intellectual delight of following an idea to its logical limit, when a runaway ship in relativistic space continues to accelerate and slow in relative time until it bursts out of our universe into a new one.

The work of a physicist, but Anderson has as well the mind of a poet, with a poet's love of language and control of emotion. Such works as *Three Hearts and Three Lions* and the Nebula-winning "Queen of Air and Darkness" are drawn from the conventions of fantasy but developed with the same hard logic and conviction.

*Hrolf Kraki's Saga* is based on legends of an Anglo-Saxon hero mentioned in *Beowulf* and written in a style that echoes Anglo-Saxon verse. The heroes of his Psychotechnic series, the rogue interstellar trader Nicholas van Rijn and the tough Terran agent Dominic Flandry, display a shrewdly bold Viking enterprise.

Anderson has been so prolific for so long, publishing all over the field, that any unity of theme seems hard to find. Perhaps he can be seen as one sane man searching for order in a world of alluring illusions. Hard science fiction shares the drive of science itself, the quest for intelligible order in a mysterious and chaotic cosmos. When Anderson is building a world, his process of choosing some challenging new assumption and finding fact and reason to support it is not much different from the mental process of a cosmologist testing a new theory of dark matter or galactic formation.

A master world builder, Anderson is as meticulous with biology and sociology as he is with physics and astronomy. He was one of the architects of *Medeia: Harlan's World*. Earlier, when Sprague de Camp said human beings could never fly, for lack of muscle power, Anderson designed a planet with very dense air and wrote *War of the Wing-Men* (later retitled *The Man Who Counts*) where they could. *Fire Time* is set on a planet broiled every thousand years as it passes close to a giant red star.

If the physics degree made him the world builder, it also helped shape the fantasist. Roald D. Tweet seems to find the scientist's concern for reason and logical order in Anderson's heroic fantasies when he writes of "the war between Chaos and Law" as the theme of such novels as *Operation Chaos* (1971), in which a werewolf and witch team is sent to harrow hell and confront ultimate Chaos, restoring the order of Law. Flandry and van Rijn, as Tweet says, "fight the same battles on a technological rather than supernatural level."

Most of Anderson's novels are clustered into series, but a dozen or so are independent. His first major success was *Brain Wave*, in which human intelligence is liberated when Earth moves out of an interstellar cloud that has been retarding it. He has written the four-volume future history beginning with *Harvest of Stars*. In the *Time Patrol* series, where Manse Everard is the main character, agents of order fight to keep history on track, ranging all the way from their far-future age to cope with threatening crises in the Punic War and early Persia.

The collected adventures of van Rijn and Flandry in their own future history fill almost a score of volumes. The Hoka books, written with Gordon Dickson, are the best of science fiction fun, the humor coming from the linguistic limits of the charming little Hokas, who have very literal minds.

Always with fine craftsmanship, Anderson has written poetry, adventure stories, historical novels (in the *Last Viking* series), juvenile fiction (*Vault of the Ages*), mysteries, a horror novel, shared-world stories, adaptations from the Danish.

Searching for any common thread through this lifetime of work, I can try to see him as a romantic, the epic poet whose heroes—men, and sometimes women, of wit and strength and daring—are rebel individualists at odds with traditional society. Often, however, I find them fighting for the order that romantic rebels are about to destroy, which should make him a conservative.

I believe he has been conservative in politics. In the shifting fads and fashions of science fiction, he has stood firm against the stylistic obscurities and existentialist despair of the New Wave. If such experimental work has refined the skills of others, Anderson himself has always kept up with the times. His vision may have darkened, but there is darkness enough to give a realistic bite to his early work.

"Kyrie," written thirty years ago, shows him already at his best as the physicist poet. It's the tragic love story of a very human woman and Lucifer, an intelligent vortex of cosmic energy, who is sucked down into a black hole as he fights to save her and her ship from it. She is left at the end listening all her life to his time-stretched dying scream. Anderson was pushing the envelope when he wrote the story, and it has never dated.

The Grand Master Nebula was invented, I believe, to honor Robert Heinlein, whose best work had been published in the pre-Nebula years. I am proud, myself, to have been let into the club and happy to confirm the welcome Poul Anderson has so ably earned.

# The Martyr

POUL ANDERSON

It's customary to include a representative story of the Grand Master's in the *Nebula Awards* collection. In the case of Anderson, however, that's a downright impossible task. Do you include one of the swashbuckling Nicholas van Rijn stories or a tale of the Time Patrol? *Tau Zero* is too long, and so is *The Boat of a Million Years,* and "The Critique of Impure Reason" (a story that mercilessly pokes fun at literary trends and that made it onto my teenage list of great stories) is too funny.

And then, of course, there's the Old Phoenix, that inn outside all universes where anybody, historical or imaginary, can drop in for a drink and a bit of conversation. But if I include "House Rule," then I have to leave out "Call Me Joe." And Dominic Flandry.

Compounding the problem is the number of his stories that have already been anthologized in award and year's-best collections. The elegiac "The Longest Voyage," "Hunter's Moon," and "The Sharing of Flesh" have all appeared in Hugo Award volumes. "Genesis," "Vulcan's Forge," and a host of others have been in year's-best collections and other anthologies.

And the mythic "Goat Song," "The Saturn Game," and my favorite Anderson story of all time, "The Queen of Air and Darkness," have appeared in previous Nebula collections. (I almost included "The Queen of Air and Darkness" anyway. This amazing novella of colonization and changelings, of myths and modern science and the planetary Fairy Hill where they meet, is absolutely dazzling, and if you—poor benighted creature—have never read any of Anderson's work, you need to read it immediately. It's in *Nebula Awards Seven.* Then go get "Goat Song"—*Nebula Awards Eight*—and then "The Saturn Game"—*Nebula Awards Seventeen.*)

I didn't want to use a story that had been in a previous *Nebula Awards* collection or that had been reprinted all over the place. And yet I wanted something classic, something representative—ha!— okay, well, then, since that was impossible, something that would at least give you a taste of what Poul Anderson can do. And something you might not have read. It was as tough a problem as Eric Sherrinford or Manse Everard ever had to solve.

But I found something. On the list of unforgettable stories I had kept as a teenager. I had not read it since then, but I had never forgotten it, or the impression its staggering, searing ending had had on me.

Neither, I would guess, has anyone else who's ever read it. In the course of trying to decide which story to include, I called Cynthia Felice (the author of *Godsfire* and *The Khan's Persuasion* and a true Poul Anderson fan) and told her some of the stories I was considering. When I began describing "The Martyr," she stopped me short, said, "I know that story," and recited the last line to me. She hadn't read it in years either. How many stories can you name that had that sort of Meteor-Crater impact on you?

No one story can completely capture Poul Anderson's genius, "The Martyr" included, and it doesn't have Nicholas van Rijn or Manse Everard, but the characters it does have are unforgettable. And it has Anderson's subtlety of motivation and cleverness at plotting and density of description. And his power to touch and trouble you, and make you think.

If you, like me, like Cynthia Felice, have read it before, you'll be excited (and a little scared) at the prospect of reading it again. If not, you're in for an incredible experience.

Here it is. A miracle of rare device: Poul Anderson's "The Martyr."

vidently we have succeeded," Medina said. "The men have captured the gods."

"Or the baboons have captured the men," said Narden.

Medina shrugged. "Choose your own analogy, Major. Just be careful not to take it too seriously. The Cibarrans have existed longer than we; they've had time to learn more, even to develop more brain…perhaps. And what of it?" An expression crossed his flat countenance, but not one that Narden could interpret. He gestured above his desk with a cigar. "It does not make them supernatural," he finished. "I've always suspected that intellect is a necessary but somewhat overrated quality. As witness the fact that baboons have killed men in the past, and now men have made prisoners of half a dozen Cibarrans."

Narden shifted in his chair. The office was a shining bleakness around him, broken only by the regulation portrait of the Imperial Mother and a map of Earth which, X light-years away in direction Y, betrayed a milligram of human sentimentalism in the hard alloy of Colonel-General Wang K'ung Medina.

"Baboons are extinct," Narden pointed out.

"They never learned how to make guns," snapped the other man. "We'll be extinct too, some generations hence, if we don't overhaul Cibarra."

"I can't believe that, sir. They've never threatened us or anyone else. Everything we've been able to find out about them, their activities at home, on other planets, it's all been benign, helpful, they've come as teachers and—" Narden's voice trailed clumsily off.

"Yes," gibed Medina. "Spiritual teaching, personal discipline, a kind of super-Buddhism *sans* karma. Plus some information on astronomy, physics, generalized biology. Practical assistance here and there, like making a Ta-Tao High Dam possible on Yosev. But any basic instruction in psi? Any hints how to develop our own latent powers—or even any proof or disproof, once and for all, that our race does have such powers in any reliable degree? If they really gave a hoot and a yelp for us, Major, you know they couldn't watch us break our hearts looking for something they know all about. But never a word. In fifty years of contact, fifty years of watching them do everything from dowsing to telepathic multiple hookups and teleportation across light-years...we've never gotten a straight answer to one single question about the subject. The same bland smile and the same verbal side-stepping. Or silence, if we persist. God of Man, but they're good at silence!"

"Maybe we have to find all these things out for ourselves," Narden ventured. "Maybe psi works differently for different species, or simply can't be taught, or—"

"Then why don't they tell us so?" exploded Medina. "All they offer us, if you analyze the pattern, is distraction. Twenty years ago, on Marjan, Elberg was studying the Dunne Effect. He'd gotten some very promising results. He showed them to a Cibarran who chanced to be on the same planet. The Cibarran said something about resonances, demonstrated an unsuspected electric phenomenon...well, you know the rest. Elberg spent the remainder of his life working on electron-wave resonance. He came up with some extraordinary things. But all in the field of physics. His original psionic data have gathered dust ever since. I could give you a hundred similar cases. I've collected them for years. It makes a totally consistent pattern. The Cibarrans are not giving out any psionic information whatsoever; and most of the intellectual 'assistance' we get from them turns out to be a red herring pointed away from that trail." His fist struck the desk. "Our independent research has taught us just enough about psionics to show we can't imagine its potentialities. And yet the Cibarrans are trying to keep it from us. Does that sound friendly?"

Narden wet his lips. "Perhaps we can't be trusted, sir. Our behavior in the present instance suggests as much."

Medina thrust out his jaw. "You volunteered, Major. Too late now for jellyfishing."

Narden felt himself redden. He was a young man, stocky and blond like many citizens of Tau Ceti II, speaking Lingua Terra with their Russki accent. The black and silver uniform of the Imperial Astronaval Service, scientific corps, fitted him crisply; but the awkwardness of the provincial lay beneath. "I volunteered for a possibly dangerous but important mission, sir. That was all I knew."

Medina grinned. "Well?"

After a pause, the general added, "It might cost us our lives, our sanity—even our honor, for the Imperium will have to disown us if we fail and this becomes public. So you'll understand, Major, that shooting a man who drags his feet on the job won't bother me in the least." Harshly: "If we succeed, we stand to gain a million years of progress, overnight. Men have taken bigger chances for less. We're going to learn from those prisoners. Gently if possible, but we'll take them apart cell by cell if we must. Now go talk to them and start your work!"

Baris Narden saluted and marched from the office.

The corridor was even more sterile, a white tunnel where his heels clacked hollowly and a humming came from behind closed doors. Now and then he passed a man, but they didn't speak. There was too much silence. Light-years of silence, thought Narden—beyond these caves, the rock and the iron plains of the rogue planet, glaciers and snowfields that were frozen atmosphere, under the keen glitter of a million stars. Perhaps a dozen men of the hundred-odd manning this base knew its location and its sunless orbit. This was like being dead. He remembered the hills of Novaya Mechta, his father's house under murmurous trees, and wondered what had driven him thence. Ambition, he thought wearily; the Imperium and its glamour; most of all, the wish to learn. So now he had his science degree, and his small triumphs in the difficult field of psionic research, and was lately a collaborator in kidnapping, which might lead to torture and murder...oh, yes, a career.

The guards at the entrance to the research area let him through without fuss. Medina wasn't interested in passes, countersigns, or other incantations. Beyond lay a complex of laboratories and offices. A door stood open to a room where Mohammed Kerintji worked amid crowded apparatus. Meters flickered before him, and the air was filled with an irregular buzzing that sawed at the nerves.

The small dark man didn't seem bothered. He glanced up as Narden passed, and nodded. "Ah, there, Major."

"All serene, Captain?" asked Narden automatically.

"Quite, and better." Kerintji's eyes glistened. "I am not only keeping our tigers tame, but learning a few new things."

"Oh?" Narden stepped into the room.

"Yes. First and foremost, of course, General Medina's basic idea is triumphantly confirmed. Faint, randomly pulsed currents, induced in their nervous systems by the energies I am beaming in at them, do inhibit their psionic powers. They've not teleported out of here, tele-kineticized me outdoors, anything at all." Kerintji chuckled. "Obviously! Or we wouldn't be here. Maybe this entire planet wouldn't be here. The facts do not, however, confirm the general's hypothesis that psionic energies arise in the brain analogously to ordinary encephalographic waves."

"Why not?" Despite himself, Narden felt an upsurge of interest. This all fitted in with his previous laboratory results.

"Look at these meters. They are set in a dowser-type hookup. Energy is required to move the needles against the tension of springs. And the needles are being moved, in a pattern correlated with the randomizer's nerve-currents. Furthermore, the work done against the springs represents too much energy for any living nervous system to carry. The neurons would burn out. Ergo, the randomizer which keeps the Cibarrans helpless does not do so by suppressing their psionic output, but merely prevents them from controlling it. Also ergo, the energy does not come from the nervous system, which is probably just the modulator."

Narden nodded. "My own data have led me to speculate that the body as a whole may be the generator," he said, "though I've never gotten consistent enough readings to be certain."

"We will now," crowed Kerintji. "We can use calorimetry. Measure every erg passing through the Cibarran organism. If output, including psionic work done, is greater than input, we will know that psi involves tapping some outside, probably cosmic force."

"Those are delicate measurements," warned Narden. "I found out how delicate, in my own lab."

"You were using humans, and had to be careful of them. Also, the human output is so miserably feeble and irregular. But look!" Kerintji twisted a dial. One of his meter needles swung wildly across its scale. "I just quadrupled the randomizing energy. The psi output increased fiftyfold. Like sticking a pin in a man and watching him jump. We can *control* this!"

Narden left, a bit sick.

Another pair of guards stood before the prison suite. It was fitted with a spaceship airlock, the outer valve being dogged shut before the inner one could be opened. Narden wondered if it helped anything except the fears of men. The rooms beyond were large and comfortable. And did that help anything except the consciences of men?

Two Cibarrans occupied a sofa. They didn't get up; their civilization had its rich rituals, but almost entirely on the mental plane. Big amber-colored eyes, and the fronded tendrils above, turned to Narden. He felt afresh, sharply, how beautiful they were. Bipedal mammals, long legs giving a sheer two meters of height, three-clawed feet, slender humanoid hands, wide chest and shoulders, large oval heads with faces not so much flat as delicately sculptured, short gray fur over the whole body, thin iridescent kilt and cloak . . . words, without relationship to the feline grace before him.

One of them spoke, in calm, resonant Lingua Terra: "I call myself Alanai at this moment. My companion is Elth."

"Baris Narden." The man shifted from foot to foot. The tiniest of smiles curved Alanai's mouth.

"Please be seated," said Elth. "Would you like refreshment? I am told we can ring for food as required."

Narden found a chair and perched on its edge. "No, thanks." *I may not break bread with you.* "Are you well?"

"As well as can be expected." Alanai's grimace was a work of art. Narden remembered the theory of some xenologists, that Cibarran "telepathy" was in part a matter of gestures and expressions. It was plausible, in a race where each individual evolved a private spoken language to express nuances uniquely his own, and learned those of all his friends. But it would not account for the proven fact that Cibarrans, without apparatus, could travel and communicate across light-years.

"I hope"—Narden dragged the words out—"I hope conditions are not unduly inconvenient."

"The nervous-energy scrambling? Yes and no," said Elth. "We can block off physical pain and prevent lesions. But the deprivation— Imagine being deafened and blinded."

His tone remained gentle.

"I'm afraid it's necessary," Narden mumbled.

"So that we can't escape, or summon help, or otherwise thwart your plans? Granted." Alanai reached out to a crystal-topped coffee table on which stood a chess set. He began to play against himself. It was a swift and even match. Brain-jumbler or not, the Cibarrans retained a mastery of their own minds and bodies such as humans had hardly dreamed about.

"I am curious as to how you engineered the kidnapping," said Elth, not unmaliciously. "I have considered numerous possibilities."

"Well—" Narden hesitated. *The hell with Medina.* "We knew your planet was sending a mission to New Mars. The world we call New Mars, I mean. One of the native tribes had asked your help, via interstellar traders, the usual grapevine, to rationalize and make beautiful its own culture. We've seen a lot of planets where you've done a similar job, and didn't expect you could resist such an appeal, even if it was way out of your normal territory. Our psychotechnicians had spent years putting the chiefs of that tribe up to it."

Elth actually laughed.

Narden plunged on, as if pursued. "What little we've been able to discover about psi indicated certain limitations which could be exploited. You can probably communicate across the universe—"

"There are ancient races in other galaxies," Alanai agreed.

A third Cibarran appeared in the doorway. "There is one entire intelligent galaxy," he said, very low. "We are children at its feet."

"Don't you think we might also want to—" Narden checked himself. "Distance can't block a telepathic message, but noise can. If you aren't actually tuned in on someone who is parsecs away, you'll receive only the babble of billions and trillions of living minds on planets throughout space—and block it out of your own perceptions. So we didn't expect you would get any hint of our plot. After all, New Mars is out in this arm of the galaxy, and Cibarra lies twenty thousand light-years toward the center.

"When your delegation arrived, it was invited to visit the Imperial *chargé d'affaires.* He knew nothing; this was routine courtesy. The kidnappers were waiting at his house, unbeknownst to him. They were raw recruits from colonial planets where the languages and cultures are different from Earth's. Our researchers had suggested that you couldn't readily read the mind of someone whose socio-linguistic background was new to you. His conceptual universe would be too different. You'd at least need to study him a short while, classify his way of thinking, before you could put yourselves in rapport. So...these men knocked you out with stun beams, whisked you onto a spaceship, and kept you unconscious all the way to this base."

Elth laughed again. "Clever!"

"Don't compliment me," said Narden hastily. "I had nothing to do with it."

"You spoke as if you did," said Alanai.

"Did I?" Narden searched a flustered memory. "Yes. Yes, I did say 'we,' didn't I? Must have been thinking in...in collective terms. I was only co-opted at the last minute, after the capture. This isn't being done for selfish reasons, you know."

"Why, then?" asked Alanai, but softly, as if he already knew the answer. And the other Cibarrans grew as still as he.

"Not for ransom, as you may have thought, or—anything but the need of our people," stumbled Narden. "It's been fifty years now ... since Imperial ships, exploring toward galactic center ... encountered your race on some of the planets there. We've had sporadic contact, from time to time, since then. Just enough to understand the situation. Your home world is much older than ours—"

"It was," corrected Alanai. "The Lost was a planet of an early Population Two star, hence poor in metals. We lingered ages in a neolithic technology, which may have encouraged our peculiar mental form of development. Physical science was carried out with ceramics, plastics, acid-filled conductors, as pure research only. The final hottening of our sun forced us to leave our home. That was many thousands of years ago; and yet we too, in a way, have known the Lost, and mourned it with our fathers—"

Elth laid a warning hand on his wrist. Alanai seemed to wake from a dream. "*Oa, Anna*," he murmured.

"Yes," said Narden. "I know all that. I know too how you have chanced to meet them. But only in the smallest ways."

"You could not assimilate physical knowledge at a much greater rate than you are already producing it," said one of the other Cibarrans. Four of them now stood in the door. Narden squared his shoulders and said:

"Perhaps. There are no hard feelings about that. We're quite able to learn whatever we wish in physics. We have no reason to believe you're very far ahead of us in any branch of it, either. You may well lag behind in certain aspects which never interested your civilization, such as robotics. In a finite universe, physics is limited anyway. What embitters us is your withholding the next stage of basic knowledge — your active hindering of us, now and then, in our own search."

Elth said, the barest edge of harshness in his tone, "You captured us hoping to make us teach you about that aspect of reality you call psionics. Or, if we refuse to instruct you — and we do — you will seek to gather data by studying us."

Narden swallowed. "Yes."

Alanai said without haughtiness (and did tears blur his eyes?), "Cibarran philosophers were exploring these concepts before Earth had condensed from cosmic dust. Do you really believe we are reticent because of selfishness?"

"No," said Narden doggedly. "But my people ... we aren't the kind who accept meekly that father knows best. We've always made our own way. Against beasts and glaciers and ourselves and the physical universe. Now, against gods, if we must."

Elth shook his head, in a slow regretful motion. "I am as finite as you are," he said. "More, in some ways. I do not believe I could find the courage to live, if I were—" He bit off his words, suddenly alarmed.

"We've got to do this," said Narden. He stood up. "Forgive us."

"There is nothing to forgive," said Alanai. "You cannot help it. You are young and raw and greedy for life. Oh," he whispered, "how you hunger for life!"

"And yet you leave us to stagnate, half animal, when we might also be sending our minds across all space?" Narden looked into the grave, strange faces. He knotted his fists together and said, "For your own sakes, help me. I don't want to rip out what you know!"

"For your own sake," said Alanai, "we shall fight back. Every step of the way."

At another date Narden remembered the words. He sighed. "It's been one long struggle."

Medina settled himself more firmly in his chair. "They haven't made any physical resistance," he declared.

"This is not a physical problem," Kerintji reminded him.

Medina had the practicality to leave his scientists alone; but he had finally demanded an informal accounting, which Narden had to admit was reasonable. Elsewhere in artificial caverns, engineers worked with the machines that kept men alive, soldiers drilled and loafed and wished they were home, technicians pondered the interpretation of measurements and statistical summaries. Here in the central office, Narden felt immensely apart from it all, somehow more akin to the prisoners.

*Isn't every man?* he told himself. *Isn't the Cibarran silence keeping our whole race locked in our own skulls?* But he knew, tiredly, that his indignation was only words. One of the slogans men invented, to justify their latest cruelty and most fashionable idiocy.

*If we could see across the universe, and into the heart, as they do on Cibarra, we wouldn't need slogans,* Narden thought. The idea straightened his back a little. He looked across the big desk and said:

"Since they don't cooperate, we've so far used them as mere generators of psionic forces. We were held up for days when they worked out some method to damp their own output. I think we have, now, an inkling of how that was done—an interference phenomenon within the nervous system itself, probably painful as hell. But it frustrated us at the time."

"How did you lick it?" Medina inquired.

"Put one of them under anesthesia," Kerintji said. "We got no response again, to nervous stimuli. More organized response, in fact, than when consciousness was present to throw out random bursts of energy with deliberate intent to confuse our readings. So we kept him anesthetized for a week. After that, the others quit their damping."

Narden remembered how Alanai had lain amidst the indignity of intravenous tubes, and how the machine's nerve-pulses had convulsed his body until he had to be strapped down. He remembered how thin the Cibarran was at last, when they let him waken and returned him to the prison suite. And yet he had looked on them without bitterness. It seemed to Narden thinking back, that the yellow eyes held pity.

"Never mind the details now," said Medina. "Have you reached any conclusions?"

"In four weeks?" scoffed Kerintji.

"Yes, yes, I know it'll take decades to work out a coherent psi theory. But you must at least have some working hypotheses."

"And some clear conclusions," Narden told him, speaking fast to hold at arm's length the image of Alanai.

"Well?" Thick fingers drummed the desk top.

"First, we've established certain things about the energy involved in these processes. It's never very great, by mechanical standards. But at peak stimulation, it does go far over the total possible output of the physical organism. That proves it must come from elsewhere. The psionic adept, to borrow the common term, puts in a small amount of energy himself; in fact, he radiates constantly in the psionic spectrum at a definite minimum level. But for purposes like doing work on material objects—teleportation, telekinesis—and presumably for all other purposes, he's more analogous to an electronic tube than to a generator. He borrows and modulates the psionic energy already there."

"What do you mean by 'psionic spectrum' and 'psionic energy'?" demanded Medina.

Kerintji shrugged. "A convenient label for a certain class of phenomena. It is not in itself electromagnetic, thermal, or gravitational; and yet it's convertible to those physical forms. For instance, it was proven some years ago by a researcher on Earth that poltergeists do work by altering local gravitational parameters."

"Then physical energy must also be convertible to psionic," Medina said.

Narden nodded, with an increase in his already considerable respect for the general's mind. "Yes, sir. The mechanism which makes the two-way conversion appears to be the living organism itself. Most species, including man, are very weak converters, with almost no control. The Cibarrans are extraordinarily powerful, sensitive, and complex converters. They can do anything they want to, repeatedly, with psionic forces; whereas even the greatest human adepts can do only a few simple things sporadically."

"I gather you knew as much before you ever got here," Medina complained. "What have you learned in *this* project?"

"What do you expect in four weeks?" said Narden, irritated as Kerintji had been. "I think we've done rather well. Having a strong, reliable psionic source at my disposal, I've been able to confirm a few tentative conclusions I'd reached previously. Besides establishing that the individual does not provide all his own psi energy, I've shown that its transmission is at least partly by waves. I've created interference phenomena, you see, as registered by detectors appropriately placed."

Medina pursed his lips. "Are you certain of that, Major? I thought psionic propagation was instantaneous."

"And waves require a finite velocity. True. But I've no idea what the speed of a psionic wave is. Far beyond that of light, certainly. Maybe it only requires a few seconds to go around the universe. After all, the Cibarrans admit being in communication with distant galaxies."

"But the inverse square law—"

"Somehow, they evade it. Perhaps psionic forces operate continuously, no quantum jumps, and have an exceedingly low noise level. Even so, simple broadcast transmission across interstellar distances is obviously impossible. You yourself, sir, realize the Cibarrans couldn't 'listen in' on all the minds in a sphere light-years across; and then there's also attenuation to overcome. There has to be some kind of tuning or beaming effect. How it works, I don't know."

Kerintji perked up. "Wait a bit, Major," he said. "You were speculating about that too, the other day."

"Sheer speculation," said Narden uncomfortably.

"Let's hear it anyhow," said Medina.

"Well, if you insist. Considering that space is of finite extent, however large, and that psi transmission is by waves, however unlike classical electromagnetics... it should theoretically be possible to establish a, uh, a standing wave on a cosmic scale. In effect, a vast total amount of psionic energy would pervade all space in an orderly pattern. Its source would be the basic psionic radiation of all life, everywhere in the cosmos. An adept could draw as much of this energy as he needed—and could handle—at any one time, and use it. Living organisms would always be putting more back, so the total would remain nearly constant. In fact, it would increase, because radiated energy isn't lost with the death of the radiator, and new life is always getting born. This adds a rather fantastic clause to the second law of thermodynamics. Physical energy becomes more and more unavailable, as entropy increases, but psionic energy becomes more and more available. Almost as if the universe were slowly evolving from an inanimate, purely physical state, to an ultimate...well...pure spirit."

Medina snorted. "I'll believe that when I see it!"

"I told you it was speculation," said Narden. "I don't take it seriously myself."

"But it would explain all the facts," interrupted Kerintji eagerly. "The mind modulates this standing wave, do you see. Oh, infinitesimally, of course, compared with the enormous natural amplitude; but the modulation is there. It can ride the standing wave with the phase velocity of the total. It can be directed and tuned."

"There are even weirder implications," said Narden, a little impatiently. "For one thing, this would mean that the mind isn't a mere epiphenomenon of the brain. The modulations of the cosmic wave may be as important to the mind's existence as the physical modifications of neurons and synapses. But don't you see, General, we can't go yondering off like that. We have to work step by step, grab one fact at a time. Fifty years from now it may be possible to talk about mind versus body, and make sense. Right now, it's a waste of man-hours that should be spent measuring the constants of propagation."

"Or getting those damned Cibarrans to cooperate," grumbled Kerintji.

Medina nodded. "Yes, I understand. Actually, gentlemen, I brought you here to discuss practical problems. I only wanted the necessary background first."

He stared at the map of Earth for a while. Then, swiftly, as if his words were a bayonet: "I expected something like this. Planned on it. But there was always a chance the Cibarrans would give up, or that you would make some breakthrough. I suppose both chances still exist. But they look smaller every day, don't they? So this will have to be done the hard way. Years. Our entire lifetimes, perhaps. Not even any home leaves, for any of us, I'm afraid. Because the other Cibarrans will wonder what's happened to their mission, and go looking through the galaxy ... telepathic...." He took a cigar from the box on his desk, stuck it in his mouth and puffed savagely to light it. "I'll do what I can to make conditions tolerable. We'll enlarge the caverns, build parks and other recreation facilities. Eventually we may even be able to bring in some prospective wives for our personnel. But"—wryly—"I'm afraid we're prisoners too."

Narden entered the suite and closed its inner valve. The six Cibarrans were gathered in the living room. He was shocked to note how gaunt they all were, how their pelts had grown dull. Alanai was almost a skeleton, only his eyes alive. Narden thought: *Being locked up this way, and probed, and watched, and always feeling the energy chaos in their nerve cells, which deafens and blinds their inmost selves, is destroying them. They're going to end my own captivity by dying.*

The ridiculous flutter of hope disappeared. *No. We have bio-chemists on our staff, who understand their metabolisms too well. Vitamins, hormones, enzymes, bioelectrics will bar that road too.*

Elth said quietly, "There is grief in you, Baris."

Narden halted. When he stood, and they sat on the floor or stretched on the couches, his head was above theirs. "I've conferred with General Medina," he said.

One who sometimes called himself Ionar and sometimes Dwanin, but mostly used a trill of music for his name, stirred. "Your determination was reaffirmed," he said.

Their understanding of the human mind no longer astonished Narden. He had learned to allow for the fact that they usually knew in advance, from sheer logic, what he would try next. "We'll continue as long as we must," he told them. "Do you know what that means?"

"Until we are all dead." Alanai's words were barely audible.

"Or rescued," said Elth. "Even unhelped by our own telepathy, our friends will suspect what has happened."

"This is too big a galaxy to ransack," Narden said. "Everyone who knows anything about the project is right here. Why are you holding out? Do you think I enjoy what's being done to you?"

"I beg." Alanai raised one strengthless hand. "Do not hurt your-self so. Your own pain is the worst one we have to endure."

"You can end it all, and go free, any time you wish," Narden replied. "We're not afraid of reprisals from your planet; that isn't in your nature. We'll make any reparation we can. But if you really care about us— Can't you see what it's beginning to do to my race, what it will do more and more as the years go by...this living in the shadow of beings who're like gods? Who own powers that make our sciences look like a child playing in the mud? If we can't have a share, even a small share, in the things and discoveries that matter, what's the use of our existing at all?"

Ionar groaned aloud. "Don't," he said. "Have we not watched

this happen before, again and again, in the long history of our race? Let us help you in the only way we can. Let us show your people how to make the cultural adjustment and be content with what they have and what they are."

Something stirred in Narden, lifted his bent head and crackled through his voice. "Let you domesticate us, you mean? No, before God! We're men, not those miserable dog-peoples we've found on too many planets where you've been!"

Elth leaned forward. "But see here," he argued, "how do you know psionics would be of any value to you? Do you envy the Osirian his ability to breathe hydrogen, or the Vegan his immunity to ultraviolet radiation?"

"Those aren't lacks which handicap us," Narden snapped. "We can send a remote-control robot anywhere one of those races can go. But how can we even know what we *are* until—"

The idea flashed through him, wildest of chance shots, but he hurried on without daring to stop:

"—our minds have also ridden the standing wave around the universe?"

It grew totally quiet in the room. So quiet that for an instant Narden thought he had been deafened, and knew a little of the horror that his randomizers were working in the Cibarrans, and wondered at a spirit which could endure it and not even need to forgive. But his feeling vanished in the upward leap of a flame.

*By Man and Man's God, I've hit a mark! They can't hide their own shock. They believed they could keep me plodding indefinitely, and hoped something would turn up meanwhile to save them. Now ... my friends, it is already too late for you!*

Elth spoke, and his lips were the only thing which moved in all that gray band of beings. "So you have hypothesized it? I did not believe any human had quite that much intuitive ability."

"And I'm going to work along those lines." Narden tried to keep his voice from shaking. His pulse roared in his ears. "Even so vague and general an idea puts me fifty years ahead. I'll know what to try, what to look for. The theoreticians can develop the concept mathematically. The biologists can work on the exact method of psi generation. Eventually there'll be an artificial generator, a mutant animal perhaps, for making controlled experiments. There's no way short of war for Cibarra to stop us!" It was anticlimax, but he dropped his tone again and added, "Why don't you help us, then, instead of hindering?"

None of them had really listened. Eyes began to seek eyes. A few words murmured in an unknown language. Alanai gestured. Elth sprang to him. Alanai got up, slowly and painfully, leaning on the other. He passed from the room. The rest followed.

Somehow, it was a procession.

Narden gaped a moment, sprang forward, and caught the arm of Ionar, who was at the end of the line. "Where are you going?" he cried. "What's all this about?"

Now the amber eyes looked down on him. "We had discussed this contingency," said the Cibarran. "We delayed, because physical life is sweet and none of us had explored its limits yet. But you leave us no choice."

With sudden unexpected strength, he broke loose and glided out through the doorway. Narden stood staring. He heard a murmur of their voices; perhaps they sang, he couldn't be sure.

Kerintji screamed through an intercom: "Get in there, you idiot! Stop them! They're killing him!"

Narden remembered in shock that every room here had a spy lens. He cracked his paralysis and ran. The main valve opened behind him and a pair of soldiers burst in.

Alanai was already dead. Elth and another Cibarran had broken his neck with a single skillful twist. They laid the body down and turned calmly to face the Imperial guns.

"Don't move," Narden heard himself shrill, and as if far away.

"Separate them," chattered Kerintji through the intercom. "Chain them up. Keep a suicide watch—"

"Whatever you wish," said Elth. "We have completed it."

He stooped and with a slow, tender gesture closed the eyes of Alanai. Yet Narden thought his tone had not entirely hidden an eagerness, like a child on birthday morning.

"They didn't do it for no reason." Medina puffed till smoke hid his face. "They sacrificed the weakened one, who'd be easiest to kill. Didn't even try to eliminate any others. What touched off their action?"

"My guess about the nature of psionic transmission wasn't too far off," Narden said. "They didn't dare let me continue my work."

"But we still have five of them! And the body of the sixth." Medina glanced at Kerintji. "No luck with re-animation, eh?"

"No, sir." The little man shook his head. "Our medics used emergency techniques immediately: opened the skull and applied direct nutrition and stimulation to the brain, as well as the usual visceral procedures. They put in a spiral jack, bypassing the damaged section of cord. By that time, any human would have been conscious again. You would at least expect the organs to respond individually. But no, the Cibarran stayed dead. I mean dead. A piece of meat. Microscopic tissue sections were examined, and even the less organized cells, such as the liver, were inert."

"Well," Medina said, "I guess we can't expect critters from another planet to die after our own patterns."

"But they ought to, sir," Kerintji protested. "They breathe oxygen, metabolize carbohydrates and amino acids, just like us. Their cells have nuclei, genes, chromosomes. Oh, there are peculiarities, of course, such as a very fine network of filaments in every cell, whose purpose we don't understand at all. But they should not be *that* different!"

Medina ground out his cigar, stared at it, and fumbled after another. "We'll find out," he said. "Maybe. You're such a good guesser, Major Narden, suppose you tell us why they did this."

"I don't know," said Narden slowly. "I don't seem able to think about it."

"For Mother's sake! Control that damned conscience of yours! We're doing this for man, the whole race, all our descendants, from now till the end of forever."

Narden remembered Alanai again, as if across ages of time. "*You cannot help it. You are young and raw and greedy for life. Oh, how you hunger for life!*" But his brain felt stiff and strange. He sat unmoving.

Kerintji said, tense in the lips, "I can guess, General. And if I am right, we had best evacuate the whole project elsewhere. At the instant he died, when he didn't really need his nervous system any longer, Alanai could have burned it out by transmitting a telepathic call loud enough to be heard at Cibarra through the interference of our inhibitor and all the usual noise. A shout to bring them here—"

"Yes."

When the word was spoken, Medina laid down his cigar and sat like a yellow meal sack, all the life drained from his face. Narden and Kerintji had to turn around in their chairs to see. Kerintji's hand dropped to his belt and a pistol leaped up. A force that tore the skin off his fingers yanked away the gun. It clattered across the floor.

Narden thought, somewhere at the back of his awareness, that he had always been expecting this moment. He looked up and up the tall gray form, to the amber gaze which could not be troubled to hold anger at him. The head was enclosed in a cage of wires and the air about it shimmered. He decided vaguely that it must protect against the randomizing energies. Doubtless only the necessity of constructing such helmets had delayed the rescue these few hours.

"I congratulate you upon your deduction," said the voice which was music even in man's language. "You need not be alarmed for your own safety. Your victims will now depart, of course, and we shall take precautions against a repetition of episodes such as this, but that concerns only ourselves. It is not our way to interfere with the freedom of others, it would be damaging to our own ethos, but we shall publicly appeal to the Imperium to desist from this research, as being too dangerous; and I think, in the course of time, that men will heed."

Narden rose. He took a step toward the Cibarran, and was halted by an unseen wall. He raised his hands. "But it is my work!" he cried aloud.

The impersonal eyes could not have pierced his skull; but the Cibarran asked gently, "Was there not a house in the forest, on a planet called Novaya Mechta?"

Another shape flashed into the office, Elth. He was helmetless— the randomizer must now be silenced—and his tendrils shivered with joy. "I have come to say goodbye, Baris."

Medina covered his face. "Damn you, damn you."

"We learned something," Kerintji snarled. "A few of us, in spite of all you can do, will keep learning. One day it won't be enough for you to commit murder and get help. There will be no help for you anywhere."

Narden stood silent once again. He had no idea if some little part of him, a rudimentary molecule which might in a million years of evolution become a true psionic organ, had caught one of the great thoughts now swirling and singing around him. It might have been subconscious logic, even. "No," he said.

"What?" Kerintji blinked. And now the Cibarrans grew still.

"Your burnout theory," Narden said. It felt like a stranger talking. "They hope we'll think that was how Alanai got the word to them. But it's another false trail. Communication is by patterns, not by chaotic bursts of energy. How could he have organized his nervous system enough, especially when he was dying? The randomizer was in operation all that while. No...remember what I also theorized...that the pattern which is the mind could be imposed on the cosmic wave, as well as on the neuron complex? He died to make the transfer complete. To liberate his mind, so to speak, from the confused body. He didn't send a shout to Cibarra. He went there himself, as a wave pattern!"

Medina looked up. "You don't mean he's still alive?" he choked.

"In a way." Narden's words tumbled over each other. He himself, his consciousness, did not know whither they led. "In a very real way, yes. But not identically with his life while the body functioned. He hasn't got physical parts or senses any longer, you see. But of course, he must have gained new psionic abilities which more than compensate. He could speak mind to mind with living Cibarrans, tell them the facts—and then, maybe, go on to the next phase of his existence, like a butterfly leaving the cocoon—"

He turned to the watching Cibarrans and shouted, "That's what you've been trying so hard to keep us from finding out, that death isn't the end! But why? You claim to be interested in our happiness. You couldn't have told us anything more wonderful than that we have immortal souls!"

The stranger vanished. Elth remained a second more. Narden realized it was a surrender: the answer given now because it would be discovered anyway, unless these humans joined in hiding the fact. When he spoke, it was with surgical compassion.

"You don't," he said.

# Alive and Well: Messages from the Edge (Almost) of the Millennium

WIL McCARTHY/BETH MEACHAM/ELLEN DATLOW
CYNTHIA FELICE/CHRISTIE GOLDEN
SHEILA WILLIAMS/MICHAEL CASSUTT
KIM STANLEY ROBINSON/GEOFFREY A. LANDIS

Nineteen ninety-seven was a tough year for writing science fiction. The stuff that really happened was so futuristic and bizarre, it was almost impossible to imagine anything to top it. There was the human genome project, the nanny trial, the birth of the McCaughey septuplets, the death of Princess Di, floods and Fen-Phen, publishing mergers, and a meteorite with (maybe) extraterrestrial bacteria inside.

The Baptists boycotted Disney, Russians and Americans orbited the earth together in a space station stuck together with duct tape and rubber bands, Mike Tyson bit off part of Evander Holyfield's ear, and George Bush jumped out of an airplane—it was all just too weird.

Even the names of 1997 seemed as if they could be characters in a science fiction story: Picabo Street, Matt Drudge, Linda Tripp, JonBenet, Ginger Spice.

It was a crazy year. And we hadn't seen nothin' yet. Like Monica Lewinsky. Or Viagra.

All of which made it hard to write a survey of the year in science and science fiction. So I didn't even try. Instead, I asked nine authors and editors to talk about the thing that struck them most about 1997. Or something that interested or intrigued or appalled them. And I got some great answers. Which is what came of asking great people.

Like Wil McCarthy. An aerospace engineer and the author of *Murder in the Solid State* and *Bloom,* Wil was fascinated by the future, and the way it's already here.

## WIL McCARTHY

For all of us who grew up reading science fiction set in the 1990s, I'm afraid the year 1997 will *always* sound like the future, no matter how far it recedes into the past. And if you could somehow fax 1997's headlines back twenty years, most of them would probably sound just about right; by 1977, modems and computer networks had begun to penetrate popular culture, and stories like John Brunner's *The Shockwave Rider* and D. F. Jones's *Colossus* trilogy (and the 1969 movie thereof) had broached the idea of some sort of global Internet. Too, the death of the Apollo program had finally sunk in enough that we were no longer expecting lunar domes and manned Mars missions by millennium's end. Really, the speculations and cutting-edge science of 1977 look very much like the technical mundanities of today.

Trouble is, today's cutting edge has gone peculiar on us. More and more scientific breakthroughs are "stunning" and "amazing" and way, way too abstract for their implications to make sense. Oh, sure, Dolly the Sheep proved that mammals could be cloned. And yeah, we had the ongoing debate about life in Martian meteors (my vote: nope), the launch of the (unmanned) Cassini probe to Saturn, the debut of Honda Motor Corporation's "P2" humanoid robot, which walks, climbs stairs, and moves its arms better than C-3PO ever could, and the ongoing silliness on Mir, humanity's first genuine Space Lemon. That one is actually a pretty fine story, full of drama and intrigue and comically malfunctioning spacebots, but like the others it's an *old* story, with elements dating back to well before the Second World War. Nothing futuristic about that!

No, the actual *breakthroughs* of 1997 carried headlines like "Distant Origin of Gamma Ray Bursts Confirmed" and "Iron-Breathing Bacteria Found in Boiling Rock 9,000 Feet Down!" Um, yeah. Cool. My personal favorite was the announcement that space, long thought to be "isotropic" or uniform in all directions, seems in fact to have a "preferred axis," at least as measured by the polarization of light over very large distances. I don't think anyone can tell you what that really means. It's not that these discoveries aren't interesting—they are—or that they're not important—they are. The problem is that they're slippery and large, offering little foothold to the imagination.

Teleportation was a nice lull, a breakthrough any child could understand, but even here we were beset with strangeness: only single atoms were sent, and not very far, and the scientists sending them kept muttering about "quantum entanglement" and "transmission of information rather than mass energy." Had they, instead of teleporting atom A, in fact destroyed or disrupted it, and then forced some hapless atom B to disguise itself in A's quantum clothing? My advice is, nobody ride on this thing until we get a clear explanation.

The "Year 2000 Bug" is a neat bit of black humor that would have gone down well in any 1977 SF novel, but SF seems to have missed the boat here; Y2K is already a "current event," and in a few more years, for better or worse, it'll be history.

My vote for the most *practical* science bite of 1997? It's a humble one that got barely any notice: the addition of blue to the family of light-emitting diodes, which had previously made do with yellow, red, and green. This deceptively simple advancement will pave the way for denser CDs, near-immortal lightbulbs, and TV screens the size of postage stamps. Or will it? Technology has a funny way of sliding sideways on us, yielding something other—something stranger—than we naively expect. Only you, the reader, looking back on 1997 from some future vantage, can know the answer for sure.

It definitely was a fabulous year for science, with shuttle missions, the Hale-Bopp comet, designer genes, and almost daily wonders brought to us by the Hubble space telescope: colliding galaxies and new planets and antimatter geysers. And of course, the marvelous Mars Pathfinder mission. And Dolly. Beth Meacham, executive editor of Tor Books, discusses the implications of the one-of-a-kind sheep who might spell the end of one-of-a-kindness:

## BETH MEACHAM

It's been the stuff of science fiction for half a century or more—cloning. We've explored the concept, the delights, and the potential problems to an astounding degree. Cloning is such a cliché that twenty years ago George Lucas could casually toss off a reference to "the clone wars," and not only did everyone know what that meant, but a large portion of the audience immediately extrapolated a complex subtext. We've thought about clones as children, clones as soldiers, clones as best friends, clones as place-markers, clones as transplant repositories, clones as immortality devices.

But on February 27, 1997, a quietly scholarly article was published in *Nature* magazine. I. Wilmut, A. E. Schnieke, J. McWhir, A. J. Kind, and K. H. S. Campbell, of the Roslin Institute in Edinburgh, Scotland, announced that they had successfully cloned a mammal from the cell nucleus of an adult. The problem of cloning suddenly left the world of fiction and entered real life.

It was, of course, the unfortunately named Dolly the Sheep, and her less well known sister Polly. The amazing facts almost immediately seemed to disappear under a barrage of jokes and religious fervor. But the facts are these: a group of clones were created from the nuclei of cells taken from the mammary tissue of an adult sheep. It's not a terribly complicated procedure, though it required a long time and a lot of skill to develop: Take an ova, remove the existing nucleus, and replace it with the nucleus of the harvested cell. Implant in a uterus. How long will it be before the first human clone is publicly acknowledged? Which future are we going to find ourselves in? And as far as I can tell, we are the only people who have already considered the alternate ramifications of human cloning. Most commentary seems to dwell on the question of whether this should be done or not, and that's moot. It can be done, and so it will. It's human nature—given the opportunity to reproduce oneself, literally, the question of how we as a society are going to view human clones is one that will have to be answered sooner rather than later.

The question of how to deal with cloning wasn't the only one preoccupying us in 1997. There was also the problem of the omnipresent computer—from Web browsers to the Mars Pathfinder mission to spam. Science fiction readers and writers spent the year surfing the Net, sending e-mail, swearing at the slowness of their modems, or valiantly trying to ignore the whole thing.

Which, as Ellen Datlow, former fiction editor of *Omni* and *Omni Internet* and editor of the fiction webzine *Event Horizon,* tells us, is no longer possible.

## ELLEN DATLOW

The Internet is here to stay, whether you like it or not. From the time of *Omni Internet's* launch in September 1996, we were fighting the prejudice of SF writers—exactly the kind of people that the public-at-large assumes would embrace new technology and new media. Producing two live interview/chat shows a week for the Internet for one and a half years demonstrated to me vividly how backward many in our community are. In order to do any kind of live interview or chat on the Web one must have a computer that can connect to the Internet and one must be willing and able to learn a few basics. I admit that the only reason I'm somewhat computer literate and Net savvy is that I was forced to become so because of the changes in my job. But writing about the future and technology and the repercussions of that technology is *your* job. So I'm surprised that so many of the SF writers we interviewed (you know who you are) were not only completely ignorant of and perplexed by the Web but even seemingly technophobic. It seems to me that the creators of the fictions of the future cannot afford to avoid a communication device that is as ubiquitous as the Web and one that is becoming a major component of that future. You may not have wanted to use answering machines, fax machines, and Touch-Tone phones at first, but now, most of you do. So explore and use the Internet—for inspiration and information, and as a tool to reach a wider audience.

But with the computer and space travel and cloning and nanotechnology and even science itself comes Murphy's Law, and other possibilities of disaster. Science fiction has always been preoccupied with disasters, especially the end of the world, but in 1997, with the millennium stomping toward us like Godzilla, virtually everybody was thinking about endings and Endings. Cynthia Felice (the Campbell Award–nominated author of *Godsfire, Downtime,* and *Double Nocturne*) ponders two possible (and possibly imminent) doomsday scenarios.

## CYNTHIA FELICE

Before science accounted for the appearance of those curious heavenly bodies known as comets, they were thought to indicate the approach of the end of the world. Likewise, Year 2000 computer experts were dismissed as prophets of doom when they said the effects of the "millennium bug" could halt civilization.

Scientists agree that a collision with a comet or one of the Earth-orbit-crossing asteroids will take place sometime between now and the year 102,000. Lesser collision events, such as the 1908 Tunguska explosion, are likely to occur more frequently, say one every fifty years, but of course randomly over time so that we cannot think in terms of being due or overdue. We have about a dozen astronomers searching the sky for Earth-orbit-crossing asteroids and comets. They can then be tracked and, if they pose a menace, dealt with by our technology. Astronomers have already found five percent of the estimated number out there, and will take only another five hundred years to find the other ninety-five percent.

Most experts agree that it's already too late to fix all the "millennium bug" problems satisfactorily, but because they were warned early, most large corporations and financial institutions—say ninety percent—will be ready with computers and programs that know the difference between 1900 and 2000. That still leaves the other ten percent unprepared—not to mention most of the federal government computers with critical systems, such as the FAA's and IRS's—and nearly all the small companies unable to meet a deadline they can't slip or ignore. Nor can they even spend the rest of the estimated $52 to $400 billion needed to fix the problem in the remaining time. Thus we'll experience everything from annoying inconvenience to the stringencies of collapse of important services while we finish replacing and reprogramming computers, which will take only three to seventeen years beyond the millennium to complete.

The doomsayers have been proven right, at least more right than wrong. One has a deadline we don't know, and the other a deadline we can't miss.

Christie Golden, the author of *Dance of the Dead, Instrument of Fate,* and *King's Man and Thief,* writes about being intrigued by doomsday predictions, too, but in her case it was the ones that didn't come to pass.

## CHRISTIE GOLDEN

For me, 1997 will be remembered as the year we quit playing Chicken Little.

The sky was going to fall on the field of fantasy and science fiction any day now. Good writers were changing their names in an effort to avoid bad-numbers disease. Those who dared write tie-in fiction were practically branded the Antichrist by those who feared that tie-ins were stealing readers away from "real" novels. The Internet was going to kill books as we knew them. We were like kids telling ghost stories, each grim tale more horrific than the next.

Then, one day, we all looked up, said "Hey, the sky is still there!" and got back to the business of writing and publishing fantasy and science fiction.

I think we all simply had had enough of scaring ourselves silly. Things weren't particularly good for our field, and still aren't. But it dawned on us that books and stories were still being published, under pen names and real names. We realized that tie-ins didn't steal readers away from Heinlein or Tolkien. There was even measurable crossover to "real" novels from the tie-ins. Nineteen ninety-seven also saw a boom in authors' Web sites. Mine went from a few hits to an average of twenty to thirty a day. It was the year that Amazon.com made it into the public consciousness—a happy marriage of books and technology.

Nineteen ninety-seven was the year the sky didn't fall.

Science fiction was taking all this in, of course, and turning out some terrific stories. Sheila Williams, the executive editor of *Asi-*

*mov's Science Fiction* magazine, comments on the trends she saw in the science fiction of 1997.

## SHEILA WILLIAMS

Science fiction is taking back the solar system—possibly even the stars. For the first time in a while, destinations like Jupiter, Neptune, Saturn, and the Moon, and comets and asteroids have become popular. Even Antares has reappeared. The resurgence of these types of tales implies a return to an enchantment with space, and some confidence that we may actually get out there. Although the richest source of SF material has always been planet Earth, it's delightful to see science fiction becoming more inclusive once again.

Getting back into space may be due in part to the influence of cyberpunk authors of the last decade who demanded that SF writers apply modern advances in technology to their fiction. Now we can see space clearly from the Hubble telescope, land an unmanned spacecraft safely on Mars, explore the red planet with a rover, and watch as the changes in information technology multiply. Our worldview is changing daily, and all that activity may have rekindled the gung-ho attitude of the thirties and forties.

Much of today's fiction is more optimistic than that of the eighties. The collapse of the cold war and the subsequent boom in the economy seem to have authors less worried about assuming that we have a future at all. Perhaps we will cure cancer and extend our life spans; perhaps the stock market will continue to soar, so we can keep our money in mutual funds and not think about the coming shortfall in Social Security for baby boomers; and perhaps we can build a more glamorous space station than the Mir.

The optimism may be misplaced. The next war, the next epidemic or natural disaster, the next stock market crash, the next mood swing in our bipolar genre may send us reeling back home and down to Earth. In the meantime it's a lot of fun to pack our bags, assume, for today, that our future doesn't have to end on Earth in fire or ice or abject poverty, and let our imagination help us flag down a spaceship bound for Pluto.

———

Space and what we might find there was present in the movies too, which in 1997 ranged (as usual) from the ridiculous (*Starship Troopers*) to the sublime (the witty and intelligent *Men in Black*) to the pretentious (*Contact*). It was even more visible on television. Screenwriter and SF writer Michael Cassutt (the author of *Dragon Season* and *Who's Who in Space*) explored the year in, as he calls it, "Sci-Fi TV."

## MICHAEL CASSUTT

I know, I've already annoyed you by using that horrid term *sci-fi* in this dignified awards volume. Tough. *Sci-fi* has won the lexicological war, and in Hollywood, especially, that giant suburb of Hollywood known as the television industry, *sci-fi* is the term of choice. And isn't *sci-fi* a more accurate name for what is offered on television than *speculative fiction?*

Names aside, the amount of sci-fi on TV is greater than ever, and more successful sci-fi, too. Chris Carter's *X-Files* has made the transition from cult series to a genuine hit. The revived *Outer Limits* has now outlasted its predecessor and has been picked up for fifth and sixth seasons. *Stargate SG-1* is a promising newcomer.

The amazing *Babylon 5* — a genuine "novel for television," the singular vision of writer-creator J. Michael Straczynski — found a better delivery system and its largest audience ever, just as it reached its penultimate year. TBS wisely planned to rerun the series from the beginning. The new WB network premiered *Buffy the Vampire Slayer,* which is certainly more horror-fantasy than sci-fi but proved to be smartly written by Joss Whedon and David Greenwalt.

And then there are the *Star Trek* series, *Deep Space Nine* and *Voyager,* in their sixth and fourth seasons, respectively, and MCA's Action Pak twins, *Hercules* and *Xena,* wisecracking and head-knocking their way through ancient times. *Earth: The Final Conflict,* based on a twenty-year-old script by Gene Roddenberry, premiered in syndication.

In the 1997–98 season there were, of course, the usual failures: *The Visitor* proved too soft for audiences expecting the same level of action seen in *Independence Day.* Sam Raimi's *Timecop* and David Goyer's *Sleepwalkers* were almost dead on arrival.

As further proof that sci-fi TV is not quite in its Golden Age, you still have to look hard to find stories set on a future Earth. Part of the problem is financial; a spacecraft interior like *Deep Space Nine* is relatively easy to design, build, and use on a weekly budget and schedule. Creating a future Los Angeles—let's not even suggest Cairo or Beijing—frightens even the most open-minded vice president of production. (My experience as a network executive and writer suggests that even conceiving a salable near-future future might be as great a challenge.)

Nevertheless, as this far-from-comprehensive survey should show, interesting and often intelligently written sci-fi is not found only in our beloved magazines, or in hardcovers from Tor, Spectra, Ace, or Harcourt Brace. A whole generation of network executives, battered by the success of one sci-fi film blockbuster after another, has been forced to become sci-fi-friendly. The writers and creators themselves, unlike their predecessors of even fifteen years ago, are well-read within the field and, in the case of Straczynski, have even published novels and short stories. The difference shows, in the variety and quality of the programs.

We love our novelettes in *Asimov's* and our Nebula-winning stories and novels, but more and more, the public face of science fiction belongs to Chris Carter, Sam Raimi, and Joss Whedon—the masters of sci-fi TV.

> But the pervasiveness of science fiction can be a double-edged sword, and Kim Stanley Robinson (the author of *Antarctica* and the Nebula Award–winning *Red Mars* in the *Mars* trilogy) shows just how sharp that sword can be.

## KIM STANLEY ROBINSON

The world has become a huge collaborative science fiction novel that we are all writing together. You see this not just in the startling SF-y newspaper headlines of a year like 1997 but in the textures of daily life, the things we do and the information we are privy to—all science fiction now.

This creates problems for us as a community and a genre. The SF community began in America as a kind of ghetto, but with the walls down, we find that the whole world is a curiously advancing macrocosm of our ghetto. One response is to feel justified. Another is to feel overwhelmed, even somehow left behind, and to try to re-erect the ghetto walls to get safe again. That won't work. We're the lingua franca now, and can never return to our little hometown.

So it feels different to be doing science fiction these days. I sometimes wonder if it is possible to do science fiction at all anymore, now that it has become the world. Of course the market category is still there, and the big audience; careers are still there to be made; but these are not exactly what I mean. I mean the art of it, and the visionary impact of the genre on the world. Can things still be accomplished in these realms?

They can be, and they are. Evidence of that may be found in this book and certainly out there in the bookstores, though it may be hard to find. The enormous pressure to become a reliable cash cow has resulted in a big portion of bookstore shelf space being taken up by franchise work, reinforcing wish-fulfillment fantasies of people in search of an entertaining escape from reality. This situation has been lamented in scores of eloquent jeremiads, and it is indeed a nasty situation for writers trying to do new and interesting work, and readers looking for same. But it is not as if this is a situation confined to science fiction alone. The particular SF novel we are living in these days is a kind of "happy dystopia," in which a technologically advanced version of feudalism rules the planet and the stupidification of the culture of the well-off is therefore a widespread phenomenon, helping to obscure the situation to all concerned.

But resistance to this phenomenon, and to the world order it masks, is widespread also, in science fiction as elsewhere. And science fiction is particularly well-suited to resist. Our business after all is depicting alternatives to the present, in a whole scattering of future scenarios that can, if constructed cleverly, question current reality. And the future is still there, of course, unconquerable—it could become anything, no matter how heavily mortgaged it seems now. It will become something we cannot foresee and cannot control.

And science is still there too, beavering away, an obdurate society extremely resistant to narrative—ponderous, collective, diffuse, unconcerned with the dramatic unities—so that it remains a major aesthetic problem to write stories about it that are both faithful to it and exciting. This society is composed of many millions of people, many of them scientifically literate to a degree that should daunt SFWA members, and many of them quite interested in reading fiction that accurately portrays real science and makes interesting, possibly subversive suggestions about what it might do next in the world. It's a big and permanent ecological niche in the world of culture, a niche that science fiction is there by definition to fill. If the niche is somewhat empty these days, that's a problem. But also an opportunity.

A year like 1997 can't really be summed up, but if anybody could do it, it would be physicist Geoffrey A. Landis, the author of the Nebula Award winner "Ripples in the Dirac Sea," the Hugo-nominated "Elemental," and *Myths, Legends, and True History.*

## GEOFFREY A. LANDIS

Living in the future we dreamed about as children, we have become immune to wonder.

Nineteen ninety-seven was a year of wonders. Nineteen ninety-seven was the year in which the discovery of planetary systems about other stars became…routine. And not just any planets, but planets undreamed of by science fiction: Jupiter-sized worlds in close orbits, glowing dull red with heat; planets of pulsars; brown dwarfs, neither planet nor star, alone in interstellar space. A sheep was cloned, a robotic rover on Mars was watched by half a billion people who live on the surface of the Earth.

In science fiction as well, it was a year of unremarked miracles. Looking over the works of 1997, I am staggered by the incredible diversity of the field. We saw new works from Grand Masters, and grand works from new masters. There were epic trips to the end of time, and stories of ordinary people in a world just half a step askew from the world we know. Media spin-offs in half a dozen popular flavors may have dominated half the bookstore shelves, but on the other half of the book-rack were books enough to satisfy any taste, from diamond-hard science to the intricately worked out societies of imaginary world fantasy. Perhaps the main problem of science fiction today is that there is so much of it that it is becoming increasingly difficult to find the best. But there is no doubt there was staggeringly good material produced in 1997. The short-story field has never been healthier. Once again the death of science fiction was proclaimed widely by critics, and once again, for the most part, the critics were ignored.

The golden age of science fiction? We're living in it.

# A Few Last Words
# to Put It All in Perspective

CONNIE WILLIS

A nd last of all, a few words for the "differently victorious," the "differently nominated," and the rest of us, just to keep things in perspective:

Neither Alfred Hitchcock nor Greta Garbo ever won an Oscar. Ditto Barbara Stanwyck, Cary Grant, and Harrison Ford. Edward G. Robinson was never even nominated. *Citizen Kane* didn't win an Oscar for Best Picture. Neither did *The Treasure of the Sierra Madre, Sunset Boulevard, High Noon, The Wizard of Oz,* or *Star Wars.* And James Joyce never won a Nobel Prize.

Closer to home, non-Nebula winners include William Gibson's "Burning Chrome," Samuel R. Delany's *Dhalgren,* Joan D. Vinge's *The Snow Queen,* John Varley's *Titan,* and R. A. Lafferty's "Continued on Next Rock." And five of the Grand Masters, including Robert A. Heinlein.

No awards system is perfect. Juries are subjective. Voting can turn into a popularity contest. Works can be overlooked, or ahead of their time, or published in the wrong year. When Frank Capra was asked what he would have done differently with *Mr. Smith Goes to Washington* if he had had the chance, he answered, "Not make it the same year as *Gone with the Wind.*"

But even though the Nebula Awards have missed a few here and there—and history will probably point out a few more—the list of Nebula Award winners and finalists is still the best recommended reading list around. Start with *Nebula Awards 33* (if you're this far, you probably already have—this message is for those reprehensible people who read the last page first). Then go back to *Nebula Award Stories 1965*, edited by Damon Knight, start with "The Doors of His Face, the Lamps of His Mouth," and go forward from there.

Or skip ahead to *Nebula Winners Twelve* and read, "Houston, Houston, Do You Read?" by James Tiptree Jr. Or *twenty-five*, and read Geoffrey Landis's "Ripples in the Dirac Sea." Or read the even-numbered volumes first. Or the primes. Or the novels.

Read the *Nebulas*. You'll have a fabulous time. Trust me.

# Appendixes

## About the Nebula Awards

The Nebula Awards are chosen by the members of the Science-fiction and Fantasy Writers of America. They are given in four categories: short story—under 7,500 words; novelette—7,500 to 17,499 words; novella—17,500 to 39,999 words; and novel—more than 40,000 words. (For a brief period in the seventies, there was a Best Dramatic Presentation Award, and in 1977 a special award was given to *Star Wars*.)

SFWA members read and nominate the best SF stories and novels throughout the year, and the editor of the "Nebula Awards Report" collects these nominations and publishes them in a newsletter. At the end of the year, there is a preliminary ballot and then a final one to determine the winners.

The Nebula Awards are presented at a banquet at the annual Nebula Awards Weekend, held originally in New York and, over the years, in places as diverse as New Orleans; Eugene, Oregon; and aboard the *Queen Mary*, in Long Beach, California.

The Nebula Awards originated in 1965, from an idea by Lloyd Biggle Jr., the secretary-treasurer of SFWA at that time, who proposed that the organization select and publish the year's best stories, and have been given ever since. Damon Knight, in his introduction to

*Nebula Awards Stories 1965,* called it "a happy inspiration," and I wholeheartedly agree.

As for the award itself, it's beautiful. It was originally designed by Judith Ann Blish from a sketch by Kate Wilhelm. The official description—"a block of Lucite four to five inches square by eight to nine inches high into which a spiral nebula of metallic glitter and a geological specimen are embedded"—simply doesn't do it justice.

It's *gorgeous.* A sparkling spiral galaxy hangs suspended in clear Lucite space above a cluster of crystals or a Jupiter-banded planet or an alien trio of copper towers. In one of the Grand Master trophies is a pocket watch. Each award is different and is handmade, developed and designed over the years by people like Alan Dean Foster and William Rotsler, and most recently by Mike Lettis. This year's contained lapis lazuli spheres—lovely blue planets and their moons—floating in the Lucite.

SFWA also gives the Grand Master Award, its highest honor. It is presented for a lifetime of achievement in science fiction. Instituted in 1975, it is awarded only to living authors and is not given every year. The Grand Master is chosen by SFWA's officers, past presidents, and board of directors.

The first Grand Master was Robert A. Heinlein, and other Grand Masters have included Jack Williamson, Andre Norton, Ray Bradbury, Isaac Asimov, and, last year, Jack Vance. A Grand Master was named again this year: Poul Anderson.

The thirty-third annual Nebula Awards banquet was held at the Hotel Santa Fe in Santa Fe, New Mexico, on May 3, 1998.

## Past Nebula Award Winners

### 1965

Best Novel: *Dune* by Frank Herbert

Best Novella: "The Saliva Tree" by Brian W. Aldiss and
"He Who Shapes" by Roger Zelazny (tie)

Best Novelette: "The Doors of His Face, the Lamps of His Mouth" by
Roger Zelazny

Best Short Story: " 'Repent, Harlequin!' Said the Ticktockman" by
Harlan Ellison

### 1966

Best Novel: *Flowers for Algernon* by Daniel Keyes and
*Babel-17* by Samuel R. Delany (tie)
Best Novella: "The Last Castle" by Jack Vance
Best Novelette: "Call Him Lord" by Gordon R. Dickson
Best Short Story: "The Secret Place" by Richard McKenna

### 1967

Best Novel: *The Einstein Intersection* by Samuel R. Delany
Best Novella: "Behold the Man" by Michael Moorcock
Best Novelette: "Gonna Roll the Bones" by Fritz Leiber
Best Short Story: "Aye, and Gomorrah" by Samuel R. Delany

### 1968

Best Novel: *Rite of Passage* by Alexei Panshin
Best Novella: "Dragonrider" by Anne McCaffrey
Best Novelette: "Mother to the World" by Richard Wilson
Best Short Story: "The Planners" by Kate Wilhelm

### 1969

Best Novel: *The Left Hand of Darkness* by Ursula K. Le Guin
Best Novella: "A Boy and His Dog" by Harlan Ellison
Best Novelette: "Time Considered as a Helix of Semi-Precious
Stones" by Samuel R. Delany
Best Short Story: "Passengers" by Robert Silverberg

### 1970

Best Novel: *Ringworld* by Larry Niven
Best Novella: "Ill Met in Lankhmar" by Fritz Leiber
Best Novelette: "Slow Sculpture" by Theodore Sturgeon
Best Short Story: no award

### 1971

Best Novel: *A Time of Changes* by Robert Silverberg
Best Novella: "The Missing Man" by Katherine MacLean
Best Novelette: "The Queen of Air and Darkness" by Poul Anderson
Best Short Story: "Good News from the Vatican" by Robert Silverberg

### 1972

Best Novel: *The Gods Themselves* by Isaac Asimov
Best Novella: "A Meeting with Medusa" by Arthur C. Clarke
Best Novelette: "Goat Song" by Poul Anderson
Best Short Story: "When It Changed" by Joanna Russ

### 1973

Best Novel: *Rendezvous with Rama* by Arthur C. Clarke
Best Novella: "The Death of Doctor Island" by Gene Wolfe
Best Novelette: "Of Mist, and Grass, and Sand" by Vonda N.
    McIntyre
Best Short Story: "Love Is the Plan, the Plan Is Death" by James
    Tiptree Jr.
Best Dramatic Presentation: *Soylent Green*
    Stanley R. Greenberg for screenplay (based on the novel
    *Make Room! Make Room!*)
    Harry Harrison for *Make Room! Make Room!*

### 1974

Best Novel: *The Dispossessed* by Ursula K. Le Guin
Best Novella: "Born with the Dead" by Robert Silverberg
Best Novelette: "If the Stars Are Gods" by Gordon Eklund and
    Gregory Benford
Best Short Story: "The Day Before the Revolution" by Ursula K.
    Le Guin
Best Dramatic Presentation: *Sleeper* by Woody Allen
Grand Master: Robert A. Heinlein

### 1975

Best Novel: *The Forever War* by Joe Haldeman
Best Novella: "Home Is the Hangman" by Roger Zelazny

Best Novelette: "San Diego Lightfoot Sue" by Tom Reamy
Best Short Story: "Catch That Zeppelin!" by Fritz Leiber
Best Dramatic Writing: Mel Brooks and Gene Wilder for
    *Young Frankenstein*
Grand Master: Jack Williamson

### 1976

Best Novel: *Man Plus* by Frederik Pohl
Best Novella: "Houston, Houston, Do You Read?" by James
    Tiptree Jr.
Best Novelette: "The Bicentennial Man" by Isaac Asimov
Best Short Story: "A Crowd of Shadows" by Charles L. Grant
Grand Master: Clifford D. Simak

### 1977

Best Novel: *Gateway* by Frederik Pohl
Best Novella: "Stardance" by Spider and Jeanne Robinson
Best Novelette: "The Screwfly Solution" by Raccoona Sheldon
Best Short Story: "Jeffty Is Five" by Harlan Ellison
Special Award: *Star Wars*

### 1978

Best Novel: *Dreamsnake* by Vonda N. McIntyre
Best Novella: "The Persistence of Vision" by John Varley
Best Novelette: "A Glow of Candles, a Unicorn's Eye" by Charles L.
    Grant
Best Short Story: "Stone" by Edward Bryant
Grand Master: L. Sprague de Camp

### 1979

Best Novel: *The Fountains of Paradise* by Arthur C. Clarke
Best Novella: "Enemy Mine" by Barry Longyear
Best Novelette: "Sandkings" by George R. R. Martin
Best Short Story: "giANTS" by Edward Bryant

### 1980

Best Novel: *Timescape* by Gregory Benford
Best Novella: "The Unicorn Tapestry" by Suzy McKee Charnas
Best Novelette: "The Ugly Chickens" by Howard Waldrop
Best Short Story: "Grotto of the Dancing Deer" by Clifford D. Simak
Grand Master: Fritz Leiber

### 1981

Best Novel: *The Claw of the Conciliator* by Gene Wolfe
Best Novella: "The Saturn Game" by Poul Anderson
Best Novelette: "The Quickening" by Michael Bishop
Best Short Story: "The Bone Flute" by Lisa Tuttle*

### 1982

Best Novel: *No Enemy But Time* by Michael Bishop
Best Novella: "Another Orphan" by John Kessel
Best Novelette: "Fire Watch" by Connie Willis
Best Short Story: "A Letter from the Clearys" by Connie Willis

### 1983

Best Novel: *Startide Rising* by David Brin
Best Novella: "Hardfought" by Greg Bear
Best Novelette: "Blood Music" by Greg Bear
Best Short Story: "The Peacemaker" by Gardner Dozois
Grand Master: Andre Norton

### 1984

Best Novel: *Neuromancer* by William Gibson
Best Novella: "PRESS ENTER ■" by John Varley
Best Novelette: "Bloodchild" by Octavia E. Butler
Best Short Story: "Morning Child" by Gardner Dozois

### 1985

Best Novel: *Ender's Game* by Orson Scott Card
Best Novella: "Sailing to Byzantium" by Robert Silverberg

*This Nebula Award was declined by the author.

Best Novelette: "Portraits of His Children" by George R. R. Martin
Best Short Story: "Out of All Them Bright Stars" by Nancy Kress
Grand Master: Arthur C. Clarke

### 1986

Best Novel: *Speaker for the Dead* by Orson Scott Card
Best Novella: "R & R" by Lucius Shepard
Best Novelette: "The Girl Who Fell into the Sky" by Kate Wilhelm
Best Short Story: "Tangents" by Greg Bear
Grand Master: Isaac Asimov

### 1987

Best Novel: *The Falling Woman* by Pat Murphy
Best Novella: "The Blind Geometer" by Kim Stanley Robinson
Best Novelette: "Rachel in Love" by Pat Murphy
Best Short Story: "Forever Yours, Anna" by Kate Wilhelm
Grand Master: Alfred Bester

### 1988

Best Novel: *Falling Free* by Lois McMaster Bujold
Best Novella: "The Last of the Winnebagos" by Connie Willis
Best Novelette: "Schrödinger's Kitten" by George Alec Effinger
Best Short Story: "Bible Stories for Adults, No. 17: The Deluge" by
        James Morrow
Grand Master: Ray Bradbury

### 1989

Best Novel: *The Healer's War* by Elizabeth Ann Scarborough
Best Novella: "The Mountains of Mourning" by Lois McMaster
        Bujold
Best Novelette: "At the Rialto" by Connie Willis
Best Short Story: "Ripples in the Dirac Sea" by Geoffrey Landis

### 1990

Best Novel: *Tehanu: The Last Book of Earthsea* by Ursula K. Le Guin
Best Novella: "The Hemingway Hoax" by Joe Haldeman
Best Novelette: "Tower of Babylon" by Ted Chiang

Best Short Story: "Bears Discover Fire" by Terry Bisson
Grand Master: Lester del Rey

### 1991

Best Novel: *Stations of the Tide* by Michael Swanwick
Best Novella: "Beggars in Spain" by Nancy Kress
Best Novelette: "Guide Dog" by Mike Conner
Best Short Story: "Ma Qui" by Alan Brennert

### 1992

Best Novel: *Doomsday Book* by Connie Willis
Best Novella: "City of Truth" by James Morrow
Best Novelette: "Danny Goes to Mars" by Pamela Sargent
Best Short Story: "Even the Queen" by Connie Willis
Grand Master: Frederik Pohl

### 1993

Best Novel: *Red Mars* by Kim Stanley Robinson
Best Novella: "The Night We Buried Road Dog" by Jack Cady
Best Novelette: "Georgia on My Mind" by Charles Sheffield
Best Short Story: "Graves" by Joe Haldeman

### 1994

Best Novel: *Moving Mars* by Greg Bear
Best Novella: "Seven Views of Olduvai Gorge" by Mike Resnick
Best Novelette: "The Martian Child" by David Gerrold
Best Short Story: "A Defense of the Social Contracts" by Martha
    Soukup
Grand Master: Damon Knight

### 1995

Best Novel: *The Terminal Experiment* by Robert J. Sawyer
Best Novella: "Last Summer at Mars Hill" by Elizabeth Hand
Best Novelette: "Solitude" by Ursula K. Le Guin
Best Short Story: "Death and the Librarian" by Esther M. Friesner
Grand Master: A. E. van Vogt

1996

Best Novel: *Slow River* by Nicola Griffith
Best Novella: "Da Vinci Rising" by Jack Dann
Best Novelette: "Lifeboat on a Burning Sea" by Bruce Holland
    Rogers
Best Short Story: "A Birthday" by Esther M. Friesner
Grand Master: Jack Vance

## About the Science-fiction and Fantasy Writers of America

The Science-fiction and Fantasy Writers of America, Incorporated, includes among its members most of the active writers of science fiction and fantasy. According to the bylaws of the organization, its purpose "shall be to promote the furtherance of the writing of science fiction, fantasy, and related genres as a profession." SFWA informs writers on professional matters, protects their interests, and helps them in dealings with agents, editors, anthologists, and producers of nonprint media. It also strives to encourage public interest in and appreciation of science fiction and fantasy.

Anyone may become an active member of SFWA after the acceptance of and payment for one professionally published novel, one professionally produced dramatic script, or three professionally published pieces of short fiction. Only science fiction, fantasy, and other prose fiction of a related genre, in English, shall be considered as qualifying for active membership. Beginning writers who do not yet qualify for active membership may join as associate members; other classes of membership include illustrator members (artists), affiliate members (editors, agents, reviewers, and anthologists), estate members (representatives of the estates of active members who have died), and institutional members (high schools, colleges, universities, libraries, broadcasters, film producers, futurist groups, and individuals associated with such an institution).

Anyone who is not a member of SFWA may subscribe to *The SFWA Bulletin*. The magazine is published quarterly, and contains articles by well-known writers on all aspects of their profession. Subscriptions are $15 a year or $27 for two years. For information on how to subscribe to the *Bulletin,* write to:

SFWA Bulletin
666 Fifth Avenue
Suite 235
New York, NY 10103-0004

Readers are also invited to visit the SFWA site on the World Wide Web at the following address: http://www.sfwa.org

# Permissions
# Acknowledgments